THE HORNS OF GRIEF

The Blood and Steel Saga

Book II

E J Doble

Also by E J Doble:

THE BLOOD AND STEEL SAGA

1: *The Fangs of War*

2: *The Horns of Grief*

REALM OF THE PROPHETS

1: *The Crescent Moon*

ISBN: 9781399947954

Cover art, design and illustration by: @diego_spezzoni

Map illustration and design by: @jogbrogzin

Dedicated to thirteen year-old me.

For self-preservation,
And having the guts to finally write a sequel.

Val Azbann
THE ICE
Casantri

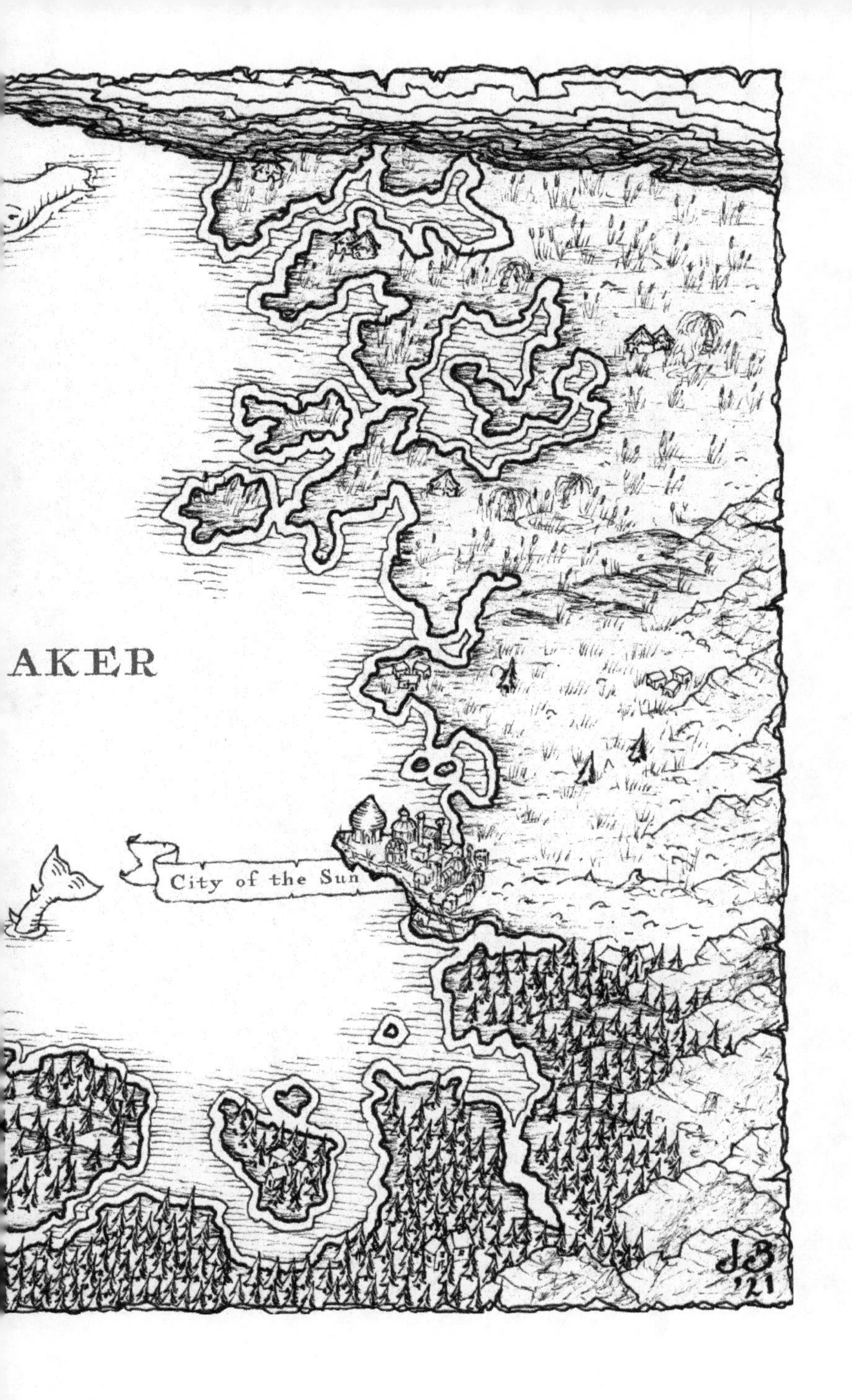
AKER
City of the Sun
JB
'21

CONTENT WARNING

This book contains graphic depictions of violence, dismemberment and bodily mutilation; frequent and heavy profanity; the kidnapping of a child; and one mention of domestic abuse.

Chapter 49 contains heavy referencing to trauma, violence towards animals, and a brief section of dialogue referring to the death and dismemberment of a child. For those readers who do not wish to read this section, I have left a brief overview of Chapter 49 in an 'author's note' at the back of the book, after the acknowledgements.

It is the duty and responsibility of writers to put the reader first, and to keep them appropriately informed of any and all sensitive content described within their work.

CHARACTER INDEX

General Cavara:
Provenci officer betrayed by her people, currently residing in the City of the Sun – found to be the Successor to the All-Mother, she is now under the protection and tutelage of the mysterious Forgotten One

The Forgotten One:
A champion of the All-Mother, summoned through the Rapture – now acting as guardian and teacher to General Cavara

General Revek:
Head of the Imperial Army of Provenci; forced into a humiliating retreat by Tarrazi forces after their defeat on the Grey Plains – now residing in the basecamp near the border wall, he is unimpressed by the change in leadership among the army, and harbours particular resent for the new Marshal in command

Marshal Lazaerys:
New joint-commander of the Imperial Army, appointed by Alvarez and sent to the front lines to serve with General Revek

Supreme Governor Alvarez:
Military ruler of Provenci after the death of the king; suffering insomnia and nightmarish visions – currently out in the field commanding the Land Army against the rebels in the west

General Ferreus:
Head of the Imperial Land Army, preparing to attack the Provenci rebels in the west who have burned much of the country – he harbours a particular dislike for their leader, Eli

Eli, Chief of the Mountain:

Husband of General Broska, now leader of the rebels in the west – hopes to avenge his husband in the coming conflict, and kill General Ferreus

Jinx (Alva):

Master thief; General Broska's sister – plans to join Eli and the rebels in their fight, and seeks her own revenge against the Imperial Army for murdering her brother

Savanta, Champion of the Iron Queen:

Former scout, who won her place as the Iron Queen's champion in the fighting pits of Val Darbesh – currently en-route to the Tarrazi capital with the intent to murder the Queen

The Alderbane:

Ruler of the City of the Sun – a mysterious figure, unsettled by the new developments within their city walls

Gaza Minesk, Iron Queen of Tarraz:

The long-assumed-dead ruler of the northern tribes – dictating the war effort from the Tarrazi capital, Val Azbann

General Broska [deceased]:

Officer of the Imperial Army, husband of Eli and brother to Jinx – murdered by Alvarez and Ferreus during his escape from the capital

Markus [deceased]:

Former scout and friend of Savanta – murdered in the arenas of Val Darbesh

Reference Material taken from the CITADEL OF SCRIPTS

Section LIV, XII, 12-32

"The Rapture & the Mothers"

The Rapture is the name given to the mirror realm that exists in the world of the Icebreaker Sea: a parallel world of physical impressions, where certain features are non-translatable and hold different characteristics than they would normally. The Rapture is also known as the 'Mother's Realm', as it is the space occupied by the four Mothers of the known world, alongside the All-Mother.

The Mothers are transient, god-like figures who reside in the Rapture, and act as conduits to the All-Mother in the transfer of information to the mortal realm. They do this by taking on the physical form of shadows – or 'Shades' – and take up residence in the capital buildings of the four main nations: Tarraz, Provenci, Sevica and Milimnir. [NOTE: the fifth nation of Rodenia does not possess a Mother, as they are a fledging nation that seceded from Provenci during a civil war – there have been no recorded instances of a Mother being 'gifted' to new nations, so it is assumed they will remain without a Mother for the foreseeable future].

As Shades, the Mothers maintain contact with the mortal realm through the leaders of the four respective nations: they offer their counsel to regulate the world and maintain a form of balance, and have been known to kill any other mortal who dares try and contact them. They have existed in this capacity since the beginning of written history, and their way of life has been unchanged ever since.

Despite once being mortal themselves, the Mothers live extraordinarily long lives: they often live for over three-four hundred years, with that only being cut short if the All-Mother passes as well [this has only be recorded as happening five times, forming what is known as a 'Cataclysm': when all living Mothers die and a complete rebalancing is required]. When a Mother then dies and a vacancy is opened, a Successor is chosen – usually the ruler of the nation they reside within – and the ruler will then ascend to take the Mother's place in the Rapture. Throughout recorded history, this process has remained flawless and the ascendency is seen as something of an honour. [NOTE: there is not enough information to ascertain how the All-Mother's Successor is chosen, so this subject remains under review].

However, it should be noted that the Rapture is not exclusively held in the Mother's sphere of influence. Certain individuals possessing unique spiritual/metaphysical mutations are able to 'transmit' into the Rapture and utilise the mirror realm at their whim. [NOTE: the extent to which these individuals can access the Rapture is debated and often varies greatly: some can only do so under great physical strain, whereas others can access the mirror realm without a single physical debilitation – more information is required]. Those who can access the Rapture have also been reported to possess other mutations and 'powers' that they can conjure within the mirror realm, and it is not known at this time whether these 'powers' can translate into the mortal realm.

Throughout history, the corruption or mistreatment of the mirror realm has featured prolifically in ancient texts and tapestries, but no recorded incidents have occurred in actuality. It has been observed through studies that the potential for corruptible elements to enter the Rapture is plausible, but remains highly unlikely…

†

Prologue

The Ides of Quiet Hell

Thirteen Nights Before…

In a quiet tower, in a black stone keep, a new era of man had begun.

Plastered across the cold walls, the frills and rivets of woven tapestries lay sombre and still. They were all depictions of ancient creatures, said to represent the corruption of man: the coiling head of a huge serpent with fangs gleaming; a great ram, steely-eyed with huge curls of bone jutting from its head; a soaring eagle, spearing out from a mountain's peak, with the silver gloss of its talons carving down across the world. Reflections, supposedly, of man's true nature. Taken from stories, told time and time again, of enemies routed and entire kingdoms brought to kneel. That there was such glory and wonder, in the vestiges of history long past. Conquering on for millennia, until one finally came to the edge of the world, and found there was nothing left.

Nothing, that was… except each other.

A new era of man had begun.

Wind howled outside; a swirling stormfront sent torrents of rain lashing across the keep and down onto the streets below. Like plates of armour, the slate-tiled houses shimmered in the low light, with the burgeoning blocks of army citadels dotted between them, alight with the flicker of torches. Like burst pipes, steel-houses stood belching smoke along the lower walls, with the echo of grinding gears and hissing steam rippling out through the din. Along the parapets, the tiny dots of blackcoat helmets stood idle in the dark, with hands never lingering far from the hilts of their swords.

A sudden tear of thunder, and a crack of blue-yellow lightning tore across the clouds above and bolted to-ground in the distance – out there, in the murky shadows of night, the decrepit shape of a single tree exploded suddenly with flame, like a tiny beacon in an unforgiving world that cared little for the cost of its hate. The tree flickered there awhile like a matchstick, little more than a tiny glint on the horizon, until the weight of wind and rain bore down upon it, and the fires began to fall away.

From afar, she watched its spark die and smiled.

A new era of man, has begun.

With a turn of her heel, she shifted away from the tall chamber window and cast her gaze across the torchlit room beyond. Stood before her like a flock of hens, the mutterings of the commanders drew to a sudden and deafening halt as they turned to attention. They stood with hands clasped and heads stooped, light skimming over their black armour like the churning waves of the sea.

They stood with fear in their hearts and bile in their throats, brought low before their mighty Queen.

"Report," she growled, rolling her thumb across her fingers.

The commanders looked among each other, sharp intakes of breath passing between, until one burly figure stepped forward, and bowed at length before her.

"Your Highness," he rumbled. "Reports from the lowlands indicate that your predictions were correct: incursion forces of the Provenci have swept through and taken several vantage points along the main roads. Within the coming days it is expected they will press on towards the Grey Plains and out west towards Val Darbesh."

"Then it appears they have seized the opportunity and taken the fight to us. And so be it: let them enjoy their time here and wallow in their *arrogance*." She sneered. "Are our forces mobilised?"

Another officer raised his hand and bowed from behind. "Three armies of four-thousand soldiers are crossing the Basra Wastelands as we speak, your Highness," he said slowly, "with a relief force pulling up behind on your command."

"Good, that means we remain on schedule. Are the cities prepared?"

"Fortifications are being constructed, with trench lines stretching out several thousand feet in every direction," the first commander added. "As instructed, we are prepared for them."

She nodded once, and once only. "Then the path forward is clear, officers: rally the forces and intercept them at the Grey Plains. Hold a securing line and drive against them. They will be emboldened by their conquests but weakened by their march. I want them driven back to their wretched lands in the coming weeks, and from there we shall bleed them dry once and for all." A fiery, unbroken stare held the officers captive suddenly. "And do not let us down… or the consequences will be *absolute.* You are dismissed."

In unabated silence, the commanders bowed their heads and gave their salutes frightfully, before turning to the exit and leaving with haste. Their echoey footsteps lay hollow across the stone floors, until only one of their number remained, accompanied only by the silent void where not even the wind dared whisper.

"You wished to speak with me, your Highness?" the burly officer muttered, still fastened to his spot.

The Queen paid him no heed, as she watched the other commanders skitter off like bugs. It was only the slam of the chamber doors at the far end that finally drew her eye away, back to the small space before her and the stern man who still occupied it.

"Yes, commander, I did," she said slowly, running a hand over the round of her scalp. "There have been a number of developments concerning the *vagrant* whom we spoke of last… the one whom our Mother leant Her eye to show me." At the mention of Her name, a tiny pulse of blue alighted through the veins in the Queen's arm, and she clicked her tongue with pleasure.

"What of it, ma'am?" the commander inquired.

"We now know that this vagrant is a woman… and more importantly, that she is a woman who neither knows nor seems to care for the sheer power that has been vested in her. She knows nothing of the Mothers; nothing of the Rapture. She doesn't seem to understand any of it. I am still baffled by the notion that the All-Mother's Successor – the champion of the known world by all accounts – is nothing but a flea-bitten wretch as common as any other… and someone so *naïve,* at that."

"I see." The officer kept his tone level. "How do you know of these things, ma'am?"

She inhaled deeply, almost with disappointment. "When the vagrant and I last faced each other in the Rapture, she was saved by a shadow-walker: those who possess a weakened connection to the void, and may access it for a limited time under great physical strain. And this… *shadow-walker*, tore a wound in the void and escaped through it with the woman, before my blade could cut her down." Her sword twinged at her side. "Yet, even with her escape it was not an opportunity wasted: for I gazed into that void, and saw upon the shadow-walker's back an imperial mark. The colours of blue and silver…"

"The standard of Sevica…" the commander said slowly, nodding at the recollection. "So the vagrant resides in the City of the Sun, then."

"So it seems, yes… and in her resides the throne to the known world, and yet she doesn't even know it."

"Those unknowing or yet unwilling to hold the mantle of supremacy… are best replaced by those more *deserving*." A shallow but potent smile coiled across his cheeks. "Am I understanding correctly, ma'am?"

The Queen produced a coy grin. "Yes commander… precisely. We must cut the head from the snake, before the fangs sink deeper."

"Very well. What are your orders, your Highness?"

She levelled her gaze. "Activate our spies in Sevica... have the vagrant located, and placed on watch. Do *not* let her out of your sight. We will hunt her down to the ides of hell if it comes to it. This will not slip from my grasp..."

"I shall see it done, ma'am."

He bowed, turning from her towards the exit.

"Oh, and commander?"

He stopped. "Ma'am?"

"Inform the Butcher of our plans, too... and of the target in question."

The officer pursed his lips, disconcerted. "You know he will expect repayment, ma'am."

"He can have the riches of the Icebreaker Sea on a plate for all I care. So long as that *wretch* of a woman is dead and I hold the throne of the All-Mother come the end of things, I will deter no action in fulfilling that aim." She paused venomously. "And I assure you, commander, that I will be *thorough* in that."

The commander gave a nod – a single glint of fear twisting in his eye – before he turned back to the exit and paced toward the doors.

As he departed, and the room fell deathly silent once more, she looked back out onto the thundering skies of the maelstrom outside.

Gaza Minesk, the Iron Queen, clasped her hands and smiled.

A new era of man has begun.

PART I

The Shadow of Loss

†

Chapter 1

The Successor

Come on!

Cavara drove left and swung out, striking down like an executioner's axe. The blade skimmed their outer leg, glancing across the fabric as if peeling an orange, before rising again just as fast. A blink later, and a counter-strike whistled past her ear. She slid on her heel, gliding out of reach, raising her blade once more to strike at their head.

Impossible speed saw her blade parried: a pirouette and her opponent was turning, striking upwards, forcing her into a backstep. She planted on the balls of her feet in response, propelling forwards, performing a lethal lunge towards their broad, cloaked chest. Yet her sword was knocked aside again like a child's toy; the robe rippled away in a flush of black and grey, as her opponent slipped from her grasp once more.

Cavara gritted her teeth, snarling with frustration and drenched in sweat, watching a victory she could have had, slip through her fingers yet again.

"Control that rage, Successor," the Forgotten One boomed with a flash of their sabre, the rivets of a smile forming across their pale face. "If the rage wishes to fight, then let it be in the mastery of one's blade… not in the screech of one's mind."

"Far easier said than done…" Cavara mumbled through heavy

breaths, hands on hips, "…when your opponent fights like the wind, and wields a sword as if it were a feather."

The robed figure bowed. "I cannot help it, if you fight too slow to make ground."

Is that right? Cavara grinned, rolling her tongue across her teeth. "Taking your head from your shoulders looks more appealing by the minute, I warn you…"

"Ah, there is no need to warn me, Successor…" The Forgotten One pulled the sabre across their chest, crouching into a fighter's stance. "Because you won't get the chance to try…"

Cavara brought her blade up to her ear, rolling the earth under her heel.

"We'll see about that…" she mused.

The dance began again.

They stood upon a hilltop of swaying grass and green fields, the City of the Sun spilling down the mountain in great reams to the south. There was a haze in the air, with low-lying clouds pressed against a bright midday sun, glazing the distant forests and slate-screened mountains in stark whites and greys. The knotted, wind-anchored trunks of great oak trees rose steadily up the hillside around them; a murder of crows circled in the skies above, harrying a lone hawk over the rocky crags to the east. It was a quiet day, by all accounts: the wind but a whisper, tranquil in its resolution, dancing over the earth.

Shattered, suddenly, by the clash of steel blades.

Cavara struck across her body: a fast, weightless motion, watching as the Forgotten One twisted out the way, the pointed end of her blade catching the edge of their robes.

The pale figure's own blade coiled up and through beside her almost immediately after, as Cavara whipped round to deflect it little more than a hair's-breadth from her face.

Three more strikes passed, each more potent than the last, skimming the length of their swords, parries and counters flourishing like the strokes of a paintbrush—

Lunging suddenly, the Forgotten One leaping backwards, a sharp upswing knocking her blade aside—

She rallied it around again instantly, a roar as she cut upward—

And the blade met its mark, slicing the robe down the front, carving several strips of the material in two.

Cavara recoiled before she hit any skin beneath, her sword slipping back to her side, but she looked with some satisfaction at the slashed cloth fluttering limply in the wind, and how she had bested a master of the blade at last.

Have that.

"Look mumma, she got them!" Evelyn cried, sat in the grass nearby with an apple in his hand, pointing with a look of joy at the Forgotten One's robe.

"She did, yes," Azura replied, stroking his hair in her lap, her floral dress spilling over the grass like rolling waves. "She fights well, doesn't she? She has a great skill with the blade."

"We shall make a champion of her yet," the Forgotten One rumbled, inspecting the damage to their clothes. "I must admit, I was not anticipating that one."

Cavara drew a heavy breath and smiled. "I may not match your skill," she mused, sheathing her sword, "but I do still have a few tricks up my sleeve."

"There is much still to learn, yes, but your... *dynamic* style of fighting shall serve you well. Especially when you face a real opponent."

"And what makes a real opponent?"

They caught her eye. "Those who wish for nothing more, than to see to your *demise*..."

Cavara rolled her shoulders, sensing shadows in the air suddenly. Images resurfaced like flickering candles in her mind, mulling over what had happened in the Room of Shadows nearly eight nights before. The passage into the Rapture, as she now knew it was called; her transit through the void; finding the totems, and the one that called to her in its strange, melodic tone; touching its face, and feeling the energy pulse through her so exquisitely. Turning...

To the Iron Queen... the woman who longs to have me dead.

Their first meeting, face to face, without the black vapour hanging over her. Sensing the venom in her very being: a raw power so unwieldy and violent that Cavara found her stomach churn at the recollection. How the shadow woman had approached, intent on her demise, readying her weapon.

How the intervention of the Forgotten One saved her life that day, and set her free.

Although free feels like the wrong word. A weight fell heavy in her heart. *I have never been more constrained than I feel now.* The words echoed through her head: a rupturing wound she longed to banish, but in the end had no choice but to accept. That destiny would prevail – her fate, in all things.

Successor to the All Mother.

What does that even mean?

"I suggest we get back soon," the Forgotten One exclaimed, drawing her back to the world. "For as nice as it is to practice the sword dance out here, there is still work to be done within the city walls." They paused, sheathing their blade. "That, and someone may need to find me a seamstress." The huge figure turned to Evelyn then, producing a half-smile that wrinkled the cleft in its skull, where the brain still pulsed visibly. The small boy looked away in disgust, pulling tighter into his mother.

"Now Evelyn, don't be like that: they're just trying to be nice, is all," Azura said astutely, looking up to the pale figure. "He takes some time getting used to new people... especially those different to our own."

The Forgotten One bowed their head. "I understand, miss... I take no offense."

The old woman produced a warm smile, the grey streaks of her hair furrowing in the wind. "Although I do agree with your talk of heading back. I have some work I need to do with the tradesmen about a new supply line for our woodworks in the north. Higher demand means a shift in priority, and we haven't got enough—"

Footsteps approached suddenly, ascending toward them: the clatter of metal with scabbards swinging. Cavara shifted her weight, hand dropping to the hilt of her blade, mirroring her robed guardian opposite.

From the south, two soldiers from the City crested the hill to the south, eyes bulging as they spied the imposing form of the Forgotten One grappling the end of their sabre. At the sight of them, Cavara squared her shoulders, scowling.

How can they know we were out here ...?

"Word from... the Alderbane," one of them stuttered, scratching their throat. "Wants to see you... when you're back."

Of course they do. Cavara waved her hand dismissively, faking a smile. "Thank you, gentlemen... we'll be there shortly."

"No," the other one said bluntly. "You come... now, with us. We have horses."

Cavara sighed, pinching the bridge of her nose. *There's no patience with these people.* "That's fine. I'll come now, *thank you*." She turned to the others. "I'll see you all later – I would accompany you back to your home, but it would appear my *duty* takes precedent at this moment in time..."

That, and every other fucking time.

She turned to the soldiers and smiled.

"Please, lead the way."

Cavara entered the throne-room with a swing of iron doors, where the same tense, unremittent air swept over her sweat-stained face. Through the wide, hazy windows that coated the back wall, warm light spilled across the slate table at the room's centre, darkening even further the shadows that dominated the throne opposite. The curling dragon bones, and the chair itself, remained sombre and still. Whether the Alderbane was hidden away in those shadows or not, she could hardly tell.

It was only when she slid into the stiff chair opposite and produced an erroneous sigh, that a pair of deep eyes blinkered to life, and moments later the full-half skull and pin-stretched skin of the Alderbane hunched slowly into view, gnarled hands sliding over the table to clasp together tightly.

"Welcome, Cavara," the voice boomed, a low rumble tapping through her ears. "I have been expecting you."

"My apologies that I couldn't come sooner," she replied. "Honing the skills of the blade has eaten into much of my time, these past nights."

"Yes: the sword dance is an admirable foe in its perfecting, but also marked as one's greatest friend in battle."

"Certainly so. The Forgotten One makes it no easy task."

The Alderbane paused, an unsettled darkness in their eyes. "Yes, the *newcomer*... I have received many reports of them since the Room of Shadows."

The memory came and went, snuffed out like an embryonic flame. Cavara exhaled slowly. "Yes... it's quite the talk of the town, I imagine!"

"Hm," the half-skull grumbled in reply.

The general felt her collar constrict around her neck. "They are... an apt sword-fighter, most certainly... and very caring and diplomatic too..."

"People are concerned, general," came the final, flat response. "Concerned over whether this *newcomer* can be trusted to their word. And, more so, whether they are safe to be within these city walls with my people." Something edged in its cold voice – *fear?* "I know of the legends, and of this *Rapture* whence it came from... I know they ally themself with the All-Mother, and has marked you as Her Successor and champion. Yet as it stands, we are only bound to those truths by their word, and by the seemingly undying loyalty they now exhibit in you. So our only gauge of their intentions within my realm... are through *you*."

"I understand your concerns, your Highness, about having this newcomer in your city – these are trying times for the entire Icebreaker Sea, after all," she said measuredly, hiding her anger at the Alderbane's sentiments. "But I can say, with my hand on my heart, that the Forgotten One has shown nothing but respect and good intention since their appearance, and has served me well as a protector and teacher since then."

The Alderbane lowered its head in some form of acknowledgement, before rising slowly from its high throne and shifting over to the rear windows. Back arched, with the porcelain rivets of its skull shimmering in the light, it stood for a long time in abject silence, as if all the world had stopped around it. There was no motion, nor recollection: it just stood as if little more than a statue, transfixed to the moment.

Cavara adjusted in her seat, the cold air suddenly stifling in her chest. The walls seemed to shudder around them, closing in at all sides—

"That is good to hear," the towering form said suddenly, still gazing off into the beyond. "And I only raise such concerns, for reasons you have already expressed: that these are trying times for us all... with enemies at *every* turn."

Something shifted within her: terror, pulling at her heart. "Has something happened?" she inquired.

"Yes."

"What... what is it?"

The answer came slowly, almost reluctantly, like a leaf caught on the wind. "A half-dozen ships appeared at the docks overnight, claiming to have blown in from out at sea," it explained. "Those working the harbour that night allowed them to dock briefly, and purchase any provisions needed for their return journey. And it was then, that a pale-faced figure in black armour disembarked..."

Her heart stopped, hands shaking. "A *blackcoat*?"

"We believe so. Supposedly, six Tarrazi vessels who were doing reconnaissance out at sea washed up at our shore after a particularly bad storm. They were only here overnight, hoping to set sail again when dawn broke… weighing anchor in our harbour even as a garrison of soldiers lined the outer wall. The workers who saw them come in did as they were ordered, and told the foreigners they were not welcome: that we were a closed dock for merchant shipping, and nothing more. They seemed aggrieved initially, but obliged nonetheless, and left with some haste thereafter. Since then, there has been no sign in our waters of any of their ships…"

"How long were they here for? Did they leave anything behind?" *They can't possibly know I'm here…*

"Reports from the workers say they came and went in little under an hour. It is believed that no-one remained when they left, and no cargo was dropped off either."

"Is that a certainty?"

That same, undulating silence spilled out between them; the Alderbane lifted its gaze. "There are no certainties, general… we cannot guarantee that no-one snuck off one of those vessels while they were moored at our docks. Only a small handful of workers were present, so many of their ships were left unwatched." It turned to her then, the piercing eyes catching at her own. "I understand your concern over this development, and I too share it… I do not want any Tarrazi in my city, and I certainly do not want them causing trouble and spilling blood here either. It would be… *damaging*, to have such things."

It cannot be. "If the Tarrazi already know I'm here, then they'll be hunting for me…" She gasped. "Are you to exile me?"

"No: you are not to be exiled under any circumstances," the Alderbane snapped. "Because if the threat you speak of is true, then whoever hunts you will search every corner of my city for you. And if they cannot find you, then they will assume you are being harboured here as a fugitive under my orders. And the last thing I need are assassins and *rogues* assailing my palace… or Tarrazi ships levelling our towns." It twitched sharply. "No: you are to remain here. There will be no cowering from the likes of *them*."

"But what will happen to me? Will I be safe? If they know I'm here – if they're *already* here – then they'll be coming for me..."

"That is also my shared concern." Something almost resembling a smile twitched across its skull. "Which is why I have arranged something for you..."

Cavara paused, frowning. "And what is that?"

"As is befitting a foreign person on Sevican land, you have been assigned a personal honour guard for the duration of your time here: two of my best officers, who will escort you about your business within the City limits, and shall be your eyes and ears against any potential threats that may arise during that time. They shall watch over you, and ensure no harm comes to you, as they have been instructed..."

Cavara ground her teeth together, puzzled and concerned. *I don't want this... this isn't right.* "I'm not sure these precautions are necessary, your Highness..."

"They are entirely necessary for your protection, general. Although I do not doubt your ability with a blade, an extra set of eyes and swords never goes amiss."

She scowled. "Perhaps – and perhaps my safety is of utmost concern to you – but that's not all there is to it. You also want to use the honour guards to spy on the Forgotten One, don't you? Because another pair of eyes on me, is also another pair on *them.*"

A look of admittance crossed its gaze. "Clever," it said.

"Exactly. Don't think I don't see through this."

"It does not matter either way: this is the nature of our new arrangement, general, and that's just the way it is." Cavara made to intervene, but the Alderbane pressed on. "Due to your... *extra-ordinary* gifts and circumstances, my liberal attitude to your being in my city is more apparent, but know that you are a distinctly rare exception in that. Foreigners, especially from the west, are usually turned away at my gates... that, or executed by my blades. This newcomer, this *Forgotten One*, is an extension of that exception, but even in my graciousness I also then have limits. They are here because they are your protector, and they are within my walls because that is also where you reside. But that does not mean I trust them as I have come to trust you, however, and... *conditions* have to made to allow for that."

"So are the honour guard designed to make it safe for me in the streets, or do they lend more of a sense of security for you, sat in that chair of yours surveying all things—"

"You shall *watch your tone,* general," the Alderbane boomed, the nodules of its fingers flexing slowly. "Do not forget who you are speaking to, and where you seek refuge. This is *my* realm, not yours."

Cavara clenched her knuckles beneath the table, exhaling noisily to dispel the ire in her heart. *Keep grievances under wraps... at least for now,* she thought. *The time will come eventually.* "My apologies, your Highness... I did not mean to disrespect you."

"Good. Then you will also not disrespect me, in refusing the gracious gift of an honour guard to stand at your side, so you may live without fear of attack within these walls... am I correct?"

She ground her teeth, fighting the urge to lunge across the table. "I humbly accept your offer, your Highness... *thank you.*"

"Then it is settled. They await your presence in the sparring court outside, and will be at your direction from that point onward." It paused, its eyes drifting off into the distance once again. "You may leave now, general," it dismissed. "I have said my peace."

Cavara stood without a word spoken, her chair grating against the marbled stone at her feet. Without looking back, she heaved the double doors apart and dislodged the guards from their posts just outside. They goggled at her, bemused, as she paced down the hallway with long, venomous strides.

They then glanced back through the doors, out onto the throne-room itself, where the Alderbane stood with its hands clasped.

And a crooked smile like glistening stone, etched across its face.

†

Chapter 2

Honour Dies in the Mud

There was no escape in reality. Only death awaited. Its idle song caught whispering in the wind; the drums of its rancour growing steadily louder. The flitting, frightful glimmers of hope dashed with each twist of the air. The burning acceptance that time was nearing its end, biting at one's heels with each step.

The soldier broke from the tree-line in a tangle of sweat and mossy debris, with branches lodged between bands in his armour. His heart was thundering and his skin was crawling and his breath boomed heavily in his ears. The sudden explosion of light was dazzling; a rally of clouds trundled overhead, splintering grey-gold sun across the plains ahead.

Or what remained of them, rather: craters furrowed the earth with felled trees split between them, shattered wood lancing skyward in a desolate cry to the gods. Stagnant pools of water as big as lakes swallowed all who strayed near. The haze of acrid decay hung like a mist in the air. The soldier witnessed it all, in that moment: the horror and debauchery of sin. The cries that had been left unrecognised; the bodies, broken and bloodied, sprawled here and there as a testament to the violence that had passed.

And the violence still yet to come.

He skimmed the edge of a great pit, scanning the twisted earth, when he heard the crackle of broken branches and the ominous lone howl at his back. Twisting, half falling over a crush of vines, he spied the hunter climbing a rise not too far behind: the six eyes and matted coat of a Kazbak Hound, jaws slathering, the rich taste of blood already stained about its gums. It took a long draw of the air – sensing the motion in the landscape before it – and almost cackled with glee that its prey was still running.

And with that, that the chase was still on.

He did not see the beast set off after him: he only heard the sharp snap of branches and the ugly bellow of a roar clip the sky. It was the same as it had been for what felt like miles, trapped in the depths of the skeleton forest. How near two hundred soldiers had set camp within its boughs, hoping to regroup at the command post to the south at daybreak. How the tension had ebbed and flowed among the tents as night descended, whispering through the night. How the sentries at the camp's edge had become alerted to motion in the early hours of dawn: that creatures were skimming the tree-line to the north. Things low and lumbering with piercing eyes and big teeth. The survivors slept cuddling their swords like children's toys, hoping the inevitable wouldn't come…

And then they had been awoken suddenly to a volley of screams: clattering metal and the foul tear of flesh as dozens of Hounds descended on the camp. Dozens of soldiers were killed almost in an instant; he had turned tail and run like the others, fleeing like them, seeking safety in any refuge they could find. He had kept running, pressing on through the unending trees until it appeared he was the only one left.

And that only death now seemed to remain.

He sailed over a felled tree, blasted apart by artillery fire. His feet landed in mud; he pulled away with a squelch and the smack of sodden grass. A thin line between the craters stretched ahead, punctuated by broken tufts of vegetation and huge slabs of stone. He stepped past one, but landed against the next, hissing as his ankle nearly rolled. Propelling away with a stumbling gait, sweat streaked, the occasional clatter of claws at his back as the Hound surged over the terrain. The sound of teeth gnashing; an unbridled savagery in the air. The tone of war, and all its malcontents, breathing down his neck with every stride.

Still he pressed on, open ground suddenly stretching all around. Open ground, left to right, marked by scenes of past carnage: he saw the broken cloth of a medical camp with ruined stretchers straddled in the mud; the banners of the Provenci standard jutting from the base of an old farmhouse, which had had its roof blown through and windows smashed by sustained artillery fire; the bodies of livestock had been left to rot in the field outside, skinned for their leather and wool. Ahead, a horse lay sprawled across a low stone wall, its flank awash with arrows – the crow that had been gorging on its eye took flight as he skittered past, circling skyward into bleeding clouds of gold and grey. Gazing up, it looked like heaven was trapped away in the gloom up there.

And as the ground at his feet gave way to a mudded cesspit, the world below gave that much more the impression of hell.

With an abruptness he was not expecting, his left leg submerged up to the shin in the pungent ooze of a quagmire. He shrieked fearfully, trying to pull away, but found his knee give as spasms of pain wracked his tendons. A whimper escaped his lips. He kicked out wildly. Three tugs and no give; his other foot started sinking alongside it having slipped over a ridge of stone. He reeled for a moment, caught off balance by a lick of wind. Turning his body abruptly—

Lifting his wrist guard as a pair of slathering jaws arched his way, the Kazbak Hound rearing into view like a goliath.

A scream: one he discovered to be his own, as the beast's curved fangs drove deep into his forearm, buckling the metal of his armour. Piercing skin like it was paper. The Hound turned to face him, throwing its head around wildly, shreds of bone and flesh ripping from his arm. He screamed again, acquainted with sickness this time. He vomited across the mud before him, his skin an odd colour of granite. The other free hand writhed, reaching down suddenly for the knife at his side.

Pulling it loose, he struck out and speared the beast in the muzzle.

The Hound produced a disapproving grunt in response, its gums thick with blood.

Suddenly the soldier was screeching, slashing across, a haze of blood and steel spinning across his vision. Carving lines across its face, butchering several of its eyes. Purple matts began to form across its grotesque fur. Not that he registered particularly: his mind was completely dormant. There was no sensation left in his arm, nor in his submerged leg. His cheeks felt numb and cold. It was oddly peaceful for such horror.

Then the Hound released its grip, its face a butchery of cuts and clefts, shaking free with snorting disgust.

And an opportunity revealed itself with frightening ease.

Watching the beast pull away, the soldier rolled backwards and prized his leg from the sludge, stumbling back onto solid ground. His mangled arm remained lifeless, little more a contortion of metal and skin. A throbbing disobedience twinged in his knee. The beast before him drew up and howled into the low winds.

The Hound surged forward, lifting its forelegs in a pounce—

He swung backwards, carving the blade down, drawing the knife across its right leg.

With a whimper, the beast landed awkwardly, hobbling to a stand nearby.

Turning almost immediately, bloody murder wrought cold in its devilled eyes.

It stooped low as it charged, aiming a lunge for his leg. The soldier stepped aside, swinging down, carving across its ribcage. Pushing deeper still, until half the knife lay buried—

Losing his grip, blood slick across his hand, as the knife and beast pulled away with a whimper and cry. As it rounded again, the Hound tried clawing at the knife with its back foot, only to find it firmly rooted.

A small victory, in the end.

Snarling at him in defiance, the Hound charged again, seemingly unphased by the metal lodged in its shoulder-blade. The soldier adjusted, preparing to sidestep, only to find the beast change course suddenly: barrelling into him, slamming him back to the mud. It rounded sharply thereafter, paws pressing down across his chest, tearing at the arm once more.

Numbed to the pain, the soldier hissed and squealed, as the sodden earth slid between his shoulder-plates and buried him deeper still. His arm flailed hopelessly, reaching out, seeking purchase in anything it could find—

To spy the glint of his knife along the beast's flank, half-buried through the rib.

He was suddenly rolling, shimmying with his legs, pulling away from the dead arm being slowly ripped from his body. Reaching, sweat-stained and shivering, the shine of steel calling to him. Pain surged again, full of malice and grief—

Wrenching the blade free suddenly, like a shimmer in the dawning light.

Driving down then, as the knife pierced the beast's throat.

A sudden, all-encompassing silence followed. The wind seemed to whisper in his ear. The Kazbak Hound, eyes still, hung like a marionette above him. The blade in its neck; the heavy jaws releasing his savaged arm. The light spilling abruptly through the clouds, as if the gods had pitied him at last.

Then the beast collapsed to the side, and the knife slipped through his fingers.

And it was done at last.

With a wheezing breath, he pulled himself up, half sprawled across the mud with little semblance of space or time. He breathed deeply with great purpose, like an ignition to his system. It acted as a recollection that he was still alive. That there was no sensation to his ruined arm beyond the adrenaline spurting through his veins, didn't seem to matter. There were just the wandering shadows of the broken plains all around, with clouds rolling thunderously overhead.

And three horses approaching from the south, the shimmer of armour on their backs.

The soldier was on his feet without second thought, swaying on dull legs, the prodigious sound of hooves growing in his ears. He followed their whispers: the snorting of stallions; the rattle of polished swords in fine-kept scabbards; the low rumble of words exchanged as they drew yet closer.

The three horses slowed along the ridge just above him, grimacing at the muddy cesspit he had fallen into moments before. The foremost rider skirted the edge and cantered gently past him, drawing to a halt somewhere behind with his face lost in a blur of grey. The other two remained before him, the leftmost figure sliding from his mount and stepping forward. The soldier traced the massive shape of his chest-piece and the shimmering gold trim of his bracer, before landing on a pair of cold, fickle eyes entrenched in a bronze face.

"To kill a Hound…" the huge man muttered, giving the corpse a terse kick, "… is no easy task, that's for sure."

"And with a knife too," the one on the horse added. "That's quite some skill with the blade…"

"Thank you, sirs," the soldier said with a smile. "I'm glad you're here—"

"Mind you though, I'm not all too sure how that arm's holding up…" The huge man levelled his finger at the mangled remains. "I'd wager there ain't much feelin' nor motion left in that thing."

"Not much use either," the officer behind added.

The soldier went suddenly cold. "It's a serious wound, agreed, but get it bound up or taken off and I'm right as rain to fight on—"

"So much blood spilt," the voice thundered behind him suddenly, "all for a *dead dog.*"

He was about to turn, to study the face of whoever had said it, before the officer ahead of him crouched down and grappled him under the jaw. With a furrowed brow, he studied the soldier intently, tracing over his eyes and his skin, and the frightened expression careening every wrinkle.

"He's got grey-ghost, that's for sure," the man concluded. "Death haunts his eyes, and we've no medics for miles around..." The officer released him, rising to a stand and wiping his hand with a cloth. "So... what are we to do with 'im?"

What are we to... wait!

"No, no!" he blustered, the fear latching hold, sensation swelling once more. "No, I'm fine! I'm fine. I just need it bound is all..." He took a step forward; swung a step back. "I'm fine... I just need time to rest." The faces of those before him provided no remorse. The soldier shivered. "I... please, *please,* I'm okay, I'm... there's no need to do anything, please." He turned to the faceless figure behind. "I promise I'm—"

The blade slid across the soldier's throat as he turned, and death struck in a heartbeat.

He stared for a moment, pinned to the spot. Disbelief leeched grey in his eyes. Finding no strength left in him as his knees buckled and swayed, he toppled sidelong into the mud, finding a death that had been all but inevitable, brought about by one of his own.

Stood behind, the commander withdrew his blade and cleaned it on the dead soldier's coat, grimacing at the mangled remains of his arm.

"I don't pity the idle fool," Revek muttered with a smile.

For only death awaits them, after all.

Traversing a narrow track between the swampy bulges of the lowland plain, the three horses made slow progress through the desolation. On the near horizon, the rugged stockade of their main outpost slowly emerged from the haze, with felled trees lashed together to form an ugly wall at its base. Set upon a raised mound, the wooden struts and spun cloth of their encampment lay dappled with thin trails of smoke, where sentries balanced at the edges overlooking the vastness of Tarraz beyond. Several stragglers lay at the camp's edges collapsed against the trees, sipping water and tending their wounds. As the three horses passed, the wounded gazed up solemnly, a mix of intrigue and resentment glazing their eyes, studying the men who passed. Wondering what would come next. Ascertaining who was to blame.

Revek looked upon them and scoffed; with a click of his heels, the horse pressed on.

I have no time for pointing fingers. He adjusted his armour, studying the broad tents of their camp as they passed, his mount weaving studiously between them. *We are at war; the fate of the nation rests in our hands.* He ground his teeth and spat into the mud below. *To hell with your pity.*

You can pass blame when you're dead.

Reaching the outpost's centre, a gazebo bearing the red-green imperial standard reared above them, with patrols of guards circling it patiently like dogs. Revek and the two generals dismounted, the commander scratching along the horse's flank, offering a quiet thanks for its service in the field. All around, the quiet ripples of flags and the customary nods of the soldiers met his eye, which he acknowledged and returned with a veneer of good will.

As if they deserve such a thing. For many nights he had watched them trickle in from the tree-line to the north: those who had survived the nightmare of the Grey Plains, and the equally-nightmarish retreat that followed. He watched them from the vantage of his command tent, sipping wine and delighting in fresh cheeses brought up from the capital: how they had arrived and gathered themselves; how they had washed and dressed and donned the armour once more.

And then they stood, and waddled about in their sorrows, and kicked at the earth like a bored horse expecting some fucking sympathy. Men and women sat in tent alcoves weeping in the night; drunkards wandered the groves to the south, shit-stained and sick with ill graces; a few stood screaming with swords at their own throats, wishing it all to end. Commander Revek had watched on with a heavy roll of the eyes as they were reprimanded and forced back to reality, wavering on the precipice between certainty and self-destruction.

Soldiers, unfit for the realities of war, so he had told his generals the other day. *Soldiers who quiver at the sight of their own blood.*

Soldiers who I'll dispatch myself, if they don't get back in fucking line.

Drawn away by the call of his general, Revek turned sharply and disappeared under the shelter of the command tent, the strike and rattle of the wind growing suddenly tame and still.

Within the confines of the tent, a congregation of some dozen officers stood awaiting him with stiff shoulders and polite eyes. Hands clasped behind his back, stooped low like a vulture, the commander regarded each of them individually, allowing no emotion to cross his steely gaze. Assessing them – drawing the line of authority at his feet – he then crossed the space and approached the makeshift table at its centre, fixing his eyes to the woman stood opposite.

And the bane he would soon come to know.

"Field Marshal Lazaerys," he mused, a half-smile clinching his jaw. "It has been... some time."

"That it has, commander," the Marshal muttered in reply, face blank and unmoving. She was tall and limber of frame, with a short wash of ginger hair slung into a braid. She wore similar armour to the commander: a polished chest-plate edged with red streaks of paint, which continued to snake up her neck into a rash of horns coiling past the bridge of her ear. Her stance came with a cold regard, almost challenging the commander before her. A testing flick of her hair seemed to illustrate that point, as Revek curled his nose up. "It appears that you have come under some considerable strain, since we last received word at the capital. Something about a *retreat,* I believe..."

So that's why you're here. The commander grimaced. "Yes, correspondence has been... *testing* at best. I can only apologise to the Governor for the lack of word from our front lines."

"It has been noted," she said bluntly. "Although it would appear that that issue has been resolved… as this *is* now our front-line, within eyesight of the border."

Revek watched the anger rise and fall like a flickering flame in the Marshal's eye, sensing his own rage do the same. "As I said, it has been *testing* at best out here," he retorted. "The hard resistance of our enemy has proven difficult to match over such a vast terrain—"

"Three separate armies set off with near two thousand men apiece at the start of this, with a thousand more in reserve as a rear-guard. It was a force designed to march, and to fight, and to draw up at the borders of Val Azbann with fire in their hearts… and yet you sit here and complain about *difficulty of covering terrain?*" She scoffed. "If you care to realise, commander, that the western detachments along the Kazbak Hills have hardly budged since the enemy rebuttal, and the coast remains largely in our control with blockades established at every port. The war effort remains alive, albeit on the defensive, with our gains being held on most fronts. So, as it turns out, the only place where the enemy have made *significant* gains… is straight through the middle. An army detachment, by all accounts, under the full jurisdiction and control of *you*."

"What are you accusing me of?" Revek spat. "If you know a thing about the logistics of battle, you'd understand that you attack when you have the best numerical advantage, and the easiest terrain to press it. It's not my *fault* that I had a depleted army when I reached the Grey Plains, and was ambushed by a force that was nearly double our strength—"

"Were the reserves contacted?"

He stalled. "What?"

"The thousand-strong reserve force waiting at the back lines, with the exact purpose of swelling the numbers of *your* army… were they contacted?"

A lump in his throat; Revek blinked heavily. "I—"

"—don't need you to answer that," Lazaerys grumbled, "because I was already contacted by another of your officers before you set off for the Plains. They told me that they were concerned that, if you came under surprise attack by a large enemy force, you would not have the numbers to repel them, by the name of…"

Darius. The memory shot back to the forefront of his mind, the anger tossing like the winter's tide. How he had paced by the river, and heard the crossbow *click.* Watching the blood jet from the general's skull, running the river purple. How good it had felt: how *righteous* it had been to put him to the mud for his treachery. The requisition of control he had felt, as he dragged the general's body across the stream and dumped it in the woods. Revek felt it bubbling within him again: that same pride and envy swelling. The thoughts spinning, wandering. *That ruinous bastard—*

"Commander."

His gaze levelled with hers again. "Yes?"

"Am I correct in understanding that the general who delivered that message is now dead?"

A hidden smile. "Yes… he died trying to save me."

"I see." She gave a slow nod. "Then we honour his memory, serving his country."

There was a stark silence, as the generals around him lowered their heads and took a moment of reflection over the loss of their friend. Revek stood at the centre, watching, the sheer loathing in his gut churning over like a sawblade. *Don't pity him… don't pity him, he doesn't deserve it… I survived, and I have been routed… this should be my pity!*

"What is this about, then?" the commander finally snapped, breaking the solemnity. "Because if you're just here to blindly lecture me on the realities of war, then I'm not interested."

Heads lifted; a few looks of disapproval glowered his way. Lazaerys was last to lift her head – and by all estimations, her disdain for him was strongest of all.

Revek ground his teeth. "Come on… *raise your charge*."

The Marshal inhaled deeply. "Among the council, concerns have been raised about your… *conduct*, out in the field," she muttered. "About the treatment of officers, and the distribution of supplies, and the somewhat *erratic* decisions that you have made in the engagement of battle. The council agreed to send me out to investigate, as Field Marshal of the Provenci Army, to see if such concerns were well founded." She rubbed the thick of her brow with a thumb. "And what I found when I arrived, was not so much an army, but rather the ashes of one... burnt, it seems, by the torchbearer's own hand." The round of her pupils speared deep into his own.

"You accuse me of misconduct ... in the organisation of the army *I* command, and have been given full authority of for the entirety of this war? An army that you said yourself, is faring in a healthy and organised state across much of the frontier?" Revek clenched a fist by his side. "I find this very demeaning, especially coming from the stately fools of the *council* back home..."

"I would also find it demeaning, if you were to call me a *liar...*"

"You dare challenge my authority over this army?"

"There's hardly any army *left*..."

"You think that's *my* fault!"

She slammed a finger down onto the makeshift table, directing toward an open map and a vast stretch of trees covering most of lower Tarraz. "Well, if it's not your fault, commander... then I want you to answer something for me." She levelled her eyes. "What the *fuck* happened in Ozban Forest?"

"I... well..." Revek stalled, his heart drawing suddenly still. "Well I... I..."

Words seemed to abandon him. A darkness cornered his mind.

Screams echoed out through his head as the memory returned...

In the dark depths of the forest, stretching on and on ahead, the day and night had no end in any direction. There were just skeletal trees and tiny shoots of leaves and the hungry lap of wind whistling through their tired boughs. Then there were the soldiers, stumbling about all around him with terror in their eyes, screeching at him for orders.

And the howls, echoing out from the gloom behind them, drawing ever closer...

"Near a thousand soldiers, your scouts reported, fled into that forest when the ranks broke and the enemy swept down from the Plains," Lazaerys exclaimed. "A thousand of our own, lost in the depths of that hellscape, hunted by roving Hounds and blackcoats on horseback cutting them down in their dozens. Good, honest people, looking for a leader in their darkest hour…"

Revek recalled the nights spent shuddering with sleepless nausea, pinned to the shallow roots of trees, sword swinging at shadows in the dark. The eerie whispers of men gone mad echoing all around, circling through the endless landscape, cut short by the death-knell of their dying screams.

Then the sound of hooves, approaching from behind one day: the familiar cry of one of his own people, there to rescue him and rally the others to safety…

"Our reports said that one of them found you, stumbling and sweating, sword hanging heavy in one hand. You were as good as dead like so many others, and had a long way to go. He wanted to help you; to rally the troops and get them home safe. And then something happened, and only you know what…"

Revek recalled an arm reaching down, and a warm face appearing aglow with relief. The snort of the horse next to him; the beat of its hooves; the strength buried in the thick spurs of its legs—

Dragging the man from his saddle suddenly, a dark plague racking his thoughts. A sword pulled from its scabbard; the pleading cries of the soldier merging with the screams of the night…

Blood on his hands and a rot on his soul, as he drove the blade down – mounting the horse and driving south, abandoning the dark where it lay…

"…all we do know, is that only three hundred of those who entered that forest, reached this outpost alive," Lazaerys exclaimed. "That seven hundred lie dead or captured in the depths of the Ozban… and that you, commander, abandoned every last one of them, just to save yourself. So I will ask, once and once only… do you have anything to *say* for yourself?"

Revek said nothing, entranced by the hollow screams still ringing out in his ears, his fists clenched white with fear and rage all embroiled into one.

So much death, he thought.

So much darkness…

Looking to his fellow officers – and their clear disappointment – he ground his teeth and turned back to the Marshal ahead, silencing the echoes of his mind.

"I did, as *any* reasonable man would've done, faced with such dire circumstances," the commander boomed. "The battle was lost, and we were routed… so I took the chance, and I *survived*. And my heart bleeds for the many dead we lost in that forest… but I will *not* be sullied for the choice I made getting out of there alive."

Lazaerys remained expressionless, sullen almost, as the commander spoke, sighing softly to herself in the din. "And it is for that reason… that you are *not* being sent back to Casantri to be tried by the military courts," the Marshal explained. "Because, despite the *clear* deficiencies in your strategy and command throughout this campaign… you did what you could to survive in the end, and at least a portion of the army still remains. So, it has been agreed with the council that you shall stay on as commander of the army, and continue to lead the forces during this war…"

"As it should be—"

"*However,* this is on the understanding that a few new conditions are met first."

Revek nearly swallowed his tongue. "What *conditions?*" he spat.

"You will be put under the supervision of several of our generals, who will remain as subordinates but will report back to me if anything goes… *awry,* shall we say." The faint glint of a smile touched her lips for a moment – *almost as if she were enjoying it*. "And, your commandership of the army will be divided between you and another high-ranking officer, to improve the efficiency on the northern and southern fronts…"

Revek spluttered. *What did you fucking say?*

"What? Who decided this?"

"The council, under orders of the Governor himself."

That covetous snake! "That doesn't make any sense… I have the Governor's favour."

"And Alvarez feels differently now.

Revek shook his head, looking up to the tent roof in disbelief. "And who is this *other* ranking officer you speak of?"

Her smile appeared in full, now.

"That… would be *me*."

The commander's eyes bulged. "You *what*—"

"I have been *appointed* as Commander of the Northern Frontier and Joint-Leader of the Provenci Army, while you command the southern legions and co-opt authority with me. We shall have equal powers and equal stead over how the war is directed, and where resources are best allocated, for maximum effect against our enemy."

"This is an outrage!" Revek growled. "I was appointed as commander of this army, *not* you. I have led the war effort, *not* you. I have—"

"Put the lives of hundreds of our soldiers out for slaughter, and have displayed a *complete* lack of discipline and tact in your strategies and morality in directing this army. Therefore, it was decided by the council to appoint a second commander to help '*ease the burden*' of your work." The smile lingered infuriatingly.

His eye twitched. "I won't stand for this."

"You don't have a choice. This was an order directly from Alvarez himself… so, if you have any problems with that order, then you take it up with *him*. Until then, I am your equal, and this army is as much mine as it is yours."

Revek flared his teeth, growling, machinations spinning through his head like needles. How the carpet had been dragged out from beneath him; how he had been supplanted by some other capital official with a point to make and a bone to pick.

Fucking ruinous authority. Embers burned in his chest. *As if the council know what's best… whispering hate in the ears of the Governor. Such a failure of sense, a failure of structure, a failure of protocol—*

Fuck!

He speared a finger in her direction across the table. "This isn't the end of this, I hope you know," Revek growled. "I will have what's mine, and you will rue the day you tried to *take* that from me."

"As you so wish, officer," Lazaerys mocked in reply. "I await to see your *responses*."

The commander turned on his heel and exited the tent with fire trailing his every step.

They think they have control of me, he bellowed within. *They think this is a game... this is no game. I have the power here.* His blade tugged at his side like a doting whore. *I have the power here. I always have.*

And no-one shall take that from me.

†

Chapter 3

Kingdom of Ash

Preening its feathers with a grey beak, the rook snapped a twig from the branch it perched upon and laced it through its wing, tugging at a deeper fissure that had proved particularly hard to reach. Methodically, it drew the twig back and forth to catch at the skin beneath. It made perhaps three passes, grumbling in pleasure, before the twig snapped completely and splinters showered its oily coat. A flush of frustration, and the rook flicked its wings open, squawking out to the grey sky through the yellowing leaves of the oak it roosted in.

The landscape beyond was serene, uncompromised by the distant roar of warfare and the desecration of the world beyond. It was an as-yet unbroken place, with rolling fields of wheat and barley, dissected with stone walls and winding dirt roads and the occasional dour shape of a windmill, its great wooden turbines jostling delicately in the low winds. The grey smudge of the border wall harassed the horizon to the north; the porcelain struts and pinnacles of Casantri were but a harsh shadow to the east. But at that middling spot where the rook roosted, neither bloody violence nor woeful politics had come to sow their seeds. For how long that would last, one could not guess, in a place where conflict was always a breath away.

And war would soon be the only answer.

The rook craned its neck slowly to the west, the persistent scent of smoke tapping at its nostrils. For out there, toward the mountains, it found a world of smouldered ash and ruined fields, coiling across Provenci like a serpent. It was like a bruise, furrowed by black trenches. Entire landholdings, bathed in flame for days long past, until nothing remained but a dust-bowl of barren, nutrient soil. The only strike of green that remained, came from the tiny pockets of woodland still intact, the perpetrators having directed the fire from their trunks to preserve something of the natural order. To show it was a deliberate act, most of all: to let the world burn, but only so far. Illustrating that fine line between control and chaos, to prove the destruction was not in vain.

That it served a greater purpose, as the bane of war rose its ugly head from the east.

The rook let out a stiff *caw* and went back to preening its feathers, not caring for war or fires or blood. Lacing the beak down the ridge of its back, it pulled at moss and debris, flicking them away with sudden jolts. Looking to and fro: from black feathers to branches, up to the sky and the horizon, seeing dust rise in the east, to the—

Snapping its neck round, the rook stopped its preening. On the near horizon, a faint plume of dust began to form, blotted out by the glare of the sun. It seemed to match the undulations of the nearest road as it snaked over the hills.

A road which passed under the very tree that the crow found itself in.

As the shape manifested, the form of a rider drew the bird's attention, donned in leather bounds with an empty scabbard at their hip. Driving the horse at a daunting pace, the rook's keen eye spied the flaring nostrils and pumping hooves of the great beast as it approached. The rider by comparison wore a vicious snarl with their eyes creased, and the sore remnants of tears streaking their cheeks.

The bird had little time to respond, or take in their approach. In the blink of an eye, the rider had crested the next ridge, and pressed on hard toward the lonesome oak.

The rook within its branches startled and took flight suddenly, squawking its concern and fear, before circling west toward the ashen realm and the war that had claimed its home.

†

He's dead.

The horse thundered beneath her, skating past low stone walls and wide grey fields on a narrow track west. The air was clear, the sky still, echoing out over wide plains – until the black smudge of destruction clouded the skyline before her, and the ashen kingdom lay bare beneath her feet.

He's dead.

Her hand lay braced across the saddle, white-knuckles bare. She had gone so long without moving, that all sensation was numb. The rope had sawn over her palms like sandpaper; a purple-ish tinge stained the bindings beneath. Yet she didn't dare let go, not until she got there and she was safe. Because last time she let go... *last time I let go...*

He died.

Arcing her head back, Jinx screamed out into the gloom.

And now only death shall prevail.

Tracing the line of the road, salt stabbing her eyes, Jinx marked a nearby farmhouse with what looked like a camp scattered at its base. It stood slightly before the scorch-line, under the boughs of a fastidious stone windmill: several dozen tents and encampments with storage carts and carrier mules, the mess-halls and open fires sprawled for almost a mile to the north. It was a demarcation, she knew: the human presence of life, just beyond the fire-ravaged world beyond. That within that camp lay the blood and steel of the entire western lands, amassed at the edge of an ashen plain.

Stood before a kingdom of their own making.

Approaching the camp at breakneck speed, it was only the sudden appearance of armed guards blockading the end of the road that forced Jinx to rein in the horse and pull to a steady pace. The horse snorted its agony, having been pushed and punished for every mile since leaving the capital, days and days on end. But with a head full of rage and a flash of pain in her eye, the thief found herself uncaring. *For the mess we find ourselves in, pain is a small price to pay,* she mused sombrely.

For what we have lost, no suffering can compare.

Slowly, both horse and rider drew to a stop, as the soldiers eased away from their shield wall and stepped forward in cautious greeting.

"This is a closed area," the foremost guard exclaimed, waving a hand. "No-one from Casantri may enter this zone. Turn back now, or face lethal force."

Don't you dare. Jinx found a bubble of anger within, quickly stilled with an outward breath. "I have the right to enter," she proclaimed. "I hold a place here. And if what I have been told is correct, you are led by one called Eli... someone I know rather well."

"And what of it?" the guard spat. "What right do you have to—"

"Because she's my sister in-law."

Like a blast of thunder, the voice echoed out over the plains, above the wind and the rattle of the camp, studding in the ears of all those present. The guards drew quiet suddenly, parting down the middle, their eyes lowered in silent respect.

From beyond them, strode a man with a head like a cannonball, and a vast forest of hair spilling from his lip to his chest. Every exhale was a storm unto itself, shifting a muscular body that lay encased in plates of steel armour. With a bludgeon hanging across his back and a mass of rings tasselled to his broad and bruised fingers, he was a formidable man to witness. A man who commanded the respect of the entire western lands; an overseer, at the helm of thousands. A man of unmatched mettle, like cast iron and wrought stone.

A man whom Jinx had so longed to see again.

"Hello, Alva," Eli rumbled, the inklings of a smile curling at his cheek. "It's been some time."

A lump caught in her throat, the well within her bubbling and breaching like a ship over vast ocean waves. She ran, uncaring of all other things – of the soldiers suddenly reaching for swords, stilled by a tiny wave of Eli's hand – and fell into his grasp, bracing tight across the cold steel of his chest. Like closing gates, the two great trunks of his arms pulled her tight, the rough of his beard coiling over her face. She found the tears reach a peak, threatening to overwhelm her, bitten down only by the calming rise of the huge man's chest.

They parted, and Jinx smiled warmly. Eli did likewise, but his face turned suddenly grave at the sight of Casantri on the horizon.

"Much has happened since we last spoke," he rumbled forlornly. "A king dead. Disloyal officers of the army vaulted into power. A war with an ancient enemy, as little more than an act of revenge... and still to this day there's no-one to answer for it." He rolled his fingers together. "And now I stand here, Chief of the Mountains, several thousand men and women in my ranks... standing against the very country I love." He sighed, shaking his head. "How has this even happened?"

"It was Alvarez," Jinx said coldly. "And Revek, and Ferreus... and all the rest of them. They've driven us head-first into this mess."

"Treachery, masquerading as order..."

"They're *butchers* and *liars*."

"And now that the tide of war has turned against them, and their legitimacy is threatened... I dread to think what comes next." He turned to his soldiers. "You may leave us... I wish to speak to my sister-in-law alone. You are dismissed."

One by one, the soldiers bowed their heads, and peeled off into the throng of the wider camp with unease weighing heavy behind their eyes.

"So, they've made you Chief of the Mountains?" Jinx mused quietly when they'd gone. "We haven't had one of those for near one-hundred-and-twenty years, if my memory doesn't fail me."

"Aye, you're right," he boomed. "It's an oddity. I stand on the shoulders of the likes of Krallos God-Splitter, the last true rebel of the west."

"That's quite an honour."

He scoffed. "It's a fool's blessing, is what it is. We are a rogue people by nature, us western folk… so to claim that I have any command out here is almost a joke in itself. The only reason they all fall in line as well as they do, is because we now have a common enemy…"

Jinx nodded. "Has there been much change in the west since the army took charge? Any greater presence?"

"You could say that. They had camps set up all across the countryside hidden away in groves of trees, conducting business out of sight and out of mind in the hopes we wouldn't catch on. And we didn't for some time… that was until the 'enforcement patrols' started scouring the villages, picking out any undesirables to send to their camps. Those that were taken were forced to work the land, and smith weapons, and provide provisions for the army… you know the type. And rather painfully, we also know that those who did end up in those camps, were rarely kept in conditions allowing them to survive for very long." A weighted pause. "Hundreds of our people were taken. Someone's brother, someone's son or daughter… someone's young child, even. All were sent to the camps… none were to survive."

"I'm so sorry," she muttered, looking to the ash-lands beyond. "What of the camps now?"

"We burned them to the ground," he growled. "Every officer we found, we killed. Melted down their shackles to make weapons, and used the wasted material to build our defences. We found none of our own left, however, in the end… only their graves, unmarked and numbering in their dozens."

Jinx found the anger rise again, overturning the sorrow and grief that had swelled within her thus-far. *Dozens dead, over the space of a few weeks, at the hands of people who were trusted to protect them.* Nausea came; she inhaled and let it recede. *And now that trust is gone… and all that's left is anger and rebellion.* Looking to the camp behind, she saw it playing out before her very eyes. *A people hurting…*

Longing to be free.

"I'm sorry," Jinx managed in reply.

Eli shrugged. "Such is life, and the nature of power in the hands of those who shouldn't wield it. What is done is done… and it's what happens next that matters."

"And what *does* happen next?"

"That will depend on how things are in the capital! How fares business there?"

She pursued her lips. "The city is under martial law: none get in, and sure as hell none get out. Patrols mark every avenue and street corner – if anyone so much as looks in the wrong direction, they're taken from their holdings by armed guards and returned bruised and battered come morning. It's… a great terror, for all involved. I only just escaped with my…"

The words dried up, hollowed, the well of guilt and swamping despair threatening to drag her down.

And for a moment, all was silent: Jinx looked up from the ground to find no sensation in her body, and no thoughts in her mind. The shells of her ears were numbed entirely, as if filled with wool. There was nothing, in that fleeting space: just the camp along the horizon, and the smoke rising skyward – and Eli, stood before her, studying her with the same quiet concern he always seemed to possess.

Then he was mumbling words, words she followed almost in slow-motion.

And Jinx found the pit of agony in her heart breach, as she realised what he was asking.

How is Arrenso?

Sensation suddenly phased back into the world around her: the soreness of her feet; the bruises over her hands; the salt-stained streaks lining her cheeks, stinging acutely around her eyes. The weight of the truth she had carried with her, from the sickened walls of Casantri across miles and miles of rolling plain. She looked to Eli – tears welling, but with not a word spoken – and within that same breath, he knew.

He knows his husband has been murdered.

Hopelessly, at the whim of a cold reality, Jinx watched Eli's jaw clench and his fingers slide together. A glassy sheen coated his eyes, blinked back furiously, a bubble in his throat forced down with a gulp of emotion. He rolled his tongue over his teeth, just to save himself from screaming, as the echoes rung out between them of a man who had had his soul ripped from his body.

Knowing Arrenso's gone.

"Eli..." Jinx muttered, tearful, her voice crackling like embers. She lifted her hands to try and console him. "I..."

The huge man held out his hand, silencing her, a stoic resolve taking shape across his face.

"Walk with me," he said plainly, biting through pain. "Tell me *everything*..."

"It turned out Bearskin was a traitor, and ... he sold us out to Ferreus and his *bastard* henchmen. So... so a battle ensued, and we lost Shivers, and Shadow was wounded in the fighting. I went after Arrenso, and Bearskin was killed in the end, and... and we escaped back through the sewers, trying desperately to get him out... but he was so *weak*, Eli. There was hardly anything left to 'im. He was just skin and bones by that point, blackened by bruises." Jinx shivered at the thought. "So we got to the pumphouse, with the outlet pipe stretching beyond the walls... and I thought we'd make it, genuinely, in that moment. But then..." Jinx stifled, forcing the words out almost as if being sick. "Alvarez appeared on horseback, obviously informed by Ferreus of what had happened. We were ambushed, and there was a stand-off, and we tried to fend him off but..."

Within the confines of the command tent – empty, beyond a single table at the centre laid out with maps and battleplans – Jinx looked up to Eli with a tearful sorrow, and bit her lip.

"I'm so sorry, Eli... I'm so *sorry*..."

The huge man said nothing in response. His face remained unchanged, characteristically muted. He simply clasped his hands tighter against the tabletop, carrying the weight of the world on his shoulders – *fearing the void that had now opened up at his feet.*

Like an echo, Jinx sensed that same fear resonate within her own heart: the thousand tiny glimmers of hope dashed in that moment, as the Governor had driven his blade through. It was unfathomable; it wrenched at her thoughts and drowned her slowly. *My brother is dead,* she longed to scream.

What do we do now?

"I am glad you are still alive, Alva," he said potently, nodding his head. "From what you've been through, I understand that's no easy task." He sighed; Jinx heard the quiver in his breath. "But it also makes clear to me what lies ahead for us, and how there seems to be no diplomatic solutions to avert the coming conflict. We have our hands tied... with only swords left to match it." He looked to the ceiling, and then back to the floor. "My heart aches, for the loss of the man who gave me such hope in my life. My dear Arrenso, I..."

His voice snapped at the last word, fearing an overflow. Eli ground his jaw, bashing a fist against the table.

"It's not your fault," Jinx exclaimed, holding his arm. "None of it is. You were his pride and joy; you were *his* light in all this. And I know... because he was my brother too." The wave rose within, but rather than repressing it, she conjured it around her. "I've lost the one person who I've always held closest, the one I could always rely on... and when you married into this family, you became a part of that. A part of *us.* And every time I saw him, he spoke of pride and honour, not just in his service and how he conducted himself, but also in *you*. In *your* honour, and *your* ambition. The one who he trusted with all his heart to look after his children. He was so *proud* of you, and cared for you and worried about you in every single way. Because, well... that was Arrenso. That was my brother... a man who knew honour, and saw what was right, and did all he could to build those bridges between the two." She exhaled at length. "I may have lost my brother, and you may have lost the man you love... but even in death, I know, he would have never lost the pride and love he held for both of us" – she caught his eye – "and the honour he had, in having you by his side."

His face hardly moved, wavering slightly, before she watched it crack into a wide smile like a warm fire's glow. Eli nodded slowly, a single tear rolling down his cheek. "Thank you, Alva," he said in reply. "I appreciate you saying that."

"It's okay, the truth needs to be heard sometimes. Besides, there's a severe fucking shortage of it going at the moment."

He raised his hands. "You can say that again..."

They looked to each other and smiled, passing the moments in silence, a quiet reciprocation of grief crossing between them.

"Now, you should go and rest," he said softly after a while. "The officers outside will guide you to your quarters. I'll send the cooks around in an hour or so to feed you." He paused, his face sinking like a stone. "Because what I have to do now, is something I don't want you to see..."

Jinx recoiled at the gravity in his voice and the sudden shift in tone. Sensing his severity, she bowed her head and made for the tent's opening, her voice abandoning the questions she longed to ask. *What does he mean? What business needs attending? Has something gone wrong? Have I said something wrong, somehow? I don't know...*

Before leaving, she turned once, and saw Eli disappear into another room along the back. From there, she heard the sudden spur of children's voices.

And her heart sank, as she realised what was about to happen.

She left the tent, peeling the door open and stepping outside into the sun.

Where an agonised scream ran out, as Camilla and Davo were told their father had died.

†

Chapter 4

Champion's Venom

They had been on the road for three days.

It had all come as a shock at first. Under the cover of night, armed guards had swarmed her rooms and seized all of her belongings. She had been bagged and bound in the furore, and had been dragged from her quarters in the nestled streets of Val Darbesh without explanation. Not a word had been spoken of why, or where she was going. Only that she should remain quiet, and hush the rattles of the chains that now bound her hands.

Reaching a ramp sometime later, she had been half-thrown into the back of a carriage, only truly realising where she was when the doors slammed shut at her back. And then she had sat there, staring at walls in an uneasy silence, with the only words being those of the driver just before they set off.

"*On, to Val Azbann.*"

Three days later, gazing out the window of her wooden carriage, Savanta watched the ashen wastes of Tarraz spill out across the landscape beyond, flinching up toward the distant mountain skies where lightning speared like falling rain. There was thunder almost constantly, she had come to realise – poetic, almost, for a nation so attuned to the drums of war. But, beyond that, there was little to discern or make sense of in the landscape around her: from the sands of the great desert to the stone crags of the Kazbaks, the land she witnessed seemed to be a new entity altogether. Broken shards of rock, dusted with an ashen soil that knew nothing of moisture; the harrowed husks of ancient trees, sprouting here and there like statues of forgotten times; the occasional chasm ripping the land in two, reaching down to far off places untouched by the human eye. There was little life in the ravaged land, so she found: the circling presence of crows; the towering form of a vulture stooped coldly in a dead tree; spurs of ground where slate-grey foxes emerged, off to hunt the wastes for whatever prey dared dwell there. The few lone creatures, ebbing out a life in the vast nothing. A place so devoid and lost. Yet, even with the desolation of it all, Savanta found not even that was the most haunting thing about the place.

As it was the silence – the sheer lack of *anything* – that ate at her soul the most.

There's nothing, she mused to herself. *Not even the whisper of the wind. Just… nothingness, as if the world is hollow.* A tension in her chest came and went; she sucked air through her teeth and found it was uncomfortably warm, like inhaling vapour. *This place is a unique kind of hell. Where is everything?*

Savanta pulled away from the window and sighed longingly. She found herself almost tempted by the thought of a few hours' sleep. Something to pass the time; to wish the world away in silence. Such was her thinking, and she almost lay her head against the wood at her side to rest, when a sudden cataclysm of noise roared into life in the world beyond, and a spur of voices and metal and fire and grand industry pummelled her ears like cannon-fire.

She shot upright once again, a fearful tumult in her mind; suddenly crawling onto the bench, peering out the window at the vastness beyond—

To find iron citadels now marked the horizon of Tarraz, as far as the eye could see.

What is this…

There were hundreds of them, constructed with more metal than she ever thought could be mined of the earth. They were towering beasts crowned with metal spears, with patrols of foot-soldiers and workers marching the base carrying loaded carts of material and fuel. From the peak of each tower, a mass of black smog thick as night belched skyward, smothering the grey-gold sky and distant mountains in an unending hale. Catching at her ears thunderously, the crackle and wrench of a thousand furnaces roared with imperious power, feeding an ever-hungry machine that creaked and groaned before her like a great dragon of old. As they passed several by, she gazed up and around them, trying to understand just how they could be built so large and in such short time. Hundreds of them, circling off to the east. A barricade of industry corralling some place that lay in the wastes of the world ahead of them.

Those words again: *Val Azbann.*

What the fuck is going on...

Almost as soon as they had appeared, the citadels receded – open land broke out before her, all dead trees and rocks again. She wondered for a moment what the point was: to have it so uniform and regimented, then to fall away for no reason.

So it was, until the metal foundations of a colossal wall sprawled along the horizon to her right, lined with towers and artillery and dotted with huge gates as far as the eye could see. The citadels were little more than the outskirts: what she now lay eyes on, was the beating heart itself. The great capital of the north.

Val Azbann.

She inhaled suddenly, the air catching in her lungs. *What have I gotten myself into?* The screech of gears sounded ahead as a set of great gates opened, and the shadow of an archway bathed the carriage in darkness for a second. *To go to the beating heart of the enemy, as champion to a woman the world thought dead for twenty-five years. To sell my life on a whim.* She tempered the void inside, forming a tight knot in her mind. *And for what? Fame? Glory? Money? A chance at a new life?*

She sighed, pinching the bridge of her nose, and looked out again to the desolation beyond. Within the metal wall, she now lay her eyes upon rows and rows of labour camps, stretching for miles across. Tiny cloth canopies, the colour of bleached bone, dotting the earth like studs. Men and woman of all ages passed between them, hobbling about in rags, dragging tools in gnarled hands butchered by the wounds of their labour.

And as she studied them, crossing from one to another, she found to her surprise that not one of them would look to her, or the carriage, or even to the open gates only a hundred feet away. Instead, they looked down to their scarred feet, absent and withdrawn, lost in the rigmarole of servitude with no hope left to spare. Dozens of them, and dozens more, milling about like ants. Grey and dour and lost and hurt. Tiny parts of a war machine.

Slaves and nothing more.

Savanta found her stomach turn, likely from hunger more than pity, and so she absently pulled away from the window—

Catching sight of a one-armed man staring up at the carriage, the only one to do so of the masses.

Suddenly she was back to her feet with her heart in her throat, looking out for him from afar: only to find he was little more than a boy, an arm tucked behind his back, playing with the bindings of his overall.

Savanta slumped into her seat, rapid breaths swelling through her throat, and eased her fingers over the bench.

Markus. The accompanying feelings welted at the thought of him: loss, hate, anger, despair. All broken, doomed to be so, without any purpose behind them. *Markus... it couldn't end any other way.* Recalling his poor face and his broken soul, as she cut him down to his knees. The sheer lack of anything in her mind in that singular moment, beyond the reality that she found herself living, and in turn ceased to be. *I had to do it,* she told herself. *I had to,* she admitted. *For the sake of what we set out for.*

For revenge.

Among the recesses of her heart, anger ballooned to the forefront, and suddenly all other emotion was moot. She sat there seething, white-knuckled, every pitiful thought of Markus snapped away in an instant.

This is about revenge, she cried. *This is about revenge, and he knew that. There was never a guarantee of survival, and he came into this with that knowledge. I was never false to it.* She gazed up to the high window, rafts of light breaching through. *I did what I had to... I did what was needed to get my chance.* She ground her teeth, rolling her tongue. *And now I am champion, taken to Val Azbann for the Iron Queen's amusement. I will be made to fight for her.* A short laugh, with something maniacal in her eye. *But I won't. I won't in the end.*

Savanta pulled at the knife-holster in her belt, and smiled. *I'm here to kill the Iron Queen, after all.*

To kill that bitch, for what they did to my father.

†

Chapter 5

Those We Have Lost

We fight a war on all fronts, Alvarez mused into the wind. *We fight a war in the north, against our ancient enemy, with all their mustered savagery.*

We fight a war within our ranks, where the truth is best left unsaid, and those who question that, are best made forgotten.

And now we fight a war against our people... those who dare oppose the unity and grandeur of our once great nation. The Supreme Governor's eyes traced the horizon, marked by ash and coiling flame, and he ground his teeth. *A thorn in my side, jeopardising our power.* He took a long swig of air and spat into the grass beneath him.

They will die for their insubordination.

"Are we ready, sir?" General Ferreus asked from beside him, their horses snapping and snorting at each other with ill-patience.

"I've always been ready, general," Alvarez proclaimed, adjusting the huge chain-link plates across his chest, glistening in the low morning sun. "The might of Casantri stands with us... we are indomitable."

"You command a great strength, for certain."

"I command *honour*, general... honour against all odds."

"Then we shall see if the rebels can match our tenacity."

A quiet smile. "We shan't give them the chance..."

Ferreus nodded. "May I do the honours, sir?"

"By all means, general: bring the ranks to the fore. Let our new enemy see what the *true* might of Casantri looks like..."

Atop the ridge of a small hill, with the sun raining down through the clouds above, Ferreus raised a horn to his lips and drew a long, haunting note.

All around, came the sudden clatter of metal; the crash of steel and jostling blades as a great force shifted into formation at their backs. The *thud* of polished boots suddenly rallied forward, as soldiers crested the ridge behind them: first dozens, then hundreds, until the entire hillside was marked by glittering silver chest-plates and the red-green standards of Provenci's Land Army. It was a zealous symbol of the might of the nation, summoned to wage war on the known world with the great capital etched into the skyline at their backs. And there was Alvarez, stood at its head: the Supreme Governor and champion of the new era, gazing out across the rolling fields of his homeland.

To an enemy on the near horizon, soon to be doused in blood.

Ten days passed... and we have rallied an army that even the Tarrazi would cower at the feet of, Alvarez cooed. *Ten days of reorganisation and planning... of rapid deployment, giving the hard-working reserves their swords. Ten days since the fires began... and here we are, with an army of historic greatness, ready to rebalance the world.*

And deliver to me my rightful claim.

"It appears their main base of operations is around that windmill to the south-west," Ferreus said, spearing a finger out toward the fire-bitten border. "That's where the largest camps converge. And I imagine it's also where that bastard Eli probably resides..."

Eli. Alvarez sensed the kindling crackle to life in his chest. *Why couldn't he just die off like his dear husband... it would've made my life so much easier.* "It'll be nice to watch him die," the Governor said.

"I long to string him up and gut him for his treachery. The arrogance, thinking he could stand against us..."

"Do not let your duties become mired by a *vendetta,* general." Alvarez pursed his lips, watching Ferreus visibly recoil. "You will have your time for revenge… although General Broska slipped through your fingers, it shall be Eli's blood that douses your hands now."

"With pleasure, sir."

"Good." He inhaled at length. "I want you to take the bulk of the army and pincer toward their camps over the hills. Have other contingents move out on either flank, and seize any towns or buildings you find along the way. Be thorough… I'll have no ruinous fucking *mountain-dwellers* catching us off-guard."

"As you wish, sir," came the cordial response.

This is our power. The Governor gazed off over the clouds, bathed in evergreen sun. *This is ours to control. They cannot have it… they will never have it.* He screwed his nose up. *They will not stand in the way of my vision. They are heretics, defilers, outcasts of no order.*

And they shall be driven into the ground for their insolence.

"General Ferreus," Alvarez boomed as the greying man cantered off down the hill.

The general turned. "Yes, sir?"

"Bring me his head, when you're done." A cold, humourless laugh escaped his lips. "I shall have it thrown in the cellar with his husband's body, and watch as the rats feed on the both of them. The wretched should stay with the wretched, after all, as that is all they deserve…"

Ferreus grinned. "Of course, sir."

Good.

He watched the general move off, rallying the bulk of the army at his back, readying the march to the camp where the rebels lay in their squalor.

This is ours to control, the Governor thought with a grin.

None shall take that from us.

†

The Imperial Regional Army formed along the eastern hillside like the scales of an iridescent fish, with snapping teeth and biting steel and the cold inevitability of hate. Near a hundred across with countless more behind, their polished chest-plates shimmered in the ample sun that breached the grey smog above. Scanning their ranks purposefully, three horses reared to the centre of their mass, with the red-and-green imperial standards billowing tamely behind.

And at that moment, Eli knew he was looking upon the shadows of Alvarez and Ferreus.

The two men who had killed his husband.

A shiver ran up his spine, threatening nausea in his stomach. *The bastards behind all of this,* he growled. The wind seemed to pick up suddenly, billowing through his beard. *How I long to strike you both down for what you have taken from me.*

And how I shall savour it.

Eli spat into the dirt at his feet and turned, giving a curt nod to the guards as they pulled their spears aside and bade him entry to the command tent. He ducked inside, passing from biting winds to warm, heavy air, studying the dozen or so rebels amassed before him with embracing smiles. They were a loyal clique: disenchanted, bloodthirsty men and women much like himself, longing for brandished steel and a turn back to times more peaceful. They inhaled as one as their Chief entered the tent, straightening backs and bowing heads as he approached the table at the centre of the room coated in layers of maps.

They believe me some kind of saviour, he found himself scoffing.

Let's see if they're misguiding or not...

As he drew to a halt, his gaze swung to the left, and between two arms he saw the frail shape of Jinx slunk down over a small chair, her head hung low and condemned. She had hardly moved since arriving: locked away in her tent, barely eating and certainly not sleeping. She had hardly spoken, either. Eli had gone to see her several times, and despite any attempt to motivate her or keep her busy, he always found her in the same state as before.

She is haunted, he acknowledged, noting the red-raw skin around both eyes. *She bears the long shadows of mourning... of guilt too. That she felt she should've done more.* He stifled his own emotion, his own grief simmering just under the surface. *She did what she could... she should not blame herself for what happened.* His face hardened. *Because the blame lies with those who gather on the eastern plains.*

And it is their blood that shall be spilt in his name.

"How is it out there, captain?" one of the officers enquired, as Eli placed his huge hands on the tabletop and sighed.

"By the look of the hillsides out there, it appears that they've amassed the entire reserve army against us," the Chief announced morbidly. The room seemed to cool around him.

"How many is that?"

He paused. "Near one-thousand soldiers, would be my estimate... all fully-armoured and weaponised, with enough strategists between them to make the gods blush."

"We number near enough that ourselves," another of them cooed in reply. "We can take 'em."

"I would agree... although I fear your enthusiasm may be slightly misguided. We may number near equal to them... but we are little more than a disparate group of workers and farm-hands at best. And against an army of the imperium, well... I don't much fancy our odds."

"But we know the lands, captain," another called out. "Better'n any of them. We know the hideouts, the vantage points... this is *our* land."

"It does play to our advantage, yes, and perhaps such things can turn the tide. But I was still anticipating half the force that they've amassed on that ridge, what with the war in the north trudging on still. But to see the full Land Army amassed, ready to raise hell against us... there is little we can do to stop them."

"What should we do then, captain?"

The Chief of the Mountains looked up from the table and gazed among his officers with tired eyes. He saw there the fear in their hearts; the feeble ruminations of dread creeping through their veins. Worried, he knew, that the cause would die before it had ever truly begun.

And then his gaze passed down to his left again, through the swaying arms of two figures, toward the absent chair where the lowly thief still sat. Looking there, Eli found that Jinx had lifted her head all of a sudden, and was gazing up to him with shiny hazel eyes that spoke volumes of the mind within. That her electric ginger hair seemed to glow like bronze in the light; that she waited expectantly as the others did for the answer they hoped would come.

The Chief of the Mountains smiled warmly, as if the skies were forever blue, and turned back to his fellow countrymen to put a hand against his chest.

"We shall have faith," Eli rumbled, steadying his breath. "To stand side by side, at the precipice of all things, and stride out against an enemy who are far stronger than we can ever be. The odds we face, can never be known, and the outcome is far from certain. I know many of you have given up so much to be here, and risk so much for fighting on. So if you choose to step away now, and preserve that which you know, then I assure you that you will not be forsaken for it. But if you choose to stay and fight with us, together... know that your sacrifice comes with greater honour than I can dream of. And as your captain and your friend, I will stand by your side gladly as we kick those bastards in the *fucking* teeth for what they've done to us." He rose to his full height, impossibly vast and imposing, spreading his arms like wings. "So I charge you, my comrades... who stands with me in this hour of need? Who shall come to the aid of their countrymen, for the greater good of all? Who shall stand by my side, as we take the fight to our enemy, and claim our right once and for all!"

A roar erupted, so loud that the roof of the tent seemed to lift from its seams for a moment. Jeers sounded, salutes and hails like drumbeats to signal the advent of war. Eli joined them, pounding his chest, booming to every bright-eyed man and woman stood there before him. A unity ringing out amongst them, that even the gods dared turn to listen to. A fissure of pride cracked open in his heart, warming like embers within him.

And in the corner of his eye, gazing up through the mass of bodies, he spied the pinprick pupils of Jinx. Her face lay awash with a smile, curling at the edges of her cheeks. Eli bowed his head to her, beaming his joy in return, before muttering two silent words from the depths of his wrenching soul.

For Arrenso…

"Now," the Chief exclaimed, turning ahead once again and raising his hands to settle their cheers, "we must get down to the business of preparation. For the enemy are upon us, and as much as I know you long to bash their heads in at every turn, our practical disadvantage needs to be addressed, so we may survive this ordeal. Is that understood?" A rumble of affirmation from the officers caught in his ear; Eli drew a hand over the map spread across the table before him. "This is a map of the central plains, covering much of the area we now find ourselves fighting over, from that new-fangled border wall to the north, down to the marshes in the south. There are several vantage points we need to make use of, particularly along the wide valley between us and our enemy. Now, Vasco?"

"Aye, captain?" a sleek woman in blue cloth robes replied to his left, missing three fingers on her right hand.

"You'll take a contingent north, along this stretch of woodland at the top of the valley. There's an old farmhouse straddling the rocks facing south; secure it, and keep your scouts there as a lookout. You'll have full view of the valley below and any enemy movements from there."

"Understood."

"Good – Baroq?"

"Yes, cap'n?" a broad figure with braided hair rumbled to his right.

"You will take a similar-sized detachment down through the south to camp along the marshes. I want a perimeter line set up in a wide arc there, from this farmhouse to the old watchtower at the water's edge." Eli indicated the points with his finger. "Hold your command post to the northern tip – if the enemy rout you from the south, push up and regroup with the main force in the valley. No heroics."

"It's blasphemy to expect no heroics, sir... but I'll make an exception."

"If it were an easy fight, I'd give you a-plenty, Baroq... but such is the circumstance we find ourselves in." The broad man have a disappointed nod in reply; Eli turned back to the fore. "Castan?"

A chiselled man with jet-black hair and a broad, unwavering smile gave a nod at his name.

"You shall accompany me through the heart of the valley with the bulk of our force... our aim is to meet them head-on and give them hell from the outset. There's a small village not far from us called Marcheg: that will be our forward command post, and likely the place where the coming battle is fought. We shall embark immediately, as I have my suspicions that our enemy have the same idea, and will try to take the village for themselves. Vasco and Baroq shall depart in a few hours' time with their contingents, and we hope to make camp by dusk. The valley allows us to use light signals to communicate, so keep your lookouts on standby for signs of trouble." Eli passed his gaze, studying them slowly. "Any questions?"

The room lay silent, an understanding passing between them, settling in their minds the hope that things would be okay—

"What if we're overrun?"

Eli turned suddenly; the crowd parted to find Jinx sat up, looking between them awkwardly, her hands trembling in her lap. "What if this doesn't work... and we're defeated?"

The huge man looked into her, almost through her, and found his words betray him. How moments before, she had been so full of life again for the first time in days; how now, cowering in the corner with the world against her, she seemed so consumed in her grief again. He saw there a quiet reflection of his own pain, eating away at his soul. A fickle thing that he begged to bury, yet which seemed to pull closer to the surface all the same. So, hoping to find the answer for her, his response was little more than a mumble in the end. Conscious thought seemed to abandon him; the canopy of the tent seemed to suck inwards like a vortex—

"We'll fight on, is what we'll do," Castan suddenly pronounced, turning to Jinx with a nod. "We do as we have always done, in times of trouble: we survive, and we regroup, and we shall fight to the last with our dying breath if it comes to it."

"And breaking the bones of the elites of Casantri... well, that would be an honourable death by any measure," Baroq growled with a grin.

"Because we stand with Eli, as we stand with you," Vasco muttered to her, a quaint smile poking her lips. "And we stand with you both, without question or fear... in the name of the great man that we have lost to this terrible plight already."

Eli sensed the quake in his heart; something of his mettle melted away. Looking to every man and woman before him, he found their heads nod in unison.

That the vengeance he sought, was as much theirs as it was his.

Jinx approached him from the side then, bracing his arm with her own, a faint but beautiful aura embellishing her. She looked out to the generals.

"For Broska," she said simply, raising a fist.

"*For Broska!*" they roared, raising their own with her.

And Eli stood for a moment as the roars boomed around him, and smiled. *For you, my dearest Arrenso,* he thought with a tear in his eye.

In your name, we shall overcome.

†

Chapter 6

Transmission

"I do not trust them," the Forgotten One muttered, as the huge bronze doors of the palace swung to a close at their backs. "I do not trust that which is so clearly a deception. Their paranoia is an exacting measure, designed to draw us close and never let go. First they were paranoid of your foreignness – then, of my presence – now, of our joint ventures into the Rapture. So they hope to leash us, like the dogs your people hold as pets, and place us under watch at every turn. Hoping we will reveal ourselves to be what they've claimed to know all along, even though we are nothing of the sort: usurpers and terrorists, here to rip the creature's throne from its hinges." Although expressionless, there was no mistaking the grind of the pale figure's jaw. "And part of me would happily do so, and worse, given half the chance..."

Cavara stifled a laugh, descending the wide steps leading to the palace courtyard, and smiled up to the shadow at her back. "I agree with the sentiment," she admitted, shrugging. "But as we are effectively refugees here, I think a bit of *diplomacy* may be needed, as opposed to outright violence. The last thing we need is an order of exile... or worse, an execution."

The pale figure pursed their lips, conceding the point. "Tactical words indeed."

"Because, sadly, we need them at this moment in time... we have little other choice."

"Hm, yes."

She nodded, then smiled. "Although, that being said, if push comes to shove... I wouldn't cry over a bit of spilt blood..."

A swell of approval formed in the Forgotten One's eye. "Just give the word, Successor..." it boomed, looking out to the horizon. "*Just give the word...*"

Sprawling out before them, sun blanched and shimmering, the sand-coloured stone of the courtyard formed an imposing divide to the grey of the palace at their backs and the bronze domes of the wider city beyond. Thick walls closed off the square from the outside, with the only access coming from two small gates on either side, just big enough for supply carriages to pass through. Like the dunes of a distant desert, fighters and archers rippled across the stone beneath them, the strike of steel and the *thrum* of embedded arrows chiming in her ears like bells.

But, despite the activity of the scene before her, none of that seemed to draw the general's eye for very long. Cavara was instead captivated by what went on at the base of the stairway they descended, and looked in awe at the fighters at work there.

"These are the Göra," the Forgotten One rumbled. The name was unusual to her ear, long and drawn like the break of thunder. "They are the guardians of the City of the Sun. They fight using an ancient technique called 'The Wave': a style said to harness the ripples of the earth, that both arise from the ground and settle from the sky, so that each blade harnesses the purity of natural balance in its very execution. It is considered a high honour to learn such a form."

"It's... beautiful to watch," Cavara admitted, stalling her stride to witness them: a hundred or so figures in brown robes, perfectly aligned across the square with rapiers locked in their hands. They moved without guidance or direction, yet every motion was performed with absolute synchronicity, almost as if they were one hive mind.

How incredible.

"It is in tune with the natural order of things, so possesses something of nature's beauty with it."

"I'd say so... it's remarkable."

"Perhaps so... but it is also, from our innate experience, somewhat flawed in the field of battle."

She turned to him quizzically. "How so?"

"Because, to understand the nature of the blade using our bond with the natural order... is to commit the sin of ignorance. It is true that the natural world may guide us with its patterns, and create art from the mastery of the sword... but how you fight, and how true battles are won, is no art. It is messy, volatile and brutal. There is no pattern involved. And if you are to survive on the battlefield, you must understand that hard truth... or you shall never draw a blade again." They paused. "And that's what makes the way of the Rapture so profound by comparison."

That word again. A cold shiver crept through her. *My destiny.* "What do you mean by 'the way of the Rapture'?"

"It is an alternative fighting technique, only accessible to those who can enter and manipulate the void. It's about sensing your opponent, and anticipating their strikes several steps ahead. Something you do quite impressively already, for that matter, perhaps without even knowing it..."

Cavara frowned. "Do I?"

"Yes. I imagine your fighting style has already been influenced by the Rapture in the few short weeks that we've been practicing, and you may have never even noticed."

She considered. "Has it... *always* been like that? Connected to the Rapture, I mean."

"Most likely not. You, by nature, have a very *erratic* style of fighting, involving a lot of quick exchanges followed by heavy strikes designed to inflict the greatest damage on your opponent. And that is often, I've found, at the expense of your own countenance."

"I fight recklessly, you mean?"

"No," the Forgotten One said simply. "To fight recklessly involves emotion... and you do not fight like that. You fight with a determination and a guile of a natural-born swordsman. So you may not have always fought with the ways of the Rapture... but you have within you an innate understanding of how volatile the mastery of a sword truly is. And that is something to cherish... and something those before us lack entirely."

"I see," she pondered, studying the Göra and their sweeping blades just ahead. "Then, what *has* changed? What makes it 'the way of the Rapture'? I feel no different?"

"Your understanding and connection to it will grow with your experience of the void, through our training and time spent navigating the Rapture. There is still much for you to learn, after all." The Forgotten One paused, then nodded. "But, next time you wield a blade in practice... take note of your attacks. Don't look at how you strike your blade, but more at how you know *when* to strike your blade. A normal fighter will find some moves unpredictable... but in the Rapture, there is no such thing."

Cavara puzzled over the pale figure's words for several moments, longing to question them more. To ask what they meant, and how the Rapture could possibly respond to her and focus her attacks, and why it happened and how it happened and as many other questions as there were grains of sand by the sea. But as the first inquiry came, the general found the black robes turn from her, and a gloved finger speared out across the courtyard—

Where she turned to find two figures approaching, with swords hanging loosely in their hands.

"We have company," the Forgotten One exclaimed.

And unwelcome company, at that.

The two stopped just short of the general, bowing slowly, their eyes never leaving the imposing figure at her side.

"So," Cavara said with hands on her hips, "you must be the honour-guard I've been told about."

"Indeed... my name is Ptolemy," the man on the left expressed, the deep crystal-blue of his eyes shimmering in the light. He had few redeeming features, with rich, smooth skin and a thin beard that traipsed the edge of his jaw like a hedgerow, and a twitch in his fingers that betrayed a deeper malice within.

"And I am Amara," the woman at his side said in turn, her voice little more than a humming noise caught in the wind. She had a dour expression, with tattooed lines around her eyes and lips like the gills of a fish. She seemed the more regal of the pair of them, likely of higher office or a different creed, but something about the man called Ptolemy held Cavara in a wary space, questioning and concerned, never sure of true intentions.

As with everything in this place.

"*Jav'gal* Cavara, it is good to make your acquaintance," Ptolemy said, in a way that made it very clear it was nothing of the sort. "We have been assigned as your honour-guard for the duration of your time here, to offer our protection and guidance. Your wellbeing is of great importance to the Alderbane, and they wish to have you watched at all times… for your safety, of course."

"My thanks… well met," Cavara replied, impressed by his fluency. "I notice you have a good grasp of Provencian."

"I was the ambassador to your imperial court for a number of years in my youth… it was considered a great honour to have knowledge of the languages, even if they were begrudging to use."

Noted. "And what of you, Amara?"

"I used to hunt refugees of your kind in the forests with my dogs," she said softly, despite the menace of the words. "I did it for many years. It was good to set a trap of trust, imitating one of their own… before the truth was realised, and the dogs came to rip their throats out." She smiled, a foul and rotten thing that made the general a touch nauseous. "I almost miss it."

Noted – although I'm not sure if I want to. "Very well. The lack of a language barrier should make things easier between us, especially as you'll be stuck to me all hours of the day."

"Such were the Alderbane's thoughts," Ptolemy said with a grating smile. "Although it is not only you who we shall be… *keeping an eye on,* as honour-guards." He seemed to bristle suddenly, as the Forgotten One took a massive step forward to cast them both in the gloom of their shadow.

"I can handle myself," they boomed, providing no emotion to grasp at. "I need not your guardianship."

"That may be so, but we come under orders of the Alderbane that you are both to be watched. So, if you want that changed, you take it up with *them*." Ptolemy turned to the huge robed figure, staring it down with a snarl. "Because if we had it our way, we'd ship you out to sea, and see if that pretty Mother you worship cares enough to send you back. But sadly, that's not the case... so here we must be, as your most *humble* servants."

"You do not know who you're *speaking* to."

"I don't care who I'm speaking to: you are nothing but scum in the gutter, *whatever* you are..."

Tension suddenly lanced the air around them. Cavara watched fearfully as the Forgotten One swung its shoulders, and the robed hand at its side lingered tentatively toward its sword. Ptolemy seemed to do likewise; Amara toyed with the hilt of a knife at her belt. The general gulped as if her heart were in her throat, watching the situation unravel. The edging of steel caught at her ear; Ptolemy smiled gleefully, sensing the anger he had fomented.

The world almost stopped.

Sensing she was alone, looking on the situation from the outside, Cavara sensed the longing to scream burn bright in her chest. That she wanted it to stop, thinking of the consequences, of their vulnerability, longing to cry out to the pale figure and make it end—

'Don't do it.'

A numbness swept across her, as if a strange cloud had ensconced her mind.

And like that, the Forgotten One turned to her without a word spoken, and backed down from the confrontation in one step.

Cavara felt her stomach lurch, the numbness receding as quick as it had risen. Anxieties resurfaced like a breaching whale – anxieties that she found pale in comparison to whatever had just come over her then.

Did it just hear my thoughts?

"I accept your terms, albeit with gritted teeth," the Forgotten One bellowed suddenly, clasping its hands together. "While we are within these walls, it is only fair that we abide by your rules and customs. Because, as I'm sure you will understand, I do not wish to offend your leader over such *petty* squabbles."

Ptolemy was taken aback, almost disappointed with the result. Instead he stood back, sneering awkwardly, and peeled his hand away from his sword. "Very well," he muttered, turning to the general. "Anything else to say, *Jav'gal?*"

"That is all," Cavara replied, only just aware of the words she had spoken. "Now please, get out of my sight."

Ptolemy smiled, receiving a reaction at last, and produced a mock-bow for his efforts. "As you wish, *ma'am.* And always remember who's watching..."

They turned and paced off toward the Göra, banking left with a self-serving certainty that made Cavara's blood boil. They made no attempt to hide their disdain, as they gazed back one more time before disappearing into the masses – where they would no doubt linger like a bad smell, watching all-too-obviously from afar, just to get on her nerves.

The general rolled her eyes. "What a shit stain of a man," she spat, the heat of the sun like a light breeze against her skin. "I've seen nicer things crawl out of swamps."

"He has a number of *detestable* qualities, it is true," the Forgotten One grumbled.

"I don't know who's a bigger threat: a Tarrazi assassin, or them."

"Always fear the wolf in sheep's clothing, for you never know their true intention until they bear their teeth." It nodded. "Although as you said before, diplomacy appears to be our best option regardless, if we're to remain peacefully here."

"Agreed... but it won't be the *easier* option, that's for certain." She sighed. "Will they honestly be watching our every move now? Are we to be studied like animals, for their own amusement?"

"It would appear so, sadly. We are not trusted, and barely welcomed, so I doubt we will now leave their sight."

"Bastards." She shook her head. "I admit, I wouldn't half mind making them disappear."

The Forgotten One allowed a smile. "Agreed. Although as much as I long to slit their throats and watch them choke on their own blood... I do offer my thanks that you dissuaded me from such a course of action a moment ago."

Cavara bristled, suddenly very uneasy, almost fearing the numbness would rise again within her. "So you did hear my thoughts..."

"It is not so much that I heard them, Successor... more that I *sensed* them."

"How can you sense my thoughts?"

"Because, without realising it, you were actually communicating with me directly through the Rapture when you told me to stand down, and did so while the other two present had no idea. And that, my dear, is called *transmitting*."

The general frowned. "What does that mean?"

"To pass information over a distance, without the use of one's voice. To project, almost, although not that simply. When you 'spoke' to me, you transmitted your mind into the Rapture for a moment... not long enough to pass into that world physically, but long enough to 'speak' to me using your projected thoughts."

"And I did that using the power of my mind?"

"Using the power of *the Rapture*." It turned to her, the sun cowering behind its robes like an eclipse. "You see, the mind is not a particularly powerful thing on its own... the mortal faculties of consciousness are very narrow, and often overstated. But within the realms of the Rapture, that changes: the mind becomes almost a voice of its own, and can communicate with other minds also within that space without a single word spoken. So any directed thought you have, can be transmitted to another attuned to the ways of the void."

They paused for a moment. "That, and you must be able to see them... transmission and telepathy are two vastly different things."

"So I can transmit my thoughts... without a word spoken..." Cavara sensed the numbness of her mind rise and fall like the contractions of breathing, a power resonating within her that connected intrinsically to the void. *Transmitting my conscience into another realm.* She struggled to make sense of it.

How is that even possible?

"You can do it, and so can others."

"How do you mean?"

The pale figure's voice hardened suddenly. "I mean, that any of those wise in the ways of the Rapture may speak to you, Successor, so long as you are within sight."

And, like day passing into night, the numbness rose to meet her.

'But you must never let them know your true power,' the Forgotten One hummed through her mind. *'That power is a key to your survival... to defeating the Iron Queen and asserting your place as All-Mother of the Icebreaker Sea. It is the only way. The fate and balance of the known world relies on it. So let no-one know the truth. Let no-one know of the Rapture... for welcome hands and stabbing knives look no different in the dark.'*

The Forgotten One turned, moving off toward the gates, and the numbness in her mind receded again. A reality returned, grounded and abject – but it was a reality she felt she understood less and less as time went on.

With shaky legs, she began to follow, the same thought ringing in her mind.

Transmission, she mused.

Be wary of knives in the dark...

†

Chapter 7

Lost Among the Trees

She thinks she's better than me: that she has what it takes to lead out here. She thinks she has some mastery of this world, as if it were some beast to tame. That this is just another game of war; a roll of the dice at her choosing. But to think how little she knows of this savage land in reality. How poisonous it is, how wrong and… and uncivilised *it is. How, if one is not strong, it eats away at every last vestige of the mortal soul, until you are left as little more than a husk. Reduced to little more than a savage yourself. You see it in their eyes, these Tarrazi… that careless hunger and hate, etched into their very bones. I have seen it… I have watched good people die at their hands. The Marshal knows nothing of their true nature… she knows nothing of the enemy who come. This is all a game to her.*

And how I so hate *her for it—*

"Sir?"

The whetstone skimmed the length of his blade and withdrew with a screech of metal; Commander Revek rolled his shoulders and stared up at the soldier in disgust. "Can I help you?"

"Field Marshal Lazaerys wants to see you sir," they responded, never quite meeting his eye. "To look over plans of engagement, I believe."

Of course she does: the high and mighty powers that be, have summoned me to nod my head and sign my life away. "Very well… I'll be there shortly. Just have a few bits to tend to first…"

"She requested your *immediate* presence, sir. Apparently it's a rather pertinent matter."

Revek ground his teeth – *of* course *she does* – and produced a chastened smile. "Well, best be on it *then*."

He made to stand, sliding his blade back into its sheath with a flush of ire, and placed it neatly within the entranceway of his tent.

The commander clapped his hands together, levelling with the messenger before him. "Come along, let us go! We can't keep her waiting. I dread to think what'd happen if I was to be late for one of her *pretty* demands..."

Revek skulked off into the wider camp with the absent soldier stumbling in tow, weaving through the colony of tents with his hands clasped at his back. Beneath a faded blue sky awash with a drowsy morning sun, the great cranking enterprise of an army on the move pulsed with life all around him: it seemed that in every direction, at every turn, his sneering gaze found soldiers at work, going about their business with a stoic efficiency and a broad, dutiful smile on their faces. The comradery, of loading carts and fixing armour and fashioning blades. A redemption, almost, of the struggles that had trounced the army in the weeks before. That now, there, on the edge of hell with an emboldened enemy never far from reach, the might of the Imperial Army seemed to shine at its brightest.

And yet when Revek looked upon them, and they in turn looked upon him, eyes were suddenly averted. Hands became idle; lips were sealed and words were left unspoken. The pride and resilience that seemed to ebb from them like an aura as they went about their day, lay suddenly misplaced and still. It seemed that in every direction, at every turn, his sneering gaze found soldiers at work. In every direction, at every turn—

But they don't work for me anymore.

As the thought came, and rotted away just as fast, Revek spied in a small opening to his left the green-red standard of the Marshal Corps, Lazaerys' new officer regiment shipped in from the capital. With fists curled, looking out into the iridescent white sun, he studied their shimmering silver chest-plates and fine steel blades, scowling at the rich and unperturbed glow of their charmed faces. They were the new recruits, untouched by the festering wounds of war, and with the world supposedly in their grasp. How they stood laughing, jostling with each other, raising glasses to the soldiers who passed them by.

They aren't my people anymore, Revek grumbled, shirking the image and pressing on through the camp. *They're poisoned, undisciplined. This is no place to be joyful. The enemy await us; their hounds are coming to tear us to pieces. The savages are massing as we speak. And yet here we are, jolly and laughing, as if we have all the time in the world.* He clawed at his head, spat across the floor. *They aren't my people anymore.*

How lost and pathetic they've become.

Ahead, through the dense compact of the camp, the sprawling canopy of the command tent emerged suddenly, imperial banners flushing in the low wind. The interwoven pathways before it were swamped with labourers and carts, and the sudden whinnying of horses made clear that their vast camp would soon be on the move. There seemed to be no idle moment, the land before him awash in a haze of colour.

But, as he began to pass through them, the thrall of bodies parted before him like the waves of some prophetic sea, with every pair of eyes cast to the floor in fear, and every horse snorting and stamping in displeasure. The commander held his head higher as he picked his way through the throng, the awkward tapping feet of the messenger following limply behind. Like a hawk, Revek leered towards the army workers, watching them cower under his gaze. The terror of reprimand quivered in their eyes. The commander found himself grinning, rather enjoying himself, until the entranceway suddenly manifested before him, and he gave a curt nod to the two guards at either side.

Who he found, to his surprise, bowed and smiled in return.

It seems I still have friends around here after all, he mused with a grin. *That could be useful…*

Revek pulled the entrance to the tent open and stepped inside without breaking pace, snapping it shut at his back to the disgruntled mutters of the messenger. Before him, the same table was lain out as before, coated in maps and imperial orders that had been scrawled over with a fine black quill. Adjacent to it, two of the Marshal Corps stood idly, tracking his approach to the table from beneath their broad steel helmets. Revek paid them no attention, and lifted his gaze.

To find Lazaerys was already studying him, her disappointment abundantly clear.

Revek produced a coy smirk. "You called, commander?"

"I did, yes," she said plainly. "With regards to our plan of action, going forward."

"How… *pertinent*."

"I thought it would be best if you were present for the final deliberations."

Final? "How kind of you to include me… although I must ask why this is the final decision, and why I wasn't involved in the planning itself. We are *joint* commanders, after all. I believe it is my place to know…"

"You *were* involved."

The commander frowned. "I was not," he spat.

"You were." She remained unphased. "When we last spoke, I made clear to those present that any future plans of engagement would be at the deliberation of *both* commanders, where we would express ideas and strategies and come to a common understanding on how to move forward. I gave you ample time to produce a report and, when we next met, we would combine our plans to find an amicable way forward." She paused. "Although, as far as I remember, when I made this point to the other officers… you had already stormed off."

His face dropped. "I—"

"But it's no problem, as we then sent a messenger to you last night to relay our plans so you wouldn't miss out on crucial information.

So I'm sure you've managed to come up with a few things" – a curl at the edge of her cheek – "unless that is, for some reason... you were otherwise engaged?"

Revek rubbed his bloodshot eyes and felt the heat stab through his neck like a snake. *How I'd love to skin you alive—*

"But, it's no matter if you have or have not," the Marshal added. "The generals and I have strung together a plan of engagement that follows some basic principles that I'm sure you can get behind."

He sighed, swallowing his anger. "Then do enlighten me, *please.*"

"Very well."

Reaching across the table, Lazaerys adjusted the topmost map so Revek could see: it was a patchwork drawing of the lowlands, stretching from the outskirts of the Kazbaks across to the Icebreaker Sea. There were vast swathes of it left entirely blank where cartographers had not been, but there was one thing he did note: a single, undeniable feature sprawling for miles across the map's centre.

The commander shivered.

The Ozban.

"This is a map of the terrain ahead of us, spanning a distance of near ten leagues. And, as the map makes abundantly clear, seven of those leagues are occupied by the great forest of the Ozban." She stalled, studying his face before returning to the map. "The forest takes on an hourglass shape, our scouts have found, with a narrowing through the middle that we can use to our advantage. As it stands there is little Tarrazi presence along the outskirts of the forest, and these narrow channels at the middle are also largely unoccupied. The problem comes with what actually operates *within* the forest itself." Her hand gestured to the great swamp of hazy trees occupying the middle portion of the map. "What information we have about the forest itself comes from old maps taken during the occupation, and from the retreat of our forces more recently. We hold defensive positions along the outmost reaches" – she gestured to several old ruins and towers marked in red – " and have a portion of the western front clear of Tarrazi soldiers. This presents us with a chance to strike clinically at the enemy, with the hopes of securing the lower sector of the forest in its entirety in the coming days."

"Optimistic," Revek said.

Completely stupid, he thought.

"Certainly, but with the state of the eastern and western fronts balanced on a knife-edge, repulsing the enemy at the centre and reoccupying a large swathe of territory will hopefully restore some balance. We're better striking now, and striking quick, for the sake of the entire campaign."

"And how do we go about this exactly? I can't see how you can enact an operation of this size in a few days."

"I think we have it covered..." With her outlying fingers, she traced the outskirts of the forest, from the channels along the middle to their base camp in the south. "I will accompany a large force along the western reaches of the forest, making inroads into the trees as we go, up until the middle channel. The terrain naturally rises here to produce a small rocky inlet, where I hope we can establish a more permanent base of operations to strike further north in the coming weeks. Parallel to this in the east, an even larger force will enact the same plan, with greater focus on making inroads and capturing the few defensive towers that lie there. Once they reach the channel opposite us, we strike a path through the middle and set patrols to cut off enemy supplies, leaving the south as our domain."

"Right." He pursed his lips. "And where do I come into this?"

"Well, you – alongside three of my most trusted officers – will enter the forest direct from the south, taking the traditional route through the central column with the intention of capturing three outposts along the river basin here—"

"*What?*"

Lazaerys stopped, sensing the tremors on her co-commander's face. "Is there something wrong?" she inquired, feigning surprise.

"Is there *something wrong?*" he spluttered in disbelief, terror and hate brawling in the base of his throat. "Do you not understand a *thing* about this place? About what's out there? Whatever goes into that forest, will *die*. They will be stalked through the trees, pummelled with arrows and mauled by Hounds the size of *horses*. The savages in there do not care for remorse, and they do not spare lives. Any who venture into that forest head on, will die… because even if the Tarrazi don't get you, the madness of that hell-hole will claim you instead. And I have seen it with my own eyes, so I *know it*." He gritted his teeth, spearing a finger at her and the map beneath. "I understand your plan is optimistic, Marshal… but this right here? This is *fucking stupid*."

Lazaerys remained expressionless. "Under normal circumstances commander, yes, I would tend to agree with your sentiment," she said simply. "But these are not normal circumstances, and this is not a normal war. And I would not entrust a lacky to direct such an important task into the heartland of our enemy. Therefore, the force entering into that forest will be under your *complete* control."

"That isn't the point! The point is it's ridiculous to send *anyone* into that fucking place!" He waved his hands mockingly. "And what of your duties anyway? What gives you the right over me to push west and establish an outpost? What right do you have?"

Her face hardened. "Because I was *told* to."

"By whom?"

"By the Supreme Governor himself."

Revek found a bubble in his throat, a shudder going through him like an eel. "He chose *you*… over *me*… to lead that mission?" It came almost with disbelief.

What the fuck is going on…

"I don't know the process by which he came to this conclusion, but that is simply how things have come to be. I will lead the army around the west and establish a base… you will lead a contingent through the middle, and retake any outposts you find—"

Revek drew the knife from his side, flicking it through his fingers. "This isn't *right*."

The two soldiers of the Marshal Corps had their swords raised in a heartbeat, pulling in toward their leader. The air tensed around them, like the billowing steam of a furnace.

But with a calming hand, Lazaerys bade the soldiers stand down and stood with her arms crossed instead, staring down the aggressor opposite her, unfazed by his show of force.

"It may be joint command, but this is still *my* army," Revek growled, knuckles bulging around the handle of the weapon. "It is an insult and an outrage that I have been demoted in this way, with complete and total disregard for my service in this campaign thus far."

"You've done nothing but—"

"*To send...* a senior commander on a suicide mission into that forest, while your contingents stand high and dry along its outskirts with no threat of failing? What a fucking piss-stain." He jabbed a finger at his chest. "Before you and your Corps came, I lead this army – I *still* lead this army. I take charge here, and I give the orders, and it is a ruinous treachery that that should ever be taken from me... especially from the likes of *you*."

Lazaerys nodded slowly. "I was just following orders... good soldiers follow orders."

"And I am telling you that I won't *stand for it*."

"You are well within your right to have issue with any plans that have been made. We are, as you say, *joint* commanders of this force. But this bravado you endeavour with, concerning the strategy and delegation of this army... as if you had an inkling of concern for the actual *soldiers* in your command... is all lies. You don't believe it. Sense isn't what drives someone like *you*."

"Then what is it, Marshal? What am I truly *driven* by?"

A quiet, almost indiscriminate smile graced her face. "It's fear."

Revek lurched back on the balls of his feet, almost in shock. Anger crowning in his soul. Ire. Venom. Hate.

"What the *fuck* are you talking about—"

"You fear the Ozban, and you fear your reputation!" Lazaerys charged, staring him down. "You fear going back into that forest; you fear that what you've witnessed in there will return to haunt your darkest nights. I see it there, behind your eyes. Behind the sleepless wash of a drunk. I see a terrified man who lost his nerve and left his men to die... I see a man who couldn't take charge, and feels the bite of that choice rising up his neck. A man who would now rather be called a weak leader, and take the easy path of no great risk, than face the realities that await him within the depths of that great forest." She shrugged at him. "So in response to your concerns, I say: by all means, commander. Do as you wish. Take the eastern path and aid the encirclement of the forest, if you so please. No-one is forcing you to go back into the Ozban; we are equals after all." Her smile returned. "But remember what it will mean, if you choose the easy path, and abandon your courage when your people most need it. Remember what it will mean... because if you don't, you know those who follow you *will*."

Revek tightened the grip at his blade, his mind roaring, a flush of red coursing from his neck to his temples. How wrong she was; how stupid it all was. It was lies. The misgivings of a manipulator. It never should have come to it. None of it made sense.

The blade tensed at his side, poised in the flat of his palm with white knuckles. The urge to lunge forward and strike her down was an easy one, like a soft kiss on his cheek. He could do it, just like that: take command, and end all of it. So close, edging closer – then drifting far away, as a thought caught in his mind.

What good is full command, if I burn the reputation that drives it?

Revek loosened the grip on his blade and slid it back into its sheath, a numbness coursing from his neck to his temples. He looked to his hands for a moment; to his boots and the floor at his feet. Tracing up – crossing the great forest at the centre of the map – and drawing back up to Lazaerys opposite him. Even in his moment of apparent indecision, there was no emotion to her gaze: no disappointment, nor smugness. She simply stood there, awaiting his decision, as if none of it really mattered. As if she were just following orders.

My reputation...

"Fine," he spat, clutching his hands at his back once more. "I accept the task at hand. I shall lead the contingent into the Ozban, and retake any strategic positions on the way." Pressing a hand against the table, he leaned in to glare at her. "And, in doing so, I will not let my reputation be ruined by some quaint *bitch* operating way above her grade. I assure you of *that*."

He turned sharply, skulking back through the entranceway, disappearing into the wider camp with a fire at his heels.

And a long silence followed in the command tent, ebbing softly – until Lazaerys placed her hands across the tabletop and smiled.

For her plan was now in motion.

†

Chapter 8

Val Azbann

Savanta arrived under the cover of darkness, within the bowels of a rattling carriage. The delicate clicks of churning wheels had ground below the boards at her feet for what felt like an eternity, with the occasional broken ebb of firelight catching at the rafters above. Through those same high windows, she spied a world beyond that was so abjectly dark, where every structure seemed to be little more than a shadow. Where the clear night sky, so open and broad above, was without a single glistening teardrop of a star. Where the firelight came accompanied with the jagged edges of huge encampments, sprawled for endless leagues into a far distant place. It was a perverse, horrifying place of twisted metal and black-grey ash, all contained within the confines of a great wall, so tall at its peaks that it seemed to rival the mountains of the broken horizon beyond. A place where not even the moon dared cast its eye.

On, to Val Azbann...

The carriage came to a resolute stop, with the sharp sound of footsteps approaching from all sides. Savanta ground her heels, bracing as the door swung open and black armoured guards swarmed in, unlatching her chains and dragging her down the ramp like cattle set for auction. From the long miles on the road, she found her bones crunch at the sudden motion, the base of her spine crackling like cinder. On shaky legs, she spilled forward through an open gateway into a cold, unlit corridor, the guards shoving at her with gloved hands.

Squinting intently, she was possessed by the sheer blackness of the passage beyond: a place so utterly devoid of light, awash with grey smudges and the deep impressions of doorways along either wall. It was pervasive, desperately so. Not even her escorts, a few inches from her face at either side, possessed any definable quality in the murky gloom. Only the tug of the chains at her wrists, and the exquisite *clink* of their steel boots, reminded her of where she was and who she was with.

And who I am on my way to see.

They swung right, descending into the intestines of the keep on wide slate steps, the murky blues and hazy greys jumping and jousting like ghosts. She often lost her step, righted a moment later by a flick of the chains and the unamused grunts of the guards: blackcoats who seemed entirely at ease in the desperate gloom, taking each step measuredly, hardly breaking stride as they reached the bottom and curled off along an echoey chamber. Part of her wondered if they could actually see in the dark: if their piercing, porcelain stares could pick apart the shadows of the void. Or if they were part of a hive mind, controlled as a unit like ants, following scent trails down into the nest.

To await the counsel of their Queen...

Another turn, and she found herself marching into a huge chamber straddled with shafts of light, criss-crossing the impossibly-high alcoves of the ceiling in warm ebbing hues. Great columns of clean-cut stone struck upwards to either side of her, sporadic horns of black metal woven within them, jutting out like teeth. The room was colossal, yet so desperately empty, like the tombs of forgotten kings. And it was then that she realised just how silent it was as well: that there was just a sheer lack of *anything,* whether it was within the shadows of the outer walls or under the orange glow of torchlight. It was a great absence, a great nothing, with the only company being that of the guards – and the crunch of their steel boots – and the chains hanging limply at her wrists.

What's gonna happen to me?

Without any clear direction, they paced to the centre of the wide chamber, and drew to a swift halt. Looking to the guards for but a moment, Savanta spied the unease blanketing their gaze, their idle hands toying with the knots of her chains. *What do they fear?* she longed to ask. But before the opportunity came to she was pushed to her knees, and with a sudden *clank* of metal the guards stood back and attached her chains to tiny rings in the floor.

Heart tensing, she was suddenly fearful, an overwhelming dread in her mind. The air seemed incredibly thin, all of a sudden. Thinking about what they'd do to her; what plans they had for her future. Frightfully, tensing her arms, she looked up again—

To find the two guards were gone, seemingly without a trace.

What the hell?

She made to stand, but her shoulders burnt angrily at how tight they had fastened the chains to the floor. Looking to one side with a glare, she manipulated her wrist around the shackles, attempting to slide free. But the bindings were tight, gnawing at her joints, and every motion she made caused a lance of pain down her arms. She relented for several moments, before eventually giving in and consigning herself to fate. Left there, buried in the deep-dark of a Tarrazi keep, in an expansive room of pillars and shadows.

With nothing but her thoughts to spare.

Why am I here? She arched her back, wincing at the pain in her shoulder as she did. *I'm meant to be champion... a fighter. Not a prisoner. What is this? Why am I in chains?* She tugged at them again, straining until the blood thundered through her head and she found her conscience almost slip. *This is pathetic!* She longed to scream, baleful and malevolent, but then her heart stuttered, a wince of fear returning.

For something was approaching from the shadows ahead.

Blinking furiously, picking apart the light and the shadows, she tried to discern what she was seeing. There was a body – a mystical, distinctly feminine body – trailing towards her, in armour that glistened in the fractious sun. They paced across the cold stone, striding toward her, something of a smile curling at their lips. Savanta reeled, blinking—

And the woman was suddenly gone.

What the fuck?

She looked about, trying to make sense of it. Challenging the shadows all around her. Discerning where she'd gone, and whether she was still there, lurking in the gloom of the beyond—

A hand laced about her neck from behind, the rasp of hot breath heavy in her ear.

"My *champion*," it said.

Savanta inhaled sharply, fear suddenly trouncing her soul.

The Iron Queen.

The grip released from her throat, as the air lapped like waves across her skin.

"A Provencian, in our midst," the Iron Queen cooed from somewhere off behind her. "How… *interesting*. Certainly not what I was expecting." Off to the left, beyond the pillars, the shadows seemed to dance and take flight, as if someone were passing through them. "Tell me, oh champion… what is your name?"

"Savanta," she muttered, a barely-audible thing that came as more of a croak than anything.

"*Savanta*… a name of the old tongue, I see." Poison seemed to drip from her tongue. "A name of Tarraz origin, at that… meaning '*serpent-soul*'."

"That is *not* a name for you to usher." An anger bubbled, blooming suddenly with a disregard for all things sane.

"Oh? And why is that?" they toyed.

It's a name my father used to call me. "Because you are not worthy to call me by that name."

"Not worthy?" The laugh rippled off to her right, a figment in the gloom. "Please, don't insult me… as if your father was really more worthy of giving you that name than I am now."

Her heart sunk, a lead weight far heavier than any chains were, before shock pulsed her back into life. "My father? How do you know my father?"

"That he was a traitorous scoundrel with blood on his hands and a death warrant to match it." They scoffed. "That old fool had it coming for a *very* long time..."

"Do not speak ill of the man you put to death, you fucking snake!" Savanta roared, lurching about toward the shadows, teeth baring. "He was a good man. Don't you *dare* sully his name with your misgivings!"

"*My* misgivings?" The words flared in her right ear; Savanta jerked violently to see who was there, to find no-one. Turning back—

To find a woman crouched before her, glaring wickedly.

"And what misgivings are those?"

The Iron Queen, stooped mere inches from her face, was a terrifying woman to behold. The eclipsed moons of her eyes, pulsing with a faint yellow glow, sat in wide sockets with high cheeks and a fanged grin. The round of her head shone like a mage's orb, the rivets of scars lacing down over her earless jaw and across her neck, where arteries pulsed in long black streaks and a silvery liquid bulged to the surface. Like the haunting image of a pagan goddess, the domineering weight of the Queen's gaze fell heavy on Savanta's mind. It was a brace about her neck, binding her arms and chest, until her breathing came heavy, and the chains fell still, and the world seemed to swallow her whole.

She's here.

"You have a strong spirit, for one brought so low," she said, lacing a finger across Savanta's cheek. "A surprising vigour, for a scout brought into my lands... to be trapped, caught, and taken to the fighting pits... to murder the only friend she has ever known, just to get here. That speaks of pain... that speaks of coldness, and a desire for one's own goals. You are a murderer, driven only by your hate for that which has wronged you. So tell me, *Savanta*... who has wronged you so?"

Caught in her moonlit gaze, the flare of resent burning within, a thousand tiny emotions prickled at Savanta's skin. That all her hate had led her there; all the pain and guilt and rage and fear. Staring into the eyes of the Iron Queen: the murderous tyrant of Tarraz, who had taken her face and her dignity, and spat upon the name of her dead father. How near fifteen years had passed since his murder, the pain ebbing within her very soul. All leading to one place, and one moment.

And now I am here, staring that bitch in the eye, chained at the wrists and completely at her whim.

To be so close, yet so far.

"I have been wronged by the blackcoats, who ruined my face," she spat. "By the commander, who gave the order from the wall to burn our forest down. By the architect, charged with designing the wall at our border to reap hell against our people. By the coward, who dictated it from afar—"

"Their leader, who wishes only death upon the people of Provenci, for their arrogance and hurt against her own kind. Am I correct?"

She said nothing, only glared.

The Iron Queen smirked, rising to her feet. "Your plan is ambitious, certainly. I can admire that much. But it is also misguided at heart. I admire your *tenacity*, and your desire not only to bleed the veins of your enemy, but to stab the heart itself… as I'm sure you're well aware, it's a policy I too live my life by. Because what good is taking names, when you can murder thousands?" A coy smile. "But I find your attempts at… *righting wrongs,* to be quite futile. That you think any of what you do will truly sate this vengeful ire that you have… you must understand it won't work."

"I will do whatever it takes to have my revenge for what you and your *savage-kind* have done to me."

"I, the savage? Coming from the lost girl who abandoned her country, went about murder and treachery at every turn, to land herself at the feet of a sworn enemy… and for what? You are here, in chains, before me. What did you expect? You are nothing. You're little more than a caged beast, at the mercy of their master. A vengeful, malevolent fool brought to heal by the weight of reality. So tell me, you conniving bitch… *who's really the savage here?*"

Savanta snarled, braced against the chains, longing to rip her throat in two.

The Iron Queen simply laughed. "You're a hard piece of work, little wretch… I'll give you that. But it doesn't matter… you're little more than a fighting pawn now. You're mine, and you will fight for me, and speak nothing of it. Because I don't care for your pain, or your hate, or your *purpose* in all this. Because you are nothing now. You will serve me…" She paused for thought, a menace about her, and took a step forward. "… and I want to hear you *say it.*"

Savanta looked disgusted, nausea breaching in her stomach. "No."

"You will *say it.*"

"I won't give you the satisfaction."

"You'll give me whatever the fuck I want."

"I'm not your slave."

"You are whatever I say you are… and you will learn to serve me. Now *say it.*"

"No—"

A sharp kick, far faster than anything she had anticipated, and Savanta's head snapped back, an explosion of pain shooting across her jaw with the taste of blood in her mouth.

"Say it!" the Queen bellowed. "Oh she who wallows in anger… *say it to me.*"

"No—"

A punch, quick as a serpent's strike, connected with her cheek; a taut sensation, as the metal pulled across her skin and she hissed with agony.

"Playing games… how *pathetic*. You'll get no sympathy from me, you little whore," the Queen growled. "Just admit it… just say you will *serve me.*"

"I will *never* serve you—"

Another punch, a crack in her jaw as several teeth rocked together.

"Say it."

"You can't make—"

Another punch, snapping across her cheek-bone. The bruising pain tore across her skull.

"Say it."

"I won't—"

Another punch, whimpering with pain. "Say it." Another punch, with tears starting to fall. "Say it." Another punch, with blood trickling from her mouth.

"*FUCKING SAY IT!*"

"I *serve you*!" Savanta wailed, tears streaming, the rupture of her soul howling desperately in her chest. Her throat seized, chest hollow and numb, losing herself to the dark. "I *serve you*..."

A hand clamped around Savanta's jaw, taut fingers pressing into the bruises on her cheek. "You do serve me," the Queen growled. "And you will serve me for the rest of your miserable life. You are misguided, and pained, and troubled... you are cold, heartless, and weak. Your existence is nothing now, beyond what I say it is; you are nothing now, without me. You are bent to my whim, and bled by my knife. And you *disgust me* because of it..."

Her mind fractured, as the Iron Queen stood and turned from her, pacing off into the shadows without a whisper. As if she was nothing: as if there was no care left for her in the world. Chained there, in the great chamber of a Tarraz keep, with nothing left for her soul to know.

With her head held low to the floor, Savanta began to cry.

†

Chapter 9

The Tide Comes

Marcheg was a quiet township, sat atop a flat hill amongst the truncating plains, with pockets of trees jutting from the earth along its southern bank. It occupied a wide perimeter, with sparse farmlands skirting the hill's base and the occasional block of an old farmhouse. Drawing steadily up the bank towards the town, a low wall marked the outermost border, with archer platforms laced between and stone ramps to the east and west for any wagons that passed through. In the orange sun of dusk, the slate rooves and grey-brick homesteads shimmered like plates of armour, with the ballooning shape of a town-hall at the centre, its pinnacle climbing skyward. It was a humble sprawl, one of many sat within eyesight of the walls of Casantri, which itself was little more than a dot on the horizon to the north-east. But, in that same breath, it was also one of the many towns that bore the brunt of imperial neglect, and as Eli approached with the mounted ranks at his back, a certain despair echoed in his chest.

Here lies Marcheg, he mused. *A once proud people, brought low by totalitarian decree.*

He gazed up at the cracked stone bridge climbing the hill into the town, where the worn stone blocks seemed to weep with pain. Weeds crawled along the gutters; sprouts of ivy clambered up the walls. The base of the hill itself was a disused bog sprouting fungi and reedbeds. There was a distinct wash of decay that caught at his nostrils: one of wet mud and old stone and tired hearts. Eli scratched at his beard and sighed.

A once great people... and the imperial pride that abandoned them.

"What a sorry place," Castan said from the mount at his side, running a hand through his black hair. "This is what loyalty to the capital gets you, it seems."

"Here we find the soul of a nation, brought to its knees," Eli replied. "Led here to rest forevermore..."

"Sobering words, sir."

He nodded. "And now they won't even know what hit them."

"At least we're doing what we can pre-emptively."

"Indeed. Have our scouting parties managed to evacuate the locals?"

"We've managed to get a number of them out from our side, but it seems the imperial legions also had similar ideas... but with less moral outcomes." He paused. "Our initial reports say that the blood of our people has already been spilt, and by soldier's blades at that..."

Eli ground his teeth, glancing for a moment to the distant speck of Casantri at the horizon. *So much for good tidings and order,* he scoffed. *Rounding up your own people and sending them to slaughter...*

Fucking pigs.

"Were the victims civilians or scouts?" the Chief inquired.

"The civilians were the prize: the soldiers planned to arrest them and cart them off to the east so we wouldn't get our hands on them. They got out of the fray without a single casualty... our scouts, however, did not get off so lightly."

"Bastards." Eli shook his head, cursing into the wind. "What's the point?"

"What is it, sir?"

"Why would they bother attacking our scouts? We're evacuating civilians, keeping our own people safe, regardless of which side they choose. They have no part in what comes next. And yet our scouts are slaughtered like dogs while trying to help them, just because of the cause they follow." He sighed, clawing at his head. "What's the *point...*"

"They wish to make an example of us, sir," Castan replied. "To show just how potent their intolerance is. Regardless of who we are, or what our mission is... if you fall on the wrong side of the line, you are just as much the enemy as the Tarrazi in the north."

The words caught in his mind, wrapping tighter like the coils of a serpent, until the air seemed to thin in his throat. That people who once sought to protect them, were slaughtering his own people simply because of which banner they flew. That his neutral concern for the citizens caught in the cross-fire of conflict, meant nothing to the enemy who now brandished their steel and murdered his scouts in cold blood. That even in the theatre of war, the lives of the innocent were an acquisition to compete for.

Eli rolled his thumb across his ring, reminding himself of just how many people had already been taken by the regime, and sighed.

"I care not for the Tarrazi or their cause in the grand scheme of things," he exclaimed. "It's all petty politics: a vast web spun by powerful people to pursue their own glories and needs. A single, massive battle, stretching on for millennia with no clear end in sight – and certainly not one in our lifetime. But the day we start condemning our own people as we do the Tarrazi in the north, as little more than butchers and savages... that will be the day that we truly lose sight of the common good in this world."

He spurred his horse on, as the last of the mounted battalion arrived at his back, and the rest of the ranks on foot crested the ridge just behind.

"We play no part in the grand endeavour of this war, Castan," he said, looking behind. "It is beyond us, and I want no part of it. We just do our bit for what we think is right, in the here and now..."

And seek vengeance against those who wield the blade against us.

†

"Bring them in."

Through the broad beige doors of the barn, three plain-clothed figures with bags over their heads swayed awkwardly in, jostled and shoved into order by the Provenci soldiers at their backs. They crossed the dry dirt floor littered with hay and weeds, with the intense orange haze of dusk leaking out through the covings above. Shivering, heads twisting at every noise, they approached the back of the room.

With a tug of their restraints, all three fell to their knees, alerted to the sound of steel-capped boots circling a table just ahead.

"Remove the bags."

Withdrawing the covers, the prisoners were met with a wash of colour and fading light, eyes suddenly straining to make sense of the world around them. They were in a barn, facing the back wall with stacks of hay to either side and a table at the centre—

As a gnarled figure in a coat of armour loomed above them, with cruel eyes and streaked silver hair and a mean sword hanging at their waist.

"Good evening, citizens," Ferreus mused. "We come in *peace*."

They stared at him, goggle-eyed and fearful.

"My name is General Ferreus, and I am commander of the Imperial Land Army of Provenci. We have come here in response to a new threat that has approached from the west, and it appears that your town has become the focal point of our strategic interests. As we speak, an army of these *rebels* have stationed themselves at the opposing end of your town, with the intention of attacking and capturing it to pursue their heinous aims: namely, the overthrow of the Imperial Army who now command from the capital. It is with great disappointment that this has become our reality, but needs must, and your safety is *of course* our top concern."

Ferreus watched their looks of concern slowly dissipate, replaced instead by those of disdain. *They think we're taking the piss,* he thought, dumbfounded by their ignorance. *They think this is a joke.* Meeting their gazes in turn, he produced a callous smile.

They will learn.

"That being said, we must also consider our *own* safety, during this difficult time. We don't want any rebel sympathisers causing us grief going forward, and I don't want them jeopardising the lives of my soldiers. So, we must take measures to avoid this happening… and that begins with *you.*"

"Are we to be accused?" one of them spoke up: a tall woman at the centre in a pale blue gown. She was fair haired, with the deep scars of a skin disease pocked across her cheeks. "Will you kill us? I… I don't want to die."

"I have no need or intention of killing you… *any* of you," Ferreus muttered, stepping forward and crouching before her. "None, that is… unless you give me reason to."

"What reason would we give? I… I haven't done anything wrong. I don't know why I'm here."

"Then by all accounts, you have nothing to be afraid of. I don't harbour any resentments for the free and *subservient* citizens of Marcheg, or any township in this region. What I do have a problem with, though… is those who do *not* hold allegiances with the imperial regime in charge here, and whose sympathies lie elsewhere…"

"The rebels?" she mumbled sheepishly.

Ferreus inclined his head, watching the other two prisoners lower their gazes. "Yes… them. The *usurpers* from the west. The unruly types who have strayed from our imperial ideals, and now threaten the very balance of power here in our lands. All while our own people die in the north, at the rotten hands of the Tarraz—"

"What's that got to do with me?"

Ferreus shot a glance left, catching the gaze of an elder man with greying hair and a craftsman's apron folded in his lap. There was little emotion to his face; little to anything about him. But Ferreus found his blood boil at the challenge he had presented.

"Why should I care?" the man reiterated.

"Why should you care?" the general growled, stepping toward him menacingly. "You should care, because it's a threat to those who are here to *protect* you. The Supreme Governor, and your leaders in the capital… the people who long to keep your *precious* little life safe… are under threat. We have worked hard, to maintain the peace and establish order after the king passed. And I will not let a miserable *rebellion* ruin that." He paused. "So if you must ask why this matters… then know it matters, because your life depends on it. To be a usurper to the regime… is to face the executioner's blade. Let's make no odds about *that*."

"I hold no quarrel with either you or these rebels… matters not to me. You do your business in the capital, fightin' whatever wars you see fit… I stay here and practice my trade, and the two never meet. Do what you please, because I hold no issue with anyone."

"Then you are a wise man," Ferreus said. "And I respect your honesty—"

"But what if we were to choose?"

The third and final prisoner glared his way: a young man, no older than twenty winters, with a scruff of wiry hair across his chin and swollen eyes that bulged in their sockets. A venom laced his tongue; Ferreus sensed an ire in him.

What do we have here?

"That would depend on what choice you are *making*," the general challenged, striding over to him with a clatter of steel boots. "And onto which side of the line you fall."

"And if we choose a path of freedom?" the prisoner spat. "If we choose the rebel cause, against an imperial force who have long outstayed their welcome and overstretched their ambitions… is that such a bad choice?"

Ferreus scoffed. "And where do you stand, young fool?" He waved his hands out with mocking certainty. "Let it be known to all those present, just where your allegiances lie…"

He almost smiled at the question. "I believe in freedom," the young man said proudly. "I believe in peace… and I believe in honour. I believe the imperial powers that be, have forgone their uses, and abandoned their ways. That there is need for change, and that such change is in the air as we speak." They locked eyes then, suddenly, with an acute gratification in the man's gaze. "And this change, it comes from the west… where the Chief of the Mountains shall rise again—"

Ferreus was at his throat before another word was spoken, clamping his fingers around the man's windpipe, watching the swell of terror as the prisoner was hoisted into the air.

"You are misguided, you miserable fucking wretch, do you understand?"

The prisoner said nothing.

"Death awaits those who are disloyal to the capital… and you have marked yourself among those condemned." The general reached for his blade. "So, I'll ask… what do you have to say for yourself?"

The prisoner stared at him for a few moments, almost looking through him as if he wasn't really there. His muscles twitching; his throat bulging beneath the general's grip. Moments, ticking by silently.

Until a smile curled across his face, and Ferreus felt his guts churn.

Then the words came.

"*Death to the regime.*"

And the knife drove straight through his stomach.

Ferreus roared with agony, blood and warmth belching to the surface between the folds of his armour.

Pain suddenly became anger; a flash of fire with embers greater than the sun tore through the whites of his eyes. Ferreus grit his teeth, bellowing, tightening his grip until his knuckles were pale—

Crushing the man's windpipe between his fingers.

With a snarl, the general cast the body of the young man to the ground and tore the blade from between his armour. It was a tiny weapon – little more than a steel toothpick in reality – but one that now lay swamped with a deluge of his own blood, up to the hilt and through. Tiny spurts of crimson dripped from the coils of his armour like a tap, as testament to its venom. The general swallowed, concealing any nausea, and looked down for a moment to the hollow eyes of the prisoner, who wore a wicked grin across their dead face.

Ferreus spat and cast the knife to the floor.

Fucking wretches.

Hand tensing over the wound, the general lowered his gaze to the other prisoners, the sheer horror painted black and bloody across their faces. His eyes then rose, up to the guards stood with their blades ready, disgusted at the wound inflicted on their leader. He sensed the malevolence, boiling in his very soul; Ferreus drew a long breath in, and grit his teeth.

"Kill all of them," he said, level and absolute, grounding his jaw like a chisel.

"The regime takes no prisoners..."

†

Chapter 10

Ascendent

Cavara drew a long breath, the sword swaying loosely in her hand, as an impossible heat scorched the plains around her from a sun set high in the sky. The weather had not changed since she had arrived in the nation of Sevica: from an orange dawn to a hollow-blue dusk, a sky devoid of clouds had reigned overhead with the blazing sphere of light at its centre. Every day, the same heat and intensity blanched across the earth below, relentless in its beauty. She had grown quite fond of it by that point, and found just how apt the name was for the great city sat idle to the south. For even then when she looked, its bronze domes and sanded-grey stone shimmered magnificently in the light.

The City of the Sun, in all its splendour.

"Successor?"

Cavara blinked, drawing back to the world around her with a long blink of the eye. "Yes?"

"Are we ready?"

She paused, then winced. "Run it by me *one* more time…"

"It's called a shadow-step," The Forgotten One rumbled, its dark robe contrasting harshly with the blue wash of sky. "It's the ability to transfer yourself into the Rapture, and back out the other side again, in a single stride. It's a transmission of your spiritual being, not bound by the physical constraints of this world. And, in battle, it means you may step *through* someone, crossing to the Rapture and back, without your opponent ever registering you have gone." They lifted their head, gazing up to the sun with pupil-less eyes. "And it is a skill you now possess... and must in turn learn how to wield like a weapon. Because someday soon, it may just save your life..."

Cavara wiped the sweat from her brow with the back of her hand and sighed. They had spent the best part of the day sparring on the same hillside as before with shimmering blades and gritted teeth, running through the same motions as she had done her whole life – only this time with newfound purpose. The honour guard had not followed them there – *but no doubt still watch us from afar* – which had given the general an opportunity to focus on the new intricacies of battle that the Forgotten One had revealed to her. Her swordsmanship; her style; the motions of the blade. And now, on top of that, learning more about the Rapture, and her deep connection to it.

And now, whatever this 'shadow-step' is on top of that.

"So I must not only learn the ways of the blade within the Rapture, but also transmit myself *through it* to survive?" she said with great exertion. "It all sounds a bit much, you know. Would be nice if it was a bit... *easier.*"

"You belong to the realm of the Mothers now, general: theirs is not a world of *simplicity*." They almost seemed amused. "That being said, as with many things in the Rapture, once you have understood what you must do, employing your skills becomes a far easier affair. Even we champions are not born with the knowledge of the shadow-step – it must be learnt."

She scoffed. "If demigods can only just comprehend this shadow-step business... then what luck do I have in doing it?"

"Because you have the All-Mother's kiss coursing through your veins... you have more luck than any mortal will ever know."

The Mother's kiss. The knot across her stomach bulged; the weight across her shoulders grew taut, suddenly heavier. *An inheritor of the known world.* Relaying her experiences: the Rapture, the white void, the shadow woman, the totems, the visions. *A Successor comes, to restore balance.* The sword conjured in her hand; an entire civilisation, on the cusp of her fingertips. *And they chose me, to be their saviour.*

'*Why?*'

'*By accident, is why.*'

The voice trembled in her skull, a numbness in her ears that shocked her for a moment. '*What accident?*' she transmitted.

The Forgotten One's mouth remained motionless, but she sensed the hesitation there. *'You were never chosen to take on this mantle as successor to the All-Mother,'* it explained. *'There was no method as to who would inherit the All-Mother's place and restore balance to this world. It was happenstance, in the end: you were just in the right place at the right time, lead nearly-dying on that sandbank in Tarraz.'*

'I saw a vision,' Cavara spluttered. *'I saw a woman... the most beautiful face I had ever seen... gracing the waves when I was dying. The mist seemed to part as they approached. I... I thought it was a dream that would carry me through to the beyond, and complete my passage in death. She came to the shore, and came to me...'*

The pale figure considered. *'If that is the case, then you have met the All-Mother in person, Successor... and it's no wonder She holds such a connection to you.'*

She frowned. *'What does that mean? How can I see Her? She's a deity... She's not supposed to be* seen.*'*

'Because you did not see Her in Her god-form,' the Forgotten One explained, then sighed at length. *'There is a certain series of events, when one Mother dies and another takes their place, which has continued on for thousands of years unchanged. The Mother senses the end is approaching; a Successor is chosen; the Mother dies; the chosen one ascends, and balance is restored. You know it, as well as I do. It is a tale as old as time itself. Although commonality, is no guarantee of the future... and we were witness to that this time round, when the All-Mother died and a Successor was not found.'*

'Is that why you killed the king?'

The pale figure paused, grimacing. *'Once I had been betrayed by my kind, and the usurper had risen in the north, I attempted to force the All-Mother's hand and reveal a Successor to her. I ended the life of the king of your people in the hopes that the next ruler would be chosen... but before the man you call Alvarez came to power, the All-Mother was already dead.'*

Cavara shivered at the call of the Governor's name. *'So, the Successor was never found?'*

'No-one had been chosen, and so the All-Mother's soul... the Ascendency, as it's known... was lost to the waves of the great sea your people call the Icebreaker, having fallen from the stars. From there it wondered for some time, lost to the world, hoping to reach land someday. I followed its course from the shoreline, waiting many days for it to come... when I found it grow suddenly warmer and brighter in my mind, knowing that it was about to reach its destination. I went to it, tracing the banks of the great sea, in the hopes of transferring the Ascendency to a good host, who could protect the transcendent soul against the usurper threat from the north.' There was a long pause, the hollows of its eyes lowering to meet her own. *'And it was there, I found you... a dying general betrayed by her people, bleeding out onto the sands... now with the Ascendency of the world nestled within their soul.'*

She took a long gulp. *'And now you are burdened with me, a foul-mouthed ex-general way in over her head, being taught the ways of the Rapture and concepts she is far too inexperienced to utilise... all because I happened to be in the exact place where the All-Mother's soul reached the shore?'* Cavara found a sorrowful pain in her chest, and scoffed. *'So much for finding a 'good host' for the Successor of the world...'*

'It is true, that a good host for a Successor was not found by my hand.' The Forgotten One lifted their arm, placing a huge palm on her shoulder, and smiled. "Because the Ascendency, found her anyway."

Cavara gazed into their pearlescent eyes and the fluctuating warmth held within there, and found the sentiment blossom within her. "You genuinely believe that I'm the one to lead this? That I'm worthy of this Ascendency?"

"You carry strength with you, as a horse carries its master into battle. You carry your love and care for those in need, as a maiden carries bread for the poor. You are dutiful, and you are adaptive, and you long for the betterment of the world far more than your own being. I believe you are right for this, Successor, but don't just take it from me: take it from the Ascendent soul that now beckons within you, and has forged within you such a beautiful bond of mortal and god. It is not a common thing, to pair so completely with it. And now, that conjoining of the Rapture and the mortal world is your power. And that is what you shall use to take the All-Mother's place as your rightful own..."

The Forgotten One stepped back suddenly, opening up ground between them, and crossed their arms. "And now, Successor, you must prove you are the inheritor of such power: you must demonstrate the bond you have forged with the Ascendent soul. So, take a step, and pass into the Rapture... then take another, and stand before *me*."

Their words seemed ethereal, as the wind snapped and the grass flickered and the crows alighted from the distant trees. The trussing and whipping of the hillside seemed to steady then, like a seafaring ship entering a quiet cove. A stillness enveloped them, her sword still wavering in her hand.

Cavara slid it back into its scabbard, flexing her fingers at her side, before a rising sensation drew up in her chest, and with a smile she stepped forward.

Where the darkness rose to meet her.

~

She stepped onto a plain of white-grey streaks, stood like the fronds of a wheat-field, and gazed out into the void of the Rapture. The same soundless, timeless numbness held her unseen body in place as before, but the nature of the world around her – a once entirely porcelain landscape with no form or colour – had slowly begun to change. With each venture she made into the void, the blotched greys that dappled the outskirts of her vision had formed into the distinct shadows of trees; the white above became far more dazzling, as it embodied the true light of the sun; the yellowed tinges staining the horizon to the south, she now understood to be the pale walls and bronze domes of the City of the Sun. With every transmission to the Rapture that came and went, she understood more of its nature: that it was not a realm entirely of its own, but rather a mirror to the true world that she inhabited. It was an unconstrained land, awash with its own mystery, yet so very grounded and familiar. A reflection, like the surface of a great lake.

And holding all the mystery beneath the waters just below.

Channelling her energy back into the task at hand, she sensed as the void twisted around her, circling around the large grey smudge just ahead. Cavara drew in a breath, the tension in her stomach flexing, and took a long step forward into blinding light—

Catching sight of a shadow approaching, out the corner of her eye…

~

Cavara gasped as she left the Rapture, jolting suddenly and missing the ground, collapsing across the Forgotten One's huge metal boots.

Spinning abruptly onto her back, cursing under her breath, she scrabbled to her feet with a sword to-hand before any such recollection could reach her.

"What's happened—"

"Someone's in the Rapture, approaching from the south," Cavara said abruptly, the Forgotten One unsheathing their own curved blade before she even had a chance to finish.

"Any idea who?" they asked.

"No, no idea." Her heart thumped against her ribcage. "Keep an eye out though… they weren't that far away."

"Understood."

They formed up, shoulder to shoulder, facing south and circling wide with blades light and looming. The wind rasped up the hillside, striking across their faces. An unnerving silence descended, with only the distant rustle of tree leaves to accompany them.

Where are you? Cavara rasped, her sword coiling in her hand. She traced the horizon – what was visible over the crest of the hill – and sensed her heartbeat in her throat. Waiting, watching carefully, a cautious patience echoing out—

A head appearing, large and thickly haired—

Eyes suddenly bulging, hands raised—

Panic, a look of shock, stooping lower—

And Cavara, lowering her blade, found it in her to smile.

"Brutus?" she questioned, watching his broad, bearded face curl into a quiet smile. "I can't say we were expecting to see you here… we nearly had your head."

"Apologies," he boomed, striding to the crest of the hill in a huge coat, bowing courteously before them. "I've been meaning to find you for some time now, but I've been… forestalled by other business." He looked to his feet, tapping his fingers gently together.

"Well, it's certainly lovely to see you. I'll have to pass on to Evelyn and Azura that you've come by."

"No need: I saw them a few hours ago, by the ford just south of the city walls. It was nice."

"No doubt he missed you dearly."

Brutus chuckled weakly. "Aye, that he did." He then looked up to the Forgotten One and, despite his own impressive stature, seemed to shrink slightly under their shadow. "Who's this…?"

"This is the Forgotten One, one of the champions of the All-Mother," Cavara introduced. "They protect those who they believe will bring balance back to the world… or something like that."

"Precisely so, Successor," the Forgotten One said, with a polite nod directed at the newcomer. "I am something of a teacher and guardian to the young general here. And I believe it was you, Brutus, who saved her from an untimely death within the Rapture some weeks ago… you have my thanks for that."

"Ah yes, thank you… I never got a chance to say," Cavara added.

"It is no matter," he replied politely. "I sensed a ripple in the void, and knew that something was wrong… the visions told me so." His gaze crossed to Cavara. "That, and any friend of Azura's, is a friend of mine."

She smiled. "I do certainly appreciate that… I wouldn't have escaped that place alive, had it not been for you."

"That may be true..." His face hardened. "But that is also why I've come to you here now."

"How so?"

"I fear that danger that we prevailed against before may have a new face, and may be searching for you as we speak..."

Her heart seized. "What do you mean...?"

The bearded man looked solemnly to his feet. "I have sensed something, within the void. Another presence, active and extremely adept in their transmission... someone who is able to pass into the Rapture and back with as much ease as you do."

The general swayed on the spot, losing her orientation as the words left the man's mouth. "How is that possible?" she gasped, looking up to the Forgotten One's grave expression, longing for answers.

Fuck...

"A transmitter? How do you know of this?" the pale figure challenged. "I have not sensed them."

"Because I have *seen* them, in the void, walking within the walls of the City. They are camped out somewhere, hidden away from sight... they use the Rapture to get around beyond the watchful eyes of the guards, searching for something." He locked eyes with Cavara. "Or some*one*."

The general paused for some time, blinking heavily, struggling to swallow. The wind had reduced to little more than a whisper around them, which seemed to make the silence all the more daunting.

Someone in the Rapture, in the City, she puzzled. *Someone searching for me, scouring the streets. How—*

"The boats," she spluttered. "The Alderbane told me that Tarrazi merchant ships had weighed anchor in the docks a couple of nights back. He said there were no reports of people getting on or off... but there was no guarantee, as it was so dark. Someone must've got off that ship, and used the Rapture to get into the City undetected."

"Then someone's been sent over from Tarraz to hunt you," came a thundering voice at her back. "And there's only one person in the whole of Tarraz who could know that you're here."

"Gaza." The name came like a frosted wind, prickling up her spine, a crackle of thunder sounding somewhere off to the north where the mountains butchered the sky. "She must know I'm taking refuge here."

"If you're being hunted, you need to get out of the City," Brutus exclaimed. "You need to find refuge somewhere that they can't find you."

"It's an idea, but I don't know—"

"It won't make a difference."

Both of them turned to the Forgotten One.

"It won't make a difference," they continued, "because of your link to the Rapture. They know you're here, and know where you will go. They're probably just biding their time, waiting for the perfect moment...."

"What do you mean? What does *any* of this mean?" she asked, with a sudden swamping dread at the thought that some unknown killer knew where she was. *How has this happened so fast...*

The Forgotten One looked out to the City of the Sun behind them, and clasped its hands. "This person hunting you through the Rapture, is one of a very small number of individuals known as 'transmitters'. They are people who have discovered the inner workings of the Rapture, and are able to transmit their souls into it as you or I can, but with greater control than someone like Brutus can manage. Your friend here requires visions and a sudden connection to transmit, and even then it is an extremely painful affair as his soul rejects the shift. A transmitter, however, does not have these same restraints, and can access the Rapture at their behest. And what concerns me about that, is that our particular transmitter not only knows *who* you are, but also *how* you can access the Rapture, and can therefore hunt you more effectively."

"Because of the Ascendent soul..."

"Precisely: think of it as a beacon upon a tall mountain," it explained. "When the beacon is lit, the transmitter knows where you are... and even when the flame has been extinguished, they will still know where to find you..."

"Because even though the light is gone, the mountain will still remain."

It nodded. "And no matter where you run, your soul shall always be there, and through the Rapture you can always be found."

Cavara ground her teeth, her breath escaping her lips in fits and starts. She found her hands trembling at her side, her whole body tense with fear. "So what choice do I have?" she said, almost pleading. "What can I do?"

"You must cut the head from the snake, Cavara," Brutus remarked. "Kill the transmitter, before the transmitter kills you."

"But I don't even know who they are!" she cried in frustration. "I don't know who they are, or what the fuck is happening!"

"It's okay, Successor—"

"It's not fucking okay!" She turned to the pale figure, gritting her teeth, hiding the tears welling in her eyes. "If they can transmit through the Rapture, and effectively perform a shadow-step, then they could have me murdered in the blink of an eye. I would be dead in seconds, and not even realise it had happened. What's okay about that? What makes it okay that I have to go back into that place with an assassin lurking around?" She steadied herself, gulping in air. "I don't want to die. I don't want to die here, on the other side of the world, knowing my homeland suffers. That I could never see the shores of Provenci again... that kills me inside." She shook her head. "But I also know I can't go back... because at least here, I'm far enough way from it all to live a somewhat-normal life, at least for now. If I went back, I'd have a new assassin sent to kill me every day until they succeed. I'd be dead within the week." She levelled her gaze with the pale figure's porcelain eyes. "So, yes, I know I must be here, and I know I must press on and act like everything is okay... but I can't see a way out of this. I can't see how I can survive, not with how little I know about the void and my place in it. I don't see what options I have..."

The Forgotten One placed a hand on her shoulder, and attempted a smile. "You must train," they exclaimed. "You must learn what it means to be a Successor, and you must go on the hunt through the Rapture. Find this transmitter out, and use your newfound skills to exterminate them and end this terror for good. For if you are cautious, and lend an ear to your innate powers... then you will retain the upper hand always."

She nodded, stifling her tears. "And if I don't?"

The Forgotten One closed their eyes, the black split of their skull pulsing expressively with the bulges of their brain. With the roaring fear tearing through her, and the flinching paranoia catching at her mind, Cavara looked upon the dour countenance of their pale face and found no answers lay there. That not even the champion of the All-Mother, in all its corporeal beneficence, could conjure the necessary words to reassure her, and save her soul from a cruel end.

Our soul, she thought, a tremor behind her eyes. *The Ascendency.* It came almost as a revelation. *The All-Mother's Successor.* As the thought came, the pale figure pulled at its robes and lowered down to her height.

The fate of the world within me.

Watching and waiting, with a great discomfort in its eyes, the champion of the All-Mother gave its response.

"If you don't, then you will die," they said slowly to her. "If you don't, you will die... and the world will be lost forever."

†

Chapter 11

Into the Ozban

As the rain fell, and the thunder rattled tempestuously overhead, Revek pulled the cloth veil closer about his head and shifted his horse into a canter.

They had departed the main camp toward the Ozban Forest with trepidation on their tongues, the horses kicking and snorting at the wall of trees as they materialised ahead. The commander, alongside three other generals he neither cared for nor wanted anything to do with, had control over a combined force of near three hundred Provencian soldiers, with a third of those being among the new intake brought north by the Marshal Corps. They were a hardy, if skittish bunch, with the Corps forming up along the flanks and funnelling the lackies across the broken earth like a snake. They appeared almost like beggars, shouldering their robes and shuffling absently forward through the mud. It was only the strike of lightning bolting through the clouds above that broke them from their trance, as shiny eyes and even shinier chest-plates watched the snap of blue come and go.

And the commander would have joined them, in marvelling at the maelstrom seizing across the skyline above, had his gaze not been elsewhere, looking back toward the main camp.

And the imperial standards still pulling at the wind at its centre.

Lazaerys. Revek found his blood boil almost on command, grinding his teeth feverishly. *How I long to cut her throat.*

They had been under the canopy of the main tent when the Marshal had chosen the three hardy officers who would brave the Ozban with him. Those who had been assigned, had made their disgust at the idea apparent before Lazaerys had even had a chance to finish: expressing how their merits were best used *anywhere* but with him. How it was a foolish business; how the commander could not be trusted. Joking often about who was really in charge there. And Revek, stood front and centre as they mocked him, quelled his humiliation with a short sermon on honour and duty – *aimed specifically at those who put personal dislike above the task at hand* – before departing quickly thereafter. He had tried to brush off their harsh words as he went about mobilising the soldiers and preparing for departure, hoping that would be the end of it.

But even two hours later, stationed at the rear-guard with a sprawl of marching steel meandering the terrain before him, Revek still felt their dismissal creeping about his neck and refusing to let go.

To think I have been seconded in place of these bastards, he grumbled internally, his gaze passing from helm-to-helm up the ranks ahead. *All of these fighters, under my technical command... and yet there is nothing. No order... no discipline... no sense of authority. I am just another officer among the rest.* As his eyes swept to the head of the procession, the grip on his reins tightened sharply, until his knuckles bulged white.

Another officer... like them.

The other three generals, stationed at the head of the detachment, rode on horseback with hoods swept across tired faces, as the ugly skeletal protrusions of the Ozban grew steadily ahead of them. The commander knew nothing of where they had come from, or why they had been assigned. All he had found out were a few small snippets of information from the passing comments of the soldiers, which had proven enough to pique his interest.

And tempt my idle hands, too.

Riding in an arrowhead, Revek marked the right-hand general as the one they called Oslo: a fresh-blood, newly promoted and compoundingly naïve. With three silver hoops laced through his nose and the kind of stubbly, angular jaw one would use to chisel stone, Oslo cut an awkward figure, and Revek watched him hunch rigidly over the reins of his horse to run long fingers through the beast's mane. The commander screwed his nose up.

Awful strange man… easy pickings for the dogs.

Opposite, atop a black stallion with silver braids through its tail, sat the swaying form of the one they called Zespa. She was remarkably tall, he had discovered: a full head-and-shoulders above the commander, and with a frame to match. She possessed a sunken face and a stout nose, with a long flush of black hair coiling across her neck like ivy and braided through with twine made of silver. As she turned to Oslo with a wicked smile that seemed to glow in the dead light of dusk, Revek found himself smiling too.

Will be interesting to see if you bark or bite.

Blinking slowly, trying to decipher the generals' conversation, it was only then that Revek realised the head of their entourage had turned in their mount, and planted their gaze squarely on him. And even from there, with the throes of the storm dicing the air between them, their disgust proved ever apparent.

And then there's you. The commander's smile fell in an instant.

The one they call Xol.

They were broad and fortuitous, sat atop their mount, with a single stretch of braided hair parting their scalp and the weaving shape of thorns tattooed around their eyes. They possessed a pale complexion, with charcoal-black sockets and lips the colour of slate. There was an intricate, indescribable aura about them: something that both captivated and nullified any ill-feeling the commander possessed. Atop their mount, with the blood-orange stain of light skimming the top of the forest behind, the world seemed to orbit around them with a quiet contentment.

Which I fear may prove difficult, in the days to come.

A heartbeat later, and Xol turned from Revek and directed their mount through the first of the trees. Moments later, the other two generals followed – and before long, Revek was watching the steel helmets of the rank-and-file disappear into the gloom behind them.

Cantering forward and stopping just before the first of the Ozban's roots, Revek held his mount steady and glanced back across the lowlands just behind. Jumping between the artillery trenches and the felled trees; the broken fields and farmhouses; the spasmodic tufts of grass and the cesspits of residual ooze. Skimming the earth, on and on toward the border, until his studious gaze fell upon the command post nestled within the distant camp. He spied the pale tents and the loaded carts and the main canopy at its centre, with the billowing flag of red and green erected at its peak.

Where that manipulative bitch still remains, plotting my downfall at every turn.

Heat rose in his neck; blood thundered through his skull. Revek ground his teeth, and was about to declare his innocence to the world – that he was wrongly dismissed, belittled with no right, brought to his knees for doing his duty – when he turned suddenly, to the dark of the Ozban behind.

And that anger, turned sharply to a grin.

You think you can control me? he cried. *You think you have the right to challenge me, within the ranks of my own army?* He inhaled deeply, as cold splatters of rain tapped against his cheeks. *If so, then I shall show you what happens when you attempt to constrain me. I'll show you what happens when you put dogs in the lion's den.*

As the rain fell, and the thunder rattled tempestuously overhead, Revek pulled the cloth veil closer about his head and turned to the Ozban Forest.

I'll bathe this land in their blood.

†

Chapter 12

We Are Not Soldiers

"Are we in position?"

Castan nodded, looking out over the dew-covered fields toward the shadows of Marcheg on the hill. "We have four small detachments stationed behind walls on the left and right flanks, with those on horseback in reserve to counter any assault from there," he explained. "We have scouts positioned along the lower banks of the hill to alert us of any approaching forces, and the main contingent are amassed along the walkway awaiting your orders, Chief. It seems to be a good day to show those bastards who's boss."

"Agreed," Eli muttered in reply, letting the wind lash his face in waves. "Although… don't call me that."

"Call you what?"

"*Chief*… I'm nothing of that, as much as the soldiers seem to think so. I'm not here to be their Chief."

"You're still a great leader to them, though. There's no escaping that."

"I'm just doing my duty."

"And you do it a damn sight better than everyone else," Castan said, slapping him across the back and moving off down the road toward town, turning once more with a smile. "Besides, being a hero out of duty sounds an awful lot like a Chief to me!"

Eli watched the youthful man slip amongst the crowds awaiting his command at the base of the bridge, and found himself smiling. He had a certain respect for the man he'd chosen to be at his side during the coming battle: knowing Castan for several years, he was almost like a younger brother, full of spirit and vigour and life. They had grown a vast network of contact across the western plains through their work as labourers, and at every turn he had been at Eli's side with new perspectives and a buoyant grin. He was, by the Chief's estimation, an excellent fit for a second-in-command, even with the farcical comments he often made about Eli's place in the world.

He's misguided, if he thinks I'm anything more than a father and a fighter who's here to right the wrongs of those in charge. He adjusted the chest-plate lashed across his shoulders and tightened the braids laced through his beard. *I believe him to be a courageous and hopeful soul, even in the darkest times. It's something I admire most. But calling me the Chief of the Mountains, facing the adversity as we are...* Eli shook his head.

What a mad world we're living in.

Drawn suddenly to the sound of approaching footsteps, the huge man turned slowly to find Jinx appear from behind an old barn, the bags of her eyes still sore and puffy from the previous day. She had donned something close to a suit of armour, slipping into whatever odd match of steel they could spare, with one shoulder-pad far bigger than the other and the awkward rustle of a loose chain somewhere on her leg. She walked with a steady gait nonetheless, striding out over the gravel path with a resilient smile. To the Chief, she looked every inch the hardy soldier ready for the fight ahead – even if he knew for sure that she was anything but.

"I wondered where you'd got to," Eli said. "I was beginning to think you'd miss all the fun."

"Over my dead body would I," she replied. "A chance to kick those bastards in the teeth for what they've done to us? I need no invitation to that."

Eli smiled. "Your spirit is always most welcome... especially at grave times such as these."

"Although, I will say I should've come better prepared... this armour is not fitting in the slightest."

"If it stops an arrow or a blade, then it'll do." He paused. "Besides, I need something to laugh at while we're out there."

"Fuck yourself," Jinx scoffed with a grin, looking off behind him toward the bridge. "Seems like you've amassed quite the fighting force out there."

The Chief looked over his shoulder and nodded proudly. "They're some of the finest people this nation has ever produced, it's true. It's an honour to have them here by our side in such trying times."

"And that's all because of you, they're glorious leader! No other person could have rallied so many with such short notice. You deserve some credit for that."

"Well," Eli muttered, recalling Castan's words, "there is that I guess."

She managed a broad smile, catching at the very edges of her cheeks. "So, where will I be positioned when the fighting begins?" she asked. "I was thinking maybe in the reserves, or along one of the flanks—"

"You'll be with me," he said pointedly, the steel of his gaze shining brighter. "Front and centre."

Her face sunk immediately. "*What?*" she spluttered in disbelief. "I don't... surely I would be safer in the reserves?"

"You'll be safer... where I can keep an eye on you."

"Surely there's somewhere else I can go to help though? Somewhere away from the violence."

"No, I need you at the front."

"I mean, maybe I can go with the supply carts and keep the logistics in check, or keep check on the horses, or—"

"Alva, *please*." A sudden well of emotion caught at Eli's throat. "I have lost far too much in my life to take any chances now. In the past few weeks I have lost more people than I ever have, and I have *suffered* for it every day since. Friends, family, comrades... my own husband. All have been taken from me... and all I have grieved so *deeply*." He turned to her, placing his huge hands on her shoulders. "You are all

I have left of him, Alva. All I have left of his blood, of his family… of the things I hold dearest to me. My children are the same… and in this war, you are no different than them. Keeping you alive, and here with us… it's my last true chance to honour those I have lost. To make things right again. So, I shall protect you with every bone in my body, and every last breath I have to give, because I know doing so is the right thing to do… and I can die knowing that Arrenso did not pass from this world in vain."

Jinx inhaled slowly, her own feelings torrenting in her chest at the sound of her brother's name. It threatened to overwhelm her, bubbling in her throat, before she conjured the faintest of smiles with the quiet of her eye, and a single tear rolling down her cheek. "Thank you, Eli… for everything," she said.

"It is my honour," he replied softly, squeezing her shoulders and stepping back.

She nodded shakily, drawing the grief back within her, and straightened her shoulders. "So… what's the plan from here, anyway? As I'm going to be in the thick of it very soon, I think it's good to know what that looks like…"

"Of course." Eli looked absently off to the horizon, the welt of his heart burning bright in the sun. "The plan… is to drive like an arrow down the main thoroughfare of the town until we reach the square, where we'll set up defensive posts in the surrounding buildings," he explained slowly. "When we get there, we will likely encounter the enemy head on, and while the archers get into position to hold the soldiers back there will likely be a lot of bloodshed in the square. I will be at the head of the charge, securing as wide of a perimeter as we can while the archers secure their firing posts. And you, Alva, will follow those archers up onto the top floor of the baron's hall, where we will have better oversight of the space below. It's our best chance of holding them back."

"Very well," she replied, seemingly chastened. "It seems like I don't have an awful lot to do then."

"And that would be a reasonable assessment, were it not for

this..."

With the click of a buckle, Eli reached round to his back and revealed a small oak crossbow that looked comically small in his hands. It was a quaint thing, with a tightly-wound draw and a pouch of bolts nestled neatly in its holster.

Jinx frowned. "Why would I need that?"

Eli smiled. "Because you'll be using one of these, and helping the archers pop a few heads for us from the balcony."

"What...?" She took it from him with a puzzled look, feeling across the smooth handle with awkward hands. "Eli, this doesn't make any sense. I... I *steal* shit, I don't handle weapons. I can't aim, or shoot. I... I don't even know how to operate this thing. Why do I have this?"

"Because you're needed... but I must also keep you safe."

"But I'm not a soldier."

"*None* of us are," Eli rumbled, looking off to the ranks of his people waiting at the foot of the bridge. "Roll it back a couple of weeks, and all those you see with armour and swords ahead of us, were tending fields in the mountains, or selling their wares at market. None of them had ever wielded anything much bigger than a butcher knife. They were common folk, like you or I. They had never dreamed of being soldiers, and never wanted any part of it. And still, to this day, they don't. None of them are soldiers: they're farmers and millers; blacksmiths and merchants; clerks and councillors. They are decent people, who have left their way of life to take up arms against an oppressive regime that has murdered and rotted its way into power. They follow me not because I have ordered them to, or because they have any greed or bloodlust of their own. They have followed me... because they believe in a common good. A common good, that all people of this realm, whether in the fields or in the rungs of high office... should be safe, and free, to be as they are. And when that is threatened, as it is now, it is those same people who shall rise up to defend those freedoms they hold most dear. Not the soldiers, or the fighters, but the common folk. People like you or I."

"Then I shall fight alongside you for this great cause of ours… no matter what," she replied brightly, raising the crossbow toward the bridge. "We will do this, together, and we'll win come the end of it." She paused, smirking. "Now let's go… the Chief of the Mountain is never kept waiting."

"Well said, Alva… well said."

Eli inclined his head and, with a great stride like a towering giant, he began pacing toward the narrow bridge with Jinx close behind, coated in a stoic resolve.

Our time is now.

As he approached, the rebels parted down the middle, faces awash with hope and fearless pride. Eli walked among them, a leader among his people, with nods and smiles and the passionate union of the common good, a power rising in his heart with every step until he reached the foot of the hill and turned to face them.

"Citizens of Provenci: today we fight!" Eli bellowed to the open skies. "Today, we shall raise our steel against those who take our freedoms! Today, we bring the war to *them*, for the soul of our nation and the people of this land!"

Cries erupted from the masses: screeches of battle-ready glee burst out over the rooftops of Marcheg and beyond.

"So, take up your swords and your axes… your bows and your knives. Take them up, and fight for your honour… and strike them down, in the name of our homeland! For together, we are as one! And together, we shall *prevail*!"

He turned on his heel, spurring into a run, roaring at the top of his lungs.

"*CHARGE!*"

†

Chapter 13

A Lamb to Slaughter

Cavara and her guardian had returned to the City as the sun began to crown the distant horizon and spill across the land below in orange waves. A hazy wash bled across the wide streets before them, shimmering across the stone at their feet, polished by constant wear. The squat blocks of salt-grey houses stood like turrets to either side, meandering along the thoroughfare as it snaked up to the great palace at the mountain's peak. The scintillating domes transfixed her gaze, as if the sky itself had ruptured, and the distant reams of heaven were leaking out into the mortal world. She looked there for a long time, passing market stalls and drinking houses absently, lost in the zealous beauty of it all.

Wondering when it would all go wrong.

All of this is in my hands, she thought in a quiet part of her mind. *I'm the only one that can save them if the worst comes.* Her gaze passed among them for a moment: the glowing bronzed faces and lustrous robes of the City-folk, smiling and gesturing to each other with all the time in the world. The merchants at their market stalls; the guildsmen, muttering outside town-houses; children, chasing each other through the legs of their elders. All people she did not know, and owed nothing to.

All people I must now save… as I am hunted by an unknown foe.

Casting her gaze out once more, a jolt of fear caught in her chest as she found people here and there watching her. A man in a hood, from behind the glass of a tavern window; a young woman studying the wares of a market-stall with a glint of steel in her eye; an elder figure, hobbling across the road, looking away with a wicked smile that set her soul on-edge. Thinking how any one of them could be the transmitter sent to kill her; how any one of them could pass into the Rapture in a single step, without her even realising, and slip a knife through her ribs. That it could all be ended – her life, and the fate of the known world – in a single, silent strike. The general reeled at the thought, trying to fight down the terror bleeding through her chest. Finding, in that desperate part of her, so many questions she had yet to find answers for. So many truths that stayed masked behind reality. So many, and yet one stood out to her most of all.

'*Why me?*'

"You seem uneasy, Successor," the Forgotten One muttered at her back, her ever-present shadow looming just behind. "What troubles you?"

Cavara found a twinge in her spine. "Many things, but nothing to worry about," she said, turning with a meek smile. "I have a lot on my mind, is all."

"It is good to speak of these things, if you feel you can... it soothes the soul to express."

I'm in way over my head. "I understand that..." *I have no idea what I'm doing here.* "But honestly, it's okay..." *I don't want to be a part of this.* "They aren't things we can solve..." *I feel trapped by destiny.* "So it's best to just process and let be."

"As you wish, Successor... your balance is your own."

Cavara scoffed. "Oh please, I haven't known balance since arriving here. Everything is new, and different... always changing... *unrelenting*."

"Such is the life you now live," the pale figure levelled. "It is a burden that afflicts all those who have been chosen to ascend."

"I just want a few quiet moments where I don't have to think about my destiny, or the Ascendency, or the Rapture, or any of it. Is that too much to ask? A few moments to myself, just once..."

"You long for a return to life as it was before... that's only natural, considering how upturned things has become."

"But I want to return to my life before *everything*: before a dead king and a new regime and the betrayal and the Rapture and destiny and..." She exhaled. "...all the rest of it."

"You wish that time had a little more patience, and good graces, and could let you live on as you always have."

"But I also know that that's a fallacy... and that such a life doesn't exist anymore, for anyone."

The Forgotten One considered for a moment, gazing along the street sagaciously. "The past is the past, it is true," they said in the end, "but what lies in the future... well, that is a stone unturned, and a path for you to decide."

She nodded, more out of habit than anything. "I hope you're right, y'know, I really do... I want more than anything to have some control over my life again, and to be free of these burdens I have. But, even then, there's a still a little part of me that has consigned that reality to fate already..."

"And why is that?"

"Because there seems to be a recurring habit in my life recently where—"

"Well look who it is!"

Cavara stopped mid-sentence and rolled her eyes in despair, as she registered whose voice was talking.

...where something always gets in the way of that.

Looking off to the left, Cavara grit her teeth as Ptolemy and Amara honed into view from beyond the market stalls, carrying the same self-effacing bravado as before. The general bristled at their repulsive smiles, hand lingering at her sword almost by instinct.

Exactly who I didn't want to see, at this precise moment in time. She shook her head, looking up to the gods.

So much for a few moment's respite.

"We were wondering when you would return from your little

adventure playing with your toys," Ptolemy mused, crossing his arms. "I must admit, my wrists grew rather tired of handling that spyglass for so long."

Of course you were watching. "Well, Ptolemy, I would say I had sympathy for you... but I would of course be lying," Cavara retorted, hardly in the mood for sardonic tones. "Besides, our business is our business, and it has no timeframe. If your choice is to spy on us... then it's your time to waste."

"You're in a fighting spirit today," Amara cooed, playing with her hair. "We could almost report you to the Alderbane for that."

The general scoffed. "Do it. It would prove to be the least of my problems at the moment. In fact, you'd probably be doing me a favour."

"A lot on your plate, my dear?"

"More than you could *fathom*."

"Well, general, I would say I had sympathy for you... but I would of course be *lying*."

"Have you stopped us for any good reason, or are you just here to piss me off?" Cavara growled. "Because if it's the latter, I'll happily be on my way, thank you."

"Now, now, hold on," Ptolemy said, waving his hand at her. "Give us a chance. We are in fact here to discuss something of note... concerning your escapades outside of the city walls."

The general's displeasure deepened. "Right... go on."

"You see, the Alderbane is... rather *uncomfortable* with how long you and this *thing* you call your protector spend outside of the city walls. It understands that you wish to practice sparring, or whatever strange business you attend... but while you remain outside of the walls there is no guarantee that that is *all* that you're doing."

She frowned, bemused. "So, the Alderbane believes we're out there conspiring against you? Seriously?"

"Evidently so."

"You do understand that that's ridiculous?"

"Well, we would say these accusations are completely unfounded… had you not made very clear on our last encounter your obvious dislike of the Alderbane, and their… *way of doing things.*" Ptolemy shrugged. "And so, because of that quite important observation, we will naturally assess *everything* as a possible threat. It's what we do, after all…"

"So this is *your* decision? You're the ones who deem it improper for us to leave the city walls at will, as every other citizen does?"

"But you aren't a citizen, are you general? As far as we're aware, you're nothing more than a *refugee*."

Anger funnelled into her lungs, rasping from her mouth like dragon's flame. "Those are bold words," the general challenged, "coming from the pawn of a mad creature who is as paranoid as they are deluded. Because why would we conspire against you? What good would that serve us? We are not a threat to you, or those in charge. We just want to live on as we are."

Ptolemy paid no attention to her, choosing to sneer instead. "It doesn't matter, the decision has been made. And so long as you reside within these walls and seek refuge here, you shall *abide* by it."

"I shall hear it from the mouth of the Alderbane before I abide by anything *you* dictate to me." Cavara grimaced at them both, before stepping forward. "Now, if you'll *excuse* me…"

She pushed past them, starting off down the thoroughfare ahead.

"You best listen to us, general," Amara warned at her back. "There will be *consequences* for insubordination."

Cavara stopped and turned sharply, staring her down. "Your place, and your word, and your *consequences,* mean nothing to me, do you understand? I am here in this city, under the good graces of the Alderbane, and the Alderbane *alone.* So it is to them I shall answer, and it is their wishes that I will respect. As for any orders you two give me, the answer is self-evident… go *fuck* yourself."

Admiring their looks of disgust for but a moment, she turned on her heel, feeling suddenly breathless and weak. She took several long steps before stopping again, sensing her ankles start to buckle and the caving sensation of the sky falling above her.

Cavara turned suddenly, looking back on the others with blurring vision. Watching the Forgotten One draw it's blade, and push past the honour guards shouting—

As the darkness rose to meet her, and she was suddenly very alone.

~

She fell into the void like a dead weight, into the oblivion of a falling star. Skin prickling, the sun lay high and forgotten somewhere above. In a panicked daze, weightless and breathless, she scrabbled to her feet and studied the porcelain walls around her, to find she was still within the City limits not far from where they had been before. But there was no sign of the Forgotten One, or the mark of its shadow. No sign of the honour guards, or the passers-by, or the hanging signs or market stalls. There was no sign of anything at all, for that matter. Just a great absence, her heart pulsing in her throat, trying to make sense of why she was there and how she had entered the Rapture in the first pla—

She stopped.

"The transmitter..."

A sudden intensity ripped up her spine, locking her legs in place. The grey impressions of walls around her seemed to glide and shift awkwardly, as if she were spinning. It was disorientating, almost to the point of nausea. Lurching about, she assessed the shadows – crossing to each one – back stepping – sidestepping – lost – confused – scared—

Something moved.

Cavara froze, studying it: an off-cut shape sliding through the haze just ahead of her. It blended with the walls for a moment, disappearing entirely, before manifesting into a figure ahead of her with a wicked grin plastered to his face.

Much like the Iron Queen had been before, the figure was a projection of their true form, with tanned skin and ringed fingers and a furrowed brow like rolling waves. A tattoo split out from their bottom lip: the tiny blades of butcher knives carving outwards down their throat like a stitch. With a striking flush of deep grey hair, she caught the glint of a tiny needle laced behind the man's ear – that, and a huge cleaver hung menacingly at his belt.

Seizing up, Cavara reached instinctively for her blade; sensing her unease, the figure drew his tongue across his lips sadistically.

"Az-Kabza, skal-thüm," *the man boomed. "Blood or death, young soul."*

"I don't know who you are..."

"Perhaps... but I know who you *are."*

"Why are you here?" Cavara blustered, holding her ground. "How do you have access to the Rapture?"

"You already have the answers you seek, general. You know what I am really." He bowed. "I am a transmitter; a simple hunter of the void. And I have been sent here by the Iron Queen to do her bidding."

"You're an assassin."

"That's a rather bold claim to make."

"I know it's true."

"How so?"

Cavara pointed toward the man's throat. "The tattoo down your neck... it's the mark of the Coven, isn't it? The hidden blades of Val Azbann."

He produced a sharp look, almost amused. "Clever girl."

"I was told they had been disbanded years ago."

"Disbanded, yes... but we are not without our uses when the price is right. Especially when the target is so... extraordinary."

"So Gaza sent an assassin of the Rapture to kill me... because she didn't have the skill to do it herself?" Cavara challenged. "Is that it? Is that how desperate she's become?"

"Far from it, general... far from it." The transmitter laughed. "There is so much here that you don't understand. So much you are unworthy of knowing. You see, the Iron Queen no longer has access to you, because she cannot enter your void anymore. She's been locked out of your transient space. And it was your newfound friend *who did it..."*

"The Forgotten One?"

"Yes. That thing *is interfering with the Queen's plans, much to her disgust. So, she sent me aboard a Tarrazi merchant ship bound for Sevica... and landed us here at the City walls, right under your nose."*

"It doesn't matter that you're here," Cavara spat, stepping forward to hide

the quiver in her hands. "You cannot harm me… the Forgotten One will come for you and close the Rapture. You'll be locked out, just as your foul leader has been. You have no power here."

He smirked, shaking his head. "Alas, if only that were true…" Suddenly, the transmitter was striding forward. "But I fear you are mistaken. Because the creature you speak of, can only shield you away from my Queen because of your joint connection to the All-Mother. It binds you all transiently through the Rapture… and the creature, as it stands, has the upper hand in that. But, you see, transmitters like myself do not require such a connection to the void as you do. We may do so of our own volition… so that means the dynamic has changed." He smiled venomously. "Your friend cannot reach you here, general… because I have locked them out…"

The cleaver was suddenly in his hand, shimmering malevolent in the half-light.

"And that means you… are mine."

The assassin made their approach, and readied their weapon.

Cavara stood back, unsheathing the blade at her side to find it weighty and awkward in her hand – wondering suddenly where the flaming blade was from before, and why she couldn't conjure it. Flexing her fingers, she felt it there: the Rapture's weapon, just hidden beyond the veil. Tantalisingly close, and yet just beyond her reach.

Betraying her, as the cleaver arced down toward her head.

Raising her weapon, their steel chimed together without a whisper of sound: instead, tiny reverberations rippled across the white around them, catching at her skin like a gust of wind. The blades struck again, and a similar sensation caught her skin, until the space between them was consumed by the vibrations of crashing blades and a wind whipped up across her face in rolling waves.

Engaging the cleaver with minute turns of his wrist, the transmitter continued to edge slowly forward, driving his weapon through as Cavara was forced to backstep. She hooked her blade back across, only to find the assassin skim elegantly around, re-engaging the cleaver like a flip-knife that forced her back again. Then another strike came, followed by another backstep; the general grit her teeth, hissing with frustration.

There was a menace in the transmitter's eye: a cold calculation that only those of the Coven possessed. With every strike – every mark of the weapon against her own – she sensed her strength ebb in microscopic shifts.

That slowly, but clinically, he was wearing her down.

"You can give in now," the transmitter muttered. "It can all be over..."

"I will not yield to the likes of you," Cavara spat, driving her blade forward with enough force that the tall man was forced to backstep.

He produced a glimmer of emotion. Surprise, almost.

"Az-Kabza..."

A spin of the heel and the transmitter advanced again, suddenly faster and more directing in his attacks. Cavara found her heart stutter; she was immediately on the back-foot again, retreating far quicker than she had hoped. Her swings became callous, her wrist jarring violently: every movement being less about attack, and more about deflection. Skimming the cleaver along her sword's edge and swiping it away fast enough so it didn't slice her fingers through. The same motion over and over, dicing through and spearing out, trying to use the length of her blade to her advantage. But with every lunge, her flank lay exposed and Cavara recoiled, fearing the weight of the cleaver snapping against her far-thinner blade. Fearing for her life, in the end.

Fearing something that almost seemed inevitable.

Her blade became taut in her hand, as the weighted strikes of the cleaver rattled through her like bolts of lightning. With each consecutive attack, the tension snapping across the sword's edge made her wince with unease. She was sweating, awash with it, the figure before her hazing and refocusing with each forced blink of the eye. Her heart pounded, throat closing.

Something had to give.

Battling on, losing ground with each step, Cavara found herself forced into an upward strike suddenly, and realised her error just as it was too late. Lurching on the balls of her feet, the transmitter's blade circled down through the middle—

And her sword shattered in her hand entirely.

Shrapnel flew like bullets; her exposed arms were butchered with tiny cuts of flying steel. She dropped the hilt of the weapon as if it were aflame, hissing with agony. Looking down, trying to stem the nausea in her chest, she watched her forearm weep an effluvial white-grey liquid where there should have been blood. She goggled it at for a moment, trying to make sense of it.

Thinking back to the totems several weeks before…

"I warned you," the transmitter said, manipulating the cleaver through his fingers, studying the stars of broken metal scattered across the floor. "If you had just yielded in the first place, we wouldn't need to be here…"

"You stay back!" Cavara growled, sidestepping slowly.

"I don't think you have the means to dictate that anymore, skal-thüm. *Because I still possess my blade… and you, do not." A step forward, then another. "So you just stay there, and stay quiet, and we can end this without any fuss. I think that's reasonable…"*

"Stay back!"

"You have no say in this." A sharp grin appeared. "But don't worry, I'll make this quick… I only want to bleed you a little bit—"

The transmitter stopped. The void shuddered around them like the beat of a drum. His eyes bulged, as he pivoted away from her—

With a sudden rush of black-grey shadow, a figure swung past Cavara and lunged at the assassin with another blade. They exchanged several strikes, with the shadow's attacks being visibly strained, appearing as a distortion in the void. It looked inhuman, unnatural even.

But when they pulled apart, and the shadow turned to face her, Cavara gasped as her heart tore open in her chest.

Brutus grit his teeth.

"Run!"

The two fighters re-engaged suddenly, the transmitter bellowing as he watched his chances slip away, the shadow pressing on with impish movements and the dull clatter of steel.

With fear in her mind and time slipping away, Cavara spun on her heel and felt her legs pound beneath her, turning to see a breach in the void closing slowly ahead.

The porcelain land around her unfurled like clouds of smoke, as the grey smudges ahead formed into a wide street with houses and market stalls; at her feet, lines appeared, separating slabs of stone; other manifestations that she recognised as people, began forming in clusters to either side. With slow certainty, voices began to prickle in her ears once again; a deep humanity resurfaced in her soul.

She looked back for a moment, glimpsing the two fighters still locked in battle, fearing for Brutus' life – before the breach swelled before her, and the darkness swept in like the tide once again.

~

She clattered across stone slabs like a battering ram, spilling down a side-street in a ball of metal and twisting hair. Air pummelled from her lungs; the crunch in her ribs sent shockwaves through her body. She collided with one building, and collapsed sidelong against the other, before finally laying still in a heap with the trickle of gutter somewhere near her head.

Cavara lay breathlessly for a moment, staring up at the open skies above and the looming rooftops of the buildings all around. She sensed the tiny trickles of blood lacing down her arms; a cool wind snapped through and chilled her soul. It was almost peaceful, in a strange sort of way. A moment of peace, in the hellish chaos that life had become. The general blinked heavily, almost inviting the joy of sleep.

Until a huge figure with a skull like the pale moon appeared from her left, and she was being hauled to her feet with words of concern pulling at her ears.

"Are you okay? What happened?" the Forgotten One rumbled, an unsettling urgency in their voice. "Where did you go? Whose Rapture did you enter?"

"I… I…" she stuttered, barely recollecting what had gone on. "I was… there was the transmitter, and I…"

"The *transmitter* found you?" Their head shot up, craning left and right to check they were alone, before settling back on her. "What happened? Are you hurt?"

"We were right about those boats that landed at the shore," she said. "The transmitter was a stowaway, and slipped ashore through the Rapture before they departed. They found me while we were in conversation with the honour guards. And I... I was attacked... they attacked me. And you couldn't help. *Can't* help. The transmitter said that they'd locked you out, or something, like you've done to the Iron Queen. I don't really know, I... whatever that means, they've done it, and it means you can't follow me into their Rapture. It means I have nothing. I... *shit...*"

"That is... a very significant problem." The pale figure paused, considering. "Although, if you were trapped in there, how did you escape?"

"Brutus, he..." Shock suddenly brandished in her mind. "He came to save me. He's still in there... he's still trapped in the Rapture with that man. I... I don't know if he's gonna be okay, or if he's alive. I... *fuck*!"

"He will be okay, I assure you," the Forgotten One replied, crouching to her level. "From what I have seen, his knowledge and control of the Rapture surpasses the skills of any other shadow-walker I've known. If any of his kind were to survive an ordeal with a transmitter, it would be him. He will survive."

"Okay... okay, that's good..." She inhaled suddenly, doubling over, an anxious wave of nausea crippling her insides. "Everything's going wrong. It's all so *wrong...*"

"I'm sorry, Cavara. Truly I am. The upturning of the world is all around us, but it hurts to see it so deeply in your own heart." A deep sorrow crossed their ancient face. "All we can do now is return to the house of Lady Azura, to rest and plan for the path ahead. That is all that is available to us. I'm sorry I cannot offer you anything more... but we have to go, now."

With little strength left in her to fight, and the gnawing fear in her throat that the transmitter could be anywhere around them even then, Cavara slipped under the supporting arm of the Forgotten One, and shuffled slowly off into the City of the Sun. Knowing peace had alluded her, once again.

And the worst was yet to come.

They entered the small house sometime later to the sounds of sobbing, with spilled cloths across the floor and mud tracked up the stairs in thick piles. It was deathly cold within the rooms, gloomy and disparate.

And Cavara knew something was seriously wrong.

"Who's... there?" came the spluttered call of Azura from somewhere upstairs, the edge of tears in her voice.

"It's Cavara... are you okay?" the general managed, numbness seizing at her limbs as if they were frozen. "Azura?"

"Please *hurry*..."

Cavara broke from the arms of the Forgotten One and, with renewed vigour streaming through her veins, ascended the stairs in bounding steps. She stumbled forward, lurching, studying each room that came and went. Until she reached the open door to Evelyn's room, and found Azura knelt crying at its centre.

The general hurried over, bundling her in her arms and locking tightly. She was quivering, her hands welded to her eyes, buried beneath the chestnut-grey sweep of her hair. Her boots lay strewn at the door, caked in mud, and the impressions in the rug told Cavara that she had been on the floor crying for a very long time.

Looking up to the wider room, Cavara could see signs of a struggle: the bed had been torn apart, with the mattress thrown against the set of drawers opposite; the books had been scattered, half-torn across the floor and up against the walls; the window at the far side had been smashed in, flapping absently in the sea winds. Everything about the scene before her pointed to a break-in, but there was one great absence that filled Cavara's soul with dread.

"Where's Evelyn?"

Azura's sobs drew suddenly still; gazing up to her, her eyes red-raw, the old woman sighed weightily. "They took him."

The general's heart went cold. "*Who* did?"

"These figures in hoods... I don't know who," Azura explained. "They came as I arrived home... I heard the commotion and ran straight up here. When I arrived and I... I shouldered the door open, they had nearly all gone. Nearly all of them... except the last one. And he just stood there, watching me, holding my dear Evelyn in his arms who was screaming like a young *lamb*..." She bit back tears.

"Who were they? What did he look like?"

"I didn't see his face... only his chin. He had... something there, some mark..."

"What was it?"

Their eyes locked. "It was a tattoo, like little knives or something, running down his throat..."

Cavara stumbled back, collapsing across the floor, air heaving through her chest as the light glinted in her eyes. She was suddenly very cold, with a weight of unbearable pain loaded across her back.

It was him...

"The transmitter... he took him," she said, looking to the floor. "That's who took Evelyn."

"You *know* them?" Azura spluttered, with a sudden and disconcerting anger in her voice.

"Someone has entered the city, from aboard a Tarrazi ship... they snuck past the guards using the same powers I have. They are an assassin, ordered to kill me by enemies in my homeland. They attacked me on my way here, and I only just escaped with my life. We were coming this way to tell you... to warn you about the dangers. I knew you weren't safe, and came as soon as I could. But I'm so *sorry,* Azura... I didn't know. I'm so sorry—"

"Of *course*."

Cavara drew silent. "What?"

"Of course it was because of *you*," the old woman muttered, a venom catching at her voice. "Of course my sweet boy was taken from me because people are after *you*. As if it would be anything else. That I have done nothing wrong... that I have never raised a *finger* against anyone in my life, to draw attention or aggression my way... until I decided, in all my good graces, to harbour you as a refugee here. And I am made to suffer, all because I wanted to *help*..."

"Azura, I—"

"I watched the *horror* in Evelyn's eyes, as he was taken from me. I saw the sheer desperation in that dear boy's heart... in my *son's* heart, as he was taken from me. I have had those I love taken from me before, with nothing to show for it... and now I am sat here, in insurmountable grief... with the fear I may lose another." A single tear coiled down her cheek, quickly snuffed out as she glared towards Cavara. "And it's because of you... it's *always* because of you. Because of you, I've lost everything again. Because of you, they have stolen my boy away from me..." A moment of realisation, straining muscles across her throat. "They've stolen my *boy*..."

Azura looked off to the window with silent tears falling, as the piercing green of her eyes grew stormy and cold.

Air caught in Cavara's throat; the well of her soul grew ever-deeper. Shame raged within, threatening to tear her down altogether. She stood there for a while, numb and senseless and frightfully alone, watching the woman who had cared for her grieve the loss of her only son. That the boy had been taken to get to her, by people she didn't even know. That Evelyn's life was now at risk, at the hands of assassins who wanted her dead. Thinking on the daunting weight of what lay ahead, if she was to prevail and make amends. Thinking of Azura's words.

I've lost everything again.

Cavara turned to the door, and left without a word. The unbearable weight of grief knotted across her neck, tight as serpent's coils.

You did this, came the quiet whisper.

And I fear it may never be undone.

†

Chapter 14

The Shadow of Loss

The quarters assigned to the Queen's Champion were far bigger than Savanta had expected. They had taken her to an abyssal room as tall as it was wide, partitioned with great pillars that ascended into the shadows high above. A squat bed was pressed against one wall, with a dresser wedged feebly at the end, looking sad and dour in the orange light. But despite the low-burning sconces dotting the walls all around her, and the rusty light they gave out, it did nothing to prevent the darkening gloom encroaching on her from all sides. It seemed that every corner of the place only existed in twilight; that the black of the alcoves high above could swallow her whole at any moment. It was a devious place to behold – as devious as its ruler, no doubt – and was a world apart from the land of open skies she had seen only days before. A sad part of her wondered if she would ever see that world again, or whether she'd have to accept what her life had become: that of a sad and murderous pet, caged in the deep-dark of Val Azbann.

A place so dark, and alone.

In the quiet recesses of that lost place, Savanta sat at the edge of her bed with a knife nestled in the talons of one hand. With methodical, deliberate motions, she drew a whetstone down its edge, the screech of metal and the rush of sparks striking shivers up her spine. She admired how the blade sat so beautifully there against her leg, with the woven hilt placed delicately in her palm. Studying its perfect, shimmering edge, now fashioned to the finest point, so that it could cut a length of rope with but a touch.

And pierce flesh like butter in equal measure.

She sighed passionately, drawing her tongue across her teeth, relishing the thought that came. *How I so long to kill you.* She had dreamt of it, in the few moments' slumber she had managed in that place: the time; the encounter; the method. All orchestrated perfectly. *I know just the right way to do it... so that it feels right.* She allowed herself a smile; she felt she deserved as much. *That I've finally come here, after all these years of torturing myself over his loss. That I can finally have my peace, and cut the head from the snake who ordered his death.* The smile widened.

I'll gut her like a fucking fish.

Turning suddenly, she was aware of the sound of latches at her door, and the slow but apparent turn of the handle. Skidding to her feet in an instant, she brandished the knife like a pit-fighter as a pair of footsteps approached.

Two blackcoats turned the corner, and were at their scabbards in an instant as soon as they caught sight of the knife. The foremost one shot a hand up toward her, stooping their head slightly in acknowledgement.

"Lower your weapon, please," the blackcoat said abruptly. "We... have a message for you."

Savanta straightened her back. "What message?"

"A summons... your presence has been requested."

"By the Iron Queen?" she asked, visibly concerned. *What could she want?*

"No... by another, who also resides in this keep. We were asked to escort you there."

"Who?" Her frown deepened. "Am I to die?"

"No." The blackcoat turned from her and gestured toward the exit.

"But you will learn..."

*

She was led deeper into the palace keep, into layers of the earth that she thought no man had ever seen before. Into the depths of a place where the souls of lost peoples cried out from the stone, long buried to the annals of history. A haunted, despotic place, weaving through corridors and chambers and stairways of snapped rock and splintered rubble. Wondering, all the while, just what destiny had in store for her in that lonely and lost place.

And what would become of her, when she finally reached the end of it.

Her guides, the blackcoat guards, told her nothing of where she was heading: they simply paced along, down into the unbelievable dark, wearing the same blank expression that all of their kind seemed to possess. She wondered if they expressed much at all as a people, beyond the reproachful malice that came and went like the tide. She wondered whether there was anything beyond that tiny inkling of hate, to give the impression of humanity in their black and corrupted souls. Or whether they were just neutral beings, uncaring and unthinking, entirely lost to the plight of common kind.

She was about to ask – to make some pointed remark about their depravity and guile – when they turned a corner sharply, and drew to a sudden halt.

Savanta stopped.

What is this place?

Turning, confused, the room ahead appeared to be little more than a corridor, the same as any other. With smooth-sided pillars along the edges, and a waning blue light echoing down from somewhere high above, the dark stone walls appeared almost luminous, with shadows dancing in the spaces between. Beyond the frightful chill that swept up her spine at the sheer emptiness of the room ahead, there was nothing unusual there to distinguish it from any other place they had passed.

Nothing, that was, except the step of a platform at the far end, and the dull impression of a throne shrouded at its peak.

Where am I?

"Step forward," the blackcoat at her left commanded. "They await your presence."

Who does?

Offering only a grimace in reply, Savanta paced across the room with slow, measured steps, aware that she could be walking straight into a Champion's test, and that even there in the seemingly empty room, her life could be on the line. As she drew closer, more shapes manifested before her: the steps of the platform ascending higher, coated in darkness; the throne swelling on the back wall, its form a mixture of rough edges and smooth slabs; the glint of a small gemstone shimmering at its very top, giving off the colour of sunset. She was transfixed to it for a moment, picking apart the scene before her with a calculating and fearful eye.

Until the dark of the throne shifted, and the gemstone disappeared from sight, as a huge mass leaned forward to study her from above.

"You summoned me?" she said defiantly, stopping just short of the platform, trying to meet the eye of whatever being resided within the dark.

"I did, *yes,*" a man's voice thundered. "I almost *remember* you."

The response took her aback – *what is this?* "I fear you may be misguided… I don't know any Tarrazi. Not that I would want to, either…"

"Always so *dismissive*… these things shall never change."

Never change? "Who are you?"

"I am… a memory."

Heat rose across her neck as she bit back her terror. "I wish to see you," she challenged. "I am the Queen's Champion, and I command it. Show yourself."

"The Queen's Champion?" The man gave a moment's reflection, then a crackling laugh like firewood. "Well, if you *do insist*…"

With a creak of bones, the figure of shadow pulled slowly forward and, like the moon appearing through a storm cloud, its pale face emerged.

Hair, long and unkempt, with wispy tendrils streaking across his face; damaged skin, with deep scars and brand-marks illustrating a tortured life; cracked lips, pursed within a scruffy beard; and the daunting, deep-set eyes of a broken man, welded into their sockets. A ruin, if she had ever seen one, comprised of flesh and skin. Savanta looked upon him with confusion, wondering why he was there and what purpose he served, but she found her words betray her the longer she looked at his face. There was something about him, even in the broken light of the lower keep, that seemed almost familiar. Almost *real.* And as she looked deeper into his decrepit eyes, and the hollow stare they gave, she realised the recollection that she felt within her was not one of memory.

It was one of loss.

"Who are you?" she spat, her heart in her throat, a thousand impossibilities ballooning in her skull.

"I am but a passing star… a ship, lost at sea," the man said slowly. "I wish I could have explained it better, once before… to make amends for what has been and gone, and right your wrongs. But choices had to be made… I had to choose survival." Their eyes locked; something within her snapped. "Because I loved you, dear girl, more than words can ever know. And you are the guilt I have worn heavy, for near fifteen years since that day…"

Raising his gnarled hands, the man pulled his wiry hair back behind his ears – where Savanta found he only had one. And on the other, she saw the tiny, delicate shimmers of three gold rings dance in the dark—

And her heart seemed to stop, as one word escaped her lips.

"Father?"

PART II

The Wrath of Consequence

Chapter 1[illegible]

[illegible] Crushing Steel

The plated woman [illegible] behind the [illegible] crashed [illegible] to the [illegible] amid the [illegible] [illegible] curled [illegible] [illegible] rapidly, lunging left [illegible] could [illegible] catch the soldier in the [illegible]. [illegible] backward to avoid a second attack. [illegible] and [illegible] melled again [illegible] the [illegible] plate. With the enemy [illegible] he took advantage of it and swung again across the [illegible] metallic [illegible] sounded as the [illegible] [illegible] the blade, [illegible] fourth part [illegible] connecting [illegible] and the [illegible] out across the [illegible].

For a brief moment [illegible] around, the [illegible].

And the last one [illegible] as the [illegible] on [illegible] again.

[illegible] unmatched [illegible] and balanced it across [illegible], deflecting [illegible] more than a [illegible] later [illegible] toward the [illegible] with a [illegible] the enemy [illegible] [illegible] enough to catch [illegible] the [illegible].

[illegible] took [illegible] the [illegible] and carried

†

Chapter 15

Crashing Steel

The soldier was on him before he'd even had a chance to unsheathe his weapon, as Eli swore and curled his fists.

He back-stepped, dodging left and swinging round to catch the soldier in the ribs. Reeling backwards to avoid a second attack, Eli struck out and pummelled against the man's chest-plate. With the enemy suddenly winded, he took advantage of it and swung again across the man's jaw. A metallic *clang* sounded as the soldier relinquished their blade, staggering about in a daze; Eli rounded for a fourth punch, connecting against their chin, and sent the man spinning out across the stone floor.

For a brief moment, the Chief looked up, hearing shouts all around, the din of battle growing stronger—

And the next one was upon him in an instant, as the fight danced on once again.

Eli unsheathed his sword at last and balanced it across his chest, deflecting the first strike of his opponent's axe little more than a heartbeat later. Brushing it aside, Eli lunged out toward their exposed stomach; with a sidestep, the enemy shifted, bringing their axe back round to attack. With quick feet, Eli adjusted awkwardly, sliding his blade through to catch it, striking out on the parry with impressive speed.

The attack scored a huge line in the man's chainmail, and carried through across his pale forearm like butter. Blood welled across the fresh wound suddenly, loosening their grip on the blade. The soldier hissed, passing the sword to his other hand, manipulating it with some deftness as he made to attack again.

Despite his discomfort using such a light and feeble weapon, Eli struck out with his sword in several successive attacks, the soldier struggling to make any dent in his rigid composure. The Chief jabbed through – struck out – lunged – recoiled and swiped up – parried elegantly – growled – spat into the dust and pressed on. The soldier seemed to flag, almost accepting defeat before it came, their evidently-weaker hand taking the brunt of each attack, back-stepping across the broken stone underfoot. An end was approaching soon, they knew.

The strike of death, moments away.

Eli swung upwards before the soldier could react, attacking with such force that their blade spun off into the distance like a lancing arrow.

And, bellowing like a mighty bear of the forests, the Chief brought his blade through and dug it up under the man's chest-plate, inching deeper and deeper until they almost embraced, the man's final breaths catching at his ear.

"You get what you deserve, you *prick,*" Eli growled, sliding the sword free and kicking the dead soldier to the floor. He spat on the corpse, wiping the blade clean before sheathing it once more, and looked upon the carnage that made merry around him with a quiet and pensive stare.

They had been a street away from the town square, when the first of the imperial forces had attacked: a small contingent, hidden away in a townhouse, who had ambushed their front ranks as they had unsuspectingly charged past. There had been a sudden call to arms, rallying forward to plug the gap before anything more could happen. It had amounted in the end to only a few moment's fighting – their sheer numerical advantage taking charge – before Eli had ordered the ranks to file out, securing the side-streets pre-emptively as the main vanguard pressed ahead.

So they had carried on with depleted numbers, surging like a river that had broken it banks, when they had rounded the final turn to see the square open out against the blazing sun—

And dozens of steel-helmed soldiers swarming suddenly before them, choking the main road before they even had a chance to get there.

And then the chaos ensued, he thought with a sigh, watching as it continued to unfold before him. They had pressed forward heroically, meeting the imperial legions head on in tight, shoulder-to-shoulder fighting. Eli had remained a few ranks behind, with the gnawing sensation in his gut telling him to order a quick retreat as more and more of the enemy appeared.

But we held, and continue to hold even now. His forces had rallied and pushed the soldiers back, securing side-streets and buildings around the outskirts, where archers now fired from high windows and barrels were thrown down into the throng of the enemy jostling impatiently below. Even as he recalled it, Eli watched a small chest of drawers slide awkwardly out a second-storey window and fall into the crowds, the crunch of metal armour only drowned out by the wicked cheers of his people in the building above.

Intuitive, the Chief thought with a smile. *We shall see how long that continues, and how long our luck holds out.* A moment's pride washed through him, before his smile quickly faded. *I fear, however, that it may not be for much longer. For the enemy keeps coming, and our numbers continue to fall.* He nodded slowly, before the smile rekindled and a warm sensation pulled across his shoulders.

Not unless I have something to do with it.

Drawing a hand across his back, he found the weighted brace of a long handle slide between his fingers. Unbuckling the heavy sheath, it slid free and Eli braced it firmly within his grasp, manoeuvring with two hands to tame the mighty weapon.

A huge bludgeon, forged of purest steel, stained black at the spiked end from the many dead it had sent to the mud. Eli couldn't help but grin.

Oh how I've missed you.

"The Chief has returned!" came a cry from his side as Castan made an appearance, his long rapier hanging at his side still dripping blood. "Are you ready for this, sir?"

"I was born ready," the Chief boomed triumphantly. "Now let's go break some fucking skulls in, shall we?"

"Took the words right outta my mouth, Chief! Let's have it!"

Very well then.

Eli took three strides forward, bellowing at the top of his lungs, before he brought the bludgeon down on the first soldier in his path. The poor fool had no time to realise, let alone react, before a weapon the size of a small meteor blotted out the sun, and crushed his skull into his neck like a tree stump. The force proved so great that his legs buckled underneath him, like a mannequin who had lost their strings, and he straddled in a bloody mess across the stone slabs below.

One.

Peeling the bludgeon from the man's brain-matter, Eli hefted the weapon in both hands and swung it around his body, barrelling into the next soldier unfortunate enough to cross his path.

The victim – a woman not much older than Jinx – only registered the ball of steel flying her way as it connected with her side like a battering ram. It almost broke her in two, her spine twisting at an ungodly angle as she connected with a stone wall opposite and faded to black in an instant.

Two.

Eli dragged the weapon away again, balancing the weighted end as he looked up into the sun—

Twisting his handle just in time to catch a soldier's falling sword, the end of which had been aiming directly at his head.

The Chief snarled, rising suddenly and stepping into the attacker's circle. The soldier leered awkwardly, and attempted to butt him in the head; Eli craned his neck to avoid the attack, and pressed a punch in the man's gut for his efforts. Bending double, the soldier coughed violently; sensing an opening, the Chief swung sharply upwards, splitting the man's legs apart and sending the bludgeon straight into his cock.

The soldier made something of a squeal, the hope and arrogance leaving his eyes as his genitals were reduced to pulp. The man stumbled backwards, making ready to be sick, but was cut short by the flash of Castan's blade as it whipped his throat open like butter, sending the bile-addled fluid jetting from his neck like the spurts of a fountain.

The convulsing corpse teetered backwards and collapsed like a felled tree; Eli hefted the bludgeon back onto his shoulder and exhaled with quiet relief.

Three.

"How are we looking... Castan?" the Chief rumbled, noting with some satisfaction how the imperial forces seemed to have thinned slightly down the middle. "Seems we're beating them back."

"We are for now, yes sir," the black-haired officer cried, dicing through another soldier with two strikes of his blade. "Although we should avoid being idle for too long... we need to press our advantage if we're to best these bastards today."

"Agreed. I want that town square secured before any potential reinforcements arrive... I'm not letting this turn into a bloodbath for nothing."

"What's the plan then Chief?"

"I'll rally the remainder of our forces and form an arrowhead into the square: we'll break through the dregs of the enemy that remain and secure a post behind that pillar." He speared a hand out, directed to the tall monolith at the centre. "I need you to move with the archers and light infantry into the baron's hall to our left, overlooking the square. Get me some eyes on the road to the east, and ready the arrows for anything that comes through. I'll not leave this to chance today... I need a victory here."

"I'll see it done."

"Oh, and Castan?" Eli called out as the officer turned to leave.

"Yes, Chief?"

"Please look after Alva for me... keep her safe."

Castan smiled warmly, bowing his head. "On my life, she will be safe. Now stop fretting, and lead your people!"

The officer pulled away under the shadow of the two-storey buildings, off toward the towering bastion of the baron's hall just beyond, leaving Eli stood alone in the midday sun with the pride of the nation all around him.

We have the advantage, he thought with a grin. *Now let's bring this home.*

Lifting his bludgeon, he strode out into the melee, bellowing at the top of his lungs.

"Rally to the fore! Take these bastards for what they're worth!"

Roars signalled all around in reply to their Chief. With several dozen swords chiming at his back, the charge began once again.

†

Showtime.

With a snap, the crossbow string locked into place, and the holster nestled in the crook of Jinx's arm like a new-born child. It was a pleasant feeling, to handle such a meticulous and finely-crafted weapon. She almost admired it, in a way.

That, and it means I'm at a safe distance, far from any bloodshed or fighting. She lifted the weapon and imitated firing it, applying gentle pressure to the trigger. *I can execute my enemy without them even seeing my face.*

And that is fine by me.

She stood with a dozen other archers on the ground floor of an old townhouse, with wide tables and chairs stacked neatly away off to one side. The air was trepidatious, heavy in her lungs. The echoes of battle whispered through from the streets outside: an unsettling merger of steel and screams, crying out under the blazing sun.

Glancing south down through the winding alleyways, Jinx saw more of the rebels jostling up the road like sheep, beckoned to the carnage ahead with roars and jeering blades. Their faces were bright and prideful, longing to spill imperial blood.

The thief shook her head in disbelief. *It seems that they are yet to be acclimatised to the realities of war. And it seems that they will learn, very soon, that this is no game when you're the one fighting…*

And the blood is either theirs, or yours.

A door cranked open at her back suddenly, followed by the mutters of order from the archers. Jinx turned to attention, and recognised the black flush of hair that had entered the room to be that of Castan's: the spry young officer who had taken up the mantle of Eli's second-in-command. With a face like burning coals, he strode over to them and whistled for their attention, waving his hand impatiently at his back. Evidently time was of the essence.

"Okay, so here's the plan," he muttered breathlessly, drawing himself to full height. "Eli and the vanguard are pressing forward as we speak, and have reached the outskirts of the square from the west side. So that means, very soon, he'll be taking a lot of heat from the soldiers ready to intercept, and likely come under sustained arrow-fire from the opposing balconies to the east. If that is left unchecked, it will likely end in a total defeat… and *we* cannot let that happen." He gestured out of the back door. "The baron's hall lies a few buildings ahead of where we are now. We don't know if the enemy are stationed in there at the moment, but we can take no chances. We need to act fast, capture the hall, and move into the upper alcoves to secure a vantage point before Eli gets in range of those archers. Am I understood?"

A few mumbled agreements sounded, with the anxious straightening of chest-plates.

"Do we *understand*!" he cried again, and a triumphant reply suddenly erupted to life, with fists raised and chests pounded and bowstrings taut as knives. Jinx looked among them with admiration in her heart, and then circled her gaze back to Castan – to find he was already looking to her, smiling warmly.

Her cheeks went suddenly red as she looked away.

That's quite a smile he has.

"Right, let's move then!" Castan ordered, striding off toward the backdoor. "No time like the present!"

In a snaking line, the archers abandoned the townhouse and moved out into the warrens of Marcheg. Jinx stayed close to the back, aware of the enemy that could be lurking in any of the streets nearby, her finger never straying far from the crossbow's trigger.

They passed along several streets under the cover of shadow, skittering like mice through the alleys of the town. The squat tiled houses loomed all around them, blanched in colours of beige and silver. A few stray cats hissed as they passed and darted off down the alleyways to shelter; crows, black and foreboding, circled in the blue skies above. The rattle and *clang* of crashing steel echoed down the streets toward them: looking right, the occasional glint of armour could be seen as more rebels entered the fray.

Pacing along behind the others, her palms doused with sweat, Jinx found herself thinking of Eli for a moment, and the dangers he faced. That somewhere down the roads ahead, he was facing the might of the army head-on, spearheading the vanguard that hoped to win the day and put the imperial enterprise to rest. That the rebels she saw charging on through the streets to her right, were rallying to the call of their chief. And that he put his life on the line, as so many others did, with death only a whisper away…

He'll be fine, she thought, more to convince herself than anything. *It'll be okay. He's a hardy soul, he can do it.* She sighed.

So long as we can do our part in turn.

As the thought came, a shadow formed ominously ahead, and the ancient pinnacles of the baron's hall stood like horns against the sun. It was a deathly old building from a deathly old time, built of worn, mud-brown stone and musty-black windows. The ruptured impressions of statues stood gaunt and bare along its alcoves: snake-like creatures with many fangs, or the hallowed skulls of half-dead rulers staring vacantly out across the town. They were harrowing, almost; Jinx found herself unsettled passing under their gaze. How long they had been there; how many things their dead eyes had seen. And how they were still standing, and were still careless to the world as it sought to break itself again.

I envy you, she cooed to herself, passing through a wide door ahead, *for your sheer lack of care for anything this world brings. That none of this matters to you.*

I wish none of it mattered to me.

She inhaled sharply, a lump in her throat, an image of her brother cresting in her mind for a moment. She shook her head, caught in the clutches of grief, and exhaled lengthily to try and dispel the quivers in her hand. *This is not the way... we are not here to mourn.* She grit her teeth, passing down a long corridor toward a huge chamber, the crash of metal armour ricocheting off the walls. *This is a time to right the wrongs of our enemy.* She nodded in defiance.

This is a time for revenge.

They entered the massive chamber of the baron's hall, fanning out across its tile-and-carpet floors to secure a hasty perimeter. The scouts manoeuvred around wide dining tables and cushioned benches – past the silver platters and serving trays of a long-abandoned banquet – and slid gracefully around the huge sconces stood atop pillars down the middle. Jinx looked left to the great doors of the bedchamber, and the balcony towering above; across to the back wall, where windows stood ajar along a high walkway overlooking the square below; and above, higher and higher to the dizzying peaks of the chamber's roof, where ornate chandeliers hung dormant and at peace. It was a magnificent place, she found herself admitting – *far grander than anywhere I've ever been.* But even in such a grand chamber steeped in its prestige, she couldn't help but feel the emptiness the room also brought. Its quiet, almost unnerving echo, as the archers skittered across the tiles like ants. The hollow notes of battle raging outside, hardly a whisper in such a vast space. She almost longed to cower away in the corners, or take to the shadows that she had for many years called her home, for fear of the nothingness that surrounded her.

I am way in over my head, she admitted, somewhat obviously. *This is more than I ever bargained for. I'm not designed for this. I'm a thief, I—*

"Alva, come here quick!" Castan cried to her right, waving to her hurriedly. "Eli and the vanguard have reached the square!"

Without a blink, she was suddenly running, vaulting tables and chairs, eyes fixed squarely on Castan as if all other life ceased to exist. Abruptly aware of time and its passage, and its ability to run out so quickly.

Please be safe.

"What do I do?" she spluttered, skittering to a halt just before him.

"Head up the stairway behind me, and get onto the walkways overlooking the square. Position yourself against one of the windows and start loading your weapon. Things are about to get hairy."

Oh, fantastic. "Lead the way, officer."

Castan produced a calm, sweet smile; she found her breath caught in her throat.

"Please... ladies first," he said softly.

And Jinx found herself smiling too.

They ascended the stairway, spiralling gently upwards until the narrow walkway stretched out before them, dissected by the pale shafts of light coming in through the open windows.

On shaky legs, with the steady presence of Castan at her back, Jinx turned to the nearest opening and gazed down on the scene below, to find total carnage had enveloped the square as the two forces collided. There were no clear lines to demark one side from the other: no areas of influence or secured zones that she could see. The south was awash with the bodies of the rebels; the north lay securely in the hands of the imperial legions. But everything between, as far as she could tell, was a free-for-all: a bloodbath of broken metal, where one could hardly tell between friend or foe. Watching axes spin and swords strike and blood jet sporadically from arterial wounds. It was sheer chaos. An anarchy that could make even the gods queasy. The horrific consequence of an imperial regime sucked into the maelstrom of—

"There he is!" Jinx almost screamed, spearing a finger down toward the centre of the square.

Under the shadow of the monolith, Eli stood in the crush of his vanguard, beating back soldiers in their dozens. They had secured something of a safe zone, where more and more people slowly funnelled through and formed a snaking path from the south. It seemed that things were going well, and the rebels were holding firm, but Jinx watched with concern as the imperial forces began to form their own lines, and struck out at weak points where the rebel influx seemed thin.

It's balanced on a knife edge.

"The Chief needs our help!" Castan bellowed down the line, to the snarls and affirmations of the others. "He won't last long if those archers get sight on him!"

His finger speared out to the balconies opposite them, and Jinx spied there the tiny shimmering points of arrows nestled among the shadows inside. She watched them shift, forming and disappearing in quick succession, as windows slid ajar and the menacing shapes of bows began to emerge. Aiming down onto the square below.

Aiming for Eli, and the southern line.

Not if we have anything to do with it, Jinx thought with a grin, pulling the crossbow up from her side and sliding the bolt into place. *You may have them in your sights.*

But we have you in ours.

"Ready your weapons!" Castan roared, as the sound of bowstrings and crosshairs snapped down the line at her side.

She marked a man directly opposite her, the pearlescent shine of a sadistic grin catching in the high sun. *This is where it begins,* she thought.

"Steady!"

This is where vengeance comes.

"FIRE!"

†

He heard the whistle of flying metal before he saw it, and knew hope had come to save them.

Turning quickly, Eli watched the first bolt make impact on the balcony opposite, where a grinning man with an arrow knocked had his eye punctured like a balloon. He stumbled backward with a cavity in his skull, crumpling awkwardly and snapping his head against the window-frame, death taking hold in an instant.

All across the second-storey, the lurking shapes of enemy archers met similar fates, with rebel bolts puncturing throats and ripping bows from hands. Eli watched it unfold with an expression of awe, and looked back across to the open windows of the baron's hall where he knew a dozen or so of his finest had just made their kill. And he wondered as well, if Alva was somewhere up there, doing her part too.

You do me proud if you are, young thief, he thought, the catch of a smile at his cheeks.

And I know he would have been proud too.

"Right, listen up!" the Chief called out to his people, rallied before him in the midday sun with sweat-sheened faces. "We have the cover of archers from the building behind us, and we have the defensive barricades making their way up the line as we speak. We have this zone secured; we have pride in our hearts and an advantage to press. So, I reckon it's about time we gave these bastards hell, and show them just what kind of mettle we're made of! What say you, my comrades! What say *YOU*!"

A united roar followed – loud enough to summon the dragons of old down from their mountain homes – as Eli's people surged forward in a battle-hungry rage, chopping and slicing at any steel they could find, pressing the enemy back on all fronts. The Chief found his blood pumping anew, with the bludgeon light and dexterous in his grasp. It was as if the air were lighter, and the weight of the world held less sway. That there was a path ahead now, a sense of direction.

An enemy to repel; a people to save.

Skulls, ready to be split.

Eli turned, watching arrows and crossbow bolts whistle over their heads, and primed his bludgeon in both hands.

Here we go.

The first soldier appeared to his left, shouldering through other bodies to get to him. Turning, Eli brought the bludgeon's handle across to catch their falling blade and knocked it wastefully to the side. He then kicked out like a horse, his boot snapping against the soldier's shin, forcing him back onto one knee. Raising his weapon, striking across their steel helmet, Eli watched with some satisfaction as it dented inward and threw the broken body out across the stones like a discarded sack.

The Chief nodded and sucked in a lungful of air, readying for the next—

A slice of pain suddenly flushed to life across the back of his right arm. Eli hissed and turned to watch the pointed end of an axe skim past, the perpetrator returning to a fighter's stance as the Chief turned to face him.

Cheeky shit, he thought with a snarl, stepping in and swinging round to catch the man's exposed flank. The soldier thought better, side-stepping and cutting through. Eli deflected with his handle, and brought the bludgeon sweeping upwards. The man backstepped, striking across again.

The Chief smacked the sword away with the ball of his weapon, watching the thin metal blade shatter completely.

Staring at it dumbfoundedly, the soldier stood with his mouth open in disbelief, the hilt of his blade still clasped firmly in his hand.

And he only then managed to snap out of it, when a gleaming ball of spiked metal curled up towards him and crushed his skull.

His death came instantaneously, fickle and resolute.

Eli smiled.

That'll teach you to try and draw blood from me—

"Sir, on your left!"

The call from one of his vanguard: Eli pivoted on the bludgeon's handle instinctively, bringing it tight to his body, just in time to feel the deafening tremors of an equally powerful weapon crash against its edge. The reverberation sent him reeling backwards, digging his heels in for purchase. He only found his footing in time to catch the next strike as the enemy moved against him again. Eli knocked the weapon aside – a broad-sword, almost as tall as he was – and brought the bludgeon back into his grasp, steadying himself long enough to observe his attacker, who—

Wait... is that a knight?

A massive suit of armour waded its way through the crowds, with red-green bands and a high crested helmet, the steel bracer across its eyes focused squarely on him. With the high-sun blaring overhead, the enemy's interlocking plates were like raging stars, forcing the Chief to squint. They were a daunting presence, shifting toward him with weighted strides. Although, in many respects, Eli did not fear the suit of armour nor whoever lay within it: a tension caught in his throat, instead, at the sight of the huge blade sat dominantly at their shoulder.

That's a mighty big weapon they have their hands on, he consider as sweat leaked across his palms. *Can't say I'm a fan of that.*

Seemingly registering his unease, the knight shifted the broad-sword to their chest, and began their advance against him.

So much for a straight path forward. The Chief of the Mountains sighed.

Nothing's ever that fucking easy.

The knight's broad-sword cut down like an executioner's blade; Eli sidestepped, letting it fall to ground, before curling the bludgeon up in return. With frustrating ease, the sword lifted away, and the malleted end of his weapon hit nothing but air as it squeezed past the knight's chest plate.

The next attack curled round from the side, intending to cut him in two. Eli blocked with his handle, the chime of steel strong enough to shatter his eardrums. He then brought the bludgeon up sharply, intending to clatter through the knight's legs – but received only a quick kick across the side for his efforts, forcing a wheeze from his lungs.

The sword rounded again; with some prolific show of force, Eli struck upwards and smashed it off course, with the dead eyes of the armoured titan bulging in shock. Compelled with dirty tactics, Eli let the bludgeon fall as he freed his left hand and punched the knight across the face, slightly dislodging their helmet. The knight returned with a backhand that cuffed the Chief across the throat; he stumbled backwards, tugging air through his larynx like a coiled rope.

Tough one aren't you, you big bastard... he growled internally, bring-ing the bludgeon back to the fore. *How about we try this instead.*

The knight took a fearless step, sword lashing down overhead. Eli sidestepped, turning his back to the enemy; his bludgeon scraped the dirt, rising suddenly over his head in a grand arc; he pivoted, the spiked ball arcing down—

And struck through the knight's collarbone.

A *snap* like a branch breaking, and the armoured titan's right arm ripped from their socket in one fell swoop. Carrying through, the bludgeon tore at the armour, tearing at chain-mail and brutalising any bone that remained beneath.

A howl like a wolf mother, and the knight was stumbling backwards, the sword limp and dishevelled in their one good arm, suddenly fearful for their life—

Eli struck out with his fist, with enough force to cave the knight's bracer through and break their nose underneath. Another scream, agonised and terrified, as the enemy lifted a hand to their face—

The bludgeon curling round, braking through the knight's knuckle as they tried to cover their face. The sounds of snapping joints; the crunch of split nails. A squeal like a gutted pig.

Eli grit his teeth, bellowing ferociously, launching the bludgeon across his body like the strike of a catapult.

Connecting perfectly with the knight's boggling skull.

Broken bones like breaking twigs. A slosh of blood like a broken dam. The armoured titan reeled backwards, legs kicking out, hitting the grave long before they hit the stone with an almighty crash of metal. The sword that had seemed unbeatable not that long ago lay dispossessed at their feet.

And a silence echoed out thereafter, with Eli stood alone at its heart. He drew up to full height, letting his gaze wander, looking out across the square to find no soldiers were left. That there were only his people remaining, stood wide-eyed and zealous about the square, among the bodies of near a hundred souls sprawled across the stones like a carpet. He looked to the east for a moment, his soul swelling, to find the street abandoned and empty. All around, from the alcoves of buildings to the shadows of side-streets, there remained no sign of the enemy. Only the Chief and his people, stood alone in the town square, bruised and bloody but prevailing nonetheless as the sun crested the sky high above.

Realisation dawned; he found himself smiling.

We won.

†

Chapter 16

A Death Wish

They say the souls of the dead are trapped in these trees, y'know? The tormented remnants of man and animal alike, screaming to be let free. And at night they whisper to us, carrying off through the undergrowth like phantoms, driving those among the living mad with their pleas. There is no sleep here. No silence… no humanity. There are only the voices trapped within the trees, screaming to be let out, drawing yet more souls out into the dark, to die and be consumed like the rest." Revek shook his head, almost laughing at the thought. "So, trust me when I say this: coming here is a death wish in itself. This is not like any place we have ever known. This is a ruined place: somewhere wretched and defiled, where the enemy is everywhere and nowhere all at once. A place where everything will find you; everything will hunt you; everything will kill you. And that is the only certainty that you'll find in the Ozban: that death is only a whisper…"

But she is always fatal.

They had been on the road for several hours, keeping a good pace through the impenetrable mass of trees, with only a single meandering path offering them any semblance of the way forward. The soldiers had marvelled at first in their hushed, disconcerted voices at how dark everything was, despite there being no canopy or vegetation: that the branches seemed to just knot into each other like snake coils overhead, betraying any light cast from the distant sun.

For it was so unbelievably black, in the depths of that place. Where the deeper one looked between the trees to either side, the more shadows seemed to form to hide it away, until not even the treeline at their feet was visible and the world beyond lay cast in gloom. The soldiers had gazed blankly off into those dark recesses, wondering what secrets lay nestled within. Wondering what foul powers held sway over such a vast and uncharted place. Looking out there, some had fallen from their horses as if in a trance, while others simply left the main path and walked off into the gloom, disappearing just as they passed between the first few trees. Only a handful had stepped among the trees at first; the soldiers had almost laughed at how strange it was.

Until the screaming had started, that was. The contorted shrieks of the mad and dying, trapped in the depths of the Ozban with no hope of escape, and no way of returning to that which they knew. The screams were sometimes far off in the distance; other times, they were close enough to hear them breathing. The soldiers had shuddered at the sounds, terrified, as if the trees were closing in on them. As if nature itself was retching, sick and rotten and foul.

Coming here is a death wish, Revek thought quietly, looking off into the trees. *And it shall consume us all in the end.*

"Should we be afraid, sir?" the young soldier at his side said, carrying a bundle of weapons in a bag on his back. Revek couldn't help but notice the look of terror that had grown on his face over the last hour. *And I certainly don't blame you for it.* "I mean, with what this place does to people..."

"Don't fear it," Revek said simply. "Be cautious, yes... but do not fear a place as dangerous as the Ozban. It is like a wolf in many ways: it will watch you, and stalk you, and track you down, and it will assess whether it can kill you fast enough to satisfy its hunger. It seeks your vulnerabilities, and fear makes you vulnerable: it is a dimming of the mind, a reclusion of the senses. You must be cautious, yet fearless, if you are to survive in this place... or else it eats you *alive.*"

As the words came, another shriek ripped through the air just beside them, maybe a dozen feet away and yet with no source in sight. It died away almost as fast as it came.

"Why are they screeching, sir?" the soldier asked timidly, white as marble.

"It is the madness of those who have strayed too far from the path. Because once you pass beyond those trees, it is as if the walls close around you. You turn, and find there is no sign of the path, or any people, or any light. And no matter where you turn, or where you go, or how far you run… you will not find the place whence you came." He paused. "Few have survived to admit it…"

"But you did, sir!" The soldier produced a smile, innocent and sweet. "You made it out alive. That's quite something."

Revek blinked. "Yea… yea, I did…"

The commander's words trailed off suddenly, his skin growing icy cold AS the memory of the events returned, bubbling to the surface in his mind…

It was the second night, lost in the deep-dark of nowhere. Tree after tree after tree after tree passing by, over and over and over through the shadows and the gloom into the night with nothing to show for it…

Four of them, traipsing with no direction through the skeletal boughs, the dry earth padding underfoot. Survivors, with crushed hopes and demons circling at their backs. Defeated, humiliated. Cast into the Ozban like rats, to scurry around until they died…

They had walked for what felt like miles, traversing the great forest until their feet ached and their eyes lapsed and the slow curse of depravity hit them. They looked among each other, tired and hopeless, with the unending span of trees stood unphased around them. Swaying, in desperate need of rest, or some remnant of sleep…

An opening in the trees, several hours later; the waxing moon high and lazy in the sky above, illuminating the grove in odd shades of blue. They sat around, sheepish and half-insane, muttering and shivering in the dark until one soul found it in him to try and light a fire: only to find the bark of the strange trees would not catch, and without burning their belongings there proved no way to start one. Instead they sat huddled together for warmth, studying their commander who hunched opposite them, a cold consolation blanketing his face…

The night ticked on, with no sleep to spare. There were only the screams of dying souls to keep him company, and the hushed tears of the three soldiers as they slowly went insane. Pacing back and forth; swearing at the trees; clawing at their faces in the hope it was all a dream. Suddenly worried about food, about water and supplies. How it would only last two days between the four of them. Whether they should employ rationing. How far they had left; what direction they should go in. What hope they had to survive…

He had watched on, as their minds slowly rotted. Watched on as they had argued and shouted and wept and cursed and wailed into the night sky. Thinking on a great number of things; thinking of the future…

Thinking of the knife he was slowly easing from his belt—

"Sir?"

Commander Revek blinked, jolting back to the real world with a groggy recollection. Frowning sharply, he looked down to the soldier still waddling absently at his side, and bunched his shoulders together.

Mad screams…

"How did you do it, sir?" they asked with a touch of concern. "How did you get out alive?"

A shudder rippled through him. *The knife…*

"Why don't you head to the front of the ranks and scout the path ahead for me," Revek dismissed, plagued with an anxious stupor. "That'll be useful."

Death…

"Sir, my apologies, did you hear my—"

"See to it, officer, that is an *order*." Fearful venom caught at his tongue; the soldier stood back, grimacing. "Question me again, and I'll walk you out into the trees on the end of a spear myself," the commander threatened, flaring his nostrils. "Then we'll see if you have any questions *left*."

The man scampered off, visibly terrified, glancing back for a moment to lay eyes on Revek's seditious grin, atop the horse with swirling shadows lacing across his back.

The commander held his smile, as the soldier disappeared amongst the trees ahead. *Poor fool,* he muttered, rolling his fingers together. *You are all poor fools, to end up in a place like this of your own accord. Only death awaits you, you know. Death and sorrow and madness and hate. It shall eat at you all, until you have nothing left.*

He looked out to the trees – to the shadows beyond – and saw their faces there: the many dead eyes he had found escaping the depths of the Ozban. How cold and lost they looked; how easy it had been in the end.

All will be taken by the shadows eventually. Revek looked forward to the army ahead.

It's just that some of us have learned to survive, and do their bidding…

†

Chapter 17

Fate's Blessing

How has this even happened.

Stood at the window in Azura's attic, looking out on the City of the Sun, Cavara conceded a painful sigh and lowered her gaze. She had remained up there for most of the day, locked away with her thoughts, as the grieving mother paced about in the rooms downstairs, muttering softly to herself. At times Cavara had heard her weeping as she crossed the corridor beneath her, entering into Evelyn's room and acknowledging his absence. The general longed to comfort the older woman in those quiet moments, as she ambled sorrowfully through the house. But she knew, in the same breath, that her presence would be unwelcome. That any kind words or sympathies she had, would be met with bitterness and unease.

And understandably so, Cavara admitted. *I am to blame after all.*

She studied her hand, pressing it flat against the windowsill to ease the shaking. The tremors had proved unrelenting since she had been told Evelyn was gone, as if her body was convulsing at the unbalance she had caused.

I've done this. The thought was heavy and suffocating. *I've brought this pain upon her. If not by my doing directly, then certainly by my presence. I've put everyone at risk. And now the one person who brought me in – who saved me and helped me when I was lost and broken – is now left grieving the loss of another child who she may never see again.*

All because of me.

She shook her head and looked off to the skyline beyond, where the distant embers of an orange-red sun dipped steadily below the horizon. Disappearing out to the west, across the great sea. Over the mountains of Provenci, most likely. Somewhere far and lost that she had not long ago called home.

And that same homeland now bleeds, because I didn't do enough to stop it. The shaking in her hands started anew. *And I have become a slave here: now I am watched at all hours for this curse that I have, that I shall never be free of again.* The tremors grew heavier, convulsing up her arms. *A woman grieves the loss of her child… because I didn't do what was necessary to keep them safe.* She caught her breath; a single tear spilled across her cheek.

All because of me.

For a while she stood tensed against the windowsill, with a dull thudding sound echoing in her ears with such force that she thought her heart would explode.

But then a crunch of wood echoed out somewhere off behind her, and she realised the thudding was in fact the sound of footsteps. Turning slowly, she watched the pale, mangled skull and heavy eyes of the Forgotten One pull slowly into view, a quiet disconcertion on their face.

"May I approach, Successor?" they rumbled gently. "I sense you are under great strain, and do not wish to burden you if my presence is not required."

"It's okay," she replied, nodding. "You may approach."

The huge figure stepped forward and placed itself on the end of her bed, the creaking of wooden boards relenting under their weight. "I sensed from downstairs that you are struggling somewhat with your mind… that you are having 'bad thoughts', as they say."

She scoffed. "If you mean I'm awash with guilt and blaming myself over the loss of Evelyn and how poorly this day has gone… then you might be correct on the 'bad thoughts' assessment."

"I sensed such feelings, and I'm sorry they plague you so. Hence why I am here, as I wondered if my company would help you to process these things." They paused. "I am… not good with your mortal emotions, or your experiences of them… but I thought it would be best to try, at least, as you are in a strange place, and these are strange times for us all."

A touch of warmth filled her heart. "Thank you, my friend."

"A pleasure, ex-general Cavara," they said softly, with something close enough to a smile tracing their face. "Now please, if you may… speak of how you feel."

The general pushed away from the windowsill and tried to draw up her thoughts, but found them muddled and broken in her mind. "There isn't much to say… or rather, there isn't any real way to say it. I… with everything that's happened, since our last encounter with the Alderbane… well, you spend your time looking into how these things came about, and where the blame lies for them."

"And you put that blame at your feet?"

"I don't see that there's anywhere else to put it. I mean, I led the Tarrazi here. I led the transmitter here. I led them to Azura, and in turn to Evelyn… and now he's gone, and they're nowhere to be found. And that's my fault."

The Forgotten One considered, looking down into their hands for a moment. "That isn't true," they said.

She frowned. "What do you mean it isn't true?"

"Because of how you describe it. I do not know much of your language and its design… but it appears you feel you have consciously caused everything to happen the way it has. That you have guided fate, almost."

"I *have* caused everything to happen the way it has… the transmitter wouldn't be here if it wasn't for me."

"That may be so, but you did not choose to be here." The deep moons of their eyes gazed into hers. "We do not know how the Tarraz learned that you were within this city. We do not know how they managed to get a transmitter all the way out here to hunt you. And until yesterday, you did not even know what a transmitter *was*, let alone what threat they posed to us. You have been forced into a new and terrifying reality, and have been left to comprehend things that no mortal has had to learn for centuries… and all of that has occurred within a matter of weeks. It's no wonder you are as overwhelmed as you seem." The Forgotten One shrugged. "So the fact Evelyn was kidnapped, and the transmitter got to him before you could, is moot. There is no point idling over that sentiment. Because you were attacked, and did everything you could to get to Azura before anything else happened. So why should you blame yourself, for doing what was best?"

"Well, I suppose, but I… well, I…" *He's right,* she thought suddenly, a sickness in her stomach. *Perhaps he is right.* She wavered for a moment, before accepting defeat. "That may be… but I still feel the guilt. I mean, what about Azura? Without a child, having already grieved the death of her own children? That's hardly right, whether I 'did what was best' or not."

"Evelyn is not dead," the Forgotten One said plainly.

"How do you know that?"

"Because the transmitter would not risk revealing themselves over something as petty as killing a child. They are not sadistic, and this is not that simple. What they want ultimately, is you: either for your subjugation, or your demise. And all that Evelyn is, is leverage to that aim: whatever plan they have, or whatever they seek from you, the child will become part of that bargain. That is why they took him: to keep him alive."

"They'll use Evelyn to get to me… because they know I would sooner sacrifice myself than let any harm come to that boy."

"Sadly so. And the transmitter most likely already knows it, too." Another long pause echoed out; a solemn look caught in the pale figure's eye. "I am sorry, ex-general Cavara, that this is the circumstance you have been thrown into. I would not wish such torture on my worst enemy. And you, certainly, do not deserve this."

"That's the thing, though: I don't know what I deserve anymore. I don't even know who or what I *am* anymore." Anxiety crawled up her sternum. "I've lost all sense of self … all sense of my *actual* purpose. Something I've had and held onto for my entire life. An actual aim, and a path forward… not to be a slave to whatever destiny has been forced onto me. And now I'm here, with the Ascendent Soul within me… and I just don't know what to do."

The Forgotten One nodded, closing its eyes. "The Ascendency is many things… but for those who acknowledge its sheer importance to the world, it is often regarded as a burden. You, Cavara, are certainly not the first to feel its burden – and you will very likely not be its last, either. But, despite your concerns, I also want to offer you some reassurance. Because, in many ways, you are more fitted to the mantle of Successor than nearly all of those who have come before you." The figure opened their palms out. "I have read so many stories of the ascendents of the past, you know: of the All-Mothers who have maintained the balance of this land since the beginning of time. There have been dozens of them, throughout history. And I can tell you that there were just as many benevolent souls among them as there were cruel despots; as many heroes as there were traitors; as many kings as there were cowards. None were ever perfect for the great gift that they were given. All saw it as a means to an end, and never actually for the beauty that it was. But you, Cavara… our new Successor, whom I have the honour of seeing in person in this lifetime… you seem to befit the mantle with greater ease than I think even you dare believe."

She produced a mocking laugh. "That can't be true. I wasn't even the one who was meant to receive the All-Mother's kiss, or embody her soul. How can I possibly be a good fit to something that was never intended for me at all?"

"Luck, most likely," the Forgotten One said with a tilt of their head. "Random chance, the last roll of the dice… there are never any guarantees in this world. On that shoreline I could have encountered a child, or a ruthless tyrant, with just as much likelihood as I was to encounter you. It was a chance in the end, that the Ascendent Soul found you… and by that same chance, it also found a capable, worthy, and entirely honourable host to take up the All-Mother's place. A perfect fit, in so many ways." They paused, nodding. "I believe that fate blessed us, the day it found you, Cavara. And I have had no reason to doubt that belief ever since..."

Looking into the pale of their eyes, with the rusty hues of dusk spilling out from the window at her back, something in Cavara grew warm and mellow then. A deep resonation sounded in her heart. The tears in her eyes seemed to weaken with each breath that came. And it seemed, in that quiet and absent attic room, that for a few tranquil moments, she finally felt at peace.

"I... I'm not sure what to say to that," she muttered, smiling at the lightness of the air around her. "I appreciate that you think so highly of me and my abilities... that I'm not just some loud-mouth army officer way in over her head. That's... it's what I needed to hear, so thank you." She paused, rolling her fingers together. "I feel it will still take some time to accept that for myself, however. If I'm honest, I still feel like the Ascendency is guiding me, and not the other way round."

"Well, there is a simple answer to that, ex-general Cavara, and one I think you're modestly missing."

"Oh yea? And what's that?"

"You see yourself and the Ascendant Soul as two separate things, entirely unique to one another, that have been conjoined by chance on a shoreline in a far off place. You believe there needs to be adjustment, and that being comfortable with your powers will take time. But, seeing you over the past few weeks, I don't believe that's ever been the case. It seems that you have this conflict within you about the Soul and your destiny, not because things need to change... but because your mind can't believe just how similar you actually are to the All-Mother's soul. You are one and the same in so many ways: a kind, caring, selfless person, who now possesses a kind, caring, selfless Soul. And this conflict you feel within you, is not conflict at all: it is *harmony*. Because you have found peace with the Ascendency, and you have harnessed its powers in ways that I cannot even begin to explain." A look of pride crossed their pale face for a moment, but was quickly extinguished by a sigh. "But that is also the reason why the Queen in Tarraz goes to such great lengths to kill you, and take the soul for herself... because you have achieved something that gives you unimaginable power. And it's something that she can never have..."

"Harmony..." Cavara whispered, some aura shifting and swirling in the depths of her chest as she spoke.

Something that felt oddly like a soul.

It ebbed and flowed, like the running waters of a quiet stream dashing over smooth pebbles. Like furrows of moss blanketing under trees with the stir of fresh morning dew. Like a cub emerging from its den after winter, to see a world of colour and life. It conjured within her a sudden strength, as if a path had been cleared, and everything before her had direction once again. A peace, rising up her back, touching at the base of her skull where a thought suddenly flickered to life.

And the world didn't seem so hopeless anymore.

"I know what I must do," Cavara proclaimed, taking a deep breath. "I have to hunt the Rapture, and seek out the path of the transmitter. Because if I can follow the transmitter somehow, then I can find where they're hiding, and there will probably be some clue as to where I can find Evelyn. I can get the honour guard to help... they can inform the Alderbane that there's a foreigner within their walls, and hopefully they'll send the imperial guard out to assist us. We can take out the transmitter, save Evelyn, and finally bring an end to this mess for good."

The Forgotten One smiled broadly. "A wise plan, Successor."

"But we need to act soon, and act fast... now that I know they've taken him, the transmitter will start hunting me again to make their bargain. We have to find him before that happens."

"Time is of the essence, of course."

"Can you show me how to find him? How to... hunt the Rapture, as you say?"

"I can... but it will take a lot of your strength to achieve, and require a far greater understanding of the Rapture than you currently have. That, and it will also be incredibly dangerous: the transmitter will be able to shift in and out of the void at will, so you need to be vigilant. So, I ask: are you sure you're ready for this?"

She closed her eyes, picturing Evelyn's face and the terror he surely felt. "I have to be ready," she affirmed. "The fate of a child is in my hands."

"Then we shall begin immediately," the Forgotten One said, rising from the bedside with a flush of their robes. "So, let us hunt, Successor. We have a transmitter to catch..."

†

Chapter 18

Shattered Glass, Glinting Steel

It was all a lie.

Savanta washed her face with cold water, the raw skin where she had clawed at herself hissing as if it were on fire. *Fifteen years... a ruse.* She picked under her nails, taking off layers of dead skin and dust. And blood. *And then I see him, my father...*

My father is alive.

The realisation came with enough force to knock the wind from her chest. The air pulsed like a vacuum around her. The urge to claw at her face surfaced once more. Instead she dug her nails into her palms. She grit her teeth. She growled under her breath. The sensation eased.

She sighed.

A lie, for fifteen years... and here he is. Alive, decrepit, broken. A husk of a man. My father.

What the fuck is going on?

She recalled just how deeply the realisation had wounded her, as he sat and smiled without an ounce of guilt at her clear and damning despair. How emotions had rallied, her anger streaming out, breaching and breaking like tidal waves. Her undaunted screams had filled the chamber until the walls shook on their foundations.

And then she had advanced, storming toward him, demanding the answers she had been denied for so long. Demanding explanation for the fifteen years that had been lost with nothing to show for it. All the blame and hurt and damage that had plagued her soul wondering what had gone wrong. Wondering how he could dare be alive at the end of it.

All for nothing.

She had been fast to reach him, she knew, but the guards had been faster reaching her: at the foot of the platform, they had seized her under the arms, dragging her away kicking and snarling like a rabies-infested dog. She had skittered along the stone floors screeching her hate as he had sat there and smiled. She had disappeared through the columned entrance out into the corridor beyond, staring back into the broken, uncaring gaze of a dishonest father who hardly seemed to register.

As if none of it mattered at all.

How can someone do that? she spat, clutching the edge of the sink. *A young girl, only eleven winters old... sent a letter with a severed ear, told that her father is dead.* She gripped the frame harder, pressure building across her knuckles. *What kind of a sick bastard does that to his own daughter? Did he not care? Did he not love us?*

How could he do it?

Savanta held her head low, accepting in the silence that no answer would come. That there was only the rasp of her breath, and the shallow beat of her heart in her chest.

And the thousand tiny ruinous thoughts traipsing back and forth in her head.

It doesn't make sense. None of this does.

Why am I even here?

She paced over to her bed and sat at one end, the hollow flickers of torchlight dancing with the shadows overhead. She rubbed her hands together; pressed her thumbs until they almost turned blue.

I loved him. Something in her ebbed closer to the surface, something pained and guilty. *As a child, I loved who he was. As a memory, I loved who he had been. A father... my own flesh and blood.*

Except, that isn't how it is. There is no love of a memory, because there is no memory. Memory implies past.

Memory, implies he's fucking dead.

The sensation rose from before: the pained and guilty thing, climbing up her larynx. Some open wound, leaking out like a plume of smoke. Its phosphorus catching in her nostrils, edging at her cheeks. Turning her knuckles white with a sudden surge of anger—

I hate him. Something roared inside of her; the tap at the sink continued to drip. *I hate what he's done to me... how he abandoned me, as little more than a child. I hate his lies, and his cruelty. His fickle fucking treachery. I hate him for what he's done to me.*

I hate *him.*

She got up suddenly, pacing back to the sink. She studied the mirror before her. Studied her gaunt eyes and her blank stare; the harsh lines across her jaw; the hollow, threadbare paleness of her skin; the shiny piece of metal blended through her cheek, the edges still knotted and blackened. She had not looked at herself since it had happened: since the medical chamber and the black magic that had claimed her face. She had been ashamed to look, for so long, at the monster she had become. And some of that shame bubbled to the surface even then, as she gazed upon herself once again.

But she also found that those feelings of shame seemed so much smaller than before. That her appearance – her twisted malformation – didn't seem to matter anymore.

I have achieved what I set out to do, she proclaimed, exhaling slowly. *I have found the Iron Queen, and I have found her with a knife still in my hand. What they have done to me, doesn't matter anymore.*

Because what I will do to them, is so much worse...

With a clenched fist, she punched the mirror ahead of her, the glass shattering and impaling her hand.

Recoiling, she lifted it to her face, studying the fragments embedded in her knuckle. With a tempestuous smile and a flick her tongue, she licked a trickle of blood as it rolled across her wrist and coated it against her teeth.

My revenge will take me wherever it needs to: whether that is at the throat of the Iron Queen...

Or through the heart of my wretched father.

A knock sounded at her door: two guards entered, and studied her uneasily as she picked the shards of glass from her hand.

"You are requested... by the Queen," one of them muttered in disgust. "She wishes to assess... your fighting skill."

"With actual blades?" Savanta asked quietly, licking the blood from her fingertip.

"Yes... swords, steel."

Her grin formed, sharp as cutting knives. "Then I shall come straight away, of course. I look *forward* to it..."

†

Chapter 19

Blood and Bond

Supreme Governor Alvarez,

In the aftermath of the fighting, I am pleased to report that we have managed to secure the northern and eastern quadrants of the town, including their main armoury and many of the local storehouses. As we speak we are setting up barricades along our flanks to secure our forces and keep the rebels out of reach. Progress proves slow, but resolute overall.

I must, however, also report that our mission to break the enemy and secure the town square has not been successful. Their archers outflanked our own, and used the high windows of the baron's hall to keep our bowmen at bay, leaving our soldiers in the square itself exposed. We were repelled, and in the end not even our knights could withstand the full extent of the rebel attack. We were forced into a small retreat because of it.

That being said, our numbers remain strong, and we did inflict significant damage on the enemy: so much so that they have retreated to the main southern road, which leaves the square between us as something of a no man's land.

Nonetheless, we shall press the advantage at sunrise and take the baron's hall, eviscerating any rebels we find there. I shall see it done personally, and I can only apologise that we did not make as much ground in the first engagement as we had previously hoped.

Signed,
General Ferreus

*

Alvarez produced a long, disconsolate sigh as he folded the letter and slid it down into his breast pocket. *This was supposed to be sorted by now.* He drew a hand through his hair; scratched at blotchy sores trapped away in his beard. *The rebels should have been put to the mud already... this was meant to be a one-day operation.* Hand resting on the pommel of his sword, he tensed the grip across the horse's reins and rolled his tongue.

They should be fucking dead by now.

Moving the horse in a wide circle, he cantered slowly down the ridge toward their forward command post, awash with the last drops of crimson sun as it dipped slowly behind the mountains in the west. His personal canopy sat squat at the centre, with the ugly beige fabric stained from disuse and the supporting struts too tall on one side. Stationed just outside were several strategists and field officers lost in deep conversation, jotting down notes on scraps of paper as guardsmen walked past on their patrols. At his approach, the gaggle of officials stilled their tongues and saluted, with one offering to help the Governor as he dismounted his horse.

"At ease," Alvarez grumbled, straightening his coat.

"What is the news from Marcheg, sir?" a greying man inquired, with a bald-patch atop his head the size of a pumpkin.

"Disappointing, but not disastrous: as things stand we have a front line secured and a rebel force held in their place." He scraped the dirt at his feet with his boots. "We have yet to drown them in their own blood so it seems, but these delays can be... *permitted,* for now."

"Well, I... we were hoping not to camp a night out here, sir, if possible... I mean, these rebels are treacherous, and under the cover of dark—"

"I know the dangers, officer, thank you," Alvarez spat. "Nothing about this is ideal; we just have to keep our heads clear about it. I will do nothing short of levelling the town if needs be. We are not without options..."

The greying man shrunk away slightly, nodding in defeat. "So… what is our next move, sir?"

Good question, that. "Well, Ferreus seems confident they can find victory tomorrow, or at the very least give the bastards a good kicking for holding us up. The plan remains to take the square and the baron's hall… although we also have to take into consideration just how fucking *persistent* these rebels are proving to be."

"What do you suggest, sir?"

The Supreme Governor paused, thinking of a path ahead with the aching desire for a drink stirring in his stomach. It made his mouth water, sensing the burn of ethanol and molasses in his throat. It was a tantalising thing. A blessing, too.

Anything to keep his face out.

As the thought came, and the night seemed to blacken around him, the shadows of the torches that danced across his command tent formed into some odd, broken shape, like the branches of an estuary driving out to sea. They swelled suddenly, morphing across each other, distinguishable features linking together like a mosaic of fabric and flesh. He blinked, almost in disbelief at what was happening, until the shadows finally stopped.

And the rotund shape of a man with haunting, pale eyes laughed at him from the gloom.

And when he blinked again, it was gone.

Alvarez shook his head, rattling his mind and restarting the headache he had been trying to suppress. He rubbed his eyes, wilted with raw skin. *I'm just tired,* he scoffed, scowling venomously at his officers. *All these sleepless nights finally catching up with me, making me see things.* The longing for ethanol dragged at his soul again. *I need this over with, soon.* He smiled.

And I think I know just how…

"Officer?"

"Yes?" the balding man replied.

"How many of the palace guards are with us?"

"Around ten, sir… why do you ask?"

Alvarez nodded, smirking. "Before dawn breaks, send them into Marcheg to reinforce our front-lines. And make sure their swords are sharp enough to cut stone."

"But sir, they're here to protect you—"

"I don't need *protecting,* officer." He flashed his teeth like a dog. "I need those rebels executed, and I need this rebellion put to *death*… do you understand me?"

"Um… um, yes, yes sir, understood."

"Good. So, send the palace guards out at dawn. Let Ferreus know in advance of their arrival. They'll reach the front-lines and take the town square with the rest of our forces, and bleed every rebel that crosses their path. I want this petty insurrection dragged to its fucking knees as soon as possible. Because I will *not* have this turning into a civil war… or there will be *consequences.*"

Without a word more, the Supreme Governor shouldered his way past his officers and disappeared into his command tent, the sweet smell of liquor burning in his nostrils. He smiled.

I'll drink to that.

†

"I'd say that was a rather successful first day, wouldn't you?" Jinx said with a smile, pulling the skewer out of the fire and tucking in to the rich meat wedged on its end.

"For certain," Eli replied, wielding a leg of lamb almost as big as his fist. "Although we should count our blessings while we can, as I'm sure tomorrow will bring yet more challenges for us to face…"

They had camped out in the great chamber of the baron's hall for the night, with the rest of his people finding refuge in the abandoned homes stretching out across the west of Marcheg. They had set watch overnight to look out for signs of the enemy and keep the sleeping rebels safe, but even so they found it unlikely that any real threat would come in such a vast, labyrinthine town. The chances were that the enemy were doing much the same as they were then: gathering around great fires, drinking and making merry under the gaze of the moon, while taking stock and forming plans and awaiting the battle that would surely come. But in the twilight, under the stars, there was no blood nor steel: only the chirp of bats, and the creak of gutters, and the shimmering hues of the Jade Sun.

As if nothing was wrong at all.

"The challenges may be great, but it's nothing we can't handle by the looks of things," Jinx spluttered, snagging another chunk of meat from the skewer.

"They're certainly a sturdy bunch, I'll give them that… I mean, it only took three of them to get this thing down." Eli gestured to the huge basin of fire before them, which three of his strongest men had politely removed from the plinth at Eli's back to give them a nice fire to warm next to. "We'll have to save them some of this cooked meat for their efforts."

"Only if they intend to prize it from my dead hands," Jinx joked, wiping gristle and fat from her chin. "This is the finest bit of food I've had in days."

"Not one for sharing, ay?"

"Not when I'm this hungry. If they try and eat any of this, I'll eat *them*."

Eli roared with laughter, spluttering and coughing with food still in his mouth. "With your skills with a knife, I wouldn't say that was far from the truth either."

"You best believe it!"

They sat for a moment laughing, tearing at great slabs of meat under the dark hollows of the hall. Eli studied the fire with a joy warming his soul, reminiscing old times that had come and gone and the memories they had shared together. Clinging to them; holding them as long as he could.

But as the silence descended once again, and the chamber echoed out all around them, the Chief sensed a coldness press across his back, and grew suddenly still. His mind drifted to other things: other memories of other times, with other people. A welt of pain followed, pulling across his feet and fingertips. Looking up to Jinx sat opposite him, he met her eyes and found she was suffering the same: a great absence that they both shared, strung out in blood and bond. A quiet inflection; a single feeling.

Loss.

"Do you remember the day I first met you, Alva?" Eli said quietly, throwing the lamb's bone into the fire. "All those years ago."

"It was a quiet summer's day, wasn't it? In Casantri. There was some event going on, I believe. I can't remember what exactly..."

"The Festival of the High Sun: when the moon and sun are said to be at their highest point, directly opposite each other. We were gathered to celebrate the balance of the world, and pray for our prosperity. I went with Arrenso, of course – he was always very involved on those pious occasions – and he invited you along as well. At the time, I admit, I didn't even know that he had a sister... let alone that you were a master thief."

"It's not something he talked of often," she said, lowering her gaze. "He... he seemed quite disappointed of me a lot of the time. For how I made my money."

Eli smiled, shaking his head. "Arrenso was many things, Alva... but disappointed in you was not one of them. He just found himself in a difficult position, enforcing the law while his sister spent her life breaking it. But he never held it against you, and never made you out as the enemy. He was determined, always, to keep you safe no matter what."

"I considered many times whether I should give it all up for him... just to make his life easier. Whether I should bury the lockpicks, and go work as some maid or craftswoman... y'know, do something polite and *legal*."

"And give up part of who you are, doing something you feel is right?"

"If it meant I took the burden off of him hiding me away, then yes."

"He would've never wanted that for you."

"Why not? From how he spoke to me, it seems like that's all he ever wanted."

"What you misunderstand, was that Arrenso wanted to keep you safe, of course… but he also wanted you to be happy." Eli leaned forward, bringing his hands together. "When I first met you, at the Festival of the High-Sun, I remember it so distinctly, because of the game you took part in that won you that money. Do you remember?"

"The puzzle game, wasn't it? The one where if anyone cracked the puzzle, they could have whatever lay inside?"

"Exactly so. And I must've stood there for hours and watched hundreds of people try it, each barely moving three tiles on that rotating board before getting stuck and giving in. It seemed impossible, and like the prize money would go unclaimed… that was, until you offered to have a go at it. I can remember how Arrenso had looked so venomous when you suggested it, but I told him there was no harm in it: it was just a game, after all." He gave a quiet, thoughtful smile. "And, I tell you what, we marvelled at how simple it was for you. We were star-struck. I mean, this was something that we had watched dozens of people fail to solve before you. And then you appeared, studying it for what seemed like a blink of an eye… and unlocked it, like it was nothing."

Jinx shrugged her shoulders, a tiny blossom of pride in her chest. "It was a neat little party trick, that's all."

"You and I both know that isn't true… and Arrenso knew it as well. Because when I looked over to him as that last piece slid into place, and that little door with the money in it burst open at the top… I had never seen that man smile like that before. Almost like he knew that'd be the outcome the entire time, because he had that much faith in your ability. He was impressed, more than anything – I mean, we all were. The skills of a master thief, playing silly games at the Festival of the High-Sun… it was quite something to witness."

"It's just what I do," she said simply.

"It's also the bit that you never quite understood about your brother… and it was something I took a long time to understand myself when we were courting all those years ago. It was that, even with the trouble your thievery caused him from a professional standpoint – with filing false reports and keeping your trail cold – Arrenso always saw it for the joy it brought you, and the good it did despite his reservations: to see the people you helped, and the corrupt bastards you stole from who the law could never quite pin down. He saw how much it meant to you, and how good you were at it. And I believe if he were still here, he'd do it again a hundred times over... just to see that smile on your face like the one you had the first day I met you." Eli inhaled, cycling a breath through his system to stifle any tears, before nodding his head slowly. "He loved you, Alva... he loved you dearly. And more than anything, he was proud to have you with him as a sister and a friend. Never forget that."

She smiled with a warm, all-encompassing glow. "Thank you, Eli... I needed to hear that. And, well... I loved him so dearly too. He just never got round to saying it to me himself."

The Chief shrugged. "Well you know what he was like: a bloody hard man to read, and an even harder bloody man to get anything out of."

Jinx grinned. "He sounds a lot like his husband."

"Oh, fuck yourself."

But he found he couldn't help but smile back.

†

Chapter 20

Destined for the Dead

The Ozban had stretched on endlessly through the chasm of dark, with the path ahead growing more congested with each bend in its meandering shape. The soldiers had moved forward in increments, fearful of the death and screams all around them as the horses snapped uneasily at their backs. Their strategists, guiding the army as best they could through the thick skeletal boughs, had unravelled their maps over and over again to try and make sense of where they were, and why it was all taking so long. A number of them made clear that they were still heading in the right direction, while a few others entertained the idea that they may have been lost or gone astray.

And in the Ozban, that meant death.

As the screams around them amplified, and the path pressed on through the gloom with no sign of stopping, terrified murmurs passed among the ranks that they may never find a way out again. That they were very actually lost in that hell-hole, with no chance of return. Their resolve had ebbed rapidly from that point on, as soldiers turned on their comrades demanding answers that they knew deep down they didn't have, praying the Forest would forgive them for trespassing and set them free again.

And, whether by luck or the benevolence of the gods, those same prayers were answered moments later, when the tree-line thinned like parting clouds and a muddy plain splayed out before them, alighting in the soldiers a jolt of shock as they realised they may not die after all.

In the opening, the remains of several rough-stone buildings stood with holes scattered across their walls and exposed beams of wood crossing between. Each one that they found lay consumed in some black-blue ivy, thick as tree trunks in places, forming roof-tops on some of the houses where it was so dense. The ivy snaked its way across the floor between them, meandering across broken stones that had once marked the main street. Spilling out to the north, down a narrow stretch to a wooden platform at the back, where the ivy coiled up across its struts like a serpent.

It was a village, or had been once, the strategists came to theorise. A place that had been abandoned long ago to the malfeasance of the Ozban. The entire area seemed to throb with disgust; the air was heavy and bitter on the tongue. Sunlight was limited, always cast in shadow, swamping the land beneath. The trees seemed to lean away at the edges like mourners, as the dying screams of those lost in the deep-dark fell away to nothingness. As if it were a harrowed place, castigated in one's nightmares, and not designed for the enterprise of mortal man. As if it were cursed, hiding behind its shadows.

Only destined for the dead.

Commander Revek sat atop his mount at the southern end of the village, watching from the outskirts as the Imperial Army flooded into the ruins and began pitching their tents among the old stone. Like termites on an arid plain, the soldiers began repurposing the old buildings and stuck drapes of cloth across the rooftops, dragging barrels of food and liquor into the shelter knowing a sleepless night of drinking most likely lay ahead. Others erected little rooms alongside the horse-carts, in the desperate hope that if something came to kill them all, they could get to the horses first and make some attempt at escape. Meanwhile, a few less-cautious souls decided to set their tents around the old wooden platform at the back, using the suspended struts as makeshift tent poles and marvelling at their handiwork. Although even they never plotted too close to the snaking ivy that seemed to twitch their way whenever they blinked, for fear of what evils lay across its roots and the poison it could seep into their veins.

As if the plants are the thing to fear here, Revek scoffed, looking off to the tree-line on his left.

They know nothing of what really awaits us in the dark.

Around the outskirts of the old village, the sentries had set about organising the perimeter of the camp, skirting close to the edge with spears clasped tight in both hands. The commander watched three of them pace the tree-line, gesturing across the open space with broad sweeps of the hand, pointing to the roots of the skeletal trees where the supposed 'madness' began to set in. Stopping to inspect an area; flinching suddenly at the groaning trees, and the echoey scrape of dirt somewhere in the dark to their left. All three spears rounded; frightful eyes studied the gloom. Finding nothing there at all, in the end.

As if the sounds were all in their heads...

The things a place like this does to you. The commander shook his head, plying at the horse's reins locked in his fingers. *Even the shadows have teeth... and their wounds hurt far more than blades ever could.* He sensed his own demons rattling in his mind at the thought, and dug his nails into his palm.

And it seems I know it more than most.

Stirring the horse into a slow trot, Revek turned and guided the beast through their ramshackle encampment, studying the half-propped tents and fumbling hands of the soldiers with a fickle glare. They were a well-oiled machine, so it appeared, both on and off the battlefield: as studious with a blade as they were with a tent-hook, pinning up sheets of cloth and fastening straps with deft fingers. They were completely unperturbed in their business, and disinterested as the commander passed. As if they hadn't even realised he was there.

Or worse, that they didn't care.

Ruinous, petty little bastards, he sneered, flicking the reins in his lap.

What is the point in having martial order if the soldiers can pick and choose their command? I should be getting bows and salutes and greetings as I pass, as is proper. Where's the respect? Where's the order? This isn't order... this is a fucking joke. He drew a finger through his moustache. *They'll learn, sooner or later... they'll learn who's in charge.* With eyes like knives, he grinned.

Either that, or I'll make them.

Looking up to the wooden platform just ahead – navigating the trunks of ivy at his feet – he spied the three officers who had led the expedition stood deep in conversation, side-eyeing him as he approached. Oslo seemed twitchy and unnerved at the sight of him, scratching at his hands like he had a rash; Zespa glanced at him with a potent curl of the tongue, rolling her shoulders; Xol nodded emotionlessly, stood tall and proud with hands clasped at their back as if the world was theirs and theirs alone.

Revek curled his nose up, dismounting his horse and lifting elegantly onto the platform.

And here are the culprits of this disorder and spite, the commander grumbled. *What a pleasure as ever...*

"You three seem deep in discussion," he proclaimed, stopping just short of them in the faint glow of afternoon sun. "Is there anything important that I should *also* know about?"

"Unless you care deeply about the maintenance and feeding of our horses," Xol muttered quietly, "then probably not."

"Because we're trying to work out what the fuck to feed them, in a place where everything is either dry, rotten or dead," Zespa muttered, flicking at her nails. "*Our* provisions will last us weeks, but the horses? Not so much."

"Can't go carting barrels of hay around, now can we?" Oslo said dumbly. "Quite a waste of time."

"The horses will be fine," Revek scoffed, waving his hands. "They're big animals, they'll find food."

"Awfully *dismissive* of you, commander," Xol retorted. "Those horses are our best way of getting through the forest to find more outposts. It's been advised that we keep them in good shape."

"And they will, just as they *are*."

"It doesn't appear that we see eye to eye, commander."

"Where we both stand doesn't matter. The horses will be fine."

Xol held their hands up in mock-surrender. "Very well, commander, very well. We will leave the horses be and entrust they stay healthy eating the dirt at our feet." A quiet smile graced his lips. "Because I know it won't be me who has to explain it to the Marshal if they don't..."

Revek sneered, his blood boiling, hands clenching at his sides. *How fucking dare you—*

But he held his tongue nonetheless, glaring at the other two officers instead.

"Although, on the topic of outposts..." Xol continued, reaching in through the top of their chest-plate to reveal a small folded map hidden away there. "We need to devise a plan to get the rest of these ruins back under Imperial control. We have a lot of ground to cover, and we don't know what the enemy presence looks like at each location going forward."

"We should go straight down the middle," Zespa exclaimed bluntly. "Follow the ruins through the trees and mark them off as you go. Keep an eye on the path ahead and kill any of the bastards you find."

The commander laughed. "Oh, that would be lovely general, but it's clearly not that *simple*," he spat, receiving little more than a grunt in reply. "The old forts weren't built in a straight line. They were built wherever the trees parted, so are scattered across the forest in random places wherever we could find a foothold."

"For the trees consume whatever does not belong there," Oslo said ominously, staring out across the horizon with blank eyes. "Only in the light may we dare make our presence known..."

"Which means we have at least three forts ahead of us that are only connected by tiny dirt roads, built probably a league apart from each other with no way to reinforce our lines between," Xol explained.

"Now, I don't fancy partitioning our forces any more than they already are, with the diminished resources we already have. With four points to defend and an enemy supposedly all around us, that would be tantamount to suicide."

Revek shook his head. "This whole operation is suicide..."

"Such calm and inspiring words from our field commander." Xol pursed lips. "Truly the man we need at a time like this."

The commander's face hardened. "I don't appreciate the sarcasm, *officer*."

"Were it unwarranted, I would perhaps apologise for any offence."

"As a secondary-ranking member of this army, I couldn't give a shit if you think it's unwarranted or not."

"The apology remains unforthcoming."

Revek ground his teeth. "You tread a thin line."

"Well, commander, here's the thing: if you disagree with my conduct, then by all means... prove me *wrong*." They locked eyes, as Xol circled their hand like an orator. "Show us the path ahead, and find an answer to this tactical conundrum of ours... and I will of *course* apologise to you."

Rounding on the general, bristling at their goading remarks, Revek felt the heat rise across his sternum and sensed the blade at his side rattle with lust. *Splitting your head would be most pleasant right about now,* he thought venomously. He was being challenged, he knew. That Xol was trying to draw him out, putting him in a position where backing down would be cowardly, but striking back would be insecure. Part of him couldn't help but be impressed - *well played, you bastard* – but the other half remained ireful and bloody. Imagining his fingers as he dug them into Xol's neck, massaging the arteries across their throat before suffocating the supply to their brain...

Revek smiled, clearing his throat. He adjusted his collar. *Make whatever remarks you want, you backstabbing little prick,* he thought.

Your time will come soon enough.

"Oslo and I shall head west to the Acolyte's Tower at dawn tomorrow," the commander explained. "We'll set up a staging post at the Tower, and establish a secure path between there and here. All other units shall remain here and fortify the village in case of enemy attack. Have a three-set rotation of the sentries overnight, so no one loses their nerve if the shadows play games. And set pit-traps along the tree-line, in case any hounds stray too close while we sleep." Revek paused, his face hardening. "I think that about covers it all, wouldn't you say?"

It was Xol's turn to smile, crossing their arms. "It appears I owe you an apology, commander. You seem to have covered everything in question rather succinctly," they replied, nodding slowly. "I just hope you still garner enough respect among the ranks for them to listen to you. They can be a difficult bunch at the *best* of times."

"They will do as I say, or be flogged for insubordination," Revek growled. "Let there be no hesitation in that."

"Always to lead with the stick, commander." Xol shook their head. "Perhaps their medicine would go down a bit smoother with honey, rather than *hornets*."

"They will do as I say, and so fucking *help* them if they don't."

To his left, Zespa gestured with a doleful smile. "Then by all means, sir... cuff the bastards into order. Let's see how they take it."

"Like a wet bag of shit, I imagine," Xol grumbled.

"Well, as you all seem to treat them like wet bags of shit... maybe there is the need for some *order* around here," Revek growled, tensing his fingers. *These people know nothing. They pander their way through each decision, like a man in a brothel fiddling with his belt buckle. A limp disappointment is all that awaits.* He looked out across the trees at their backs.

And I am not one of them.

"See that my expeditionary force are mustered and put in order for sunrise tomorrow," the commander ordered. "Oslo, make any preparations you feel are necessary for the journey. We will probably encounter the enemy when we arrive, so I will want swords sharp and eyes peeled. I wouldn't want anything to *happen* to you, after all..."

With a sharp grin of his pointed teeth, Commander Revek turned from them and waved his hand dismissively. He bent low and slid off the platform into his saddle, securing the horse's reins in his grip and guiding the beast back off into the ruins.

†

The three officers watched as their commander moved off through the makeshift camp, the darkening clouds overhead proving something of an omen to them.

"I don't trust that one," Xol said quietly, looking to their feet, "and I don't trust his intentions."

"Seems the type to screw someone over with a turn of his hand," Zespa scoffed at his side. "We've all heard the rumours about the Grey Plains… how he supposedly killed his own soldiers and stole their horses just to get out of the fighting and then out of the Ozban alive."

"It was something the Marshal warned us about, before we set off: beware the wolf when it feels threatened, for it will bite friend or foe without fear."

"You think he'll… you think he might try and hurt us?" Oslo muttered with sudden fear in his voice.

"No, Oslo… he *will* try to hurt us." Xol tracked the commander as he disappeared behind an old stone wall, and shook his head. "The question will be, when he chooses to do it…"

"I'll skin him from head to fucking toe if he comes anywhere near me," Zespa said with a snarl.

"But I'm… I'm going to the Acolyte's Tower with him… he'll be in command, alone, without…" Oslo scratched at his knuckles, ripping at his skin until the pores were red-raw. "Am I gonna die?"

"Just keep your wits about you, Oslo, and you'll be fine," Xol replied, placing a hand on the general's shoulder. "Remember he is only one man, with one weapon, and you will be commanding over fifty of our most loyal soldiers…"

Xol looked skyward, and saw the faint shadows of crows circling high above.

What's the worst he can do?

†

Chapter 21

The Fire Burns

"Well, Cavara, this is certainly… *unusual.*" Ptolemy took a swig of his drink, rolling his tongue across his lips. "To what do we owe the *pleasure?*"

The three of them sat in a drinking den known as the Tyrant's Bluff, which lay along the same road as Azura's house at the outskirts of the market square. It was a quaint hovel, full of high-backed benches and thick wood tables and the delicate flickers of candlelight. Homely, almost. The bar was quiet, with the casks plugged and left to stand; there were hardly any patrons, as the midday sun still crested the sky outside. Other than the doddering shape of the innkeeper polishing glasses to their right, and the faint creak of floorboards above them as the servants got dressed, the drinking den was entirely empty. It was only Cavara present, sat with her hands clasped on the table top.

And the effortless silence all around.

"I didn't want to have to do this, trust me," the general muttered, setting her jaw square. "But I didn't really have a choice."

"You sound desperate," Amara mocked.

"Perhaps because I am."

"And who says we'll help you?"

Cavara sighed, rubbing her face. "Because something in me holds out… that maybe you aren't as much of a waste of space as you come across being. That maybe – just *maybe* – you can actually help me out for once."

"Sounds like she means to insult us, Ptolemy," Amara grumbled. "What d'you think?"

Ptolemy remained unreadable, with no emotion crossing his cold grey eyes. "And why should we listen, Cavara?" he inquired. "Why should we hear what you have to say?"

"Because if you don't, then you can explain to the Alderbane how you failed to protect me when a rogue Tarrazi assassin slits my throat and runs rampant through these city streets. Your choice."

She received an unimpressed grunt in reply; Ptolemy waved his hand. "Let's hear it, then... let's get it over with."

"My thanks for your *courtesy*." Cavara inhaled deeply, shifting her gaze between the two of them. She hated how uncaring they were; how fickle and dismissive and brash they were toward her. How they were there on orders, and not because they had any respect or dignity in their position. Her honour-guard. Her so called protectors. *Righteous bastards with not an ounce of good in them.*

But we save those grievances for better times... as this is not one of them.

"I have called you both here today, because it has become apparent to us that the perceived threat of an enemy assassin within our walls, is *real,*" Cavara explained. "We have discovered that someone did in fact disembark from one of the Tarrazi ships that washed up at your docks a few nights ago, and that they are now within the city. And not only are they in the city... but they are also hunting me, with the intention of ending my life."

"How do you know this?" Amara asked.

"Because I met them, last time I was with you... it was where I disappeared to. They... took me into their world, so to speak."

"What do you mean, *'their world'*? We saw you disappear, but where did you go?"

"I..." She stopped suddenly, realising the secrecy she was sworn to about the Rapture and her powers.. "I..." *Shit.* "I cannot disclose that, I'm afraid. I'm sorry."

"And why not?"

"It's a secret, kept between the Forgotten One, the Alderbane and myself… and is not something any of us want circulated to other people." *Especially not people like you.*

Amara looked to Ptolemy and scoffed. "Sounds like a hot crock of shit to me… what say you?"

Ptolemy scratched at his chin in thought. "I would say much the same," he muttered. "But, then again, the Alderbane made clear that our business would include a lot of secrecy… that, and we did see her disappear the other day before our very eyes. That was no trick of the light, you know." He shrugged. "So, whatever it is that's being kept from us, we must at least admit that it's real… and in turn, that there is indeed an assassin in our walls."

Cavara was taken aback, holding her breath. "Thank you, I… I do appreciate your—"

"But the Alderbane also said that you were likely to lie to us, in an act of rebellion to being placed under watch…" Ptolemy leaned over the table, studying her intensely. "So who says that that isn't the case right now?"

The general rolled her eyes. *Never mind.* "What would I gain in lying to you, honestly?" she spat, exaggerating a shrug. "I don't call counsel with you people unless I have a damn good reason to… and believe me, *I do.*"

Ptolemy rolled back in his seat, seemingly satisfied with the answer. "You could be nicer about it," he muttered with a grin.

I want to break your nose. "Well, my apologies for the *harsh critique.* I shall be more professional in the future."

"It would make a nice change."

"Right, look, I'm not here to play fickle little games, so if you'd kindly dispense with the sarcastic remarks—"

"Get on with it then, what else is there to say?"

The general gripped the leg of the table hard enough for it to creak under the pressure, digging her nails into the varnish like talons. A few moments passed, before she composed herself and sighed.

"What I am trying to stress in all this, is that I am not the *only* person who has been targeted by this assassin... and as it stands, a fellow citizen of yours has been abducted, and is being held somewhere within these walls. A child, at that."

"Do you mean that old lady's boy, who you're staying with? That child?" Amara asked dumbly.

"Yes. He's..." She held the quiver in her voice. "He's been taken by the assassin, and hidden somewhere... I don't know where, but all I know is that they want an exchange, my life for his, so they can finally capture and execute me. But if I die, then a lot of things are going to happen that are far, *far* worse than this. Things the likes of which this world has never experienced before. And that is why the Alderbane is so protective of my life, and why he assigned you to me in the first place" – *or so it claims.* "So my situation, I hope, is clear: I cannot die, but I also cannot let the life of an innocent child be taken in my place."

Ptolemy nodded. "And what are we to do about that?"

"I need your help in finding the boy," Cavara muttered. "I need the Alderbane informed of the situation, and I need every soldier and guard available to find out this assassin and rescue the child. That's why I'm here... I'm asking because his life is in danger, and I cannot lose him and cause his mother so much grief. I have to save him. So I'm asking you, please, to help..."

As her words failed, Cavara looked between them both in the dull light of the inn and whispered a tiny prayer in her heart. Ptolemy remained sprawled across his chair, watching her intently, a finger toying with a lock of hair at his chin; Amara, fiddling with a tiny blade in her hand, smiled blindly at her without concern. The innkeeper continued polishing glasses behind the bar, as if there was nothing wrong with the world.

Cavara found prickles across her spine; her skin was suddenly itchy. It was so silent and the air was so thin, stifling her breath. She was trapped there, almost, lost in a daze, waiting for an answer—

"From what you say," Ptolemy mused suddenly, "it seems that

your life is certainly very valuable, and that we are doing a great service to our most magnificent ruler in protecting you. People want you dead, and it is in our interest to make sure that doesn't happen. And although you take some *reservations* of us and our way of doing things, we can at least have mutual agreement that your death brings no benefit to anyone." Ptolemy paused, nodding imperceptibly. "So, yes, we will inform the Alderbane of the new threat that now walks among us and hunts you through our streets. They will likely send out an alert, and inform the city guard of the enemy at large. They will ensure that no harm comes to you." Another pause; the honour guard produced a muted laugh. "However, that courtesy is not all-encompassing, and does not extend to anyone else *other* than you. Because our prerogative, you see, is the continuation of your life... *not* the lives of anyone else who may have been caught up between swords. That is not our business, and not of our concern...."

The general's face took on a shade of thunder that seemed to make the whole room tremble. "So, you won't help in finding Evelyn?" she said, dumbstruck. "You will leave an innocent boy to die, because it's '*not your business*'? Honestly?"

"We have been assigned to protect *you*, and ensure that *you* survive. Not to go on merry little adventures saving children who walked down the wrong path. I am sorry, *truly,* that he is not our priority... but that's just the way it is."

"Do you not care? Does none of this really *fucking* matter to you?" The tremble in her voice was lost: she caught herself snarling with flared nostrils and hateful eyes. "Have some humanity, for gods' sake. Have some general fucking sympathy for those affected by this. Are you seriously that cruel, to let a child die?"

"Cruelty has nothing to do with it," Ptolemy growled. "We do our jobs – those that have been assigned to us – and nothing else. Because if we don't do our jobs, we don't get paid. Or worse, we get *killed.* So I'm sorry that your sweet darling Evelyn is expendable in all this, but at the end of the day... I. Don't. *Care.*"

"Don't you *dare* speak his name, you filthy piece of *shit.*" Her fist clenched.

"Or what?" Ptolemy goaded, smirking coldly, leaning across the table. "What are you *actually* gonna do about it—"

Cavara reached down to her right and hoisted the spare chair by its leg, swinging it across the table like a battering ram.

A sudden cracking of wood and cartilage followed, as the seat seemed to explode into pieces across Ptolemy's face. The squelch of blood spat through the air; the wheeze of a broken nose caught in her ears; the awkward squeal of an arrogant pig burned like fire in her veins.

Without blinking, the general was standing suddenly, and flipped the table sidelong. With no time to react, it crashed across Amara's body and sent her spinning away across the floor.

Ignoring her, charging forward with adrenaline coursing through her body, Cavara bent low and drew Ptolemy up by the scruff of his neck, his face lulling from side to side in a half-conscious daze. Completely lost; utterly astonished by what had happened—

Cavara swung with her fist and connected sharply with his cheek, enough to knock a tooth loose that spun off like a bullet to their right.

Another punch, the same place, purple bruising already forming.

Another punch, twisting his jaw like a door hinge.

Another punch.

Another.

Another.

Screaming, biting, howling.

Another, venomous.

Another.

Hatred.

Another; the snap of bones.

Another

Anot—

Hands reaching, sliding under her shoulders, dragging her back to a stand as she relinquished her hold on Ptolemy's bloodied collar.

Cavara stood swaying, grinding her teeth, lost in his foul little face.

How selfish they were, the pair of them. How self-serving and undignified. A gross waste of human life. She spat in his face, toes curling in her boots like grinding gears. Thinking of Evelyn locked away somewhere, fearing death – Azura, grieving her son – her own pain, deep and welling within, and the guilt that swamped her with each day that passed. How dark she felt inside; how cold the world had become to her.

Shrugging off the two servants that had dragged her to her feet, Cavara wiped her hands clean of Ptolemy's blood, and left without a word.

†

Chapter 22

Turning Tides

The ranks parted before him, like the shifting waters of a great sea, all bowed heads and hungry eyes and the quiet shuffling of feet. He strode through them, among them, passing and assessing, pulling at shoulder pads and chest plates and straightening the brows of high-crested helmets. Striding across the stone streets of Marcheg, under the watch of a rising sun, General Ferreus studied his army with thoughtful eyes.

And a burning desire to shed more rebel blood.

We've been held and challenged by these peasant scum of the west, he thought with gritted teeth. *How they burn our lands so recklessly, and march against us with swords raised... how they strike out against the might of the Imperial Land Army without a word of honour among them. Those wretched little shits in their cloth shirts and stained breeches, under the command of a treacherous beast. It disgusts me, to see them foment such disorder. It disgusts me, and beckons correction. For we must claim back what is ours... we must amend this great wrong in the world.*

And we must do so with bloodied blades, killing all those that we find.

For a moment, he looked off to the north through the trees, out over the rolling plains of Provenci: knowing that somewhere out there just over the horizon, the ugly black smudge of the Tarrazi wall still remained, and the battlefield still wept imperial blood in the rotten lowlands beyond.

We have a centuries-old enemy marching against us as we speak, spilling our beautiful Provencian blood and threatening our borders with their ruin. We have a true war, against a true foe, right at our doorstep. And yet here we are, camped out in the streets of a forgotten town in the middle of nowhere... fighting an enemy of our own people, strayed too far down the wrong path. He flicked a bug on his hand, drawing a nail across his thumb. *They must understand that this is a farce... that their grievances do not serve the greater good of the nation. Do they not see that we are at war, and that we possess a common enemy in this time of need? Do they not see it... as they bite at our ankles like disobedient dogs, longing for the sting of a master's leash.*

I won't stand for it. He drew to a halt, skidding on his heel at the fore of the army. *This rebellion must be exterminated, and their faith must be forgotten. We must leave no trace of their pitiful cause. We have a war to fight, and a true purpose in the world. We are the gods' ordained.*

And the hand of the gods will never fail us.

Turning slowly, he was alerted to the sound of scurrying feet: a messenger appeared in beige overalls and bowed to him frightfully, caught under the steely glare of the field general like a fish at a butcher's knife.

"What is it?" Ferreus snapped, leering above him. "I don't have time for any dithering. We're preparing for a battle here, if you couldn't tell."

"Yes sir, I... there's..." the messenger spluttered.

"Spit it out!"

They gulped, followed by an awkward smile.

"Reinforcements have arrived, sir..."

Ferreus frowned, looking down the alleyway of soldiers ahead of him to discern what the messenger meant. It took seconds until his eyes began to widen, and he pushed the messenger aside with a dismissive hand as he realised what was making its approach. The catch of a smile coiled across his cheeks.

Yes they have...

Steel chest-plates and leg guards like shields. Chain-gloved hands with joints like scales. Green and red trim lacing the shoulders – hanging as a sash at their waists – ringing around their necks like medallions. High crested helms laced with red, extending down to two points like fangs across their mouth. Swords hanging at their sides; serrated spears shimmering brilliantly against the sun. Passing the crowds of soldiers in perfect rank-and-file, the rhythmic clatters of heavy boots chiming in his ears. It was a marvel to see, drenched in the warm glow of dawn. A perfect symbolism, almost.

Now this… *is a soldier of Provenci.*

"Greetings, sir," the foremost palace guard boomed, stopping just short of the general and kneeling at his feet. "We are glad to have found you well, and are honoured to be at your service for the coming attack."

"The honour is mine," Ferreus said devilishly. "Now please, stand… let everyone see what a *true* fighter looks like."

The palace guard stood, swelling their chest to the awe and wonder of the other soldiers stood idly at the edges.

The general nodded. "Very good… now, to what do we owe the pleasure?"

"Supreme Governor Alvarez wishes for today to go as smoothly as possible, and for the rebellion to be stamped out in the next two days if possible. So, to ensure this outcome, he assigned us under your command to assist in the coming attack, to be utilised sparingly should the enemy prove too difficult to overcome. The Governor does not wish for our direct and complete involvement in the fighting, but rather as a securing force in case gaps appear in our flanks or the enemy make any significant gains. Beyond this, we take any and all orders from you, sir."

Ferreus inclined his head, flexing his fingers. *I will ignore the sleight that the Governor feels my command of this army needs assistance from other forces… and I will ignore the fact that they only plan to engage in the event of a fuck-up.* He rolled his finger and thumb together at his side. *So, if they wish to play the game like that, then I shall of course oblige… I will use the force I have to exterminate this rebellion, and they won't even have to get their hands dirty. I will do as I set out to do, with the army I originally had. Because no-one questions my command.*

No-one.

"Very well," the general proclaimed. "If that is the case, then please organise yourselves among the rear-guard and be prepared to engage if the enemy split our forces. I want to leave nothing to chance though: if we need tides to be turned, I expect you all to step up to the task."

"Of course sir… as you wish."

Like the delicate coiling of a sand-snake, the palace guards rippled apart as they marched back down the street whence they came. They were silent as they did so, impervious and resolute in every motion. General Ferreus watched them move off down the causeway, and couldn't help but feel a sense of pride adrift within him.

They are good, fine officers of Casantri: of that there is no doubt, he mused. *Not fighters of the field, admittedly, but they are fighters nonetheless. And had it not been for the Governor's sly sentiments, I would almost feel sad not to use them.* With a wave of his hand, the main army closed back together again, forming up behind him as he turned west to the road ahead.

But no matter. This is a day of victory, and this is a day of death. The rebellion is lost, and its ringleaders will be slaughtered.

"Form up!" he cried to a rattle of steel.

And I'll make sure of it, by my own hand if I have to.

"*MARCH!*"

†

Chapter 23

Grief is a Cruel Mistress

A blue light swamped the room, carried down from the cracks in the ceiling as light ebbed its way through from the surface. Starting as golden rays of sunlight, butchered by clouds and the smog of the furnaces, it spilled down into the earth in great reams, growing colder and colder. Burrowing deep through the rocks – little more than a reflection of the yellowing beauty it had once been – until stopping, finally, at the edge of a vast chamber of pillars and broken rock, illuminating the empty space in hollow shades of blue. A forgotten chasm, in a forgotten part of the world addled with sin.

Never to see the true light again.

Savanta heard the doors close at her back, as the guards who had lead her down into the chamber disappeared into the dark once again. The noise echoed out for some time, ricocheting off the broken walls, spitting and biting at the shadows that lined the outskirts of the room.

In the spaces that the Iron Queen was probably lurking, awaiting the Champion's first move.

I want to hurt her, but I don't want to fight, came the first echoing thought. *I want answers... I want to know what's going on. I deserve to know. I will fucking demand it. I will break her bones and pluck out her eyes until she tells me that which I seek. Why have things become so foul? Why am I made to sit alone in the dark for days on end?*

Why is my father cooped up in an antechamber of Val Azbann, rotting away, supposedly dead for fifteen years...

She unsheathed her blade – or rather, the pitiful blade they had given her in place of her own. It was an awkwardly-weighted short-sword, which handled as if it were made out of tin and loaded with tiny stones. She had scoffed at it when they had presented it to her; she scoffed at it again as it lay limp in her hand, with the dusty shade of rust catching along its edge.

Hardly befitting a champion, to wield something like this, came the second thought. *I'd stand a better chance with a skewer than this fucking thing. It's a mockery, that I'm brought here to spar with the Iron Queen – a champion, challenged by their so-called master – and I am given a rusty sword that handles like a mallet to do so. A joke, surely?* She turned the blade in the hollow light and shook her head.

A death sentence, if not.

Her eyes crossed to the shadows, deciphering them like the gears of a clock. The faint licks of motion: a gust of wind, or a rippling crack in the wall. The shapeless movements, almost like mist. And within that void, somewhere, she sensed another presence. Something human, acutely vulgar, dancing through the gloom. The occasional glint at the corner of her eye; the twitch of the sword in her hand. Watching, waiting patiently.

Where are you? came the final thought.

"*I am all around,*" came the response.

Savanta's head snapped to the fore.

A shadow manifested ahead her, with a skull like the moon and eyes like broken blades and the glint of two rapiers hung delicately at the sides. Striding forward, stopping several paces from her. A haunted, tainted smile curled across her cheeks.

"Gaza," Savanta exclaimed, attempting to hide the tremble in her voice.

"Champion," the Iron Queen replied, studying her. "It is nice to see you again."

"The feeling is not mutual, I assure you."

"Oh, my dear… there is no need to lie to me. I know that that isn't true." She gestured with her blade. "You've been wanting to see me for some time, really…"

"I want *nothing* to do with you."

"That may be so, but you still *need* me. You've needed me all along. For who else can answer all of these questions you have, about the old man locked away in my keep? Who else can finally speak the truth about your poor, *poor* father…"

Savanta channelled her anger, a bitterness biting at her tongue. "What do you know?"

"It's not what I know, my dear… but rather how this has come about that astonishes me. How is it that I kept that man locked away for years in that chamber, feeding me information on the country he abandoned… only for his poor little daughter to appear before me, chained and bruised, fifteen years later? It's incredibly to think of really. I mean, you didn't even know he was *alive*…"

"*What* do you *know*—"

"I mean, imagine the pain and *anger* you must've felt, when you found out that your father did not in fact die at the hands of your enemy. When you found out that, instead of abandoning you, he chose to fake his own death to escape you, and pursued a cause so against everything you've ever believed in. The turmoil that must have caused you…" She shrugged, grinning. "So tell me, champion, if you will… how does that make you *hurt*?"

Savanta winced. "Stop this."

"Knowing your father is alive…"

"*Stop* this."

"And you… have *nothing*…"

Six strides and a lunge of the blade: Savanta cut into her circle, forcing the Iron Queen to sidestep with a click of her tongue.

Gaza brought her own weapons through, catching at Savanta's blade, the two intertwining and snapping aside like shattering glass.

Another strike. Another. Another. Blades chiming, sparks dancing off their edges. The shadows reeled fearfully all around, locked in the gloom. Thunder seemed to crackle somewhere above.

As the dance pressed on unperturbed, in the deep-dark-blue of down below.

Savanta cut across with a glancing blow; the Iron Queen stepped in to meet it, bringing down her second blade, forcing the champion to recoil and relinquish her attack.

She struck out again, teeth gritting, this time with more force – only for Gaza to swipe it aside, using her other sword to force a backstep and claim back the lost ground in a heartbeat.

Savanta snarled; she spat across the stone underfoot, her knuckles pink and white.

"Tell me, champion, now that you have seen him," the Iron Queen said, drawing her blades together, "do you wonder why he left? Why he abandoned you? Do you have any idea why he chose to take our cause over yours?"

"The question has crossed my *mind,*" she grumbled, wiping her brow.

"It's because he despised you, for who you were, and what you had become. He feared you, and ran away before you could hurt him so." She paused. "I mean, you already know what that looks like, to destroy those you hold closes to you… just look at what you did to that poor man, back in Val Darbesh…"

"Do not *speak* of him!" Her eyes were red embers. "You know nothing of the sacrifice I have made to get here."

"He was your only friend, the only one who ever stood by you… and you cut him down in cold blood in front of thousands, just to get to *me.*" Gaza scoffed. "And to think you look upon your father now, as the wreck of a man that he is, and scold *him* for abandoning his principles?" She smiled. "What a fucking *joke…*"

Savanta screeched and swung out again, forcing a parry from the Iron Queen that she knocked aside easily. Another strike followed, beating across Gaza's blades; Savanta screeched and broke one away from her defence, forcing the Queen to backstep or face a sudden, exquisite end. Savanta stood, tears biting in her eyes, with an unhinged laugh catching on her tongue.

And a madness in her heart.

The Iron Queen advanced again, making an upward strike that was easily deflected, but Savanta spied the second blade coiling past and stepped aside fearfully. She pulled away for a heartbeat; Gaza lunged forward immediately, blades twisting, striking in two different directions. Savanta brought her limp blade up to match one of them, twisting on her ankle to avoid the other—

A crunch in her jaw, as the Iron Queen brought her fist across and connected with Savanta's cheek.

She stumbled awkwardly; Gaza's knee bucked upward and ripped the air from her system, forcing her to wretch. She collapsed to her knees.

A sharp strike across the side of the head like a mallet, and Savanta spilled across the floor in a flay of limbs, the black and blue spinning all around as the Iron Queen disappeared into the shadows once more.

Savanta heaved in great lengths of air, nausea biting in her stomach. The stone was cold against her back. A violent agony pulsed in her skull. Lights flickered and faded in the gloom above her. Alone and dark and cold and so certain she would die.

"*Pathetic,*" came a voice from the shadows, somewhere in the dark of beyond. "*Such a waste...*"

"What do you want from me?" she spluttered, lungs burning. "I just want to know... I just want to *understand...*"

"*What is there to understand? You are lost and alone, and have nothing left. All the things that you held close to you, have either been killed and cast away. You are lost, champion, and you are worthless...*"

"Please, I..."

"*A father who abandoned you... comrades you let die... your only true friend, murdered by your hand...*"

Markus's face flashed before her: his final, pitiful stare hoping for mercy, as she run him through like a gutted fish. How little it had mattered then. How deeply it hurt, seeing it now. His face, as the light had receded from his eyes and blood had welled in his chest.

And the last vestige of what had been, ceased to be altogether.

"I have done wrong… I have wronged *so many* to get here," she admitted, pleading almost, trying to find the energy to sit up. "I hate everything… I *hate* everything. I hate the cruelty; I hate its misery. I hate every single last person who has tried to cross me. I hate the dead and the living and those who deserve it and those who don't. I hate the gods and the beasts and the hell of what this land has become." A flash of tears; her heart boiled in her chest. "I just want to find my peace… I just want to end this *torment*. I want to live free again, I want to… I…"

She pulled herself upright, and ran a hand across her cheek. The blunted ends of her fingers prickled against the knotted flesh of the plate embedded in her cheek. A wound from a lifetime ago, tainted with blood and effortless sin. A wound that had lead her to the heart of the enemy: to the fangs of the snake itself. How they had called it a suicide mission when she had set off, and yet there she was, not dead.

And yet somehow, not quite alive either.

"I don't know what's left for me," Savanta admitted, studying the shadows. "I don't know where this ends. I fear for my soul… I fear for the ruin of all things. The grief, it… it eats at me… and the anger too. How I *hate* it… how I want to *burn it all…*"

A figure manifested from the gloom before her, striding across the chamber floor with the sharp *click* of boots. A skull like the moon; a wicked smile; two rapiers hanging loose at her side.

Then a hand grappled her throat, and a voice whispered in her ear.

"If you long to burn this world, Savanta… then you can burn it, *for me.*"

†

Chapter 24

Leave Nothing to Chance

Show-time.

Eli hefted the bludgeon over his shoulder, the weight of its steel slotting against his collarbone welcomingly. Strapped head-to-foot in pads and leather bracers with metal plates lodged in between, he looked in that moment every inch the Chief whose mantle he had taken on. And, beyond the reams of sweat trickling down his spine in the stuffy chamber of the baron's hall, he was starting to feel like one too.

There's a lot on the line today, he thought, inhaling at length. *We need leadership, and we need direction, and we need to hit the bastards where it hurts.*

Because if we don't, everything else is lost.

"Are we ready?" he asked, looking out on the main doors of the hall just ahead.

"As ready as we'll ever be," Jinx replied, latching her crossbow in place at his side. "Reckon it'll be a tough fight today?"

"Like no other." Eli nodded his head. "The Imperial Army will be chastened from their lack of progress yesterday… and I imagine General Ferreus would have had some choice words to make when reporting back to the capital."

"You reckon they're unimpressed?"

"I reckon they're fucking furious."

"Things not going to plan?"

Eli scoffed. "It's the Imperial Army… when does it ever go to plan?"

Jinx laughed. "You may have a point there…"

The sound of echoing footsteps emerged to his left: one of his scouts emerged from the corridor there and approached them briskly, something of a smile catching at their face.

"Welcome, lad… anything to report?" Eli inquired, turning and grappling the man's forearm in greeting.

"Nothing out of the ordinary, Chief," the scout replied. "The main column of soldiers are marching back along the eastern road as expected, and making good headway toward the town square. Although, there is something worth noting: we believe that their *general* is manoeuvring among the vanguard, directing the attack from the front this time round. We've tried taking a few pot-shots at them, but to no avail. As I said, they're moving at quite some pace…"

Ferreus. Anger bubbled in his heart like a cauldron. *We'll have to see to his demise quickly.* "What about along the flanks?"

"There's limited activity to the north and south at the moment, as far as we know. The archers are fanning out to a few areas looking for vantage points, but their movements are nothing substantial. It does genuinely seem like the entire army is comprised of that one column in the east, marching to meet us head on…"

The Chief produced an inviting smile.

Then I'm happy to oblige.

He turned to Jinx for a moment, placing his hand on her shoulder. "Are you ready for this?"

"Ready as I'll ever be," she said with a grin.

"Good answer." Eli winked. "You'll do us proud… all of us. Just do exactly the same as you did yesterday: up on the balcony, using the pillars for cover, and keeping the archers off our backs where you can. Maybe look for some more targets in the square below if things ease off… and if you spot Ferreus among them, then please, crack his skull like an egg for me. As much as I want to be the one to cave his head in for what he's done, I'll leave nothing to chance."

Jinx bowed her head. "I'd be honoured to."

They embraced each other tightly, his huge arms pulling her in like a great winter coat. "That's the spirit," he whispered softly, a warm kinship in his heart.

"Now, we best get going, sir," the scout said insistently, biting at his lips. "The Army will be here at any moment."

Jinx and Eli parted; the huge man squeezed her shoulders, his face awash with pride. "Good luck up there, Alva."

"Stay safe, Eli."

"You have my word... now go pop some heads."

Looking down to the crossbow, she clicked the first bolt into the holster and smiled. "With pleasure, Chief."

She skittered off across the wide chamber floor, disappearing up the spiral stairway and out along the balcony above with a spring in her step and bolts rattling at her side.

Eli turned, wrapping his arm around the scout as they moved off toward the rear exit, his bludgeon shimmering like a star.

They emerged onto sunlit stone surrounded by the dour grey houses of Marcheg, turning sharply left down a side-street awash with streaks of shadow. The scurrying feet of rats ricocheted across the walls as they disappeared into the sewers. The tip-tap of a loose faucet trickled out from one of the homes as they passed by. The lone *squawk* of a crow sounded overhead, circling clouded skies with hungry, studious eyes. Yet Eli heard nothing of the coming violence as he paced down the alleyway: nothing of the blood and pain that was soon to come. Only the chatters and mutters of the calm before the storm, in a world that did not care for the cause of man and would remain uncaring long after they had hit the mud.

It is all a dream, to them.

It was only as the baron's hall fell away to his left, and the dim glow of the main road honed into view, that the thundering drum-beats of war began to rise, as dozens of bodies lined the streets with steel boots and steel hearts. Eli found himself swept up in it, drawn to it like the sweet scent of fresh bread: that this was home, and these were his people.

And this is where I belong.

He entered out amongst them, shifting through ranks of bright-eyed faces, clasping shoulders and whispering prayers and nodding graciously. The corridor of buildings collapsed to either side of his vision, like the parting gates of the heavenly realm, as he looked upon a marl sky of shifting clouds and the delicate glow of the sun.

Reaching the top of the road, he moved in amongst his vanguard, where the largest rebels in shining steel helmets stood with their axes and mallets to-hand. The foremost fighters had broad shields strapped across their arms that they had seized from the city's armouries, forming up like scales to protect their Chief as he hunkered down next to them.

"What's the situation?" Eli inquired to the woman next to him.

"It's confirmed that General Ferreus is among the vanguard stationed opposite us," she explained. "It seems he will be involved in much of the fighting today."

Oh isn't that nice for us. "It seems that he's confident of success today."

"Either that or there's something we don't know." She paused, blushing slightly. "I'm sorry, sir, that was quite—"

"No need to apologise, Mora: it is best to err on the side of caution with these things." She seemed to glow slightly at the use of her name. "As you say, he's either a damned fool looking to get killed, or has a subtle trick up his sleeve… and knowing how much of an insipid bastard he is, I would put my bets on the latter…"

"Agreed." She looked forward, craning her neck with wide eyes. "Look sir! They're approaching!"

Eli lifted his head above the crest of their shields, and watched as shimmering steel helmets emerged from the buildings opposite like a shoal of tiny fish. Floods of them, dozens upon dozens pulling up along the edge of the square. He noted how their swords had been gleaned; how their armour had been polished and their boot-straps had been tightened. The Imperial Land Army of Provenci, honing into view with the red-and-green standards billowing in the wind at their backs, looked ready to spill rebel blood.

And somewhere amongst them, skulks a rotten little shit with a thorn in his side who I'd quite like to see maimed…

As their front-lines fanned out into formation, Eli spied the greying hair and deathly-pale skin of the General lurking among his men, like a wolf through snow-capped trees. It set his heart on edge to see him in the flesh. An adrenaline-fuelled lust for revenge corralled in his chest; the bludgeon tensed in his hand.

You will die for what you've done to me, he growled silently. *You will die for your sins… for executing an innocent man, because you were nothing more than a paranoid little prick with a point to prove. Jinx deserves better. Arrenso deserved better.*

And I will show you the full force of my wrath, as I bleed you in his name.

"Ready yourselves! Shields high and swords sharp!" Eli bellowed, rising up from behind the shields to the hushed concerns of his vanguard, crashing a fist against his chest angrily. "Be ready to march! The time has come! We shall make them bleed, and we shall make them *suffer!*"

A roar sounded in reply, rippling across Marcheg like ocean waves, shaking dust from the walls and alighting birds from the rooftops.

"*Ready!*"

The sweet chime of blades being drawn echoed at his back; the crunch of drawstring sounded as bows were drawn taut. Everything held for a moment of silence, until the final words came…

"*CHARGE!*"

Steel broke. Steel flew. Steel thundered all around like cannon-fire. Like tiny droplets of rain, arrows and bolts were cast overhead in a perilous exchange. Eli found the drive in his legs, picking up pace alongside his people. Their gleeful cries echoed out through the alleyways of the town, rising over the frantic and suddenly-fearful faces of the Imperial Army as they set upon them like dogs. Snapping teeth and hungry eyes and blade hilts warm in their hands. All was glory and all was hate.

And then the carnage ensued.

Eli caught the first one before their blade had even left their sheath: his bludgeon impacted across the side of their head as their nose exploded like a squat plum. They reeled in pain, sword releasing, hands clawing at the shrapnel of their face – before one of Eli's vanguard stepped forward and ran him through quietly, whipping the blade out with a coat of blood.

The next one ran at him faster, with an axe curling up to one side. Eli caught it along the bludgeon's handle, brushing it aside and landing a heavy punch against the soldier's helmet. A woman's voice cried out from underneath: stumbling back, she swung suddenly upwards, half-blind and without direction.

Caught off-guard, the Chief backstepped, grappling the bludgeon like a lever and hefting it skyward.

A crunch of bone sounded as it connected with the woman's wrist; there was a sheer, brutal agony in the screech that followed as she dispossessed the axe.

Eli stood back, gritting his teeth, and swung the bludgeon around his body—

Where the woman's neck, and all the connective tissue lodged between, snapped to the side like a door bust from its hinges.

And no noise escaped her lips as the light went out in her eyes, and she hit the floor moments later.

The Chief exhaled shakily, straightening his back, ignoring the twinges in his shoulders. Looking out on the wider square, darting from helmet to helmet.

To spy a squat figure with a short-sword and mean-looking eyes rushing toward him, readying their first attack.

Come and get it then.

The soldier lunged at his exposed flank like skewering meat, forcing Eli to suck his gut in to avoid being impaled. The Chief adjusted on his heels and swung his bludgeon in response, forcing the soldier to back-step and stumble over another soldier's corpse. It seemed to have a nullifying effect on them, to see the dead eyes of their comrade, as the next three strikes were limp and non-committal against the fury of Eli's weapon. Several more came and went with no clear direction, as the Chief dictated the fight with a commanding rigour, until the soldier swiped across in fear—

And the sword shattered completely in their hand, reduced to nothing in the blink of an eye.

Fearful suddenly, with recklessness swelling in their doleful eyes, the soldier ran at the Chief with hands extended, hoping to wrestle the weapon from him.

But Eli simply smiled, pulling the weapon back and launching it up into their gut, lifting the hapless figure from the ground. Legs bucking, squealing like a pig, the soldier rolled off the end and crashed hard across the stone, the blue-grey sky spinning high above. They lay splayed there for several moments in something of a daze, marvelling at the vastness of the world above.

Until a black shadow fell into his vision, like the sun falling from the heavens, and the soldier's skull exploded across the cobbles in an ooze of bone and brain.

The Chief of the Mountains heaved in great lengths of air, suddenly alone in a clearing of the battle with the clash of steel numb in his ears. Sweat stained, dusted and aching, twangs and spasms caught across his legs. The bludgeon lay heavy in his hands. The flow of battle formed like river currents, dicing all around. A cold wind seemed to catch at his face, gracing through from the east. In some far off place, he thought he heard a songbird chirping from a rooftop. And for a moment, there in the din of hell, it all just seemed so perfect.

What anarchy, he mused, caught in a ray of sunlight. *What anarchy and peace.*

He steadied himself, looking out to the clouds, preparing to sigh at the futility of man—

When a thrumming sound caught in his ear like twisted branches, and an arrow embedded in the meat of his shoulder.

Eli hissed through gritted teeth; he swore and sighed and growled. Grabbing at the shaft in an attempt to wrench it free, he felt the barbed ends of the arrow tear at his skin and threaten to draw more blood. Thinking better of it, he snapped the wood between his fingers and cast the remains to the floor, stamping them underfoot and leaving the arrowhead nestled in his arm.

Lucky shot, he scowled, retrieving his bludgeon and sighing at the pain now shooting across his collar. *And a potentially lethal one at that.* He looked over the scene of the battle, and saw the hungry eyes of idle soldiers lock on to him and begin their approach, with swords and axes glistening in their hands.

This needs to end quickly. Eli hefted his bludgeon and snarled.

And where's that bastard Ferreus?

†

I see you.

Jinx charted his path through the crowds: the silver wash of hair through the silver wash of steel, like a fish swimming upstream on a pearlescent river. Directing the attack; barking orders; snarling and snapping like a weasel. At one point pushing past two people, and driving a knife up through a young man's chest, twisting the blade deeper with a malice in his eye. A grin as he pulled the knife away, laced with gore, before discarding it and moving off again to cuff more soldiers and marvel at more wounds. General Ferreus, murderer and traitor one and all—

Just out of her line of sight.

Had I not the risk of killing some of our own, Jinx thought from the balcony of the baron's hall, *I would make no hesitation in ending you.*

She drew her gaze away, looking out on the wider battle below. The landscape was merciless carnage: the fighting broke out in waves, contracting and swelling, as the sun ticked by steadily overhead. From the bird's-eye as she saw it, much of the battle remained inconclusive. Skirmishes broke out in the wider streets. Reinforcements drew in from the sides, joining the crush of bodies to fill the gaps. Messengers trickled through the swarm of imperial soldiers, dispersing across the battle and then returning to the eastern road, relaying their reports to the command posts no doubt stationed somewhere beyond. *And they're probably all saying the same thing,* she concluded.

People are dying to no avail.

Jinx levelled her crossbow at the crowds beneath, and let one of the bolts whistle out across the square. With pinpoint accuracy, it reached a small opening that had appeared at the base of the pillar, and pierced a lonesome soldier in the throat as he cried out with glee. Reaching for his neck suddenly, gargling and retching, he crumpled to the floor like a stack of paper.

And Jinx couldn't help but smile.

A small victory, she concluded, loading another bolt.

But we can't do this for long.

She searched across the battlefield then, her heart in her throat, and exhaled with relief as she caught sight of a huge metal sphere arcing overhead and crushing a soldier's head into their neck. *There he is.* The bludgeon drew back, and she watched as Eli brushed his brow with the back of his hand and set to work on the next foe in his path.

It is good to see him fighting well, and leading his people with honour. She closed her eyes for a moment, looking back down to him and finding her chest knot. *But I can see it's also taking its toll...*

As the thought came, Eli hefted his weapon across his side and propelled a soldier six feet across the square, lost in the stampede of other fighters struggling to stay alive. It was an impressive feat, she had to admit – but as he recovered, Jinx noted how he drew his hand across his shoulder and found blood on his fingers.

That wound is going to get worse the longer this goes on, came the fearful cry of her mind. *He's in danger.*

We all are.

"Alva?"

She turned suddenly to the sound of her name: heat rose in her neck, as she watched Castan ascend the stairway, producing a broad and merciful smile.

"It's good to see you... I'm glad you're well and alive," he said softly.

"It's good to see you too. How come you're here?" she inquired.

"Well, Eli sent me to come and check if you were okay."

She frowned. "But I haven't seen you with Eli this whole time..."

He opened his mouth to respond, but his words seemed to fail him. Jinx saw a redness catch at his cheeks.

"Okay, so maybe *I* was the one who wanted to check if you were okay," Castan admitted.

Jinx felt her heart flutter. "And why is that?"

"To make sure you were alive and well, and to see if you needed anything. I remember you stressing to Eli that you were not entirely comfortable with facing a battlefield..."

"Very true," she cooed, smiling. "Although I believe I'm handling myself pretty well so far."

"Well, I've watched a few heads pop from the balcony and was starting to wonder if any of them were your doing."

"I may have had a hand in their demise."

"And you should not be second-guessed on that, I'm sure." He caught her gaze; something glistened there like gemstones, as he approached the window and looked out on the square beneath. "How are things looking from up here?"

"It's a shifting tide, but there's nothing definitive as of yet. Reinforcements keep arriving from either side to plug holes, so it's hard to say we're *winning* as such."

"I tell you, they're a bastard to try and break down, especially in circumstances like this."

"That being said, you can tell they're uneasy with how little progress is being made."

"What makes you say that?"

She stepped closer and felt the heat rising from his body. She found it comforting, almost. "They've had messengers moving through the battle more frequently as it's worn on," Jinx said, charting one such figure through the crowds with her finger. "All moving back along the eastern road… where I recently saw Ferreus scuttle away as well."

"I wonder what he has planned…"

"I'm thinking that too. I don't want Eli caught out in the open if something bad happens."

Castan stepped back, studying her as he bowed politely. "Then do allow me to report to him about what you've seen, my dear, so that your worries may be put to rest. I wouldn't want you fretting over him any longer."

She smiled back, imitating a curtsey. "Well how charming of you, good sir… please, by all means."

"My pleasure."

He turned and disappeared down the staircase, leaving Jinx to turn back to the window with a warm emanation in her heart. She looked over the battlefield below, crossbow in the crook of her arm, and sighed softly.

How charming of you…

†

To leave me in this fucking mess again.

Ferreus skulked down the eastern road with fire at his heels, snarling at every stray soldier and feeble messenger who passed him by. The road was effectively empty, with a few stray supply carts propped up against houses and snorting horses penned up along the outskirts. The ugly yellow-grey clouds overhead brought a muggy thickness to the air that sent streams of sweat down his spine. He despised it, as he shielded his eyes from the sun. He despised all of it.

I despise that military incompetence addles my every move, he grumbled to himself. *No-one seems to be able to get anything decisive done around here.*

And that the only solution to my woes, is an act that accepts failure.

He turned a corner sharply, entering a small courtyard where the red-green banners of Casantri swayed vigorously in the wind. A few gnarled trees curled up the walls at the edges; flower beds lay half-dead and sun-blistered along the skirting. The stones underfoot shifted like sand as he crossed over them, approaching the silver-red coats of the infamous palace guard with a pained feeling in his gut.

Anything but this…

"We wondered if we would see you again," the foremost guard said simply, crossing their arms.

"I am here regrettably, it should be known," Ferreus replied. "But as it so happens… circumstances mean that I must."

"The battle fares poorly?"

"The battle is going perfectly fine, *thank you*." He ground his teeth. "We simply require an additional touch to… *exterminate* the rebels in their entirety. They are treacherous bastards, and I want their throats cut at the earliest convenience. We've already suffered an hour in this heat…"

"Are we to engage then, sir?"

The general produced a sigh, punctual and self-defeating. "Yes, you are to engage now… so take your people and do what must be done to end this mess."

"Of course, sir," the leader said without a hint of smugness, inclining his head to the general.

With the signal given, the other guardsmen rallied around their leader and marched off toward the main road, swords glinting and malevolent in the low light. To watch them mobilise was as terrifying as it was impressive, Ferreus admitted.

And even more so, for the rebels that will face them.

"Officer?"

The lead guardsman turned to attention. "Yes, general?"

"If you find Eli, do gut him like a fish for me," Ferreus said with a grin. "I shall return him to the capital, and use his intestines to hang his husband's corpse over the city gates." He licked his lips. "I'm sure it would be most fitting to have them reunited in death..."

†

The Chief wiped sweat from his eyes, blinking into the wind, staring at clouds and the blur of the sun as it crossed midday and beyond. He saw crows circling high above, perching atop silent chimneys and peering into silent homes. He watched as they sensed the air, interpreting the violent human sounds that seemed to explode all around with intelligent charcoal eyes. They studied from their vantages a wide town square of baked stone and polished metal, where the blood of many dozens painted the land purple-blue. A dirty, forsaken thing, the enterprise of battle proved to be. But as Eli watched one of the crows circle down and rip a dead man's eye from their socket, he knew it was no crueller than nature could be.

And certainly just as careless.

Eli shifted the weight of the bludgeon across his shoulder and grimaced at the conflict still blooming before him, readying for the next attack. The battle had become disjointed now, with tight-nit clusters of tired and ill-functioning people thrashing it out like sea-waves. Bodies littered the floor; steel clattered underfoot; the stench of blood drew tears at his eyes. And still they fought on, two sides of the same coin with no sense nor feeling, and no time to spare.

And the sun continued to pass idly overhead, coated in a glean of cloud, indifferent to it all as it had always been.

How I envy you, for being so free, Eli thought quietly, looking down and locking eyes with a soldier who turned sharply to face him. *And here I am, battered and aching, in a blood-soaked square against the Imperial fucking Army of Provenci, with nothing to show for it but an arrow in the arm and breaches that stink like a cesspit.*

The enemy advanced.

And still they come again…

The soldier whipped their sword up and through, glancing off Eli's arm guard and skittering away. The Chief smirked, using the bottom end of his bludgeon to jab up into the man's chest. They buckled over, biting their tongue and squeaking with pain, snapping their blade up again to counter. Eli backstepped, the blade whistling past his nose, and brought his bludgeon across. A sharp crunching sound, and the metal ball broke across the soldier's side; they groaned, side-stepped and hobbled back, spasms seizing across their chest. Eli grit his teeth; he stepped forward and jabbed a fist into the soldier's nose like a bullet. The warm, oozy crunch of broken bone meshed between his knuckles. The soldier turned deathly pale, the colour of watery sick – stumbling backwards, tripping and falling, staring lamely off into the sky.

Blacking out moments later, as the falling bludgeon sent them to the stars.

The Chief pulled his weapon away with a nauseating squelch and leaned heavily against it, panting. There was a welting pain in his chest; the air filling his lungs tasted like sawdust. Knees buckling, he used the bludgeon almost as a walking stick, wincing at the shooting pains up his thighs. The thin column of wind sweeping across the battlefield did little to dissipate the heat, as sweat continued to peel down his spine and sting across his eyes. Hell on earth beckoned all around, and deep within his own soul. He sighed.

I'm too old for this shit.

He looked up, conscious of the battle still raging around him, and smiled suddenly at the sight of Castan approaching from the baron's hall. *Good lad, coming to give the old man a hand.* Eli watched him draw closer, a joy in his heart to see his second-in-command again.

But as the haze left his eyes, the Chief noticed Castan's expression, and felt a weight pull across his skin. Castan was waving at him, and he was shouting, and there was a deathly fear in his eye.

What are you trying to say? Eli listened closer, flinching, trying to hear past the dull ringing in his ears. The world around him was still spinning, all soft colours and ill-defined shapes.

Until there were footsteps, Castan approaching, and his words were suddenly clear.

As the great weight of something incredibly strong broke across Eli's back like a meteor.

The Chief was thrown forward, landing heavily, his weapon clattering at his side. Pain exploded across his shoulders; across his back; across his skull and bones and sorrow. Looking forward suddenly, he saw shadows form and weapons loom, a banner skimming the skyline somewhere behind—

The draw of a blade at his back, as Castan appeared to his side.

"We need to move sir, *now*," the officer whispered in horror, pulling Eli up under his arms.

"Why?"

"No time, sir."

"But what's going—"

"We've been looking for you, *Chief*."

Eli turned to the voice, watching the hazy shadows part across his vision. He saw armour suddenly manifest, all silver steel and red-green cloth. He saw sharp, curved, venomous things hanging loose in gloved hands. A dozen of them, fanning out to either side, studying him from beneath the guise of their tall helmets. His heart sank; something in his stomach opened like a rift in the earth. Stood there bruised and battered, quaking on his feet with his bludgeon as a cane, nothing seemed particularly useful at that moment.

Not when he was staring death in the face.

"Ferreus was hoping you'd still be here," the foremost guard cooed. "He wanted to send his regards."

"You keep back from him," Castan challenged, threatening with his sword. "I'm warning you."

A number of them scoffed; their leader stepped forward. "You'll need to do more than that to stop us from taking his head, *pretty boy,*" they said with a grin. "Now let's get this over with, and send you to the mud where you belong…"

Eli hefted his bludgeon, bellowing like thunder; the enemy charged toward him.

Chaos began anew.

†

Chapter 25

False Pretences

They say that the Acolyte's Tower is cursed, sir, did you know that? That... that there are things living in it, with fangs and claws that crawl out the walls and... and they tear your eyes from their sockets. It's horrible to think of, to think of those... *things* living there. I mean, people have gone mad when they behold the tower, so the stories say. They say that the gods have come to save them: fleeing hell to the heavenly sanctum. That from the sundial atop its roof, it is believed that one can see the passage to the afterlife. And... and people have *killed* for it, sir... soldiers and travellers alike, they've... *slaughtered* each other in the hopes of finding the sundial and attaining that power. To go to such lengths for nothing more than a myth... it's a madness, sir, a rot on the brain. I... I don't know what to do, really. I fear the place and the madness; I fear ushering its name." Oslo shivered, adjusting his collar. "It is said that the tower seeks out the souls of the undeserving, in its plight to claim the world, so that the deserving may live on as it's acolytes and seek out the dregs of hell. And I admit when I first heard that story, sir, I thought little of it. But now that we're here, in the depths of the Ozban itself... it does make one fear which side of that line we fall on..."

Revek grumbled in response, guiding his horse off to the right as it followed the narrow path north through the trees. They had been marching for several hours, passing along a dirt track with thin boughs and finger-like branches to either side. Arrow-shafts of sunlight danced through the canopy, breaching the perpetual shadow that marked the Ozban for miles across. Sixty bobbing heads marked the path ahead like a herd of sheep, swords steady in their hands, cautious eyes fixed wholly on what lay ahead.

And not the deep hell of what lay beyond.

It's simple really, to keep everyone safe, Revek mused, watching the uniform line snake ahead of him. *Give them easy orders: 'march forward, two abreast, follow the path'. Guide from the back, and let the scouts lead from the front. Give a disciplinary or two to even them out, and everyone does as they're told. It's simple.* A snorting, coughing rasp of breath at his side, and the commander rolled his eyes. *With the only issue being that, in this strategy, I have also landed myself next to the most annoying fucking man this country has ever produced.*

And will ever, if I have anything to do with it.

"Do you believe it's true, sir?" General Oslo said softly. "Only, I was hoping to hear your own thoughts—"

"There is no curse on that tower, any more than there is on the rest of this hell-hole," Revek spat. *Gods I wish you'd shut up.* "What drives people mad in this damn place is the false pretence that everything is under control. The stupid idea that we somehow *understand* this place, just because it has trees and human settlement. But there is no understanding a place like this, not even remotely. Because in a place like the Ozban there are only two modes of life: survival, or a long, suffocating death. And survival is a cruel thing in itself, out here. Survival is to live with your eyes to the floor, counting your blessings… knowing that any tree or any shadow – as much as any tower – can rip your soul from your skin in a heartbeat." He shook his head. "Because we are in hell, general… and there's no escaping it…"

"But surely there's a better way?" Oslo whimpered. "Surely there's a way to harness it… to tame a place like this?"

"And you'd be right: there is a way to harness it… but that does not make it tame in any respect. Because the secrets of this place, and the ability to harness it, are not held by those who bleed the same as we do…"

"The Tarrazi."

The commander nodded. "Only they can traverse this land without succumbing to its rot."

"How… *disconcerting*." Oslo's eye twitched.

"Indeed. In many ways, they are not unlike the acolytes in the story you spoke of: a plight on the world, guided by a great evil to bring destruction wherever they go…"

"Is that what happened to the main army, sir, last you came here? Did you fall to the same fate?"

"Well, I… I…"

As the words fell from his mouth, Revek drew his horse to a stop. A silence crept in on him, twisting like the wind. A great stillness surrounded them, like clouds parting in his mind.

As the rains thundered down suddenly, and the memory beckoned to life…

He saw hounds loping through the trees, big as bears: snarling, snapping, biting beasts tearing at the legs of his soldiers as they fell, scrabbling through the mud screeching terror. He saw as others were struck by arrows whistling through the trees, impaled in their skulls and vertebrae, with the black armour of the enemy shifting through the dark behind and gone again moments later. How one man screamed, staring off into the nothing in the depths of night, carving his own throat out with a pocket knife.

Succumbing to the hell of the Ozban.

And then one face picked out from the rest, crawling through the dirt beneath him: a young man, his legs savaged by a hound's great jaws, the pale-white of his face begging to survive.

The commander had sat there on horseback for what seemed an eternity, watching the tiny, ragged arms of a desperate corpse pull their way closer to him. He admitted, he had found nothing in his heart in the end, staring into his dead eyes. Because looking there, he only saw the truth: that kindness got you killed.

And cruelty got you killed slower.

So he had turned, guiding the horse away as arrows ripped across the canopy overhead and his men died all around him. He had traipsed off into the gloom with no direction, guided only by the screams of the dying man crawling through the dirt at his back, and the knowledge he would be dead soon.

And Revek, would not.

"Yes, general… we fell to the same fate," the commander said softly, spurring his horse on again through the columns of trees.

And the Ozban shall claim us all…

Several long miles had passed, marching through the forest in an unending line, before the first falsely-joyous call went up that they had reached the Acolyte's Tower. A sudden activity took hold of the line soldiers as they meandered through the trees: like a ship at sea with the wind suddenly in its sails, the entire battalion seemed to accelerate. Glowing eyes and relieved faces emerged, hungry to be free of the forest. Pressing on ahead toward their hope, with their commander watching them skitter off toward the light.

Knowing the truth was in fact far darker than they could ever imagine.

"Is this it, sir? Are we here?" Oslo asked sheepishly, watching the path open out before them onto a wide, dusted plain. "Is it… safe?"

"Yes, this is it… and no, it is not safe," Revek replied, shaking his head. "You *are* in the Ozban, general. Nowhere is safe anymore…"

Drawing their mounts into the light, they entered onto a wide plain of dry earth and strange, moss-like plants, which clung to the ruined cobbles half-buried underfoot like skin. A strangled stone wall marked the perimeter of the plain, with the roots of trees twisting between them and tearing them apart. Reclaiming what they had lost, so he perceived.

As if being here is an act of sacrilege.

Revek shivered, acknowledging the reclamation going on all around by the malicious hands of the forest. Where there had once been outhouses built by Provenci hands, there now lay only stone scraps and the mirage of old walls. Tents and their pillars had been eaten away by the clawing dissolution of weeds; the firepits that had been dug by their forebears were now little more than puddled holes, with the squirming shapes of parasites tracing across the water. The place was a mistake; a rot in the world. The commander studied it all with a steely eye and a brute lack of conscience, assessing the nightmare as it came, until his gaze finally drifted left and rose steadily skyward to behold the Acolyte's Tower in all its foreboding grace.

The tower stood alone on the empty plain with stone as black as night, appearing as the evil twin to the famed Citadel of Scripts. Its walls seemed to hum with intensity; the same vines of ivy as they had seen before snaked up the outside, curling up the stairway to the door like fingers. Tiny, flat turrets stuck out like teeth at its peak, where Revek was pretty certain he saw a skeleton dangling. And even then, several hundred metres away in the saddle of a stallion, he felt it call to him: the terrible pleas and promises of the tower demanding of his subjugation. Demanding acolytes and tributes; lusting for its blood and hate. Drawing him closer, closer again – until he drew his eyes away and shook his head, looking off toward the sun.

A terrible place, the commander concluded, dismounting his horse with a sigh.

We should never have come back here…

"It's remarkable, sir, to see such a… to be in such a place," Oslo muttered, dismounting his own horse and staring up at the Tower. "To see something so old, and so strange. Just think of the stories that reside in those stones… think of all it has seen, and all that it knows—"

"All it takes, and all it *poisons* too," Revek growled.

Oslo turned sharply, bristling, brushing himself over awkwardly. *Snapped out of a trance, almost.* "Yes, yes of course... a place like this can play tricks on you... and is certainly not something to take lightly," the general muttered.

"No, it is not." Revek smiled. *Although if you find yourself wandering sheepishly into the dark and get lost... I guess that's just fate in the end.*

"What should we do now, sir?"

The commander straightened his back. "We should set up camp in the open, away from the walls of the Tower and away from that ivy stuff we keep seeing. Don't organise any patrols, either; have everyone camped at the centre of this plain and have no one stray toward the trees whatever you do. We stay close, and we stay quiet, and we make a full assessment of the tower while the sun is still up. Because when dusk hits we need to return to camp and wait out the night with no fires..." A scream echoed off somewhere at their backs; Revek didn't even flinch. "This place wants to consume us as it is... let us not go lighting fires and disturb the shadows even more."

Or death is all that will await us.

Under Revek's guidance, and the looming darkness of the Acolyte's Tower, the camp assembled with a prodigious uniformity against the rising tide of dusk. Like a pupil at the centre of the plain, the tents were pitched inwards to face one-another, turning their backs on the dark trees of the great beyond where they hoped no one would wander. They had repurposed the stones of the old buildings wherever they could be found, trussing them to wood planks and crafting makeshift benches for the soldiers to rest their legs. It proved the only luxury that could be afforded, however: there was no room for fires between the tents, and all alcohol had been drained into pits, so as to deter the soldiers from making merry and drawing the enemy in from the dark. The few horses they had were given the freedom to roam as they wished – but, as the commander had expected, they stuck quite resolutely to the camp perimeter, skirting the edges of the tents with frightful snorts and the stamping of tired hooves. It had taken some time to accomplish such a task – and to meet Revek's ignominiously high standards – but as the soldiers lay down their tools and looked upon their completed camp, a certain joy passed among them that the job was finally done. That things could be safe, even if just for a few moments.

And they may yet survive to see morning.

We shall see what fate brings us, as night descends, Revek thought quietly, with the Tower looming uneasily to his left. *We shall see if this is enough to save them, when the true hell begins.*

And they won't even know what's coming…

He thought back to Lazaerys for a moment – how dismissive she had been, and how little she seemed to care about the dangers of the Ozban – and Revek found his concern conjure abruptly into hate.

These people have no idea what's coming for them… and they don't know because they've been lied to by that bitch and her merry-men, he scoffed. *Those who refuse to see the danger of what lies directly in front of them; those who think the Tarrazi are impish fools with no sense or tactical skill. I learned that they aren't the hard way, I will have the decency to admit… but even after that monumental fuck-up, they still don't believe it.* He ground his teeth. *To think I may well die in this godforsaken shit-hole, and what do I have to show for it? Nothing more than a bad attitude and a long list of people I want dead.* The tension in his jaw eased into a grin.

A long list that I plan to make shorter very soon…

"Sir!"

Footsteps approached to his left: one of the soldiers strode over from the tower draped in a woollen overcoat, with a grave, threadbare look worn heavy on his face.

"What is it?" the commander grumbled, unamused at the disturbance.

"We found something, sir," they replied plainly. "Thought we should let you know."

"Unless its dead or still breathing, it's not really my concern."

"Well, sir, I can assure you that what we've found is definitely dead... or rather, *they* are definitely dead."

Revek frowned. "What do you mean, *they*?"

"General Oslo said for you to see for yourself sir, it's... not something we can quite put into words."

He grimaced, and sighed in reply.

So be it.

Without acknowledgement, Revek marched past the man and made off toward the tower, passing under its looming shadow as a red-grey dusk set in behind. The soldier turned sharply and followed at his back, cautious not to draw level for fear of some reprimand that would see him hung by his guts come morning. The commander smirked as he reached the tower's door.

He's wiser than he looks.

Within the dark stone walls beyond, everything was a blur of motion. Soldiers in their thin cloth coats milled about tending to various duties, looking fearfully over to their commander as he entered in amongst them. A messenger skittered past and seemed to jump at the sight of him, bowing their head awkwardly and filing out the door again without a word spoken. Revek remained unphased and pushed his way through the crowds, locking eyes and scowling as he went until the general honed into range with a look of surprise on his face.

"Ah, commander! Thank you for coming so quickly. We've had something of an issue—"

"What's happened?" Revek growled, his face awash with disdain.

General Oslo frowned, chastened by the interruption. "We've found something, within this Tower sir. And it's not very... it's rather unsettling, sir, if we're honest."

"That's great *officer*, now can someone please explain to me what is—" An odour caught at his nose, pungent enough to skin a man alive. Revek's eyes began to water. "I... what the *fuck* is that?"

Oslo's face remained blank, his lips pursed.

Without blinking, he turned his head toward the north wall, gesturing to the far corner. "See for yourself, sir… if you can stomach it."

Revek sneered at the general and wiped at his eyes, before striding over to the north corner where the stench seemed to originate from. The soldiers parted as he approached, and a wide space opened out before him, where he noticed a large hatch was set into the floor with its door hanging wide open. Scrunching his brow, Revek peered over the edge of the hatch, to find it was nothing more than a black, indecipherable abyss plagued with grey morphing shadows. There was nothing that he could make sense of in the passage below. Nothing that seemed real. There was only the constant *pang* of dripping water beneath his feet – that, and the insufferable smell that plagued his senses with each uncomfortable breath.

"What's… down there?" he inquired, pulling a hand up to his face.

General Oslo said nothing as he approached, and made no sign of giving the answers that Revek sought. Instead, he turned to a soldier at his side, and took from them a glowing torch that crackled with an eerie orange glow. Holding the torch aloft over the open hatch, Oslo sighed breathlessly.

"See for yourself," he repeated, and dropped the torch below.

Revek looked down into the abyss and gasped.

What in the fucking gods…

Bodies everywhere. Dozens of them, lining the walls of the pit. Each lay half-mutilated: corpses of peeled skin and matted hair and snapped bone, like a grotesque spider puppet. Hollow sockets looked up from the shadows; the terrified expressions of those sentenced to death peered up toward them. Bony hands reached up toward the hatch in desperation; their blood painted the walls purple and black, oozing with old blood and residue. The stench of rot funnelled upwards in a chokehold, consuming their senses and churning their stomachs.

By the gods, the commander gawped in shock. *What could've done this…*

And then he saw it. At the centre, at the base, he spied a hole: a wide, perfectly circular tunnel, into which the torch descended like a star. It spiralled end over end, deeper and deeper into the earth to reveal more tunnels and burrows along the walls, where more bodies lay broken across the mud in ugly, brutish contortions.

Bodies, he saw, with the puncture wounds of fangs.

This... this isn't just a mass grave of our kin, the commander realised, his eyes bulging.

This is a creature's lair.

Revek stood back, steadying himself, his face pale and expressionless. Grabbing the edge of the hatch, he pulled the door closed with a single swing, and turned to Oslo slowly.

"We *never* should've come here..."

†

Chapter 26

Breadcrumbs

"What happened?"

Cavara stood at the attic window with her hands clasped behind her back, looking out on the beige walls of the City and the aquamarine sea just beyond. The mirror to her left was still spotted with water, and the sink beneath it had the pearly droplets of diluted blood around the rim of the plug. A mound of emplastrum flowers the colour of roses sat pressed against one of the taps, having been used to soak and clear the wounds laced across her knuckles.

Several hours had passed since the incident in the Tyrant's Bluff, and the image of Ptolemy's broken face had not shifted from her mind. It made the bruising and cuts across her hands throb with pain; it produced a churning sensation in her stomach like kneading bread. Looking out on the waters beyond with a great silence echoing through the house, the general had almost forgotten what the world was like outside that tiny attic room. It was only her, and the window, and the sink – and the distasteful consequences of her actions spinning through her head like silk. Knowing that what she had done, had been done with anger and bitterness: that her conduct had been untoward, even if the intent was still pristine. She had knocked a woman unconscious, and beaten a man to a bloody pulp, on the floor of an inn in the middle of the day. And even if the pain she had inflicted had been so thoroughly deserved, and part of her felt so good to have done it, *I don't know whether it was worth it.*

And I don't know if I'll die now because of it.

Cavara sighed, releasing her grip on the windowsill and turning to face the room beyond. She pursed her lips, trying to hide her disappointment, before looking over to the left-hand side where the Forgotten One stood waiting, their wandering eyes thoughtful and plain.

"I made a mistake," the general admitted, nodding slowly. "I let my anger get the better of me… and I let my grief take control… and now Ptolemy is in a medical chamber having his face stitched up, after I beat him to a pulp in broad daylight. It wouldn't half-surprise me if Amara is rallying support for my execution as we speak…"

The Forgotten One held their lips still for several moments. "I see," they eventually said. "That is a problem."

"And now I don't know what to do. I'm frozen here, lost in a daze, just waiting for the city guard to march up those stairs and drag me away to be killed. I'm expecting as much. Either that, or they take me out in chains and set me loose in the forests, letting Amara's dogs have the final say on if I live or die." She shrugged hopelessly. "I know what I did was wrong… I know it was stupid, and callous, and driven by my guilt at losing Evelyn. And I know, equally, that there will be consequences for that. But what that looks like, I don't know… I have no idea if I'll even be alive come morning."

With a patient gaze, the pale figure nodded and closed their eyes, letting the silence ebb out for a while. "You fear the repercussions, because you know that they will come," they explained. "You fear death, more so than normal, because you believe that will be all that is left for you. And, perhaps, under different circumstances, you would be entirely right in that assumption. Brutalising an honorary guardsman of the Alderbane is, I imagine, quite a damning offence. But, Cavara, these are not ordinary circumstances… and you are no ordinary subject." They looked past her, off to the blue skies outside. "No matter what you have done, and who you have done it to, the

Alderbane will never give the order to end your life. You are far too important – and far too *dangerous* – to be killed or exiled. To kill you, would be to extinguish this power you have and the potential benefits the Alderbane may get; to exile you, would be to hand that power over to another... and we both know they are far too paranoid to allow that."

"But I don't understand: what power do they hope to gain from me being here? What does the Alderbane expect of me, if they go to such great lengths to keep me alive? What do they know?"

"They *don't* know... and that's the point. *That* is your power, and how you will stay alive in this place. No-one here knows what being the Successor to the All-Mother actually means, nor what importance that carries – and neither do they need to know. It is an illusion to them, one that they fear. And so long as they believe you are powerful but don't know to what extent, then you will never come to any harm under the Alderbane's command."

Cavara considered. "I suppose that's true."

"Although, with that being said, there is also another side to that coin," the Forgotten said forebodingly. "The Alderbane may not wish to bring any harm to you, it is true... but be wary of those who do not express such restraint, and would not fear running you through with their blades."

"You think the honour guard would go against the whim of their leader?"

"I believe any mortal with an inkling of corruption can do foul things, even if it goes against direct orders. I mean, you've been victim of that yourself."

The knotted wound across her stomach tugged under her chest guard as they said it, reminding her of a time long-past that she had almost consigned to fate. Cavara bristled and squared her shoulders. "That is also true," she replied. "Although I doubt Ptolemy and Amara would be capable of something like that. They are maniacal, yes... but to murder me against the Alderbane's will, while an actual Tarrazi assassin stalks these streets? No, I don't think they would."

The pale figure inclined their head. “Very well, you make a good point. But I would still exercise caution: for a snake will only bear its fangs when it’s close enough to kill.”

“Understood.” *Although I’m afraid of what you mean.*

“But, anyway, enough of that. There’s something I’ve been meaning to show you – or rather, there’s something I’ve been wanting to *teach* you.”

Cavara frowned. “*Teach* me?”

“Yes… to teach you something rather important in your understanding of the Rapture. And also something that will prove imperative in locating this assassin, and in turn your young friend.”

“Okay, good… yes.” Her heart ballooned at the thought of seeing Evelyn again. “What is it?”

“It would be easier if I showed you, Successor.” They turned to the staircase, gesturing for her to follow. “So, if you would… let us go to the street outside and see if we can find what I’m hoping to discover.”

“And what is that, exactly?”

The Forgotten One smiled.

“Breadcrumbs.”

Breadcrumbs?

They had navigated down several alleyways into the quieter parts of the City, with a burgeoning sun bathing the world in golden rays. The Forgotten One had not spoken, nor made any indication of their destination, until they appeared in a small square between several blocks of houses and drew to a sudden halt. The general had looked around them – studying roof-tops and gutters, and staring down a particularly quizzical alley cat – before admitting she was completely at a loss. There was nothing around her that seemed significant, and nothing that provided any answers to the Forgotten One’s cryptic words.

What do they mean?

"So, why are we here?" she inquired, looking up to the pale figure's content expression.

"As I said before," the Forgotten One boomed, "we are in search of breadcrumbs. A trail, to catch a thief."

Cavara frowned. *Do they mean that literally?* She looked to the floor almost on instinct, in search of some sort of debris, before cursing herself for thinking it was that simple and looking up into the sky. "Where would we find these 'breadcrumbs'?"

They paused, as something close to a smile graced their face. "What if I told you, that there was a way of tracking people through the Rapture who have passed by recently? As if they had left footprints in snow, just waiting to be found..."

"Is that a thing?" the general said in disbelief. "Can I do that?"

"I believe you have a firm enough grasp of the void and its powers to do so, yes. But it is not something that is done easily, let me warn you."

"How so?"

"Because the tracks that you will find, are called a 'spirit-trail'. They are the impressions that a soul acquainted to the Rapture leave behind when they traverse the void. You leave them when you enter the void, and so do I."

"Do you think that's how the transmitter found me the other day?"

The pale figure considered. "Most likely, yes. I imagine they stumbled upon your trail by accident and followed it to it's source, thus being able to target you and draw you into their Rapture."

"And why is following such a trail hard to do?"

"Because you are looking for remnants of a person's actual *soul:* you, a physical being, are looking for a spiritual impression in an otherworldly void. To bridge that gap requires an incredible amount of power and concentration, and can be very dangerous if misused." They inhaled slowly. "Which is why I have brought you here."

"Where is *here?*"

"A place to begin, where half the task is already complete," the

Forgotten One explained. "So, please, step into the Rapture and let me show you what I mean. To see it, is to understand it best..."

Cavara nodded, fearful and unsure of what the pale face meant. *A dangerous power.* The world seemed to sharpen around her. *Looking for the impressions of another's soul.*

Her mind drifted for several moments as if caught out at sea, before she sensed the sudden numbness coursing at her finger-tips, and the darkness rose to meet her in its enveloping embrace.

~

"Welcome back."

Cavara inhaled slowly, taking in the void once again: the ribbons of grey and sunlit gold dancing through an ethereal gloom, with the lines and etchings of houses occupying quiet spaces.

"It's always strange being back here," Cavara echoed, tensing her hands. "To be both lost, and yet completely at home. I don't know if I'll ever get used to it."

"It becomes easier, over time," the Forgotten One rumbled next to her. "When the Rapture reveals more of its mysteries, things become clearer. But such things take time, of course. As you like to say, 'nothing is ever easy'."

She allowed herself a smile. "That sounds about right."

"But, you are becoming accustomed to your powers a lot faster than I was previously expecting, so perhaps the process will not be as long for you."

"We can only hope." She sighed. "Part of me still thinks this is all a dream."

"How so?"

"Part of me still thinks I'm in some vivid nightmare, and that one day I'll wake up back in Casantri with the king still alive and no war at our borders. That everything that's happened – my betrayal; the All-Mother's kiss; the Room of Shadows; the shadow woman – will simply cease to be, and I can go back to the life I had and not have to deal with any of this anymore..."

"You want your life to be peace once again."

"I do, yes."

"But do you think that life will be enough, with everything you've come to

learn now?" the Forgotten One asked.

"What do you mean?"

"Say you woke up from this dream, and everything was back to the way it was… would you really feel the same as before? Going to council, and seeing the faces of people who vaulted themselves into power and butchered hundreds of innocents. Hearing talk of the Mothers in quiet drinking dens, speculating realities that you know to be true. Watching every report from Tarraz come in, awaiting the day that everything goes silent and the ships come for your harbour again. Seeing the man who betrayed you, and the officer who gave the order, knowing that they never did such a thing in reality, but that in their hearts they could so easily do it again." The pale face looked to her. "Peace, Cavara, is when ignorance becomes a way of life. When acknowledging the facts is second to keeping everyone happy. And whether you stand in a dream or not right now, doesn't really matter: for you have experienced just how much is at stake in this world, and just how easily this 'peace' you desire can be broken by idle hands and petty tyrants. You have seen the truth through the reeds now, because of it. You understand human nature and its cruelties in so many ways, because of your experience as Successor to the All-Mother. And I believe, genuinely, that if this were a dream and you were to wake up one day to a life as it was… you would feel even worse than you do now. To watch the world collapse around you like you always knew it would, but not having the power or fate intertwined to stop it and make things right for all. Because peace is when ignorance becomes life… and bliss is only denial of the inevitable."

Cavara blinked when the Forgotten One had finished, and realised her hands were shaking violently at her sides. A swelling in her stomach rose and fell, as if she were about to throw up. She inhaled noisily through her nostrils, steadying herself, calming the shudders that coursed down her body. Her mind spun on an axis, fearing what she now understood. What the truth of the matter really was: that this was the only path for her now, and that life could never be how it had once been. That she knew too much – understood too much – to go back to a life of naivety and bliss. That there would always be doubts in her mind, now, and she would spend her life fearing the worst. That in the end, the fate she had been bestowed as Successor came almost as a blessing.

Knowing that peace would in fact be so much worse.

"I apologise, general, I... did not mean to upset you or cause you alarm," the Forgotten One muttered, a genuine sadness in their eyes. "It appears I may have said too much..."

"You haven't, I promise you," Cavara replied stoically, finding balance on her feet again. "Because, in the end... you are right. I cannot honestly go back to the way things were. I can't go back to a world where everyone is ignorant to the realities; knowing the end is nearing but doing nothing about it. It would sicken me, and... and drive me insane. As you said, I think I would feel so much worse than I do now if this ended up being just a dream. Because I'd go back to a life feeling utterly hopeless, seeing the truth written across everyone's face... knowing I could do nothing about it, when the inevitable finally came."

"I am glad you see it that way, Successor – it is something I've been meaning to discuss with you for some time now, because I know how much of a connection you hold to your past life. I'm just sorry I caused you such distress in doing so."

Cavara opened her hand out and pressed it against the pale figure's robed arm. "You know, for a big demi-god with unimaginable powers... you can be a right softie sometimes."

They smiled, with a look almost amounting to a blush. "I only have you to thank for my grasp of human emotion. I have not been well-acquainted to it before."

"Well, if I'm your teacher in that regard, then gods' save us all." Cavara allowed herself a laugh. "You'll end up being stubborn, pig-headed and rude in no time."

"You do yourself a disservice, general... you are so much more than that."

The general smiled, gazing up into the moons of their eyes. "Thank you, my friend... that means a lot."

They imitated a bow. "It is my pleasure, Successor, I assure you."

Cavara nodded, looking down at her feet with a friendly warmth in her chest, as if a thousand of her problems had been solved in one and the air was now that bit fresher. "Now, anyway... to the task at hand," she said, scanning the floor beneath her. "How does one locate a 'spirit-trail'?"

"Well, in the same way as if one were looking for footprints," the Forgotten One replied. "Find the tracks, and follow their path."

"So, in that same line of thought, you're saying that if I just..." The general lifted her foot, and almost gasped at the strange, blueish impression her boot left in the void beneath her. "That's so strange... have I always left footprints like that?"

"You have, although your limited grasp with the Rapture has hidden them from your sight so far. So the fact that you can see them now, means my theory must be true... and your powers are growing."

"Incredible." She stood in bewilderment for a few seconds. "So, the transmitter's spirit-trail looks exactly like this, and I would be able to see it if I found it?"

"Precisely so, Successor. Exactly the same as this."

"Okay... where should I start looking?"

"Well, that much is the easy part, because although it may take the fun out of it, I've done you the service of locating one of their paths already, so as not to put too much mental strain on you following your first trail." They gestured with an outstretched hand. "It is actually in this square, somewhere right in front of you."

The general frowned. "There's... how...?"

Cavara craned her neck like a stork, as if the trail would just reveal itself to her at whim. She found her gaze focusing on the impression of a stone wall opposite, with an alleyway snaking off to either side. With a biting intensity that caused a pinching pain in her temples, she was able to focus in and pick out each individual block of stone before her, and each huge slab wedged in the earth just beneath. It was an unusual observation, seeing everything so white-washed and grey-scaled. She realised she was squinting to try and take it all in. The pinching sensation intensified the longer she looked, almost as if she weren't meant to see what she was finding.

Until she saw a blueish tinge on the floor just ahead of her, and the pains began to ease in her mind.

"There," she exclaimed, pointing to the marks and stepping forward.

As she approached, the impressions became clearer, and the blueness intensified until they almost mirrored her own steps. At first, she wondered if there was some mistake, and if the footprints beneath her were actually her own from a previous journey. But as she studied them closer, she realised they were much wider than her boot, and passed with a far bigger stride than she could manage.

"These are from the transmitter."

"They are, yes. And they seem to head off to the right here down the side-streets," the Forgotten One said. "I wonder where they go."

Cavara smirked.

"Only one way to find out..."

Turning right, with the pale figure like a ghost at her back, she paced off down the half-realised alleyways pursuing the spirit-trail at their feet, a sudden hope building in her heart at the thought of finding Evelyn and setting things right again. As the walls reared up around her in smudges and loosely-defined lines, she imagined Evelyn's tired, lost face trapped behind them crying out to be freed. How confused he must have been; how scary everything had become. Cavara feared for him: feared for his life and his safety. That he may never get out. That he may never see his mother again.

And all her efforts would be for nothing.

She inhaled softly, tempering the pain in her skull as she pursued the blue marks, which continued to snake on through the City ahead with no signs of stopping. The general noticed as she walked how the transmitter's gait would change occasionally: how they drew closer together at street corners to survey the path ahead, and shifted sideways every so often to let someone pass. The steps were sporadic, heading in an indeterminate direction, but there was one thing she knew for certain: that wherever they were going, they had a destination in mind.

"How are you faring?" the Forgotten One asked.

"Well... the pain is minimal, if that's what you mean," she replied, turning another corner.

"That's good, I am most pleased to hear that. And, from a casual observation, it would appear our transmitter is walking at quite a pace through these streets, so you're doing well to keep up with them and follow the trail with such ease."

"It's because I don't focus in on the footprints themselves: I'm only following the blueish tinge they leave in the void beneath us. It requires less concentration that way."

"Very intuitive, Successor."

"Although, it may start to put a strain on me if we're gonna be covering as much ground as we are currently. This trail seems to go on for miles..."

They passed down two more alleyways and crossed a wide thoroughfare where the smudges of people shifted past in angular, disjointed motions. They wore hazy impressions as she passed them, with shivering eyes and trembling lips. She heard the tiny pinpricks of their voices, too: echoing and broken, as if they were talking through glass panes. She marvelled at just how unreal everything was – at how alien the simplest things seemed to be. How she was sweating, but saw only a faint golden glow in the sky where the sun should've been; how she passed under shadows, but nothing seemed to darken in her eyes to prove it; how she could put her own hand out in front of her to see something so perfect and defined, and yet from the waist down she appeared as nothing but a ghost traversing a forgotten plane.

The general seemed lost in thought for several moments, suddenly overwhelmed by the world around her, when she looked down and realised the spirit-trail at her feet had slowed.

And how a few paces ahead, it disappeared altogether.

"What?" Cavara spat, studying the area where the trail ceased to exist.

"What is it?"

"The trail disappears here – look."

The Forgotten One stood alongside her and studied the ground, frowning profusely. "How unusual..."

"It doesn't make any sense."

The pale figure looked closer, assessing, before a coy smile appeared on their face. "Ah... I see."

"What is it?"

"It is not that the spirit-trail has disappeared: rather, that it has left our visible range."

"How do you mean?"

"The footprints turn left at the last second – see here? – and then if you

look closely, there's half a step disappearing behind this wall here."

Cavara followed his indication, and looked up to the grey surface beside her. "Which means, if they've passed through here... then this isn't actually a wall..."

The general put her hand out and placed it against the grey, where the void seemed to pulse and ripple like waves around her fingers. Sensations burst against her palm suddenly: she was touching something cold and hard and smooth, and definitely not stone.

"A doorway," she deduced, looking back to the Forgotten One. "This must be where the transmitter is hiding out." She paused. "How do we get in? Do we need to break in?"

"No, Successor... nothing as callous as that is required. The easiest way to get through this door, is actually using the powers you have."

Cavara frowned. "I don't follow."

"Well, something you should know about the Rapture, is that nothing in this realm is physical like it is in the real world: everything is just an impression *of the real world," the Forgotten One explained. "It holds some of the same qualities, but not all of them. You can see where walls should be, or where people are in the real world, but they're not actually* there. *It's all a projection of what your mind is seeing. And, because of that, there are certainly rules that can be... bypassed, shall we say, in this realm compared to your own."*

"Okay." She stood puzzled for some time, trying to make sense of it. "So this is not a door... it's just where my brain knows a door should be?"

"Precisely so."

"So, if that's the case and this realm isn't physical, then can't I just... you know, walk through walls?"

"Not quite: remember, even though this is only an impression of the real world, it still follows some *rules. For example, a wall is still a wall in the Rapture: a flat, immobile surface that you cannot pass through. But doors, like the one you see before you, are more unique. Because a door has hinges, and can be opened, the Rapture responds differently when it encounters one: as the impression of working hinges and locks are too complex, the void just registers every door as being permanently open."*

"So the Rapture can only project simple shapes and environments, but can't project anything more than that?"

"Correct."

"And whatever door I encounter in this realm... I can just walk straight through it as if it isn't there? Like walking through curtains?"

The pale figure nodded, gesturing to the door in front of her. "And that means that the impression you see here, does not actually exist at all. It's just a projection your mind has made of what a door should look like... not how it works."

Cavara nodded, impressed. "Well, if that's the case..."

She stepped forward and pressed into the impression of the doorway, which she found to be viscous and heavy like walking through honey. She pressed through with her hands, pushing her knees up and out like mounting a fence. The whites and greys of the void around her pulsed chaotically as her head breached through, and somewhere in the space behind she heard the Forgotten One cry out in wavering tones.

Then sharp spikes were bristling up her spine, and the impression of the doorway collapsed behind her. A darkness lurched at her feet, biting at her ankles, forcing a silent scream from her lips as she fell, spilling out with nothing left to give.

And the void rose to consume her whole.

~

Cavara collapsed onto a flat stone floor like a lead weight, her hands jutting out just in time to stop her nose caving into her head. The air snapped from her lungs; a coughing splutter escaped her lips as the numbness receded, and an over-sensing reality flushed back across her skin like mites. Several seconds passed where she had no understanding of the world at all, sprawled across the cold stone wheezing quietly.

Then her mind spurred to life like a bolting horse, and air funnelled through her chest, and her eyes bulged as she realised where she was and just how serious things had become.

Fuck!

She threw herself to her feet and unsheathed the blade tucked neatly at her side. Stumbling for a moment, she found her footing, scanning the room ahead—

To find seven hooded figures turn towards her and pull knives from the folds of their robes, approaching her from all angles like a pack of hungry wolves.

Cavara tensed suddenly, biting her lip; she flexed the sword in her hand. The ceiling seemed to pull in above her.

Hell broke loose.

†

Chapter 27

Champion's Scream

Savanta had just settled down for a few hours of elusive sleep, down in the depths of her subterranean chamber, when the blackcoat guards had shouldered their way in and told her she must ready her weapons. At first she thought, rather surreally, that Val Azbann was under attack, and that she could finally display her prowess with a blade against whatever aggressor had come at the surface. She had gone for the knife hidden under her pillow with a childish glee just thinking of it. But as she went about putting her armour on and fastening straps into place, she realised the guards who had woken her had no sense of urgency to their request, and that the look they wore was not one of impatience and fear, but was instead one of disdain and boredom. The Champion's shoulders had slouched, as the truth finally bubbled in her mind: that this was not the call to action she had been hoping for. That this was not a chance to prove herself, and finally make something of the title she had earned. This was just another game, orchestrated by a ruthless Queen. Another test of her patience and will, as she was ground under the thumb of a tyrant.

And in the end, all she did was laugh.

For what else was there to do?

So she had followed them once again into the labyrinth of hell, descending down wide stairways big enough to house giants, as the air grew thick and still. There was a heaviness in her lungs, as if they were coated with phlegm. Her skin seemed to crawl like the legs of giant centipedes. Her eyes could hardly adjust to the darkness that consumed her, where she was guided only by the glint of the blackcoats' armour, and the pale, unrelenting moons of their eyes. She was so desperately alone, in the labyrinth of hell.

All the while wondering where it would end.

And the answer came suddenly, when it finally did: stopping abruptly along a narrow corridor, near enough falling into the guard who led them. Savanta goggled in confusion at first – wondering why, of all the places, they had reached their destination there – before she turned to the right as the black-coats did, and observed an old iron door with intricate locks and hinges addled with rust.

Where the hell are we? She scowled, squaring her jaw. *Why am I in this fucking place? What's the point?*

The guards alongside her offered no answers or explanation; the right-hand one reached around to their belt and unhooked a bronze key from its chain.

Is this a cell? Some kind of holding pen?

Why the fuck am I here?

With a single twist of the key, the blackcoat unlocked the door, and pushed it gently open to reveal an unusual orange glow just beyond.

"Enter," they exclaimed plainly, without meeting her eye. "The Queen awaits you."

"Where am I going?" she spat.

"To learn a lesson, *shlaktum,*" the other guard scoffed. "Now go."

Savanta baulked, wondering in a mutinous part of her mind how easy it would be to stab the two guards to death where they stood. Imagining the blood as it leeched from the bodies; imagining their savage eyes roll into their heads as she plunged her blade deeper...

No point. A waste of my time. She pressed a hand against the door. *There's only person I'm here to kill.*

She stepped into the light.

And I hope it fucking hurts when I do.

Savanta entered out into a long tunnel that smelt of damp earth and faeces, with an orange glow like the dawn sun exploding across her vision at the far end. Passing from the depressing corridors into the brilliant light sent stabbing pains through her eyes suddenly; she hid her gaze behind an outstretched hand and studied the sooty earth at her feet. The dusted floor was the colour of charcoal, diced with prickling black stones; the walls of rust-coloured rock around her morphed as if they were made of clay. It looked natural, almost, compared to the Azbann keep at her back. Part of her almost believed that she was back at the surface. But as she approached the end, and laid eyes on what was beyond, the Champion understood that such a belief was a farce.

And that there was nothing natural about a place like that, destined for the damned.

She entered out into an ancient arena carved into a massive cavern, with the jagged ceiling above so impossibly high and coated in layers of shadow. The echoing notes of dripping water quivered across the cavern like a bowstring, reverberating between the walls and around the canal of her ears. All around her, the mud-brown stone had been carved to look like turrets, spearing up and into the walls in strange contortions; the shimmers of precious ores laced their way through them in shades of granite and amber. Along the wall's upper reaches, massive bone horns had been embedded into the rock to deter things from escaping – but what exactly could escape over the ten-foot walls in such a place, Savanta dreaded to think.

And considering the dusted ground beneath her, and the pinkish-blue tint to the sand, she had a feeling she would be encountering such hellish creatures very soon.

What is this place? Another arena? the Champion scoffed. *I've done my share of pit-fighting. I don't have time for this. Have I not proven myself already?* The knife hilt was comforting at her side. *Yet more games at the hand of her majesty, forever testing my patience—*

"Hello, Champion."

Savanta jumped, turning suddenly to her left to find the Iron Queen propped up against the wall, flicking at her nails like a disinterested cat. A coy smile marked her lips under the orange glow of torchlight.

"Care to explain what all this is about?" the Champion said with a grimace, gesturing to the arena. "I thought I was done with the pit fighting."

"Apologies for the misunderstanding, of course," Gaza replied mockingly, "but some things need to be addressed first."

"What more could you possibly want from me?"

"Oh, dear, your ignorance is so *pretty*."

"I've earned my right to be here, have I not? To stand before you as your Champion… what more do you need? All this about 'burning the world for you', and yet here I am wasting my time."

The Iron Queen shifted to a stand. "This is not about your place as my Champion: in fact, none of what you've experienced here so far has been. As you say, you've earned that right already. So this is for something very different… and something I'm very much looking *forward* to."

Savanta tensed her hand around the knife-hilt. "What do you mean?"

"Well, you have met many challenges so far, my dear, and have bested them all at every turn…" The Queen paced forward, circling her. "But I do wonder, all the same, what will happen when the enemy *within* finally hunts you down…" She stopped directly opposite her. "I wonder what will happen, when the only thing left between you and ultimate power… is your own *shadow*…"

Gaza stepped aside; Savanta's eyes locked to the arena behind her.

And there she saw her father, ambling across the pit, with a sword hanging deftly in one hand and his head held low in shame.

"*What?*" the Champion gasped. "No, I—"

She looked beside her to find the Iron Queen had gone, disappearing without a trace once again. And with her absence came the foul realisation that there was only the fighting pit ahead, and the form of a man who had broken her soul shuffling slowly towards her.

I can't do this. Savanta sensed nausea rise in her chest. *I can't do this. I can't. Or I don't think I can. I don't think I… or…*

Or is this exactly what I've wanted all along?

The Champion raised her arms, looking between him and the wider arena. "So this is it? This is where we finally meet to talk again? In a *fighting* pit, with a sword in your hand? You've got to be *joking…*"

"It is as the Queen commands," her father said glumly, never lifting his gaze.

"*'As the Queen commands'*? You're not her fucking dog."

"It is respect."

"Respect? *Respect*? You abandon your family and traipse off to kiss the feet of the enemy, and you stand here and tell me of respect? Who leaves their child like that, not even twelve winters'-old, to mourn their supposedly-murdered father with only his butchered ear as a token? It's cruel, and foul… so don't you *dare* tell me of respect."

"I did what I had to…" He lifted a hand and coughed violently, the crackle of his lungs like charred wood. "I *survived* you."

Savanta grit her teeth. "You *sicken* me."

"And you disappoint me."

She drew her knife, a beautiful shimmer of light catching along its blade. Hate burned in her eyes. "Why is that then, you *bastard?*"

"That you are still, after all these years… a pestilent *child.*" Her father raised his hood, laying eyes on her for the first time. The intensity of his stare hit her in the chest like a gut-punch; he seemed uncaring, and if anything slightly amused. "Always blaming others… always so hungry. Naïve. Futile. Fifteen years… you are still the same. Nothing more than a desperate hound… baying for blood."

"I am not the desperate one here, I promise you that. I'd rather have forged my own path and risen from the ashes… than to be a morally-corrupt pet locked away in a dungeon at the hands of a sick tyrant."

"I have played my cards, and I feel no shame for it." He manipulated his sword against the torchlight. "Can you say the same?"

"The only shame I feel, *father,* is that I wasted so much time mourning you when it meant nothing. You did not deserve an ounce of it… and you deserve nothing but hate now."

"These are just words," her father rasped, clutching his chest. "Just words…"

Savanta snarled, stepping forward. "Then how about I show you what happens, when my words become concise fucking *actions*, hm?" She stepped forward, imitating strikes with her knife. "Let's see what fifteen years of grief does to a woman, when she meets a decrepit little shit like you again…"

Despite being shrouded in shadow, she saw her father smile under his hood. He lifted his blade to his chest.

"Do your *worst*."

Savanta hesitated, the knife wavering at her side, allowing a space for her father to strike and force her to back-step away. Snapping from her trance, she lunged out toward his stomach, bringing the knife across to deflect his blade. It skittered away, allowing her a space to cut through and slice a ribbon from his robes – but before she could press the advantage and draw blood, her father started circling her, managing the distance between them with sweeping steps just out of range of her knife.

The Champion mirrored him, studying his movements: how his left leg limped slightly with each step, and how the degeneration in his right hand meant it was unsuitable to handle a blade. A quiet smile graced her lips.

If I can wound his hand, then he'll be forced to relinquish his blade, she analysed, moving closer to her father.

And then I can slit his throat, like the fucking traitor he is.

Like a viper, she struck out and twisted her knife toward his hand; her father circled with his sword, and sliced a hole in the fabric of Savanta's cloth shirt, a hairsbreadth from her flesh. The Champion spat and brought the knife up again toward his chin, hoping to embed it under his jaw. Before she had a chance to connect, however, her father angled his own blade in toward her liver and Savanta lurched backwards, her boots skidding against the dust underfoot.

She allowed no time to recover, as she bellowed and lunged out again toward his chest, skimming past his outstretched blade with surprising ease. Her father side-stepped, grunting with irritation, as Savanta's knife twisted in to try and spear his ribs. A heartbeat, and she looked ready to end his life; another, and she was twisting away, spying the dancing shadows above as his sword plunged down toward her head.

That was close.

The Champion found herself behind her father, manoeuvring faster than he could manage, and took the opportunity to strike: with a single, punishing kick like a horse, she lashed out into the back of his knee, and the responding crunch of bone showed she had met her mark.

Her father buckled, stumbling forward, dragging his left leg with no strength left to give. Using his sword as a walking-stick, the dereliction of his body finally showed its true colours. How old and frail and broken he was; how bitter he had become. Savanta had known the fight would not last more than a few moments. She had known just how old and weak her father had become, trapped away in the dark and desperate recesses of the palace keep.

It almost made her wonder why they had fought in the first place.

"You talk of naivety..." Savanta paced around him, studying him: the pain in his eye and the hateful glow of his skin. "You talk of all bark, and no *bite*..." She swiped his sword away with her boot, and watched him topple head-long into the dust, a shuffling mass of robes trying to turn onto their back. "And yet you are here, beneath me, broken and lost, because you have been *bested* by me wielding nothing more than a knife. How *pathetic*..."

Her father rolled onto his back, coughing painfully, his hood pulled back to reveal the horrific, threadbare skin around its sockets and the cavities across his cheeks. There was a grotesque absence of life in his face; she envisioned a reanimated corpse clinging to each breath as if it were their last. It disgusted her, more than anything.

He disgusted her.

"I hope it was all worth it," she scoffed. "I hope the pain you have caused was worth it in the end. I hope you can look me in the eyes here, and think on your sins as I embed this knife in your skull and watch that fucking *despair* drip from your eyes." She paused. "And oh, I hope it hurts..."

She loomed over him like a wraith and raised the small curved blade above her head, studying his dour expression with fifteen years of venom in her heart.

"When you die, I hope you know it was your daughter who killed you, and that I savoured every *moment* of it."

Her father looked up then, catching her gaze, and managed half a smile. "Perhaps... I would," he spluttered, pursing his lips.

"But you are no daughter of *mine*."

Savanta baulked, her soul shattering in her chest. An empty vacuum opened up and threatened to swallow her whole.

Until the anger swelled through her like the torrents of a storm, and the tears forming at the corners of her eyes vaporised against her cheeks. She opened her mouth, releasing a scream that shook the very walls of the cavern above, and drove the knife down toward her father's head.

Plummeting.

Hate in her eyes.

Meeting its mark—

A sword sweeping in and batting it aside, inches away from her father's face.

Savanta, wide-eyed, looked up to her left where the blade had struck from, spying steel boots and black leather bracings and elegant hands laced with rings.

"So close, Champion," Gaza said with a grin.

Savanta felt something connect with her temple, and the world went suddenly black.

"And yet so far..."

†

Chapter 28

The Hatch

Silence, echoing out over the Ozban Forest.

Dusk set along the horizon, an orange glow like candlelight bleeding across the sky. The shadows, black as coal, thickening between the pale trees. The rustles and whispers of their twigs and leaves, setting the dead to sleep.

An opening, amongst the vastness of trees, where a sombre camp lay still. No fires were alight between its encampments; no merry songs echoed out. The horses at the far edge held their heads low in mourning as the night set in. And, sat huddled at the very centre of the camp, the soldiers studied each other with twitching hands and nagging swords. Gazing up, looking out across the sky as it grew suddenly darker, and the looming shadow of the Acolyte's Tower swamped the camp completely.

Under the moon's eye, a figure crossed towards the Tower with long, purposeful strides. Their eyes like a hawk's, piercing the gloom. Leaving the camp unnoticed, crossing the threshold to the Tower; ascending the thin stairway with hands clasped at their back.

Disappearing within without a whisper.

Inside, the crunch of metal on soft stone. The pitter-patter of water trickling down walls. The strange, ominous howl of the wind, biting through cracks in the old structure.

The figure stepped forward, approaching the back wall, reamed in shadow. With hands unfurling, they reached for the sealed hatch embedded in the floor. With deft fingers like a mortician, the lock slipped apart and was placed gently to one side. Sliding iron, and the hatch peeled open.

A suffocating stench smothered the air. The sound of liquid sloshed somewhere in the chasm below. A splutter, suppressing a cough, and the figure wedged the hatch ajar.

Stepping back, grinning malevolently; turning back to the Tower entrance.

Silence, echoing out over the Ozban Forest.

The smell of death ripe in the air.

†

Chapter 29

A Breath of Savagery

The camp lay silent and still, as the shadows of night shifted across the tents like the clawing hands of ghosts. The trees of the Ozban lay still in their slumber, finding comfort under the pearlescent gaze of the moon, where the dead screaming between their boughs were finally put to rest. A low fog clung to the earth at the soldiers' feet like a great lake of silver, coiling off in rivets towards the foot of the black Tower looming assiduously off to one side. Even from afar, the tiny snaps and skitters of motion could be heard from within its curved walls, as creatures of the dark crawled from their refuges to prowl the night once more.

Commander Revek looked up to the Tower from the north edge of the camp and tapped his fingers against his leg. *It's like a sentinel,* he thought, chewing his lip. *It stands there and watches us and waits... and we're left here to question whether we'll die or not, under its lonesome gaze.* He peered through its tiny windows, imagining eyes within there, watching out across the camp. *Many of us will die, and it will watch without fear.* A tiny smile, as Revek shook his head.

How the Ozban cares so little.

"The camp are all asleep, sir," General Oslo said, shifting between the tents and placing himself in the chair beside the commander. "We have lookouts along the perimeter of the tents as instructed. Everyone is staying well clear of the, uh, of the tree-line sir... it, um, looks to be a long night."

"That it does," Revek replied forebodingly. *We'll be lucky to see morning, knowing what this place does to people...*

"We should... maybe we should rest too? In case we're needed... need to be sharp and alert, after all!" There was a hesitancy to the general's voice as he spoke, accompanied by unusual flutters of his hands. He scratched at his thighs like a flea-bitten dog, looking off toward the tower and back again.

He's shit scared, Revek mused, rolling his fingers together.

Smart man.

"You're welcome to get some sleep, general, but I shall remain here for some time yet. I don't trust this place enough to allow any respite."

"I see... hm." Oslo paused, opening his collar. "Should we... should we all be this concerned about it, sir? About sleeping in a place like this?"

"If you have any sense you should be: you don't walk into a place like this with wool over your eyes, unless you plan on being eaten alive."

Oslo gulped. "There are... there are things here that can *do* that?"

"Do what?"

"Eat someone alive."

Revek smiled at his ignorance; he shrugged his shoulders. "Perhaps there are... in a place as vast as the Ozban, where people are lost by simply straying between the trees, who knows? This is nothing like the plains of Provenci, I can assure you that much."

"I was always told Tarraz was a place for the defiled."

"And whoever told you that, was right. This is a savage land full of savage people, after all. But it is not only the people, general... this place *breathes* savagery in its very being. It forms it in the soil and the roots beneath our feet; it taints the air in our lungs. The disgusting retches who live here have tamed it to their whim... whereas we outsiders are not so lucky."

Well, most of us aren't.

"But what of the hatch in the Tower? You said... that we *'never should have come here'*, when you saw it... should we be concerned about that? Why did you say that?" Oslo flinched at a snapping twig somewhere in the trees far behind them.

"I said it," the commander explained, "because we never *should* have come here, general. That's the simple fact in all of this." He gestured out to the wider forest, prickled with moonlight. "There is nothing here worth the price of finding it. No strategic point, or landmark, or area, or outpost... this place is a vulgar absence of all natural things in this world, and we've walked straight into it. This is a savage place of a savage people... and that hatch and what lies beneath it, just proves my point." Revek turned to him, acquainting with the horror in his eyes. "Because there are things in this place, stalking under our feet and amongst the trees, that will rip your throat out just for existing. And if you aren't watching, you'll never see it until it's far, *far* too late."

"I... hm." The general nodded slowly, shivering. "Understood, sir, understood, yes... understood."

"Although, then again, the savagery of this place is not unknown to us: the Ozban has been the source of many bold and horrifying tales over the decades. Even when the occupation began after the Collapse, and the first forts were built out here, many believed this place was cursed as thousands of soldiers got lost in the trees. In a way, we know this place almost as well as it knows us... but we would be foolish to think that we know any *better*."

"So... so there's a chance to survive, you say? If we keep our heads down and, and keep our wits about us... we may yet prevail?"

Revek considered. "Perhaps, yes. It's why the camp has been arranged how it is; why the fires remain unlit; why all the booze has been dumped. We maintain something as close to the natural order as we can, without disturbing things too much... and maybe, just *maybe,* the Ozban will be merciful."

Oslo nodded his head, some colour returning to his cheeks. "They were wrong about you, you know, sir."

Revek frowned, turning to him. "Go on."

"You do have the soldiers' wellbeing at heart," he explained. "You do care for the men and women under your command. I... I was warned, before I came out, to expect trouble from you. That you would try and... *sabotage* us, in an act of revenge. But I don't see it; I don't believe it anymore. Watching you, and how you lead... you do care, and you do understand, and... well, they were wrong about you sir. Very wrong."

Well, how about that. "Thank you, general... your words are pleasant to hear, and I'm deeply honoured by your sentiments," Revek replied, patting him on the shoulder. "I have often been painted poorly during this campaign for my conduct and my methods in leading this army. It's why you and the other two generals watch over me now, after all. But I do always act with the best interests at heart, and I will always do what is required of me to keep this army and its people safe. And that's how it should always be, I believe."

"Admirable words, sir. I completely agree." Oslo smiled with a trusting gaze; Revek hid his smirk in reply.

He is right in so many ways, the commander thought, looking off to the moon. *I do care for the army. I care for order and discipline. I care that everyone mucks in and does their bit. But even that has its limits... I am only human after all.* A foul smile crossed his face. *Because if blood has to be spilt, and the pests who desire my power die before me...*

He looked north to the Acolyte's Tower and grinned.

Then who am I to stop that?

†

Chapter 30

Courage by the Blade

Patience is a virtue, apparently.

Cavara brought her sword across and carved the hooded figure's chest open, sending him reeling backwards into a stack of boxes as the next attacker pounced, a knife the length of her forearm taut in his knuckles.

If only I'd realised that fucking sooner...

Dodging a lunge, Cavara swung through and sliced a length of cloth from the man's robes, before bending awkwardly to avoid a knife in her gut. She stepped back for a moment, lunging forward and spearing the man with a fist across the bridge of his nose.

Through the shadows of the hood, she heard bone crack, and the figure was reeling backwards suddenly like a startled animal, clawing at their face.

The general made to run the man through and finish the job, thrusting out with her short-sword, when another knife appeared to her left and she pulled back to deflect, smacking the tiny blade away and kicking out against their leg.

Before she could rally, however, Cavara spied another figure approaching to her right, and sensed the walls close in around her. Her blade lay taut in her palm; her skin crawled with prickles of sweat. She jumped forward suddenly, skimming along a stone workbench and landing in a wide space opposite, turning sharply to spy the hooded figures approach her once again, knives glinting in their hands.

Cavara forced a smile and shook her head.

So much for an easy way out.

Looking out to the wider storehouse, three of the assassins had already hit the mud, and lay sprawled across the stone floor in odd and freakish contortions. Their blood pooled across the grey slabs like spilt wine, dripping from the stacked boxes in small rivers.

They had been average fighters, attacking vociferously and keeping their distance, but as soon as an opening had emerged Cavara had swung in with her blade and sliced through flesh like butter. It was light work, she admitted: for a general of the army with twelve years under her belt, Cavara had picked them apart comfortably. But after the second body fell, the third had proven difficult – and once they had gone down, the four fighters who remained all bared down on her like a pack of wolves, with sharp teeth and hungry eyes. Wearing their prey down; closing their jaws slowly around her neck, until the killing blow landed and ended her world for good.

She sensed it, even then: the four assassins spreading out across the storehouse in front of her, loping about with their knives poised, closing the circle around her like a noose. Cavara swallowed, clamping her jaw tight.

The walls close in... the prey lies waiting, she thought. *The end seems near...*

The general smiled softly, looking to the sword in her hand.

But not for me.

The first figure carved through in a weaving pattern, cutting down toward her hands; Cavara slung her hand back and thrust out with her blade, catching the figure across the side and drawing blood.

A second assassin approached to her left, navigating between the tables; the general grappled a metallic jug from her side and lobbed it at their head, smirking as it bounced off their forehead and sent them stumbling back across a table—

As a third came in from the right immediately after: Cavara swept across and used her sword to dish the knife aside, parrying an attack from the figure in front of her in the same move. The general sidestepped, sweeping across with successive attacks against the third assassin, putting them on the defensive almost immediately. Her attacks were relentless; their knife was nearly beaten from their hand under the force—

Cavara kicked out like a horse and sent the assassin flying into a stack of boxes—

She twisted her blade across her back instinctively, deflecting another knife that had been spearing toward her spine—

Swivelling on her heel, she rounded and brought a fist across to catch them in the side, knocking the wind from their system. They buckled forward, clutching their stomach, some disjointed Sevican prayer slipping from their tongue—

Cavara drove her blade through their gut and up into their ribs with a single, driving thrust, planting her shoulder into their chest and charging forward like an ox. Dying breaths rasped in her ear; bloody saliva dripped across her neck as the assassin succumbed to their wounds. Death knocked; a second passed; a knife scraped across the metal plates of her back—

She slipped her blade free of the corpse and pushed out with her hands, throwing the dead assassin into one of their comrades like a sack of shit.

Turning again, Cavara inhaled sharply and stopped a knife coiling toward her neck, grunting as a fist then connected with her stomach and sent bile up into her mouth. She growled in frustration, slinging the knife aside and kicking out at the assassin's shin; they stumbled backwards, and narrowly missed the general's sweeping attack destined for their throat.

Cavara swore under her breath, readying for the next one and—

Sucked her stomach in suddenly as a knife slipped through on her right, glancing off the reinforced leather pressed against her abdomen.

Poor choice there pal.

Like a viper's fangs, Cavara lunged down for the knife with one hand, and speared her sword into their wrist with the other.

A hideous snap, and the tip of the blade embedded between the wrist-bones, digging in through the tendons, blood exploding across their skin like a broken sewer. They screeched like a hog, dropping the knife from pale fingers; the general snatched it up feverishly and swung across her body—

Impaling the assassin in the eye, pushing deep into their skull.

The body seized, spasming furiously. Cavara let go of the knife. The haunted face of an old man emerged from beneath the cowl, staring absently at the ceiling as they tipped slowly backwards, toppling like a felled tree across the stone.

Their head slapped against the ground at her feet.

Death was instantaneous.

The general stood, stepping back, wiping her brow with a ruined sleeve...

As footsteps approached from behind her, and she sighed tiredly.

These bastards just don't let up...

Cavara clicked her neck; rolled her shoulders; turned to meet the attack as it came: two knives from two different directions, both angling through toward her jugular with venomous intent.

Bringing her sword close to her chest, the general batted one blade away with a turn of the wrist, and cut through against the other to avert its path from her neck. She managed another weaving attack before deflecting again, back-stepping and cursing under her breath. Several more followed shortly after, interspersed by hapless jabs and the occasional glancing blow.

This isn't working, Cavara acknowledged, sensing the numbness in her movements and the hazy light dancing across the ceiling above. She had lost track of time, and the world beyond the four walls of the storehouse seemed continents away in that moment. There was only one six foot circle, occupied by three fighters and their blades, and the quiet but certain understanding that only one of them would walk out of there alive.

And something needs to change, or that someone won't be me.

She glanced left for a heartbeat, out past the nearest assassin, and a glimmer of hope emerged.

Unless...

Rounding on her opponents, she struck out viciously toward the one on her right, forcing them to stumble backwards and lose their poise; turning, the general then lunged into the assassin's chest in front of her, as they darted to the side and opened a path up to the table she had spied moments ago.

Wasting no time, she leapt forward and tucked up into a tactical roll, spinning across the dusted stone floors and rising again just as fast, twisting back to her opponents like a sea serpent as they charged toward her again.

The foremost one approached with a snarl, manipulating the knife through their fingers. Approaching a lethal prey, weakened but not down. The tension strung out over the room like a spider's web.

The assassin closed in...

They stepped in for an attack—

Cavara brought the mallet across and hammered it against their skull, gritting her teeth as she did so.

A grotesque *crack* of bone and the assassin spun away, the whites of their eyes stained pink as blood seeped into their cavities. Stupid, bubbling clicks escaped their mouth as they tried to remember how to scream. Tumbling off into their comrade, who gawped in horror as the body hit the floor like a cannon-shot, limbs contorting at ungodly angles as they lay to rest forevermore.

Cavara grinned.

Most effective.

Lifting the mallet and sword across her chest, she levelled her gaze with the last one.

"Let's finish this, you *prick*."

The assassin bellowed, hate in their eyes, and seemed more than happy to oblige—

When a shimmering blade speared up through their chest and tore the life from their eyes, as they slumped to the floor and revealed the unsettled form of the Forgotten One just behind, studying the body with a clear disgust.

Cavara relaxed her shoulders at the sight of them – grateful that they were okay – and held her arms up, watching the pale figure assess the room before frowning towards her.

"You've been busy," they said facetiously.

"Yea, a couple dead bodies to spare, *thanks*!" Cavara replied. "Where have you been?"

"I have… I was busy."

"With what?"

"Getting in."

The general frowned, gesturing to the door.

The Forgotten One rolled their eyes. "It's not that easy."

"How so?"

"Because something was blocking my access to this room."

Cavara considered. "Is that why I came out of the Rapture when I entered through that doorway?"

"Yes… it appears that whoever has been using this storehouse, has placed a 'void-trap' on the room, which activated when you walked through that door and made it impossible for me to follow you in."

"Okay… what's a *'void-trap'*?"

"It's a binding between the Rapture and your realm, caused by the meddling of a transmitter," the Forgotten One explained, looking across the walls. "These walls are present both in your world and in the Rapture… but as we have discussed before, in the void they are only *impressions* of the real thing. And because of that, these impressions can also be altered."

"So, what you're saying is the transmitter used the impressions of the walls for this storehouse… to make a cage to trap me, so the assassins could kill me easier?"

The pale figure nodded. "They disconnected your ability to use the Rapture, so once you stepped through that doorway, you were cut off from the void, and I had no way of getting in to help you."

"Could you not break down the actual, *physical* doors and get in?"

"I could have done… but I would have seen nothing but white shadows if I did so. Because the void-trap doesn't just lock you out of the Rapture… it locks your soul in the physical world too."

"But if that's the case, how the hell did you get in just now?"

The Forgotten One allowed a smile. "Let's just say that, when you have as much knowledge and experience of the Rapture as I have… dismantling a void-trap is almost like picking a lock. It takes a few tweaks and a lot of fine-tuning… but it comes apart all the same."

"So the void-trap is gone?"

'Yes, Successor, it is,' they said through her mind, the familiar and surprisingly-welcome numbness sweeping through her body.

'Thank you for doing that… and for coming to assist me,' she replied in a measured tone.

'Please, general, you need not thank me: you did most of the work yourself.' They turned to the wider room. *'Your intuition and skill with a blade is remarkable.'*

'That's what twelve years of the finest sword-training in the Icebreaker Sea gets you, I'm proud to say.' She found herself smiling.

'You do it a great justice.'

"I hope I can see it again one day…"

She spoke the words aloud, and felt a trembling in her heart as she did so. It was the first time she had thought of her homeland in several days: of the plight of her people, and the war that no doubt ravaged the kingdom she had known and loved. She felt guilty, almost, for having her thoughts occupied by other things. That she had drifted somewhat from the true goal she sought.

To return to my people, she proclaimed.

To make things right again—

"What's that?"

Cavara snapped back to reality with a sharp inhale of breath, burying the thoughts as quickly as they had arisen, and followed the Forgotten One's outstretched hand to the tabletop at her back.

Where she spied a folded letter atop a stack of paper, with dirty prints along its edges.

"Do you reckon one of the assassins had it?" she asked.

"It would make sense... it's rather tattered, compared to the other papers there."

The general walked over and plucked it from the stack, peeling the torn edge open and sliding the letter out. Opening it, she was shocked to find that it was written in Provencian, with long, flowing letters elegantly woven across the page. Her eyes flicked along the lines with an almost insatiable intrigue, darting between spaces and numbers and details until...

Until she saw the last line, and gasped.

'Deliver the kidnapped child to The Cellar and await further instruction – I will be in contact soon', she read, blinking heavily.

And it's signed by someone called the Butcher.

And if that's the name of the transmitter, then that means...

The Forgotten One appeared alongside her. "What does it say?" they asked.

Cavara turned to them with glowing eyes and a newfound hope in her soul. "We have to see Azura... now," she said, folding the letter into her pocket and turning to the door. "I think I know how to find Evelyn..."

†

Chapter 31

Death and Choices

We're running out of time.

Eli brought his bludgeon across to deflect the palace guard's blade, propelling it off to one side in a heavy sweep of steel. The imperial man recovered quickly, however, and brought the sword back through, forcing Eli to back step. It took the sheer weight of the bludgeon to hold his balance, as the rebel leader swung forwards again and heaved his bludgeon toward the guard's chest – a sudden motion that left them stumbling backwards, narrowly avoiding the steel ball.

This is anarchy.

Despite wielding a longsword, the palace guard used it with as much ease as a knife, lunging through with an extended arm designed to pierce Eli's gut. The rebel leader swung backwards as a result, handling his weapon awkwardly as the muscles strained along his bicep. He hissed and dug his heels in, arcing the bludgeon overhead and nearly shattering the guard's hands, opening up the space between them just long enough to catch a breath.

The tide's turning against us.

Eli was about to re-engage and strike back, only to find the palace guard occupied by another stoic rebel coming in defence of their Chief. They were only young, maybe eighteen winters' gone, brandishing a short-sword stolen from the armoury. Too young to be fighting any real war; too inexperienced to be challenging an elite officer. And Eli knew it. He knew it clear as day. And saw it, too, as the young rebel made three attacks and overcompensated on the last, allowing the palace guard to step in and slice his chest open in one. No words escaped the young man's lips; no life dripped from his tongue as the blood welled across his leather cuirass.

It was only when an enemy soldier approached from behind and speared him up through the ribs, that the young rebel found it in him to scream.

Eli struggled to swallow, watching the chaos unfold before him. His skin seemed to crawl with their pain; the sun was so impossibly bright in the sky.

And it was only the approach of the palace guard – unphased by the horror of the past few seconds – that brought him back to reality and the grip on his bludgeon, numbing the reminiscence of the many dead who could never be mourned again.

We're running out of time.

"Sir!"

A howl, echoing off to his right: Eli turned to see Castan charging towards him with his sword raised. His second-in-command stepped past and deflected the palace guard's longsword, using the fluidity of his short, curved blade to dice through and push them back.

"We need to move, sir… we're outnumbered!" Castan shouted, gritting his teeth as the longsword swept through for another attack.

"What's happened?" Eli roared, bringing his bludgeon across to catch the guard along their flank.

"We've been routed, sir! Enemies are swarming in from all angles… we can't beat them back!" Castan stepped back and lunged in, timing the attack perfectly to drive the palace guard away and into the throng of more rebels just beyond. "We're regrouping in the baron's hall. It's the only secure location large enough to hold us."

The Chief glared at him, wide-eyed. "That's where our archers are! Why are we regrouping there?"

That's where Alva is.

"Exactly! We have the high ground there, sir, with support from the balconies. Out here we're exposed!"

Eli ground his teeth and shook his head, a million muddled thoughts racing through his mind with no clear direction to any of them. *Alva's there... I need to keep her safe... I have a duty to the rebels, left to die out here... the baron's hall is our only sanctuary... we can secure the outskirts easier... but it puts her in the firing line... could never forgive myself if...*

Fuck!

"Okay, let's move," the Chief said with a grimace, looking to the ground and the many dead who lay there like a mosaic. "We don't have much time."

Or much hope, in the end...

He turned on his heel, pulling the bludgeon close and retreating back down the western road with several dozen of his people in tow. The sun beat down on their backs like heavy drums; the fuzz and haze of the shadows ahead seemed to vibrate with energy. All around them, scattered bodies lay with their mouths agape: broken metal and twisted limbs and purple rivers of blood weaving through the cobbles like a delta. The slosh of bodily liquid against the rebels' boots was nausea-inducing in of itself – but accompanied by the poisonous, acrid scent of death, it proved near-unbearable. Battalions of flies numbering in their millions alighted as the rebels marched past, swarming skyward, falling prey to the hungry crows jostling on the rooftops above.

The many dead... two sides of the same coin, the Chief thought, observing the horror. *Maybe in life we can be so adverse to one another and our ways of life. But in death... in death we are just corpses, one human soul after another.*

The same, and never again.

Eli steadied his stomach and set his sights on the baron's hall just to their right, looming majestically against the clear-blue skies in towering pinnacles of grey. Scanning the structure, from its highest point down to the column's base, he realised the two huge metal doors that had been sealed shut before now stood slightly ajar, with the familiar green-brown cloth of his people milling about just beyond. Castan gestured to it from his side, the faint glow of a smile on his lips.

"We'll get everyone in through there and seal the doors shut at our backs," he announced. "Once inside we can set up a defensive position and ready ourselves."

"I expect there will be a lot of blood spilt," Eli said forebodingly.

Castan nodded. "Aye sir… we'll just have to pray it's theirs."

The Chief pursed his lips.

That we will…

Approaching the massive doors, Eli flinched as an arrow whistled past his head and skittered off across the cobbles to his left. Looking back for a moment, he saw the colossal forms of the palace guards shadowed against the sun, with the thin branches of bows lining up alongside them to pummel the rebels as they fled.

"Get into the hall *now!"* the Chief roared, sliding through the narrow gap with his gut sucked in and Castan trailing just behind as a volley of arrows hailed at their backs and sent three rebels to the mud.

Eli half-collapsed into the vast banquet chamber, steadied only by the straining grip of his second-in-command. Lowering the bludgeon against the stone, the Chief turned to the sounds of more screaming, watching as another of his people collapsed against the door with clawing hands and an arrow in their neck.

A heartbeat passed; he dispossessed the weapon and launched over to the doors, pressing a shoulder against its side and pushing hard. Several others joined him, palms flat against the iron with bare-white knuckles, until the door's massive gears started to grind and nearly a dozen of his strongest souls forced the door to a close.

"Hold it!" Eli growled, directing people to the opposing door as the sound of clattering steel echoed out from the other side. He heard the commands of the palace guards; the muffled, straining voices of the imperial soldiers.

Time ticking slowly by…

He watched as Castan detached from the crush and grappled the door's massive locking mechanism, pulling an iron bar toward his feet with veins bulging in his arms. He growled, biting and snapping – planting his foot against the metal and drawing harder.

Releasing, finally, as the mechanism slipped into place, and two wooden pillars snapped across to seal the door as one.

Eli took a step back, holding his hands out; the other rebels alongside him did likewise. After several unnerving moments, with the soldiers attempting to enter from the other side, the Chief found it in him to lower his arms and release a heartfelt sigh.

"We're secure."

We're alive, for now.

He lifted his head, a tightness pulling in his neck and shoulders as the rebels around him caught their breath and doubled over with exhaustion.

Gods do I ache. He flexed his fingers as knots of muscle strained in his knuckles, heaving air through his half-broken nose on his half-broken face.

Gods, does this hurt. The floor beneath him was splodgy and dim; nausea curdled in his empty stomach. Voices muttered all around him as little more than gusts of wind. His fragile, decrepit body swayed gently with a burning hate in his eyes.

Gods, do I want to break that general's fucking jaw.

The Chief rose to his full height and stood wearily, tiresome pains gnawing at his joints like the chattering teeth of rats. He looked out to his people across the hall: looked at their haunted but expectant faces, gazing back at him with admiration in their hearts. He realised how heavy his own heart felt, in that moment.

Loss comes for us all.

"Are you okay, Eli?" Castan muttered, walking over and placing a hand on his back. "You're looking a bit worse for wear."

"I'm in fucking agony and I've been shot, Castan," Eli said slowly. "But, yes… thank you for asking."

A meek smile from his second-in-command. "Nice to see the heat and the fight haven't knocked your humour, sir."

"Knocked a couple of bones out of line I think... but no, my humour seems relatively unaffected." He let out a heavy breath. "Is Alva okay?"

"You can ask me yourself."

Before he had a chance to look up, a pair of tiny arms wrapped about his chest and a fluff of ginger hair nestled against his beard. Eli smiled, as he drew a hand around Jinx's shoulders and embraced her tightly.

"It's good to see you well, Alva," he muttered quietly, lying a cheek against her head.

"And you, Chief," she whispered in reply.

They parted a few moments later, with Jinx looking up to him and a warm gratitude glowing in her face at the sight of him alive.

How glad I am to see you too, my dear, he thought with a smile.

More than you can know.

"What's our status?" Eli asked, turning to his second-in-command again. "How many of our number remain?"

"We managed a quick evacuation when the palace guards first appeared, and got at least half of our forces clear of the town square from there. Your stoic defence made that possible, above all else," Castan explained, nodding proudly. "Although, from the initial skirmishing we've lost roughly a quarter of our forces out in the square, and those that remain have had to retreat further back to form a defensive circle. We still hold much of the west, but any gains made yesterday beyond the town square have been taken. This hall is our furthest point east, as it stands." His mouth became a hard line. "So many lives lost..."

Eli rolled his tongue across his gums and closed his eyes. *The dead number in their hundreds.* The sheer number seemed impossible on reflection. *All for the sake of a few streets.*

What have we become?

"How fares the front line now?" the Chief inquired.

"All districts around us are secured and well mobilised. Initial reports suggest that the Imperial Land Army has retreated back east for the day along both flanks, facing similar issues with exhaustion as we are no doubt. And, at that, we believe that the only enemy force that still remains a threat… are stationed right outside that door." He speared a finger behind them to the sealed entranceway, where the hushed rattle of voices could still be heard.

"Do you reckon they'll attack?"

Castan shook his head. "We have near a hundred souls within this hall… I would have thought they'd be mad to try and take us on alone—"

A sharp, terrifying sound of snapping metal echoed out across the banquet hall just as the words left his mouth, and the chamber doors bucked violently inward at their backs.

Eli turned, horror-stricken, and retrieved his bludgeon from the ground in a heartbeat.

They've got a battering ram…

"*READY YOURSELVES!*" he bellowed, as the panicked spasms of running feet padded across the carpet and stone all around him, buckling armour and snapping helmets and drawing swords with a hiss of steel.

"Get into formation—"

A second strike cracked across the door; the Chief watched Jinx bolt up the stairway to his left with the crossbow loaded in her hands. To either side of him, the rebels formed up into tight ranks with gritted teeth. Eli swallowed, chewing his lips, a fresh bloom of adrenaline eclipsing all other thoughts. He studied the space ahead, as the spine of the huge doors pulled ajar for a moment, revealing the light and open air of the world beyond.

And the huge trunk of wood edging slowly backwards, preparing another breach.

The air drew silent.

Eli held his breath.

The battering ram connected like a fist in the jugular. The wooden pillars of the locking mechanism split in two. The doors burst open.

Footsteps sounded.

Here we go.

"*FIRE!*"

Snapping drawstrings. Whistling bolts. The thunderous clatter of boots. Roaring voices. Palace guards swarming forward, swords raised. Howling metal skimming armour. Ricocheting bullets. Biting flesh. Collapsing. Gargling blood with bolts through throats.

Still they ran.

The rebels engaged, swarming them. Angry faces and gnashing teeth and fearful eyes. Jabbing and lunging from different angles. Innocent souls with butter knives. Farmers and smiths and merchant-men. A single sweep of a palace guard's longsword, carving limbs from torsos like butter. A head spinning off, tongue lolling like a pig's. Slinging blood like paint across a canvas. The muttered prayers as a rebel ducked a guard's blade and speared them up through the armpit. Shock and despair and hate and hope; tired eyes. Bloody words from bloody mouths. Light fading.

Still they pressed on.

Clattering steel. Biting knives. The heat of battle ascending once more. The Chief of the Mountains stood dead centre, watching it unfold around him. The chaos; the horror. The sheer depravity of human ignorance.

Watching the doorway beyond as the dust fell. Focusing through the light and the haze and the din.

A figure approaching. Grey hair and butchered skin and a poisonous ire in his eye. Gazing out on the carnage; centring on the rebel leader stood opposite.

Ferreus smiled.

"Hello, *Eli.* I was hoping you'd be here…"

"You have a lot to answer for, you fucking snake," Eli spat as the old general approached him.

"As do you." Ferreus stopped just short of him, his sword swaying at his side. "You have made an embarrassment of us, you know?

Burning scars across our great nation with your barbarity… tearing people from their homes and their farms in the midst of a war, all to swell the numbers of your *pathetic* cause. Pitting Provencian against Provencian, blood-kin against blood-kin. And for what? A chip on your shoulder? An ugly wound in your heart?"

"You've vaulted yourself into power at the expense of dozens, and you've ripped holes through families with your cruelty. People have bled and people have died because of your cowardice. So with all due *respect,* general, I am not the one with a '*chip on their shoulder*' here."

The general scoffed. "We've done what was needed to bring order to this place. To fill the void left by that sorry excuse of a king when he kissed the mud. We in power did what was necessary to bring about this order… and those who died in the process of that, mean *nothing* in the face of—"

"You murdered my *fucking* husband, you treacherous little prick!" Eli stepped forward, looming like a giant. "He was one of your own, a general like yourself… and you had him tortured and beaten for it, and stood by as he was murdered as if it were *nothing*." Heat boiled in his throat; grief racked his soul. "You are a liar and a cheat, general… but more than that, you are a fucking *coward.* A paranoid, despotic little coward. And I will greatly enjoy breaking your face for the sins you've committed… mark my *words.*"

Ferreus inhaled slowly, studying the rebel leader with slate-grey pupils.

Then, with sadistic glee, he grinned and levelled his blade.

"You can *make me*—"

The bludgeon rounded before the general finished, arcing through the sky toward his head at terrifying speed. Ferreus side-stepped quickly, flinching at the cracked stone where the metal ball made impact, his sword wavering at his side. Eli balled a fist and swung upwards with a lunge; he caught the general in the stomach, relishing the groan that escaped his lips.

Backstepping almost immediately, Ferreus growled and lashed out with his sword, a flurry of strikes reigning down on the Chief with venomous intent.

Eli pivoted, manoeuvring his hands and dodging the attacks until he had both hands along the bludgeon's pole, and swung it round to counter—

Forcing Ferreus to drop down onto his front, as the rush of air curled across his back and the metal ball skimmed overhead. The general felt the vibrations as the bludgeon clattered across the stone to his right; he lifted back to his feet and struck out like a spear.

Eli lurched backward, gasping and biting his tongue. Dropping the bludgeon, he curled a fist, swinging out—

Connecting with Ferreus' jaw like a boxer.

The general stumbled backward, clutching at his chin, his mouth little more than a thin slit. A trickle of blood seeped down from the corner of his lip.

"You'll pay for that," he growled.

Eli reclaimed his bludgeon and smiled.

"Your move, *asshole*."

Gritting his teeth, Ferreus surged forward with a powerful exchange; Eli rounded the bludgeon, using its shaft as a shield to knock the blows as they rained down, wincing at the grating metal as it slid dangerously close to his fingers. Sweat blanched his skin in pools, stinging his eyes. Exhaustion bit through his arms.

Time ticked effortlessly on...

A stall appeared in the general's attack; Eli dug in against the stone and hefted the bludgeon round.

Ferreus dropped to the ground on his back – an impossibly nimble move – and struck out with the heel of his iron-capped boot.

The boot cracked across Eli's shin with a deafening sound. The Chief groaned, stepping back, his bludgeon falling lazily to the side. Ferreus twisted, lunging out with his sword, forcing a backstep—

But Eli prevailed, adrenaline consuming him and rounded his weapon with an incredible roar.

Ferreus stooped into a crouch and leapt away like a frog, sprawling across the red carpets as the huge weapon crashed down where he had just been.

He hissed, turning, fearful eyes and—

The Chief of the Mountains loomed down, dragging him up by his collar, his sword left discarded across the stone several steps away.

Time seemed to stand still…

Watching the old wolf writhe in his grasp, trying to claws his hands apart, Eli smiled with satisfaction at the sheer power he possessed, and how fate seemed to rally beside him.

"I will enjoy this," he said simply, holding his gaze, "for what you have done to me and my family… and for the pain you've wrought against thousands, in the name of peace and *order*." Images of Arrenso crossed in his mind, pulling at his heart. "I condemn you to *death,* general, for your sins…"

Ferreus drew still, lowering his hands without a word spoken, and seemed to accept his fate. A quiet, unshakable moment wrung out between them, when the clashing metal ceased and the light grew dim and the biting force in his heart fell still. As if nothing in the world were wrong, or ever would be again.

As if time would stop forever.

And then Ferreus smiled, flicking a knife from the folds of his armour, and drove it deep into Eli's flank.

He leaned in close to his ear and spat.

"*To hell with your family.*"

The knife withdrew with a flick of his hand; the Chief stumbled backwards, clutching at his side, all sensation receding in his legs. A single backstep and his knee buckled; another, and he collapsed onto his back, husky breaths tightening in his lungs. Light receded in his gaze, as the shadows threatened to swallow him whole.

Ferreus stood before him, easing to a stand and brushing himself down, shaking his head with a mocking smile.

"You should've listened," the general exclaimed, stepping closer, eclipsing the sun high above. "You and your *insolence*, costing the lives of hundreds… all for a cause you neither deserve to lead nor are fit to follow. You're a vengeful, sad man with a broken heart and only a sword to make sense of it. Your husband would be *sick* at the sight of you, if he were alive. You have ruined what was left of his good name with your barbarity." The bloody knife twisted in his hand. "And now you will die, and join him in your *failure…*"

The general took a single step, lunging the blade down toward Eli's throat.

The Chief, lost in the valley of the gods, looked up to the balcony high above – spying there a single figure, etched out in fuzzy streaks, gazing down upon them through the fray.

The blade edged closer.

The figure on the balcony twitched—

And the general's kneecap shattered entirely, as a crossbow bolt struck his leg.

A screech like a strangled deer: Ferreus bellowed in agony and collapsed onto his side, pulling at the bone shrapnel that now constituted his knee joint with retching turns of his mouth. He waved his hand skyward, screeching, garbled words spewing from his tongue. A plea to the gods, perhaps, that his sin would be undone.

Eli watched on hopelessly, battling with his wound as he dipped in and out of consciousness. It was all so heavy and cold, suddenly; so dark and alone in the vast and desolate room…

The glint of steel plates and high-marked helmets swept across his vision like fish through a cove: the palace guards formed a defensive crush in the space before him, shifting their weight down to collect their felled leader and drag him to the streets beyond. From there, everything was motion suddenly, as the imperial legions fled the scene and rebels swarmed against them. Leather cuirasses crossed Eli's vision; glinting swords swept out toward the enemy.

All the while, the Chief looked on, and slipped slowly from reality. Every blink came heavier than the last; the light twinkled like stars. It was not death, but it was not quite life either.

Some delicate space in between, looking up to the balcony above where his saviour stood.

With Jinx's ginger hair billowing in the wind.

†

Chapter 32

The Sun Still Rises

My son is alive.

In the alcove of her living room, bathed in the amber light of dusk, Azura lowered the crumpled letter into her lap and let out a dishevelled sigh. The shadows that coursed around the room before her seemed to flicker like candles, pulling in at the edges as if ready to consume her, dicing with the emotions she held knotted in her chest. She rubbed her red-rimmed eyes as the darkness swelled, almost hoping to banish them, but she knew all the same that such things were futile. The shadows had become as much a part of her as they were a part of life. They claimed her, almost, like a king covets their jewels. All-encompassing; ever present. Grief had been her solace, trapped away in the gloom – and light, therefore, had only sought to break her apart.

My son is alive, she rasped, her throat constricting tighter and tighter with the sheer realisation of it all. *He lives, and is still among us now...*

So why do I feel so lost?

"We found the letter in the storehouse where I was attacked," Cavara explained, sat on the armchair opposite her with the looming mass of the Forgotten One just behind. "It has no recipient, but it is signed by someone called *'The Butcher'*... who we can only assume is the name of the transmitter who's taken Evelyn. Which also means, according to that letter, that he is not only alive, but being held somewhere in the City… and that means we can find him."

"How do you know this… *Butcher,* is the right person?" she asked, chided by the general's optimism.

"We believe the marks you saw on the kidnapper's chin and neck when they took Evelyn were tattoos of butcher's knives," the Forgotten One rumbled from the back of the room. "Thus we made the link between the transmitter and the person who wrote the letter."

Azura considered, her mouth a straight line. "It says something here about *'The Cellar'*, too. What does that mean?"

"That's the bit we're unsure about," Cavara admitted, rolling her fingers together. "We know that the transmitter is using a network of Tarrazi sympathisers throughout the City to find and capture me, but the exact whereabouts of these groups is unknown. We stumbled upon the one today by accident, for example, while following another trail. But the problem is… any one of these groups could be guarding this 'Cellar, anywhere in the City. So although that letter reveals that Evelyn is alive and being held somewhere, exactly *where* that is, we don't really know…"

"Do you have any knowledge of a 'Cellar' such as the one detailed in the letter, miss Azura?" The Forgotten One inquired. "Maybe an abandoned building, or a sacred space…"

"Nothing comes to mind, no," the greying lady replied, looking to her feet guiltily. "I'm sorry."

"There's nothing to be sorry about Azura, I assure you." Cavara stepped forward and knelt in front of her, looking up to her with shimmering hazel eyes. "Because even if we don't know exactly where he is, Evelyn is still *alive,* somewhere within these City walls. It'll only be a matter of time until he's found. We were most likely correct in our assumption that he would be used as leverage to get to me, which means they will keep him alive so long as I'm here. And I promise you, as a friend and a woman of the army… I'm not going *anywhere* until Evelyn's found and returned to you. You have my word."

Azura sat still for a moment, lost in the deep of her thoughts, and examined the general crouched before her making promises in the dark. She assessed her feelings as they came, bubbling up from her chest like a geyser. At first she recognised the weight of resent: here was the woman responsible for the kidnap of her innocent child. Here was the army officer betrayed by her people, hunted by assassins that Azura knew nothing about, because of a war in their homeland that should have been little more than harbour gossip for the City of the Sun.

But then there was also sympathy: to have everything you've ever known stripped from you, as you muddle around in a foreign place with people who want you banished. To be a product of one's circumstance; to have any semblance of stability torn from you by forces you didn't even know existed.

And from that, the old woman found another sensation rise in her chest – one that shocked her, and left her hands trembling at her sides.

Guilt, she thought, looking off to the orange sun. *I feel guilty for blaming her… when she was really as clueless as me.*

Azura sighed, and let a single tear pull from her eye and trickle down the wrinkles of her cheek. She looked into her palms for a moment, studying the light and shadow dancing between her fingers, and closed her eyes to the world like a dying saint lying to rest.

She's only ever wanted to do what's right. She lifted her gaze again. *And who am I to deny that?*

"Thank you…" she muttered, swallowing through a bubble in her throat. "Thank you for not giving up on me… and on my boy, wherever he may be. I don't know what I'd do without you."

"It's the very least I can do," Cavara said with a warm smile and a glossy shine across her pupils. "I just want things to go back to the way they were, because… well, it's something I can never have again, and I know how much that disconnection can hurt. I can't go back to my life before… but I can return Evelyn to your arms, so you can."

Azura leaned forward suddenly and pulled Cavara into her arms, embracing her tightly, tucking her head against the general's shoulder. A quiet plea escaped her lips; she found herself crying, sobbing quietly in the gloom. She heard the whispers of tears in her ear too, as Cavara locked arms across the grey woman's back and pulled her closer. Like a cocoon, they nestled together, witness to each other's pain. A thousand tiny burdens ebbed in the space around them, flowing out like an ocean breeze. Azura thought the known world would cave in on itself in that moment, as she fell deeper into the well of her soul – until the general pulled away and wiped the tears from her eyes, placing hands on the mother's shoulders.

"I won't let you down, Azura," Cavara said determinedly. "On my life, I won't."

"I know, my dear," she replied, managing a smile. "You never have."

The general nodded slowly as if she were about to cry again, her face a knot of relief. A moment passed, and she stood, squeezing Azura's shoulder before turning back to the Forgotten One and drifting slowly from the room.

Azura watched the general move off through the kitchen toward the stairway at the back, where she would no doubt return to her attic room and begin preparations for the task ahead. The old woman marvelled at how determined she was; how driven she was to right the wrongs of the world, no matter how vast they were.

And in that quiet moment, with the orange haze of dusk sweeping in, Azura sensed a new feeling blossom in her chest: something small and bright, tapping delicately like the wings of a butterfly. A beautiful thing that she has almost forgotten.

Something like hope.

†

Chapter 33

The Burning Candle

She waited in her chambers in the deepest pits of hell, sharpening her blade and sensing the shadows as death marked her soul and bled her dry. She sat shining the perfect edge of a perfect knife ready to cut imperfect flesh like rotting wood. She sat patiently, perched at the end of her bed with the hollows of orange torchlight to keep her company, methodically turning it over in her mind.

Imagining their necks as she carved them open, and spilled all the dirty corruption in their blood.

Savanta lowered the whetstone and studied the blade in her hand, noting how her fingers shook and her palms were coated in sheens of sweat. It was as if she'd been struck by lightning: there was no thinking nor sitting still; breathing came in quick, stuttering rasps like a panic attack. Everything was constant motion, both in of herself and the world around her. She vibrated on the spot; the shadows quivered like waves around her. Her skin crawled and was yet so desperately cold.

As if there were parasites under her skin…

Lost in the reams of her dislocated mind, she didn't register as her finger slipped and the knife cut across her thumb, where a bloom of red appeared almost immediately and wept down her wrist in a thin line. She hardly flinched at the pain; hardly realised that it had happened at all. Studying it for some moments – marvelling, almost, at the calmness it seemed to possess on her shivering hand – before she inhaled softly.

And licked the blood from the wound with an almost feverish joy, coating her gums with it until her teeth stained pink.

A heartbeat later, and the latch sounded at her door. Steel boots walked down the corridor toward her.

Savanta gripped her knife.

Fucking bitch, she growled, grinding her heels across the stone at her feet. *Fucking bitch, I know you're there... I know you're there you bitch. Come and let me see you. Let me bleed you. I want it.*

Fucking bitch!

"Hello, Champion," the Iron Queen mused, stepping into the light ahead of her. "I hope you don't mind the intrusion, I was—"

Savanta pushed up from the bed and launched at her, screaming like a rabid animal with her knife curling upwards—

Offering little more than a fickle smile in response, Gaza twisted her arm around the outstretched knife and locked her shoulder, forcing the blade from Savanta's hand under the pressure.

The Champion blinked for a heartbeat, watching the knife clatter across the stone – as the Queen kicked out and buckled her legs, before backhanding her across the face with such force that she spun out across the floor and coughed blood across the stone.

Fucking bitch...

"Pathetic," the Iron Queen laughed, clicking bones in her hand and pacing the room alongside her. "As if it would be that easy... as if I would just 'let you' kill me like that, over something as petty as hate. Truly pathetic..."

"Why didn't you let me... just *kill* him..."

"What was that?"

Savanta turned over, glaring at the Queen with a bloody mouth. "*Why* didn't you just let me *kill* him!"

"Because what good would have that served?" Gaza studied her intently. "What good would have come if I just let you murder him so... *childishly*."

"I have a right," Savanta rasped.

The Queen scoffed. "You have nothing of the sort. You lie here, bruised and bleeding like a sad fucking rat addled with poison... and you think you have a *right* to anything? How ridiculous."

"He's my father."

"But you're hardly his daughter."

The words cut deep – deeper than any wound she had sustained by the tyrant's hand. She grit her teeth, hard enough that her jaw ached, and exhaled shakily through her battered lungs.

"I have a right to kill the man who abandoned me and took so much from me, and then had the *audacity* of staying alive long enough to see what it's done to me," the Champion boomed. "I have the right to slit his throat, for all the years I mourned him hopelessly, even though he had never died at all."

"The fact he still matters—"

"He is *dead* to me, don't you fucking get that?" Savanta lifted onto her hands, jutting her neck out at the Queen above her. "That's the bit you don't understand. That's the bit that doesn't seem to make any fucking *sense* to you, as you toy with me and push me around like an old dog. Because, you see, I don't *care* about him anymore. I don't *care* about who or what he is, or what he means to you. I think nothing of him, other than as a memory of the past I long to *extinguish*. He is a wasted soul. A piece of shit lost to the world and in need of divine intervention. He should have died when he had the chance: when he abandoned me fifteen years ago, with nothing more than an ear as a fucking *souvenir*. He is dead to me, and he should be dead... and with the blessing of the gods and the curse of the hate within me, I shall be the one to exact that. To take his life, and step forward from the shadows... and be rid of that which has burdened me for so long." She speared a finger out. "So, I say to you, your *Highness*... that if you intend to stand against me, and deny me that as your Champion, then do as you fucking-well *please*. Because I will still find a way to him, and I will still end his life, and after that you can do with me whatever you wish. I don't care after that... justice will have been served, and it will be done by *my* blade."

With a tension in her chest and venom scolding the tip of her tongue, Savanta lay snarling up at the Queen with twitching fingers and an unrelenting fire in her eye. A thousand tiny machinations reeled through her mind, like scalping layers of flesh, as she gazed deep into the blackened marks of the tyrant's sockets and sought there the answers she hoped to find...

In turn, the Iron Queen looked down upon the quivering, hate-driven creature sprawled across her chamber floor – her Champion, thrown into the fire of the enemy – and found she was almost impressed by its flawed and fatal form. That this woman possessed the audacity and the guile, after all that time, to stand up and challenge her: a half-god woman who commanded the legions against her homeland, whose name sparked fear into all those who heard it. That even with that reality – and that undeniable fact – the broken creature bruised and bleeding at her feet still managed to bare her fangs. A part of her was almost impressed by it.

And the other part had expected it all along.

"Very well, Champion... I heed your warnings," Gaza said with a smile, turning back to the door. "And I hope you heed mine, in return: remain here, and think on your sins, and be ready for when I next call on you. Because as much as your father means nothing to you... you also mean so very *little* to me." She nodded, passing into the shadows of the corridor. "Besides, I have you exactly where I want you: under *lock* and *key*..."

The tyrant slipped from sight, whispering something to a black-coat guard just outside the room as they fumbled with their chains and sealed the chamber door shut. The rattle of keys echoed out through the Champion's room for a long time after they had gone, dancing with the lights and shadows in minute waves.

And, thinking on the Queen's words with blood lacing her teeth, Savanta started laughing.

Time for the wolf to go hunting...

†

Chapter 34

Our Price to Pay

The night passed like the gentle breaths of a sleeping child, with the fog like a blanket pulled tightly across the camp. No noise emanated from the forest at their backs, beyond the faint rustle of wind through the branches; no life stirred in the undergrowth, or coiled its way through the walls of the Acolyte's Tower. The camp lay slumbering patiently, and the Ozban lay dormant.

And Revek remained alert, all the same.

He rolled back on his seat, arching his spine against the frame of the chair, gazing up into the star-lit sky spinning high above. Admiring the peacefulness of it: the placidity of everything. How strange it was, to see quiet in a place so ruinous. Camped amongst the knotted branches of hell, and yet entirely ignorant to the forest around them. Where the enemy scoured amongst the trees sharpening their killing blades, as beasts of ungodly terror skulked through the dark on the hunt for naked flesh. Where the dying screamed for days and the dead melted into the trees; where the whispers of the wind could drive a fool mad, and bring an end to their life in a heartbeat. And yet, in the suffocation of night, with the moon's glow bursting across the Tower like shards of bone to his right, the camp remained entirely uncaring all around him, snoring in its slumber.

Entirely unaware of the terror that would come.

“Awfully quiet out here sir,” Oslo muttered from beside him, rubbing at his eyes. “Seems... seems too quiet, would you say?”

Revek smirked. “Not at all: this quiet is the good type of quiet, where you can still hear the wind and the trees at your back. But when the wind stops and the branches hold their breath... *that* is when you should be worried.”

“You have a keen sense for this, sir... I feel somewhat comforted in your presence, out here.”

The commander hid a smile. *Your first, and last mistake.* “I only know how this place works from experience... after spending eight long days trapped within the trees, things start to make more sense.” *And those who are expendable, become more apparent.*

“I heard what happened... on the Grey Plains, when everyone was scattered through the Ozban. Those who escaped were lucky to have their lives.” He paused. “There were rumours about you sir, about how you escaped... I, I don’t believe them myself, but there *were* a lot of rumours... about people disappearing, lost in the dark...”

“Don’t believe everything Lazaerys tells you, general,” Revek said pointedly. “She has her reasons to blacken my name.” *And I have my reasons, in wanting to bleed hers.*

“You’re saying the rumours aren’t true?”

“I’m saying the rumours aren’t worth hearing.” *The truth is a different matter.*

“Understood, sir... understood,” Oslo replied sheepishly, nodding his head and settling back into his chair.

“Besides, it’s better to face the now than question that which came before...” the commander expressed, looking up to the Acolyte’s Tower.

Because we all have our sins... and we all have our price to pay.

Several hours ticked by without disruption, as the moon continued its arduous transit across the night sky. Silence prevailed, as the whisper of the trees at their backs drew to a quiet rustle, and the wind pulling across their legs eased its sweeping attack. The commander remained alert, assessing the world before him with bloodshot eyes and flexing hands, as the officer at his side drifted in and out of consciousness with the muttering flinches of nightmares.

Looking out on the camp, Revek observed how the shadows and moonlight danced across the sides of the tents, illuminating the wires that held them aloft like phosphorescent seaweed. The fog pulled across the bare earth with an almost electric glow from the moon, thinning as it reached the base of the Tower, which stood in its corrupted blackness entirely unphased. The commander studied its edges, and how the light seemed to repulse from it: a black turret of ancient stone as sinister as it was barren.

Such a strange structure... so laced with hate, he thought, pulling a hand through his hair. *Stood here for millennia, revelling in the death of the many souls who dare come here and lay eyes on it...*

With his gaze lowering, dropping down each storey until fixing to the wide door at the top of the stairway, he noted how the shadows seemed to coil and sift awkwardly in the light.

How strange... I wonder—

His thought stopped entirely, as shock claimed his mind.

And something pale and pulsating curled across the floor of the Tower, descending the narrow stairway towards them.

"*General.*"

"What, what is it?" Oslo said, stirring from a half-conscious daze and sitting straight.

"*There's something here with us.*"

"What? Where? Should we..."

He made to stand; Revek shunted him back into his seat and glared. "*Don't move a fucking muscle, do you understand?*"

"Yes... sir," he replied, his voice dropping to a whisper.

Revek raised his right hand slowly, directing a finger over to the Tower. "*Something is moving around the base of the Tower... something long and white.*"

"A serpent?"

"Not that size... and certainly not in the Ozban."

"What could it be?"

"I don't know, we'll have to wait and—"

A spasm of clicking sounds echoed off to their right suddenly, circling the edge of the camp, changing pitch and speed at random intervals. Revek held his neck stiff, fastening his hand to Oslo's chest so he wouldn't panic and try and run. Instead he sat with his heart thundering and blood rattling through his head.

As a scraping sound drew closer, clawing through the fog toward them.

"*Don't move... don't fucking move.*"

Out of the corner of his eye, Revek saw it move towards them: a creature of bulging white flesh, scuttling on massive pointed legs revolving along its huge body. There was no sign of a head, but the commander heard the snapping of pincers ease slowly past them, and the twitching of mandibles that made his feet squirm. Spanning the length of an entire military convoy, the creature was horrifying to behold, as it circled the northern edge of the camp sensing the air for its prey. It was only when the creature was safely beyond the line of tents in the distance that Revek relinquished his grip and managed a shaky breath.

We are in deep shit...

"*What was that thing?*" Oslo spluttered, hands tensing over the arms of the small chair.

"*That... was one of the foul creatures that stalk these lands,*" Revek explained, trying to trace the monster's movements around the camp. *"Something very fast, very lethal, and extremely dangerous... and it's best to avoid it at all costs."*

"But what do we do now? How do we keep it at bay? Can we get rid of it somehow?" Oslo seemed to whimper. *"Are we gonna die?"*

"No-one will die, providing we all keep our wits about us. All we need to do is remain perfectly quiet, and avoid drawing any attention to our presence here. Because as soon as that first cry goes up, or there's any sign that the

creature's prey is here... there's nothing to save us from that thing."

General Oslo did not respond – he found no response in him, sat in the crook of an old chair quivering like a hypothermic child. Revek paid him little notice – and had little time for him, at that – as he eased forward in his seat and listened out to the tiny, almost-indecipherable noises that told him where the creature was. The clicking, pulsing, snapping, rasping, undulating sounds; the sounds of stomach acid and cooling metal and the birth of children. Sounds that felt wrong, like an abscess in such an ungodly place. All emanating from the body of a massive white creature that circled the camp with predatory intent, sensing the air for fresh meat with hungry, rotten eyes.

This is quite a problem, Revek thought facetiously, curling his tongue across his teeth. *Because if anyone makes any noise, then we're all dead. Ripped to pieces, throats torn out... dead.* His eyes crossed to the Acolyte's Tower, and something of a smile caught on his face.

Dead, that is... unless you know where to hide.

Looking back through the tents, the air thinned in his lungs as ripples of white passed along the southern verges of the camp. It was like watching a great porcelain maggot, swaying slowly with its bloated stomach scraping the floor beneath. There was a menacing glean to each of its pointed legs. Blue-purple tendrils twitched delicately along its sides, sensing the fabric of the tents as it passed.

Wondering what prey lay inside.

"*It's at the southern edge of the camp,*" the commander explained, tracing its movement with an outstretched finger. "*Snaking its way back toward the Tower.*"

"*Reckon it's gonna leave?*"

"Not likely... it just hasn't sussed us out yet."

"When will it?"

Revek turned to him. "*When someone starts screaming...*"

A haunted look suddenly claimed Oslo's face; the commander watched him claw at the armrests of his chair like a trapped rat. Somewhere ahead, another spasm of clicks rippled through the night air, carrying through the fog between the tent posts.

Revek's gaze shifted toward the Tower, and a knot formed in his heart as the creature seemed to disappear entirely. Nothing beyond the tents moved: no white nor shining silver could be seen. There was only a perpetual stillness, jumping at shadows.

Where have you gone?

"*Uh, sir...*" Oslo muttered fearfully.

"*Yes, what is it? What do you see?*"

An audible gulp chimed in his ear.

"Where did we leave the horses?"

Revek stood abruptly, eyes on stalks, and looked out through the haze across the camp—

A sudden spurt of neighing caught his ear: all stamping hooves and gnashing teeth.

A rumbling like thunder eclipsed the air. Gravelly clicking sounds echoed out through the fog—

The horrific snap of bones ripped through the sky, as the creature's mandibles tore through the horse's body and put it to death in an instant.

Then a mashing sound erupted like cold stew, all blood and flesh and skin.

Shit—

In the silence, bodies stirred across the camp. Motion shifted between the tents.

Blades were unsheathed.

Revek turned to Oslo, terror in his eyes—

The first scream went up.

"*Run!*"

The commander propelled from his chair like a launch-pad and bolted along the outskirts of the camp, with General Oslo following fearfully behind. Wind whipped across Revek's face as he ran, biting across his cheeks; his heart thundered in his ears. Exhilaration and nausea claimed him all at once. The moon seemed impossibly bright above them for a moment, almost mockingly so. The commander scoffed.

Welcome to hell...

To his right, tent debris and snapped poles exploded across the night sky. Bellows sounded. Screams wailed as bones snapped. Flesh and mud mangled into each other. Clicks seized the air. Terror echoed out over the Ozban in all its maleficent beauty.

...we are at your mercy.

Flinching suddenly, Revek spied the beast curling high over the encampment to his right, hailing the gods in a surging, porcelain mass: he spied its huge black skull and silver-scale horns; its twisting mandibles and blood-soaked jaws; its beady eyes surveying the carnage with glee. Spiralling skyward, with spear-like legs twitching and flexing, cresting against the moon with a snap of its jaws...

Tearing back down into the camp like a landslide, ripping through cloth and wood and steel indiscriminately as it went, as dismembered bodies volleyed skyward in mangled limbs and gore.

This is bad, Revek thought quietly to himself, studying the chaos as it unfurled. *This is really bad.* A smug grin flashed across his face.

I told them...

"What do we do sir!" Oslo shouted from behind, stumbling over his own feet. "It's tearing us apart!"

Revek screwed his nose up, spitting into the dirt at his feet. *Survive, is what you do.* Eyes flitting across the camp, tracking the beast's undulating body as it tore through several dozen half-conscious soldiers, the commander watched as a number of his soldiers fled the scene and ascended the staircase into the Acolyte's Tower. They disappeared within its walls like scurrying beetles, and some time later their shimmering chest-plates emerged on the Tower roof, lighting torches to direct other soldiers their way.

How about that, Revek scoffed. *Soldiers with half a brain...*

"Get everyone into the Tower!" he bellowed. "We'll be safer there... the stairways are too narrow for the creature to attack properly!"

"Aye sir!" Oslo cried in response, his stomach rolling as the crunch of bones echoed through their ears. Somewhere nearby, the clicking sounds chattered with joy, revelling in the violence.

And the screams of the dead grew steadily louder.

They banked slowly left along the outskirts of the camp, passing under the daunting shadow of the Acolyte's Tower like two mice fleeing a cat. They reached the bottom of the stairway; Revek drew to a stop, grappling Oslo under his arm and pulling him close.

"Get a torch lit, and stand at the door behind us," he commanded. "Get the attention of any survivors you can see, and direct them here. We need to save as many people as we can." Revek released his grip and slapped the general across the back.

"Okay, but, wait… what are… what are you gonna do, sir?" Oslo muttered.

The commander pulled his blade loose.

"I'm gonna buy us some time." He grinned. "Now go!"

General Oslo stalled for a moment, before turning and ascending the stairway to stand at the door at the top, addressing a soldier to bring him a torch and secure the interior.

Commander Revek turned to the decimated camp with a long exhale and took several strides forward, sensing the eyes of his people looking down from the roof of the Tower at his back. He ground his heels in the dirt; rolling his shoulders, he bellowed at the top of his lungs and pounded his steel glove against his chest, sending a torrent of noise across the camp for all to hear.

Sliding between the ruined tents – a porcelain white against the bleached grey fog – the creature raised its head and turned to face him then, accompanied with a melody of curious clicking. There was a moment's consideration, with light twitching in its six bulbous eyes, before the creature chose its course and snaked its way through the debris toward him.

Revek levelled his blade, pulling into a fighter's stance as the creature stopped a few feet in front of him, studying him with a primal intrigue.

Why am I doing this? Revek thought with a sigh. *Risking my life so callously against this... thing.* He twisted the sword in his grip, grinding his teeth together like a wash-basin. Beyond the creature's winding body, he spied a number of shivering souls lift themselves from the ruined camp with fearful eyes, looking up to the torches on the Tower with a glint of hope.

Perhaps I do it for them, because it's the right thing to do... because they respect someone who leads them, and fights for them. He produced a snarl; the creature sensed the air with its tendrils. *The Marshal might have taken my leadership by decree, but I still hold sway here. This is the right thing to do, for everyone involved.*

Because this is what gets me back into power.

Revek took a step forward, lifting his arms as if consulting the gods, offering an open challenge to the beast twitching before him.

The black skull quivered as he approached, its mandibles tapping in rapid pulses: the beast sensed the threat, and lifted its head to meet it. Revek stood his ground, and studied the white-pink contortions of its stomach: the translucent skin with organs swimming beneath, and the two ugly welts of flesh that seemed to have once been arms. The tendrils across its neck fluttered with a grotesque beauty, like the flushed petals of a meadow, whipping and flicking through the air – sensing the commander before it, as the beast produced a low growl and the clicks drew still.

"Come on!" Revek bellowed, raising the challenge, crashing a fist against his chest. "Come on!"

The creature hunkered low to the ground, circling in front of the Tower with its eyes spinning violently. Tiny rows of needle-like teeth shimmered in its wide mouth, stained with the pink-red blotches of blood.

Revek circled opposite, his sword drawn close to his chest.

Come on you bastard.

The creature bunched up, with stabbing legs and twitching teeth and the rhythmic clicks of mandibles.

"Come on!"

Teeth gritting, lunging with his blade.

"Come on!"

The creature growled; the clicking stopped.

"*Come on you bastard!*"

Lunging like a phantom, the beast surged toward him on scuttling legs, its tendrils flaring and its teeth grinding—

Revek crunched his knees and rolled to the right as the huge black skull charged past, its mandibles snapping closed like the doors of hell.

Lifting to a stand and turning, the commander spied the beast rounding on him again almost immediately, dispelling the fog at their feet with its sheer mass and speed. It seemed to wind toward him like a snake, ready to spear out and slice his body in two – and it was a good plan, had Revek not dropped at the last moment, with the massive head and translucent body whistling overhead as he lay pressed to the dirt just below.

Sensing something was wrong, the creature ground to a halt, using its tendrils to sense the air and determine where the attacker was, jostling on the spot with an intensity—

As the commander swept out from underneath its body and drove his blade up into its flesh, penetrating deep into the organs beneath, twisting up between a pair of legs as blue-black blood exploded over the dry earth.

Revek steadied himself and smiled; the beast screeched with a torrent of violent clicks. He pulled his sword free and went for another strike—

To find only the bubbling remains of his hilt left in his hand, as the blade dissolved entirely, and the toxic blood from the creature's body started to eat away at his armour—

Swearing, he grappled with the straps along his wrist guard and tore the glove free, casting the hissing metal out toward the Tower in a smoking ball of vapour, looking up again to see the enemy—

As the nearest pair of legs snapped out and struck him in the chest, with enough force to throw the air from his lungs and pull him off his feet.

Cast backwards, Revek landed heavily on his spine, the dry earth crunching between the folds of his armour. An uneasy warmth bit across his stomach; his ribs pulled like broken strings; the old wound from his previous encounter in the lowlands twinged viciously. Reminders of life flashed before his eyes.

And death's sweet kiss drew suddenly near.

He pulled himself up, scrabbling with his legs; the world ahead was little more than a blur of white-black-grey as the beast shifted toward him with a slow and fatal certainty. His eyes like flickering candles; the beast's mandibles snapping in a melody. A coursing nausea in his stomach.

The walls closing in.

Looking for a moment to the left, he saw the last few soldiers of the camp swaying up the stairway into the Acolyte's Tower, with Oslo's torch still waving like a beacon at the door. He saw the faces of his people on the Tower roof, cast in the orange glow of torch-light, looking down to their leader with fearful eyes and prayers on their lips. The pride and beauty of the imperial standard emblazoned on their chests; Revek produced the visage of a smile.

The plan has worked, he considered, turning back to the beast as it pulled up from the earth and made ready to strike toward him.

Now it's time to survive it.

Like a meteorite cast from the heavens, the beast plummeted toward him in a revolving mass of flesh and pumping skin.

Revek pushed up and rolled to the side deftly; the beast's head twisted away, as its front leg jabbed into the earth mere inches from the commander's head.

Another roll and he was on his feet, abandoning any notion of success against the creature; he kicked out with powerful strides and started running, moving off toward the Acolyte's Tower as more furious clicking seized the air at his back.

He covered the ground in heartbeats; the thundering, scuttling legs of the snapping, clawing creature loomed somewhere behind, making ready for its next attack—

Revek pivoted up the stone stairway, pulling at the walls and ascending with great lunges toward General Oslo at its peak, who stood dumbstruck and terrified at the door.

"Move, you bastard! Come on!" the commander roared, pushing past him and turning sharply left toward the winding steps.

Oslo, ripped from his trance, wailed as the beast rattled up the stairs toward him with its jaws flaring. Turning to the steps, the general propelled after the commander as the creature threw itself into the tiny room, its body threading in behind like reams of ribbon bunching up across the stone.

The two officers clambered up the stairway, reaching the second storey in seconds, sweat-plastered and panting. Looking to the other stairway next to them – across the black walls illuminated only by the torch in Oslo's fist – Revek gestured off in that direction.

"We need to keep moving," he exclaimed.

"I thought you said that thing couldn't attack—"

"Reality is often cruel, Oslo… get fucking used to it."

The general pursed his lips, nodding slowly and stepping forward toward the opposing stairway—

To face an explosion of splitting stone, as the beast's massive head broke through the floor and breached up next to them, its clawing legs pulling tar-black stones away to drag its body free.

The commander's heart seemed to stop.

Oh fuck…

"Move, *now!*" he roared, pushing past the general and charging up the stairway to their left, with the grinding of needle-like jaws ricocheting through the chamber just behind as the beast continued to emerge.

General Oslo scrabbled behind on unsteady legs, horror leaking from his soul as the creature broke through and the six piercing eyes honed in on him. A sob in his throat, he clawed at the stairs ahead of him, his face a contortion of terror and despair. His torchlight spilled out, the beast scuttling behind him—

And the stairway suddenly caving in beneath his feet, as the beast lunged out with its huge skull and tore the stone apart, cracking the steps below—

Oslo leapt, clutching at slabs with bloodied palms, gasping and spluttering as the world collapsed beneath him, staring up into the dark void of the chamber above.

And the dead eyes of the commander looming there, watching on with intrigue.

"Help me up!" he barked. "Help me, please! Sir!"

Revek looked at him – through him – and smiled.

The general screamed. "Please, sir! Sir… please, oh gods—"

"I always did hate you academy officers," the commander mused, shaking his head. "How you came out here and took everything from me… everything I had worked so hard to achieve…"

"*Sir*… please… I'm begging you…"

"But it doesn't matter, in the grand scheme of things: you were little more than a grain of sand in the end. A distraction that I needed to get *rid* of…" He bent low, studying the general's sad eyes with a venomous grin. "And all it took, was a turn of a latch…"

Oslo looked at him – through him – and all hope sunk in his face. "You unlocked the hatch… you let that beast out of its lair." It came in disbelief; his breath became shallower "And all of it… all of the death and hate that we've seen… was just to kill *me*…"

Revek rose to a stand and shook his head. "Goodbye, General Oslo…" He stamped his foot down across the general's knuckle.

"And good fucking *riddance*…"

Oslo's fingers slipped from the stone; a screech escaped his lungs.

The creature coiled up beneath him with insatiable hunger, its mandibles opening like knife-blades.

The general fell, looking up into the eyes of a maniac, as his limbs torn to shreds in the maw of the Ozban beast.

And silence claimed them all, once more.

The commander smiled, rolling his shoulders and revelling in the moment, before turning from the desecration at his feet and climbing the stairway at his back.

Beautiful inevitability, as exacting as ever, Revek thought as he climbed. *No matter the cost, and no matter the crime.*

It bathes in blood all the same.

At the Tower's peak – stood in the cold, unsettled air of midnight – he emerged to face the three dozen soldiers who had survived the ordeal below, sensing their hopelessness as the sound of mashing bones echoed up from the Tower beneath.

"Okay listen in… I have some news for you all," the commander said, gesturing for them to draw closer with a solemn gaze. "I regret to inform you that, while making our escape through the Tower, the beast who has ruined our camp and taken so many lives this night pursued us into the building, and exacted a terrible toll. As we ascended the second stairway, the creature tore the floor open at our feet… and as I was ahead, I turned to try and help our General Oslo, but realised it was far too late… as the general was seized in the creature's jaws, and ripped from my hands so cruelly." A moment of reflection passed; the moon cast a heavy gaze over them. "So, in light of that information – and with the beast still at large somewhere below us – I believe it's best that we wait for it to return to its lair at dawn, and head back to the main camp as soon as we can to report on what's happened here." He hid a smile, balling his hands at his back. "And as there is no general among our number, that means the full jurisdiction of this force now falls to me… which I understand may be a shame, as I'm sure we're all missing General Oslo *deeply*…"

The commander looked among them as the words left his mouth, studying their faces. Watching their gazes lift, jostling among each other like dogs. The moonlight glowed high above; the beast growled beneath.

And their smiles began to appear, one by one.

†

Chapter 35

The Wrath of Consequence

Wake, wake, slumbering rise;
silence your screams and still your eyes;
sing, sing, mourner's cry;
fate has come, and they shall die...

Cavara stirred from her sleep, with reams of moonlight peeling in from the attic window to bathe the room in shades of blue. It was a cold night, and her skin crawled with goosebumps under the thin quilt, forcing her to pull it tight around her neck and preserve any heat she dispelled. Her armour sat upright on a chair next to her head; her sword sat in its scabbard adjacent to it. Reaching up under the pillow at her head, she sighed with relief at the knife that still lay hidden there in case of emergency.

Must've just been a dream, she deduced, turning back over and letting her eyes slide shut again. *Nothing to worry about...*

Until she bristled, caught by a sudden rush of cold air, and a creaking sound like a footstep echoed out in the room behind—

Cavara turned sharply and grappled for the knife under her pillow, silencing her breaths and studying the motionless room beyond for signs of an intruder. Her heart thundered in her throat; her knees bent, curling up toward her chest defensively. The space beyond lay dormant, uninterested by her concerns. Shadows merging with shadows, with only moonlight to discern between them.

The general held herself steady, blinking slowly, as the gentle rhythms of sleep called to her again. That the warmth of her body seemed to bloom in the bed beneath her. It all seemed so enticing, so opportune. She blinked once, twice, the third time almost drifting away—

When a shadow darted between two beams opposite her, and disappeared without a sound.

What?

Cavara rose from the bed with the glinting knife in her hand, and eased her feet against the cold wood floor. A number of creaks sounded as she moved – a number of creaks that the shadow should have made, too, had it been a real person.

Jumping at the dark, thinking things are there when they aren't, she scolded herself, shivering at the burst of cold now sweeping down her spine. *Why would anyone come to me here anyway? With the Forgotten One moving downstairs, it'd be tantamount to suicide stepping into these walls. No-one can reach me here.* She lowered the knife in her hand, before clutching it tighter suddenly.

No-one, except the Butcher.

She scoured the room again, pulling apart each shadow and moonlit alcove over and over, fearing the enemy was upon her. Up there in the attic of an old woman's house, in her cloth shirt with a blade in her grasp and only the darkness as company.

Entirely unaware of the hand pulling past her left ear, slipping slowly across her mouth—

Until it clamped against her jaw, pulling her in close, and Cavara let out a stifled scream.

The darkness rose to consume her once more, with the echoes of laughter all around.

~

She slipped into the void as if caught on ice, steadying herself with outstretched hands as her feet ground to a halt. The Rapture seemed to convulse around her as she did so, baulking at her presence like a dog unsure of its master. Her eyes and lungs felt heavy, as if they were bound to iron chains. Every sense she encountered was wrong; the air tasted uneasy.

This is not my Rapture, *she realised.*

And then he appeared.

Manifesting from the white ahead of her: a grey-black figure of hulking proportions, grinning pointedly with two butcher knives swinging at their belt. Sauntering toward her, his armour peeling across his skin beneath a bloody apron; his hands flexing, diced with tiny cuts and scrapes. Fear lanced into Cavara's heart as he drew close and stopped several feet before her, a cold and ireful gaze locking to her own.

"Hello, usurper," the transmitter mused, blinking slowly.

"What have you done with Evelyn?" Cavara spat, gritting her teeth, her legs fused to the spot. "Where is he?"

"He's alive, if that's what you're concerned about. Yes, alive and well… as it stands."

"He's an innocent child, you fucking monster! *Why have you involved him in this?"*

The transmitter scoffed. "You already know the answer to that."

Cavara pursed her lips. "Leverage."

"An eye for an eye."

"And what good does that serve you?"

"It means I get what I want… and I don't even have to work for it."

"And what is it that you want, exactly?"

The Butcher smiled. "An exchange is what I want, usurper. Someone must bleed, and I hold the knife… the only question is, who meets it? You… or the child."

Her heart jumped at the thought of Evelyn coming to harm; she sucked cold air through her teeth. "You can't do this."

"I can… because I don't encounter the same moral issue that you do. I don't have to debate whether my life is worth more than a child's… knowing what it will mean for the balance of the known world. That is no concern of mine. I was sent here for one reason: to get paid, and kill someone called General Cavara. And if the boy dies in the fulfilment of that arrangement,

then so be it... you will still die all the same, in the end."

"You won't win," the general snarled, taking a step forward – noting the surprise in the Butcher's face. "We know more about you and your little operation than you realise. No-one will die, except you... and when I put my blade through your chest, send that bitch Gaza my regards."

"Hm," the transmitter considered, smirking. "Bold words... especially from someone with no weapon to spare. Bold words indeed..."

Cavara frowned, studying the Butcher to see if he was bluffing. But, lifting her left hand, she found she had in fact been dispossessed of her knife – and, watching the transmitter unhook his own menacing weapon, the look of horror could not escape the general's face.

"What are you gonna do to me?" she asked, more out of fear than curiosity, sliding back in tiny increments.

"I will do nothing to you, don't worry," the Butcher replied, drawing a finger along the blade of the butcher knife. "Because if I attack you, you'll summon that flaming sword... and because I know you can't summon it of your own volition, I'll just leave you dispossessed." A smile curled across his cheeks. "That, and it will make this next bit all the more satisfying..."

Her throat closed up. "What?"

"You said you knew more about me and my 'little operation' than I realised... that you know what my plans are, and what the field of play looks like between us." The Butcher started circling her; she tracked his movements like a hunter. "Yet, with that creature *you call a guardian locked out of my Rapture, and your clear inability to use the powers you sadly possess... I can't see how that's possible." He shifted behind her. "Unless there was something else going on as well, that is..."*

Cavara turned to him, and saw a kneeling body at his side; her heart seemed to stop.

The transmitter grinned.

"Unless you had help from someone else..."

"Cavara..." the figure moaned in a deep, pained voice.

"Brutus!" she yelled in reply, taking a step forward—

"Ah, ah!" The Butcher levelled his knife with her, forcing her to backstep and hold her ground. "You can stay right there."

"Don't you fucking dare lay a finger on him."

"I don't think you're in a position to contest that."

"Save… yourself…" Brutus mumbled through the black smog of his figure, before the transmitter cuffed him across the jaw and silenced him.

"Why are you doing this?" Cavara spluttered, relenting against the weight pulling taut against her skin.

"Because it's the only way you'll understand just how serious I am… when I say I will kill that child if you don't hand yourself over to me."

"You're a fucking monster."

"I'm doing my job. So, will you hand yourself over to me, so I may kill you and crown the rightful heir to the All-Mother?"

"I can't…" Cavara felt defiance rise and fall in her chest.

"Will you?"

She looked into the dark, broken pits of the Butcher's eyes. A thousand possibilities flickered through her mind. "I…"

"Will you?"

She sighed. I have to.

"I—"

"No… she won't," Brutus rumbled from beside them, his dark form shifting in the void. "She just needs to retrace her steps."

"Oh yea?" the transmitter challenged. "And why's that?"

The void pulsed; Brutus looked up to Cavara, and she thought she saw a smile there.

"Because that's where the truth is… and I'm gonna choose for her."

Brutus lifted suddenly from the ground and turned toward the Butcher like a wraith, the black shadows of his body straining against the void.

Cavara gasped and started running, trying to close the distance between them as she realised what was happening, but found it was all too late.

The transmitter stumbled back as the shadow approached, his eyes like tiny fires as he struck out with the butcher's knife—

A line of dark matter arced off into the white, staining red as it hit the earth at their feet. Brutus's shadow stumbled forward, spewing the same black-red liquid, and collapsed in a heap moments later.

Cavara screamed; the Butcher studied the blood across his hands with wild eyes, and turned to her in disbelief.

The general bellowed at the top of her lungs and felt the flaming sword conjure in her hand—

As the void collapsed around them, shattering like falling glass, and everything went dark once again.

~

Cavara spilled out across the attic floor in a tumbling mass of limbs, crashing against the far wall and coiling up in a ball. Air heaved through her system; her eyes strained with anger and tears. The moonlight sweeping in from the window stilled her thundering soul, albeit only long enough to make a conscious thought.

He's dead... another gone because of me, she thought, grinding her jaw together. *Another taken.*

She heard motion in the house beneath her, and the heavy boots of the Forgotten One diving through the kitchen toward the stairs.

The Butcher can't win. This can't be how this ends. I can't have another innocent taken at the hand of that fucking psychopath. There has to be a way.

The pale figure appeared at the top of her staircase and hurried over to her, as she considered Brutus's last words.

And I think I know how.

"What happened, general? Are you okay?" the Forgotten One said in a panic, searching the room for any intruders. "Are you safe?"

Cavara looked up to them with quiet certainty, and inhaled slowly. "We have to find Evelyn tomorrow, and we have to return to the storehouse to do so," she replied, closing her eyes. "Because if we don't, the Butcher will win."

And Evelyn will die because of me...

PART III

Plight of the Ascendant

†

Chapter 36

Madness Casts Long Shadows

Supreme Governor,

Today has been a hard-fought day, and the soldiers stood strong in the face of the enemy for many long hours in the sun. The rebels put up a stiff resistance, it is noted, but with my coordinated attacks and the interception of the palace guards you so graciously gifted to us, we were able to break their defences and take the town square for ourselves.

As it stands, the rebels have been routed, and their numbers have been decimated, but I regret to inform you that they continue to hold the western sectors of the town, and still hold the strategically-important baron's hall. Our gains may have been significant, but it was not enough to exterminate their pathetic rebellion once and for all, and I can only offer my apologies for not achieving the primary objective.

However, we are not to be undone by this minor setback. Because, despite sustaining an injury in the line of duty today at the hands of little bitch Alva, the medical officers have cleared me to resume my active duties tomorrow, so that we may put an end to this fighting and return to our true cause against the savages in Tarraz. I shall see it done for you, sir – you have my word.

Hail Provenci, and Glory to our Leader.

Signed,
General Ferreus

*

Alvarez screwed the letter into a ball, tightening it in his grip until his knuckles went white, before exhaling slowly and throwing it to the ground.

Two days of fighting… and for what? He ground his teeth, squinting his eyes shut. *I give them an army… I hand over my own palace guards to bring about a swift end… I more or less hand them victory, on a silver platter.* He shook his head, rolling his tongue across the roof of his mouth. *And yet here we are, with dusk approaching on the second day… and the rebellion still hasn't been quashed. Two days of fighting gone…*

And nothing to show for it but bodies.

The Governor clasped his hands behind his back and scowled. He stood on the ridge overlooking the brown smudge of Marcheg, where smoke trickled up toward blood-red clouds seeping out from a distant sun. The grassy plains rippled like inlets of the sea, their tiny waves braking across jutting rocks and the tiny congregations of trees. Birds circled above the town: massive ravens with deathly-black wings, spearing down into the streets in search of the fresh dead. No doubt the rats were already clawing through the sewers awaiting their feast when nightfall came; no doubt the flies were already there in their swarms, their maggots twisting through skulls and nestling deep into the flesh therein. The foulest, most destitute creatures of the known world, flocking to the town at the scent of blood, as the green havens of the wider plain swayed gently back-and-forth as if nothing had happened at all. How nature ticked on regardless, forever uncaring.

As we once again tear ourselves apart in our quest of perpetual madness.

"Sir."

Alvarez gritted his teeth; he turned and smiled. "Yes officer?"

"We've had reports from Marcheg, sir… and it doesn't sound good," the soldier exclaimed politely. She was a young woman, with an angular face and a close crop of hair, and the unblemished gaze of someone who had never seen a corpse spouting blood. She was also, as far as the Governor could tell, entirely unable to read a room. "We've sustained heavy losses across the front lines..."

"Yes, I've just been reading something similar in my reports," Alvarez dismissed, a knotting venom biting through his throat.

"The enemy still hold much of the west, sir..."

"Yes, I *do know*..."

"It appears they're putting up a stiffer resistance than—"

"*I know what it fucking looks like officer!*" the Governor bellowed, rounding on his heel, spittle flying. "I have my reports. I know that it looks like fucking *anarchy* down there. It's a chaotic, senseless waste of time. And to think, I wanted this *done* tonight! I wanted this burnt and brushed under the *fucking* carpet, and I can't even have that. I wanted to be back on my throne, in my palace, away from this nightmare... planning for a fight that actually *matters,* in the north against Tarraz. I wanted to enact my wrath on every poor savage north of that border wall... and to finally lay claim to power that should be rightfully mine... and yet here I am, stood on a ridge, sleeping in a command tent, overlooking a town where my people are dying and a bastard rebellion is picking my reputation to *shreds*." He exhaled. "I don't have time for this..."

"If I may, sir," she asked sheepishly, lowering her gaze, "why do you not engage yourself? You are one of the finest commanders this nation has ever had... why not show them how it's done?"

The Governor pursed his lips. "No. No, I won't show them... because I shouldn't *have to.* Because they should do it themselves. Because... I... becau..."

Alvarez stopped suddenly, like the failed hands of a ticking clock. His mouth carried on moving in little trembling motions, but no words formed at his tongue. Instead, his gaze was locked, transfixed almost, to the bow of the ridge as it drifted gently down towards Marcheg. A shifting plain of rippling grass, glistening like scales in the low light. A great nothingness, indifferent to any other.

Other than the hazy impression of a figure steeped in smoke, stood watching him with yellow eyes.

No…

Alvarez swayed, an anxious sickness souring in his stomach, creeping up his neck like a fungus. The figure before him billowed and twisted in the coursing winds, with the faint definitions of an arm and leg along the right side bound in the reams of a robe. The face remained expressionless, but the eyes were all-consuming: yellow slants staring into him like dissecting blades, glowing like embers in the low light. It was nothing more than an impression of his mind, he knew. It was a glint of terror that had followed him from the walls of Casantri, and paced about the camp like a wraith every day since. A shadow; a darkness, howling with the winds, reflecting out from his soul. It was always the same figure, and always had the same eyes – and as he stared deeper into it, and almost through it, he found the same voice too echoing within, ushering the words that had haunted him since the first day he had heard them.

'Destiny will prevail… and you, shall die.'

Alvarez blinked; the smoke and shadow dispersed. Only the swaying grass and the flickers of wind remained.

The Governor lurched around, fearing its presence, studying the confused soldier at his side with a gaunt white face and bleached eyes. He turned his back on Marcheg; he stumbled forward and shoved past her, on toward the camp at the bottom of the ridge.

With a terrible leak in the tyrant's heart, and the taste of sweet liquor on his tongue.

†

Chapter 37

An Arrow in the Wind

Cavara lowered herself into the squat stone seat and lay her forearms against the long table, studying the dragon-horn throne ahead of her and the murky shadows within. The room was warmer than she remembered: reams of sunlight glinted through the mosaic windows around them, dashing over the tabletop like twinkling stars, and the air felt thick and heavy in her chest. Stifling, almost.

As if it's comfortable breathing here in the first place.

She squared her chest and winced at a tension pulling across her shoulder-blades, as if there were thistles under her skin. *The last place I want to be, and yet it's the first place I find myself in.* She sensed the other presence somewhere in the dark ahead of her, no doubt watching her and plotting devious schemes to further frustrate her hopes.

A 'courtesy call', was what Azura called it. The general scoffed.

Not that I think they deserve one.

"May I speak with you, your Highness?" Cavara prompted, trying to keep her voice as level as she could bear.

"Yes" – with the grinding of bones, the Alderbane leaned forward in their chair, the half-skull emerging bound in robes like a druid of the dead – "I think you can. To what do I owe the pleasure, general?"

"I felt it was important to give you an update on my circumstances, and the events that have occurred over the previous few days."

"Hm, yes. I've heard certain *whispers* about what has been going on in my city… I am aware that blood has been spilt, and something has been uncovered."

"It's partly the reason of why I'm here, your Highness. To tell it as a first-hand account, and alleviate any *inconsistencies* that may have occurred." Cavara levelled her gaze.

The Alderbane raised their bony hands to the table. "And what might they be?"

"That will depend… who did you receive your reports from?"

"From the same people who were also attacked that day in a local inn in broad daylight, left bruised and bloodied by a, I quote… '*disgraced lunatic foreigner*'." Although their face did not move, she sensed their lips go taut. "Does that sound familiar to you at all, general?"

"I will not sit here and deny that the use of violence was employed against Ptolemy and Amara during our last conversation in the inn… but I will also not *apologise* for doing so. Because, your Highness, I was goaded, dismissed and belittled by them at every turn, when all I asked for was assistance in the pursuit of the kidnapped child so he may be reunited with his mother. I believe that was quite a simple task to agree to, don't you?"

"That is not their duty," the Alderbane replied bluntly. "They are required to protect you – not to assist in your separate, personal aims."

"And if those aims put me at risk of harm?"

"Then you are not only naïve, but also incredibly reckless."

Cavara sensed herself bristle, like the heckles of a hound.

Don't let them get to you…

"I was hoping that there was some humanity to them, when I asked for their help in finding the child," she said resolutely. "I was hoping that they could forgo the limited scope of their duties, and see that sometimes there are bigger things in life than just what they've been ordered to do. I was hoping a young boy in danger – at the hands of a dangerous criminal, at that – would be enough to move them to action. But all that I found instead was a disappointing selfishness, and a complete dismissal of my concerns."

"So you proceeded to throw a table at Amara, break a chair over Ptolemy's head, and beat him to a bruised pulp for it?" Something guttural escaped their voice, almost like a scoff. "You are like a dog with no leash, who cannot be brought to bay..."

"I simply did what—"

"You do whatever you please *unrequitedly*, general, because that's the kind of person you *are*." The Alderbane hunched over, the black of their eye sockets burying into her own. "You are untethered, like an arrow in the wind: let loose, only to fly off course and hurt everything that lands in your path. Tell me, how many lives have you ruined, to amend a problem you yourself caused in the first place? And how many more will yet die because of it?"

Cavara lurched out of her chair and pressed her palms flat on the table, lifting a hand to point at her chest. "I am *not* the enemy here, your Highness, do you understand that?"

"That may be so, general... but you make a monster of yourself nonetheless."

The general eased back, balancing against the table with her fingertips, and ran her tongue across her teeth. Thinking of Azura's salt-stained eyes and the sleepless nights she had foregone; thinking of the assassins in the storehouse, and their bodies lain bloody across the stone floors; thinking of Brutus, entirely innocent and only ever wanting to help, meeting his end at the blade of an enemy intent on Cavara's demise. The path she had taken so far; the arduous task of what lay ahead. Wondering if the Alderbane was right, and she was becoming the very thing she sought to destroy.

I've always wanted to do what's right, and bring correction to the wrongs of the world, she thought, closing her eyes. *It's why I long to return to Provenci, after all. My homeland bleeds, and I wish to return and heal it. I want nothing more than to see my countrymen saved. It's all I've ever wanted.*

And yet I'm here, facing a failure of my own making with a child's life on the line, wondering what it will take to fix it – and wondering, too, if I've already caused too much pain for it to be worth it anymore. She sighed, looking up to the Alderbane once again.

But it is still worth it. For Evelyn, and for Azura. To end the reign of terror exuded by the Butcher and their cronies. To right these wrongs – to amend things that never should've happened – is always worth the pain of the path ahead. Because I know where the path ends now.

And I know what I must do.

"I am no monster, your Highness, and I am certainly not the enemy," she said simply. "You may have your reservations about me, and about my people, because of your own life… but I know where my faults lie, and I know that saving the kidnapped child is not one of them. I am no monster for saving the innocents; I am no enemy for hunting an assassin through the Rapture so you may be free of his terror. These things do not define me, because I don't *let* them. So if you wish to mark me as a threat, because of my resolve to help people and right the wrongs I have caused, then do so… because I am proud of the choices I make, and the path I walk, knowing I can do good in this world come the end of it."

The Alderbane studied her for a moment, emotionless and still, with the tiny flickers of white light tapping in their eyes. Pondering her words for a moment; Cavara opened her collar.

"Very well, general," they replied eventually. "If that is how you wish for it to be, then so be it. I am in no position to deny the notions of grandeur you clearly perceive, so I make no attempt to. But, you must also understand that, after all that, I am left with a question… where does this path take you, exactly? What comes from this, when so much has already been taken?"

She grated her teeth, swiping the remark aside. "I will return to the storehouse where I was attacked yesterday, and continue my search there through the Rapture to locate the transmitter and save the kidnapped child. I believe there are a number of clues there that may ascertain where they are."

"I advise against such actions," the Alderbane said forcefully, as the room became suddenly colder. "It is best you steer clear of that place."

"Why should I? I was attacked there… there were signs that the transmitter was using that building. Why would I not go back?"

"Do not attempt to disrespect my wishes, *general.* Do not forget who allows you refuge within these walls." A darkness clouded across the half-skull for a moment, and Cavara swore she saw the shimmers of gold somewhere beneath their robes. "I will not have any more blood spilt so callously. The citizens are already afraid of whoever this transmitter is… let alone of assassins occupying buildings throughout the city. Let us not draw unnecessary *attention* to things."

"I am simply concerned with the threat at hand, your Highness."

"And I am concerned with the control of the state, and the well-being of all those within my walls."

The Alderbane slid back into their chair and disappeared into the shadows, as the half-skull faded from view like a serpent slipping beneath the sea.

"*Remember your place,*" the tyrant growled from the dark, "*and do not attempt to defy me when you do…*"

Cavara made no attempt at a response, holding her lips still and measuring the room defiantly.

If that's how you wish to play it, then so be it.

She turned from her chair and approached the two doors behind her, placing her hands against the cold metal as a thought suddenly coursed through her mind.

I never told them about the attack yesterday, or about the assassins – the Alderbane already knew. She squinted, sensing eyes burrowing into the back of her head. *Which either means the Alderbane knew the assassins were there… or someone witnessed it and reported to them.*

She pushed the doors open and strode through.

What are they hiding?

†

Chapter 38

Right Beneath Our Feet

Son of a bitch…

Eli grit his teeth, grinding his jaw as the surgeon wiggled the arrow-head out of his arm. It was embedded deep within the muscle, igniting fresh plumes of blood with every twist, tearing at whatever sinews lay within. The surgeon's steel implements wormed their way into the cut like two tiny pincers; the sensation of metal under Eli's skin almost made him sick. The lights flickered; he exhaled slowly.

In the dark expanse of the baron's bedchamber among the quiet streets of Marcheg, the Chief of the Mountains swore violently under his breath as the arrow-head finally came free.

"The money I'd pay… to gut the bastard who did this to me," Eli growled, curling his nose up. "The money I'd pay…"

The surgeon beside him placed his implements to one side and started stuffing the wound with emplastrum flowers, watching as they shifted from pearly white to rosy pink and absorbed the blood within.

"An inch to the left, and I reckon the arrow would've impaled your ribcage," Castan muttered in reply at the Chief's side, perched at the edge of his chair like a doting mother. "You're lucky that it didn't do any more damage than what you've got."

"Yea… I suppose that's true."

"And, with that being said," the surgeon interrupted, reaching for a roll of bandage, "it is also recommended that you avoid using the arm for the next few days while it heals, as is quite normal with this type of wound."

Eli nodded his head, smiling facetiously. "And that's what I'm *recommended* to do, is it?"

The surgeon smirked in reply, looping the bandage around his arm in tight weaves. "Well, I am a village healer by trade, sir… and I will be the first to admit that I am no battle strategist in any sense of the word. So any recommendations of rest that I make are purely based on your health, and often don't meet the brute and… *delaying* realities of warfare."

Eli met his gaze. "The two don't usually go hand in hand."

"And truer words have never been said, sir." The surgeon reached the end of the bandage and tied a substantial knot, nodding with some satisfaction as the emplastrum held and the bandage remained crystal white. "It appears on first inspection that the wound is sealed, and the bleeding has stalled significantly. Although that comes on the understanding that it remains in a fixed position for the next few days… and I believe our enemy may have *other* plans." He slid an arm under Eli's bicep. "Twist the elbow joint in a circle for me a moment, sir?"

The Chief did as instructed, rotating his forearm left and right like a pendulum with minimal pain. "It feels fine… very little pain."

"Good… now, could you extend the elbow up and down, so it flexes the muscle?"

With a delicate upswing, Eli contracted his bicep and brought his hand towards his head, flaring his nostrils at the shooting pain that lanced across his collar. "That one hurts a bit more…" He let his arm loosen again, lying it flat against his leg, only to find the shooting pains were replaced by a throbbing numbness that tore across the muscle like a virus. "…and it doesn't seem to ease up either."

"That is expected, I'm afraid, because of how deep the arrow embedded… however, I can inform you that the wound is unlikely to reopen in its current state unless it is put under significant strain."

"And I guess hefting a bludgeon into battle falls into the category of *significant strain?*" Castan jested.

"It falls *well* within that category, I assure you," the surgeon replied, shaking his head with a smile. "Although, should you choose to use the bludgeon tomorrow, I am still here to rebind the wound if it opens at all and needs attention. Idle hands do the sinner's work, after all."

"I appreciate it my friend, thank you," Eli said, lifting his hand and gripping the surgeon's forearm tightly. "It is good to have someone as skilled and eloquent as yourself by our side."

The medical officer returned the gesture. "A pleasure, sir. And as for the eloquence, well: you don't get trained in the Casantri College of Medicine if you don't remember your manners."

"Is that so?" Eli chuckled. "Well how about that..."

"Indeed, sir. Four years of study."

"Then I must ask, out of curiosity," Castan added, "what landed such a well-educated person like yourself out here with people like us? Surely you would profit more from working in the capital with the guilds?"

The surgeon turned to him and nodded reflectively. "You're probably right: I would earn more working for the guilds in the capital, tending to rich clients and what-not. But then again, I'm not, and neither do I want to be, and it's for the exact same reason that I joined this cause in the first place. Because it feels good to help the everyday people in this world who don't have life as easy: to help the hardy types who work the fields and tend the mills and build the carts. To do my bit, for people who know how to do theirs. It's... it's the right thing to do, being out here. It feels like what I do actually matters." The surgeon paused, grinning to himself. "Besides, it's a lot more interesting too. I'd sooner be stringing someone's hand back together after an accident on a farm than picking splinters from the fingers of some rich prick in the capital... over my dead body!"

At the surgeon's words, Eli erupted with a laughter that seemed to shake the dust from walls, bracing a hand across his chest to stop him coughing. He steadied himself after several moments, red-cheeked and smiling, before he placed an appreciative hand on the surgeon's shoulder and squeezed tightly. "Truer words… have never been said, my friend. Thank you."

"Thank you, sir," he replied with a smile.

"And with that wonderful insight, I believe you are free to go… thank you for your work here today. A bed will be awaiting you somewhere in the chambers above us."

"My honour, sir… and may the prayers be with you for tomorrow."

"My thanks, friend."

The medical officer turned from him and disappeared up the winding staircase at the back wall, taking each step measuredly with his box of surgical equipment nestled under one arm.

"He's a good man," Castan exclaimed when the surgeon had shifted from view. "It's reassuring to know we have people like him on our side."

The Chief lowered his gaze, nodding his head. "It's a shame that there are sides at all, really. That people like him are dragged from their work and forced to take up a thankless job like this."

"He doesn't seem to mind."

"Perhaps, but I imagine it's still something of a burden for him."

"It's a burden for all of us in our own ways, sir."

"I'll have to make sure everyone is reimbursed when the time comes for it…"

"Especially with the magic he's worked on that arm of yours…"

"Without a doubt…"

The sound of twisting locks echoed out from the chamber doors to their left suddenly, and Eli turned to spy a bushel of ginger hair slip through the gap and pace across the stone floor toward them.

"Ah, Alva, it's good to see you again," the Chief said softly, the vestiges of warmth reanimating in his heart.

"As it is to see you," she replied with a smile. "How's the arm?"

"Sore, and it hurts like a bastard when I shift the muscle, but it could be worse. The surgeon said that the emplastrum has sealed it over nicely, so there's less chance of it reopening when the fighting starts again tomorrow."

"That's a relief… we need you out there with us."

"I'd be out there whether it was medically advised or not, Alva, have no doubts about that." He lifted a hand and squeezed her forearm. "How are you after yesterday, anyway?"

"I heard about your heroics," Castan added, looking to her with ember-filled eyes. "It sounded quite impressive."

Jinx hid the warmth in her cheeks and nodded. "It was terrifying, if I'm honest… how every shot could save someone's life. I spent half the battle trying to steady myself… and then when they broke into the baron's hall and I saw that conniving little shit skulk in, all of that went away. It was just me, and him, and a single silver bolt destined for the back of his head." She sighed. "I can't believe I missed…"

"You saved my life nonetheless, Alva. Regardless of where you intended to hit, you were the reason that we survived. Incapacitating the general did enough to force a retreat… and just as good, considering the damage I sustained." The wound in his chest where Ferreus had stabbed him twinged for a moment, as if to remind him of that fact. "I thought I was a goner."

"But you're still here, with us," Jinx exclaimed, oozing defiance. "And that means we can fight on, and we have a chance."

Eli rolled his shoulders and looked solemnly to his feet, imagining the walls of the chamber curving in around him. "And I wish I shared your optimism, Alva… but I'm really not sure anymore."

"Why?"

"Well… because we got lucky today, is why. We all did. We were caught off guard, and nearly paid the price for it. I mean, had it not been for the evacuation plans, and our escape to the baron's hall, we would've all been slaughtered the moment the palace guards arrived. Had you not shot that monster in the back of the knee" – he waved a finger at Jinx – "I would likely be dead now. Because we were lucky today… we escaped with our lives, by the skin of our teeth. It was the sheer unpredictability of battle that saved us, nothing more. And if that proved to be a close encounter with death… then tomorrow is little more than a suicide mission."

"C'mon, Eli," Castan interjected, "you know that isn't true…"

"It is true," the Chief snapped, "and the sooner we accept it, the better. Our numbers have been decimated. Many of our best fighters have been killed. The Imperial Army control vast swathes of the town, and our outlying defences are only just holding against them. There are twelve heavily-armed and incredibly dangerous palace guards ready to cut us into ribbons, at the hands of a maniacal man with a bone to pick. That is what we face… and all we have left to face them with, is our honour and our belief in this cause. Noble qualities, it is true, but beyond that… we are in the end little more than farmers and village folk, and if we go out there tomorrow in the position we're in… we'll all be dead by dusk, and everything we've fought for will be gone."

A silence descended, ebbing out from the shadows. Castan lowered his gaze, mirroring the grave expression plastered to Eli's face. His was one of contemplation, and demoralisation. Regret, too. Like the clawing talons of defeat digging their way into his neck, pulling at his arteries like bowstrings. Acknowledging, for a moment, how everything seemed to hang on a knife-edge.

And how it teetered dangerously into their enemy's favour with each hour that passed.

We are at the end of the road. The Chief shook his head, studying the bindings across his arm with wincing expressions of pain. *There is no end, really… only absolution… but I see no way out of this either way. I've done all I can in the end.*

And in the end, it wasn't enough.

Eli lifted his head, studying Jinx stood opposite him – finding, to his immediate surprise, that she was hiding a smile.

"What is it, Alva?" he inquired, frowning.

Jinx ran a hand through her hair, shrugging like a mischievous child. "As dreary as things may seem at the moment, Chief... your assessment of imminent failure may not be *entirely* true..."

Eli sat forward. "Why?"

"Well, while you were recuperating after the battle, I decided to explore the baron's hall a little bit to see what I could find. I went searching in the vaults beneath our feet mainly, where they keep the records and financial legers and shit like that. Most of them were just dusty old tomes of no particular relevance, but then... then I found something else: a book of the town's initial urban planning, dating back nearly sixty years."

"Okay... what did you find?"

The young thief smiled.

"A way to win the war..."

"Okay... what am I looking at?"

Jinx drew her hand across the parchment, careful not to apply any pressure with her fingers against the very old markings. "This is one of the copies of the original urban planning maps used when Marcheg was first built," she explained. "Although the city itself is several hundred years old, it appears that this town and many others in the valley underwent a massive redevelopment about six decades ago, and the original maps that they used had to be copied and have the new plans drawn on top of them. You can tell which is which by the thickness of the lines."

Eli hunched over and placed both hands flat on the table, studying the old map sprawled beneath them. It was yellowed and water-marked in several places, curling at the edges as the paper hardened with age. Across its surface, a massive sprawl of thin, wiry lines indicated the base of the city in an oval shape, demarking houses and streets and larger structures, with a distinct absence in the middle for the town square. And, as Jinx had explained, in some places thicker lines had been etched over it where buildings had been added or renovated. There were large turret shapes across the baron's hall where they camped; a number of extensions on an old bath house in the east; and, quite unusually, a number of broken lines traced in sharp angles that spanned across half the map.

"I see what you mean by the thicker lines," Eli mumbled, "but what are these broken marks here? They don't follow any particular street or district… they seem to clear straight through entire buildings, in fact. Are they sewer systems?"

"Not *exactly*…" Jinx smiled.

"They're tunnels, aren't they?" Castan examined, smiling back to her with a glow in his eye. "Tunnels built under the town, right beneath us…"

"What? Surely not…" Eli frowned, scoffing at Castan's suggestion – before he turned to find Jinx nodding her head with pride, and he promptly studied the map again. The Chief's eyes widened. "By the gods… I didn't even know…"

"And you aren't the only one, because I'm pretty sure the enemy don't know about them either…" Jinx added, tracing a finger along one of the tunnel routes. "They were built before the cessation of Rodenia in the east, back when the foreign taxes were high and income was good. The Tarrazi of the time were still independent, and had started threatening our borders with raids. There was talk of an invasion everywhere, long before any war was ever considered. So, with trepidations high, the king devised a new redevelopment scheme to bolster the outer reaches of his kingdom, with the aim to help evacuate towns in the advent of an invasion. And he called them the Warrens."

"Which is what these tunnels are…"

"Exactly so: narrow passages built to navigate the city undetected, kept in the hands of the barons as a secret. We're probably the first people to see these plans in near twenty-five years…" Her finger stopped at the end of a tunnel. "And as you can see here, this particular tunnel leads right across the town… and also, as it turns out, right behind the enemy lines."

Eli and Castan looked across to each other,

Perhaps all is not lost after all, Eli thought warmly. *Perhaps our redemption will come.* "How deep behind their lines does it go?"

"At least four streets back, we reckon," Jinx replied. "Which would put us just behind their rear-guard."

"And where does it come out to?"

"In a small courtyard I believe, behind what appears to be a large tree. The markings on the map don't show it very well, but the notes I saw indicate some kind of hidden space."

"How do we access it?" Castan asked, a charming boyishness in his cheeks.

She tapped a finger on his chest. "And *that* is the beautiful bit..."

Looking past the Chief, she tilted her head toward the fireplace built into the back wall of the chamber and smirked.

Eli frowned, turning to it. "*There?*"

"See for yourself... lift the rug for me, would you?"

Furrowing his brow, the Chief took several long strides over to the old fireplace and studied the burgundy-woven rug sprawled across the floor in front of it. Kneeling down and pulling at one side, he folded the rug over with a flick of the hands...

...and studied the tiny handle of a stone hatch beneath it.

"By the gods..."

"And there it is," Jinx cooed, running her hand over Castan's, "a way to win the war, right beneath our feet."

Eli turned back to her, a bloom of hope building in his chest.

We may prevail after all.

He turned back to them. "Castan?"

"Aye, sir?"

"Inform the leading rebels of our discovery. Have them convene in the hall's main chamber at dawn tomorrow for a briefing..." Inhaling, swelling his chest like an eagle, he looked down on the stone hatch beneath him and nodded. "Let them know we have a plan... and let them know we shall *win*."

†

Chapter 39

The Wolf

Smells like shit, this stuff.

The blackcoat fastened the door-keys to his waist-guard and grimaced at the bowl of gruel that had been slapped into his hands by the cook. In the plain grey dish, the green-ish liquid looked almost like reconstituted sick, with tiny lumps that he thought were vegetables but had the distinct feeling were not. It was an off colour in the low light, looking as if the gruel was ill. And it certainly smelt that way too: producing a putrid, violent odour combining spice and herbal relaxant, designed to calm even the most unsavoury of captives. Even then, every breath the guard took brought more of the aroma to him, where it cavorted through his system until he felt close to passing out.

Awful stuff, this gruel, the guard considered, lowering the bowl from his eyeline. *Filled with enough intoxicant to fell a troll, and unappetising enough to shit yourself thin come morning.*

"Who's this batch for?" the cook asked in front of him, sealing the basin of gruel with a heavy metal lid, and setting the ladle down next to it.

"Her majesty's *Dartunma*, I believe," the guard replied, screwing his nose up. "Down in the lower chambers."

The cook seemed shocked. "And the Champion is being fed *gruel?* How strange."

"It is... but I don't ask questions. I just do as I'm told."

"I overheard that she tried to kill that old man the Queen has kept in the *Qul'ta* Chamber. Have you heard that? Sounds like this *Dartunma* is quite violent..."

The guard scoffed. "Violent? I doubt that. If they had any sense, they wouldn't dare disrespect her majesty like that. Not unless they want to start losing fingers."

"Either way, do go careful when you go down there."

"Oh, *kü'gal*, it'll be fine. It's just another day."

"Very well... *Tol-tun, besyan.*"

"*Tol-tun.*" The guard turned to the door and stepped out into the long hallway beyond.

Nothing to fear.

Descending the third set of stairs, hissing at the pain pulling up through his ankles, the blackcoat guard turned left and paced the torch-lit corridor with long, balanced strides. The high ceiling above echoed with the sound of his boots; the torches quivered in their metal cages as he flowed past like the wind; the bowl of gruel in his hands sloshed delicately like stomach bile. The smell, which had been bad to begin with, seemed to become even more repulsive the longer it was exposed to the air – to the point where the guard had almost retched traversing the last staircase.

Who would reasonably eat this? He looked down into the bowl, and found its chundering consistency enough to make his intestines turn over. *No amount of relaxant would make me eat this... none.*

I'll stick to rat meat and pig's liver, thank you.

His pace slowed as the doors passed by on his right, counting each in turn until he reached the seventh and drew to an abrupt halt. He stilled his breath, listening out through the silence for signs of the Champion beyond the door: this famed fighter that few of them had even laid eyes on. He was intrigued, by the presence of the first

Champion in nearly seventy years – and he was astonished, that they were rumoured to be a Provencian.

Although I'm not sure how much of that I believe, the guard thought. *Those bastards in the south never had enough guile about them to succeed for very long… I doubt her majesty would pick someone of a race so unbecoming.*

Or foolish enough to let a wolf roam among our flock.

He pilfered through the keys at his waist-guard and plucked a long iron one from the fray, unhooking them from his side to approach the lock. With the bowl of gruel balanced precariously in his other hand, he plugged the key in and twisted it with some force until the *clunk* of a metal latch sounded.

Steadying any nerves that snapped across his sternum, the blackcoat guard eased the door open gently, peering into the dim chamber just beyond. The sconce on the wall was hardly burning, coating the room in shadow and hiding away the occupant that lay somewhere within.

I'll have to get that relit, he considered absently, pushing the door open and stepping in—

To find the door rebound against him and snap his elbow against the wall. His eyes bulged; the gruel dropped from his now-senseless hand, landing delicately against an outstretched foot and rolling silently off into the dark beyond.

He had little time to think, and even less time to scream, before a figure cast in shadow turned the corner and raised a knife toward him, a predatory hunger glowing in her eyes and the metal plate in her cheek…

†

Savanta slipped through the doorway like a python and grappled the back of the blackcoat's head, pulling him in close to slit his throat with a quick turn of her knife.

Blood exploded across her hand, gushing from the Tarrazi's neck as he attempted to form a scream – failing to, as a spluttering, ruinous cough escaped his lips and splattered the Champion's face with red. His legs kicked out, scuffing against the stone underfoot; spasms of energy coursed up his arms as he tried to reach up for her. With an embarrassing ease, Savanta ignored the attempts and swiped the keys from the guard's out-stretched hand, which he stared at dumbly as the white of his eyes turned pink and death suddenly took hold. She held his gaze for some moments and eased him gently to the ground, where she placed his head against the stone and sensed his soul drift off through the air. She regarded him slowly, with a cruel and ireful indifference, before pursing her lips and lifting to a stand and traipsing off down the corridor to her left.

She thinks she can keep me corralled down here like her little pet, Savanta growled, her leather shoes gliding with an effortless silence over the stone floors. *Like some fucking dog, that she feeds and toys with and beats for misbehaving. As if that's right... as if that is the grand total of what I've earned by coming here.*

I've earned more than that. I've hurt more and killed more, and I deserve more than what I've received as my dues. She tries to keep that from me. She tries to keep me in line, as if I'm something to be tamed. But she won't keep it from me any longer.

Because now it's mine to take.

She turned to a staircase that appeared on her right, with one side descending down deeper into the labyrinth and another climbing higher to the surface.

The Queen said that depravity was best kept out of sight... The Champion grinned.

So someone as depraved as my father, must be down below...

She started off down the staircase into the gloom, hardly able to recognise the steps as they formed beneath her feet. The torchlight seemed frightened down there, as if its existence were a battle and the battle was being lost. Every footfall seemed to envelop her more in the darkness, until even her hands were little more than grey smudges jutting from two stump-like arms.

Need to find a mobile light-source soon, Savanta admitted, nearly slipping on a shorter step. *Or if I can prize one of the torches from those metal cages, maybe I could—*

She ground to a halt; a chill crept up her spine.

A laugh echoed out somewhere behind her—

She turned sharply, looking up into the dull light of the corridor above—

Where she swore she saw the shadow of a person slip suddenly from sight, sliding off into the gloom without a whisper more…

The Champion ground her teeth together and snarled, turning back to the stairway below.

It's just the shadows, Sav. She shook her head.

Just the shadows and their knives…

†

Chapter 40

Darkening Skies

Like the snaking tail of a predatory fish dicing through murky water, the survivors emerged from the folds of the Ozban in a sombre, meandering line, returning to the camp with heads held low and the skies black above their heads. The rest of the soldiers turned to study them and found trepidation biting in their stomachs: looking at the bandaged heads and mangled arms and the stricken, haunted eyes as the survivors filtered out through the tents aimlessly, carrying with them their lives but not much else besides. They realised, with absolute dismay, just how few of the original force were actually returning – and they wondered, too, about what the hell had happened the previous night to have killed so many so quickly. They watched on, working through the options in hushed tones, before spying their commander emerge from the tree-line at the rear of the snaking column: bloody and bruised but otherwise unaffected, with the wicked ruminations of a grin catching at his cheeks. A man who appeared no different as he arrived to when he had left.

General Xol crossed their arms and watched him closely.

I don't trust this for one moment.

"The monster skulks back to his lair," Zespa muttered softly next to them, propped against the platform at the centre of the derelict village. She, too, watched cautiously as the commander approached, pursing her lips and tapping at her thighs with hesitant, long-nailed fingers. "The survivors are few to name."

"Reports say they encountered a creature that lived beneath the Tower in a tunnel system," Xol explained. "Apparently at night the beast emerged and the camp was overrun. The only survivors were those who made it to the top of the Tower before the beast could slaughter them… and our commander, here, was the only leading officer to survive."

"The only leading… wait, Oslo's *dead?*"

Ah, I forgot I didn't tell you. "I'm afraid so. General Oslo was killed in the line of duty… killed by the monster who terrorised the camp, so they say." Xol locked eyes with the commander skulking toward them.

Although which *monster that was, I'm not entirely sure…*

With a disconsolate sneer and a flick of his hair, Revek drew to a halt several steps before them, exhaling noisily through his nose.

"Morning, officers," the commander introduced, craning his neck to study them. "I must apologise for our… *sudden* appearance. Although, with a giant subterranean insect tearing through our camp and massacring our people, I think you can perhaps understand why we're here."

"We've seen the reports," Xol replied bluntly. "Care to elaborate for us?"

Revek bristled, but remained otherwise unperturbed. "Well it was a tragic and sudden turn of events, you see. We set camp as instructed within sight of the Tower, and *I* suggested it would be a good idea to keep the tents all packed in close together with no fires lit, so as not to draw attention. General Oslo concurred, so that's what we did." A pause. "However, we also discovered a hatch within the Tower itself, where we believe the creature emerged from in the night to stalk our camp. We set watch to—"

"Wait… what's this about a *hatch?*"

Revek grimaced, making his disgust at the lack of respect very clear. "We found a hatch inside the Tower, on the ground floor. It lead into some pit covered in corpses, down into a tunnel system below. We had it locked and sealed when we first found it, to keep us safe… but evidently something – or *someone* – decided to reopen it in the night, allowing the beast to emerge and decimate our camp."

Xol nodded. "I see. Was the hatch checked at dusk?"

"Yes, it was."

"So you were the last person to see it before the camp settled?"

"I was the last person to see it… *to my knowledge,* yes." Revek grit his teeth, sensing Xol's tone.

"But if you set a night watch, then anyone sneaking off toward the Tower would have been spotted, and you would have been alerted, as is the appropriate chain of command when assessing and neutralising a threat."

"Well I wasn't notified of any disturbance, so someone must have slipped through… and you can have my *apologies* for that," Revek spat.

"Apologies don't explain how that creature got out and tore through your camp, however, commander. Something doesn't seem to be adding up…"

Revek took a long step forward, entering Xol's circle with a baleful menace. "We lost a lot of people last night general… a *lot* of people," the commander growled, his eye twitching. "What happened was, unquestionably, a *terrible* accident, at the hands of a massive creature. It was only by sheer luck that we survived at all. So, *officer,* I'd appreciate it if you'd dispatch with the snide remarks, and leave any questions about my leadership *unsaid*. Am I understood in that?"

Xol smiled, nodding their head slowly. "I understand perfectly, commander. Of course."

Revek's cheeks reddened. "Then why are you *smiling*?"

"Because… I'm still trying to work out when you decided to start *caring* about people. When you decided to start looking at the soldiers of this army, as more than just cogs in a machine. *'They know what they're getting themselves into'*, as I believe you put it before. So, I really must ask: what changed, commander? When did you start caring?" Xol leaned in closer. "When they were dying before you in their dozens, in the jaws of a foul creature… or when you realised their deaths might actually cost you your *job*—"

Revek lunged out and grabbed for Xol's throat before they had a chance to finish.

Catching his arm, Xol twisted his wrist with a flare of the nostrils, shaking their head.

The commander winced, gritting his teeth, reaching suddenly for his blade—

"I wouldn't do that if I were you."

Xol relinquished their grip on the commander's arm and stood back, savouring the look of despair and pain that crossed Revek's face as he realised whose voice had spoken. Both of them turned to attention, offering appropriate introductions as the newcomer approached – but Xol sensed the commander boil beside them at the sight of his co-leader, as if the sun were set to swallow him whole.

"Evening, officers," Marshal Lazaerys bellowed, standing before them with a steely disposition that would've made the gods cower. "Can't say I was expecting my field general and joint-commander to be drawing swords on each other when I arrived, but disappointment seems to follow like a bad fucking smell at the moment."

Revek shifted in front of Xol, puffing his chest out like a peacock. "I can assure you, Marshal, that this incident—"

"Ah yes, Commander Revek," Lazaerys interrupted. "Just the person I didn't want to speak to and yet still find myself engaging in conversation with. As far as my reports have indicated… you have quite a lot of explaining to do."

Revek seemed to shrink like a limp cock, gesturing awkwardly with his hands. "Well, you see… a lot of stuff happened, a lot of terrible things… and well, I… well, you see, what it was, was…"

"Okay, commander, I'll stop you there. I see you're struggling to accept even a tiny-*fucking*-modicum of responsibility, so how about I make it easier for you? I've received reports that, because of your inability to maintain control of a situation and your complete negligence of security in the face of a possible threat, over half of the force that set out to the Acolyte's Tower are now *dead*, and the survivors who remain all look as if they've just watched their families be executed." She scoffed in disbelief. "I thought the reports were some sick joke at first: I mean, who could fuck up and cause the deaths of so many people so quickly? Seriously, we haven't even been out here a week, and look at this army! It's in *tatters*!"

Xol watched Revek wave his hands dismissively, refusing his part to play. "This can be explained, *Marshal...*" he began.

"Can it? Really?" Lazaerys spat. "Because, *commander,* ideally I would want to hear it from the general in charge of this little expedition, as part of a joint-report signed and stamped on my desk back at base. But as far as I understand it, you've even managed to fuck that up, because apparently he was killed in *'a debacle'* in the Tower... and you were the only other person present." She looked him up and down with a sneer. "So if this can all be *'explained'* as you say it can, commander, then please, try and explain *that one* to me..."

Xol looked between the Marshal and Revek like two pit-fighters matching up in the arena, as the commander squirmed like he had maggots in his ears trying to conjure the right words to say.

Let's see what story you enlighten us with, sir, Xol considered with a smile. *I'm sure we'd all love to hear your side of events...*

Revek adjusted his collar, managing his distress with a sharp cough. "We were... we were climbing through the tower... and it was dark, with only a torch between us. We charged up the stairs... and that *creature* was tearing through the floors after us, clawing at the stones at our feet trying to get us. The rest of the soldiers, they'd already made it... I had stayed behind to make sure of it. And on the last stairway to the rooftop where they were, I turned one moment to see Oslo clambering after me, thinking we were gonna make it... but when I turned again, I stood and watched helplessly as the floor exploded behind him, and he... he just fell through, down into the broken hollow of the Tower with the beast snapping at his legs..."

Revek sighed. "I didn't see any sign of him after that. All I heard was a crunch of bones and a short scream… and I just knew he couldn't have survived." His eyes dropped to the ground at his feet. "There's nothing I could have done that would've saved him, you see… we were both running for our lives trying to escape that creature, and… and he lost out. That's all there is to it."

For a long time after he'd finished, Marshal Lazaerys studied him with a furious intensity, dissecting his words like a cook pulling meat from a spit. Trying to anticipate the truth; to derive fact from fiction. And despite being held under her gaze, the commander remained steadfast, with nothing more than a sincere solemnity painted thick across his skin.

Xol stood patiently, tensing their hands against their back, awaiting some kind of response. They noted Zespa doing likewise, rolling her tongue across her gums incessantly. Time seemed to tick by endlessly, almost without fault – until Xol watched the Marshal relax her shoulders and produce an erroneous sigh, conceding the truth with a nod of the head. A truth that Xol also acknowledged, with equal parts acceptance and regret.

Whether you're lying or not… we have no way of proving it.

"If that is the case, and the whole truth… then I offer my condolences for the loss of General Oslo, and I am grateful that you are still with us to lead the survivors back to camp," Lazaerys said measuredly, bowing her head to her co-leader.

"Thank you, Marshal," Revek muttered through pursed lips. "I appreciate your understanding and sincerity."

"Although, this does not disregard the issue concerning your lack of leadership – nor why the creature was able to emerge from its lair when the hatch in the Tower was supposedly locked shut. These things still remain… *questionable,* to say the least."

A smile curled at Xol's cheeks; they watched Revek glare their way with enough poison to fill a chalice.

Actions have consequences, commander, Xol mused silently, clicking their tongue against the roof of their mouth.

And I hope yours hurt.

"So, with that in mind, I have decided to delegate all of my prior operations along the forest's outer borders to my subordinate officers, effective immediately," Lazaerys pronounced, "so that I am available to take *joint* control of what remains of this battalion, alongside my fellow commander, from this point on."

Revek's face soured instantly, as if all the colour had leeched from his skin. "*What?*"

The Marshal glared balefully. "Is there a problem, commander?"

"I... what are you hoping to achieve by doing that?"

"To coordinate, strategize, regroup... to clear up this fucking mess that you left behind, perhaps?"

"But... why are we looking to coordinate and *strategize* after what's happened? Why are we looking for ways *forward* in this? Half your expeditionary force were just eaten by a giant maggot with *tendrils,* for fuck's sake! What the hell are you talking about?" The rage in his voice flowed, crackling sharply like embers on a fire. "If you or anyone in command has any fucking sense left in your empty, vacuous skulls, then it should be *obvious* that we should be in full retreat! We're in the fucking *Ozban* – when you see a warning sign in a place like this, and when people die here in *droves*... you should never look back. You should pack your shit, and go. Because people have been massacred... and more will be massacred still, if we don't get the *fuck* out of here, *now.*"

Lazaerys shook her head. "Thank you for the impassioned hysterics, *commander*... they were really befitting our conversation," she replied mockingly, pinching the bridge of her nose. "Now look, I am not ignorant to the dangers of being here, or of the enemies we may face. I know the risks involved in staying put and fighting on, and I know that may raise some questions among the rank-and-file of this army..." She speared a finger out toward the commander. "But may I remind you, *again*, that it was under *your* command that near seven-hundred soldiers died on the Grey Plains and in the subsequent retreat through the Ozban, as well as another three dozen lost last night to that creature while under *your* watch. So, before you question my tactics, *commander*, please consider your own accountability in this matter. Because I have not let hundreds die while I flee for my life... and unlike you, I have no intention of starting now."

Revek remained silent, animate only in the twitch of his left eye, and the wavering hand lurking close to the hilt of his blade at his side. But behind his pupils, however, Xol observed the machinations of an unhinged man losing his way with power, awaiting the perfect moment to strike and exact some heinous revenge.

He is dangerous, the general considered, inhaling slowly. *Perhaps even more so than the Ozban itself.*

"Anyway, now that we have the *pleasantries* out the way, I believe a plan of action is in order," Lazaerys boomed, waving a hand toward Revek. "If I *may?*"

Revek said nothing; he seemed to just stare off into the distance like an absent bug, oblivious to the world and any words it spoke to him.

The Marshal frowned. "Very well... Xol, you will organise the survivors from the Tower and get them the supplies and medical treatment they need. Make sure they have tents and beds available, and ensure everything is kept dry in case of any prevailing showers that may come overnight."

"Yes, ma'am," the general replied, bowing their head.

"Good – now, Vespa, you and the commander here are in charge of fortifying the northern side of the camp in anticipation of enemy attacks. Use whatever supplies you can to form the barricades; maybe dig a few trenches by the main roads to deter any horses or Hounds overrunning the tents. See it done as quickly as possible, and utilise whatever free hands you can."

"Yes ma'am," Vespa replied politely.

Lazaerys awaited Revek's response in turn, only to find none forthcoming.

"Is that *clear*, commander?"

Revek tilted his head slowly. "Clear as day, Marshal."

"Good – then if that's everything, I'll be in the command tent if anyone needs me. You're all dismissed."

She turned sharply and paced back through the camp, giving waves and acknowledgements to the soldiers she passed who gazed sheepishly up to her.

Xol traced her steps as she disappeared from sight, sensing a weight leave the air as she did so, before they turned their attention back to the two officers just ahead: to Vespa, as she made to leave to start gathering supplies, and then to Revek in turn, who looked to the floor and his mud-stained boots with a foul grin on his face. A great unease gripped the general, watching the angular, despotic twist of the commander's cheeks like a mischievous child.

But this is far more than mischief, he knew, saluting to Vespa as she turned from the platform and walked off into the northern reaches of their camp. *This is something far more sinister.*

Xol remained silent, studying Revek as he looked up and glared their way, the swell of his irises like tiny daggers as he made off after the other general, lunging forward in long strides. Moving almost with a sense of purpose; almost like there was something to exact. As if there was something hidden within the shadows of his mind.

And when we work out what it is...

I wonder if we'll be too late.

†

Chapter 41

Retracing Steps

Cavara stepped out into the morning sun, glazed in yellow and gold, and looked across the walls of the storehouse from the previous day with a weight against her chest. Knowing what she had to do, and what it would cost if she failed.

How the life of a child lies in my hands.

"What is the plan, Successor?" the Forgotten One said behind her, closing their eyes and sensing the air. "What must we do?"

The general inhaled slowly and turned to them. "Before he died, Brutus said something to me in the Rapture," she explained. "He said I needed to *'retrace my steps'* if I had any hope of finding Evelyn… or learning *'the truth'*, as he called it. And at first, I didn't think anything of it, but last night… I think I realised what he meant." She tilted her head toward the storehouse. "I think the answer to where Evelyn is, is somewhere in that building… and I think Brutus found out, so they killed him for it."

The Forgotten One nodded. "An honourable man, marks his sacrifice by saving the lives of others… so if that is the case, then let us return to the storehouse, so he may not die in vain."

"Agreed," she replied. "Let's go."

They turned the corner and paced down the side-street to the storehouse's double-doors, which stood ajar with the sound of voices mumbling somewhere within. Cavara cursed – *I had hoped for no guards* – but held her resolve nonetheless, grateful at least that the Alderbane was taking the threat seriously.

And then there's the case of my honour-guard. Cavara tensed her knuckles and felt her blood boil, trying to make sense of it. *So much arrogance... so much hate. And for no good reason. Beyond our last encounter, I have never wronged them once. It cannot be purely prejudicial... can it?*

She shook her head, looking along the street to see if they were still watching her – only to find empty stone in both directions. *I haven't seen them since the fight in the inn... I don't know where they've gone, or what the arrangement is now. They were ordered to watch me at all times. Have they been recalled? Have the plans changed?* She sighed. *I don't know. It doesn't make any sense, I...*

I just don't know.

"Forgotten One."

The pale figure stopped suddenly. "Yes, general?"

"Whatever happens in there... or over the next few days, with the Butcher and the Alderbane and the honour guards... I just want to say thank you. I know that I haven't known you for long, but you've been the only certainty I've had since the Room of Shadows and I... that goes a long way, for a person like me. So, y'know, thank you for that. For sticking with me."

"It has been a great honour, Cavara, to stand by your side during these troubling times," they replied, placing a hand on her shoulder. "You have proven so fortuitous in the face of adversity, considering the odds you have come up against. To be the thing bringing balance to your life... is something I take pride in most." They leaned in close to her ear. "*And besides, you need not fear the Alderbane or their appeasers, general... because I'll gut any bastard within a hundred leagues who plans on harming you. You have my soul on that.*"

Cavara smiled, managing a quiet laugh. "Well, you have my thanks for that too then, friend."

They bowed their head and smiled. "A pleasure."

They both stood for some moments, looking into each other's eyes admirably, before Cavara cleared her throat and nodded. "Now, anyway... to the task at hand." She turned to the open double-doors of the storehouse.

Time to face the truth that awaits us...

She paced forward and turned the corner, entering the wide building where a half-dozen Sevican soldiers milled about looking over surfaces and searching drawers. Two of them, stood at the centre exchanging words, turned at the sight of the general and her companion and immediately went for their swords, pacing toward them with long strides and threatened faces.

"Dolco no pelos micatarni, co'dezoa!" one of them growled, waving his hand to direct them elsewhere. "Co'dezoa!"

"It's alright, we're here with the Alderbane's permission," Cavara replied, bowing her head. "We just have to follow up a few things from the attack yesterday."

The guard stopped in his tracks, recoiling like a startled cat, and looked to his fellow soldier with a perplexed gaze. "You... are Provencian woman? The one who..."

"Was ambushed here yesterday? Yes, that's me." She nodded to make the point clear. "The Alderbane has given us permission to search over this area again for any clues as to where the kidnapped child may be found."

"Hm," the guard replied.

"But... what you see that we not see?" the other soldier said, making a stoic attempt to master Provencian. "What else is here?"

"Certain things are often hidden," the Forgotten One boomed beside her, "unless seen by the one who seeks them."

"Just... trust us," the general added. "We'll be out of your way in no time."

The soldiers regarded them cautiously, weighing up their options, before slowly parting down the middle and accepting their words. Cavara smiled to them both in turn, steadying herself with a long draw of breath, before gliding effortlessly between them and out onto the main floor beyond.

That could've gone a hell of a lot worse, she acknowledged, closing her eyes and exhaling through pursed lips.

"We have survived our first ordeal it seems," the Forgotten One said, pulling up alongside her with hands clasped against their chest.

"By the skin of our teeth, too."

"Did you actually get the Alderbane's permission to return here?"

Her cheeks curled, thinking back to the throne-room earlier that day. "That may have been a *slight* fabrication."

"Sometimes following orders, and doing what's best, don't always align…"

"Yea… something like that."

The pale figure gestured across the room ahead of them. "So, general, I recall that you said something about *'retracing steps'* to gauge some idea of where to find the missing boy. Something about '*the truth*'?"

She nodded in reply.

"What do you think Brutus meant by that?"

"Well, it can either mean one of two things: we're either missing something we can see…" She pointed out across the floor just ahead of them. "…or looking for something that no-one else can."

She had sensed them when they had first walked over, like a deer alerted to a wolf skulking through the bushes nearby: the faint, hazy blue imprints marked across the stone floor, exactly the same as those they had followed through the winding streets yesterday.

"You see the tracks?" the Forgotten One asked, gesturing toward them.

"Yea… although, how can I see them without accessing the Rapture? That shouldn't be possible, I would have thought…"

"In any other instance, you would be absolutely correct in that, Successor. It should not be possible. But when one has as much exposure and connection to the Rapture as you do, through your Ascendent Soul, the boundaries between our realm and theirs begin to merge slightly, allowing certain abilities that would otherwise be out of reach."

"So what I'm looking at is *their* world projected onto *ours,* rather than the Rapture which is the other way around?" She paused for a moment. *How weird.*

"Exactly so, general. It is a melding of two realities, conjoining on a temporal level. And the fact that you can see it, means that you are either very apt at your ability to interpret the void... or a blood vessel is about to explode in your head, and kill you outright."

She frowned, looking up to him with fearful eyes. "Seriously?"

The pale figure remained still, before a huge, awkward smile pulled across their cheeks. "Got you."

Cavara rolled her eyes and shook her head. "You scare the shit out of me sometimes, you know..."

More than I care to mention.

Turning back to the footprints tracing across the ground ahead, Cavara felt the pull of the Rapture suddenly in her mind. Taking a few steps forward, as the spirit-trail formed more acutely beneath her, she noted how they moved off toward the back of the room and disappeared behind stacks of boxes. Making off into the shadows: into a place where there were no doors or access points that they knew of. Which would have made no sense, in any other circumstance.

Unless there's something else awaiting us there.

"Around that corner, behind the boxes," she directed. "The same spirit trail as before."

"It seems quite recent, too," the Forgotten One considered.

"Are you thinking the Butcher returned here after the attack?"

"It's possible... although I'm not sure how much we will find here if they have."

"Why's that?"

"Because, as you can see spirit-trails, I don't believe the transmitter would be foolish enough to return to wherever they're hiding, knowing you would be able to discover it quite easily. They may have already moved whatever it is, and are now leading you in circles."

Cavara rolled her tongue across her teeth, a disheartened weight forming in her chest. *Perhaps they're right... perhaps we are too late.* She siphoned through her thoughts, trying to find some semblance of hope there that all was not lost – and returned to her conversation with the Butcher the previous night, where she recalled a certain detail they had discussed.

The Butcher believed that I had been using Brutus as an informant to learn of his whereabouts, as he was the first one to see the transmitter in the City.

But if he thinks it was all Brutus, then…

She gasped.

"I don't think the Butcher knows that I can see spirit trails," she spluttered.

"How so?"

"I think they had Brutus killed because they genuinely believed he was the only way I could find the transmitter without you, and that with him gone I wouldn't even consider coming back here. I mean, why would I return to a place that was used as a trap to have me killed?"

"He assumed you would be naïve… and that if any more spirit-trails were found here, then I would dismiss them as part of the Butcher's trap."

"But because of what Brutus said, I know that these footprints we can see here are not just part of the trap. And if that's the case, then the transmitter didn't come back here last night to move whatever they've been hiding…"

"They came here to secure it," the Forgotten One inferred, studying the room with porcelain eyes, "because the best hiding place is always somewhere you'd least expect it to be…"

Cavara moved suddenly, anticipatedly, following the blue-tinged footprints manifesting beneath her like a dog that had caught a scent. She moved off into the shadows at the back of the storehouse where the high windows could not reach, banking slowly left behind the stacks of boxes as the spirit-trail illuminated below. Keeping her head down, with the echoes of voices and her clattering boots reverberating through her eardrums, she sensed the walls narrow alongside her as she entered a short corridor toward the back wall –

where she looked up and stopped suddenly.

Realising the trail was gone, and all that remained was a single heavy box against the back wall.

What? She frowned, puzzled. *That doesn't make any sense, it can't just stop. Where does it—*

"Cavara."

She turned at the sound of the Forgotten One's voice, stood like a grey statue in the dark, and noted their outstretched finger pointing to the floor just ahead.

What? The general looked back down to where the footprints stopped, trying to make sense of what the pale figure meant, when she spied the faintest glow of a footprint just beneath the box, tucked away like a doorstop.

"They go underneath," she remarked. "Do you think...?"

She grappled the edge of the box and tested its weight; the Forgotten One stepped past her and moved to the right side.

With a count of three, and the muscles in her forearms bulging, the general and her guardian dragged the heavy-set box to one side. The pressure across her shoulders tightened suddenly; the pale figure flared their teeth under the strain. As it shifted slowly to the left, Cavara noted the wooden square underneath it, sealed at the edges with metal slats and thick steel bolts. An oddly familiar shape, like many she had seen back at home.

And with a final heave, the box planted firmly in the far corner, revealing a wooden hatch just beneath.

Cavara scoffed. "Well I'll be damned..."

She bent low and slotted her fingers under the handle, pulling upwards with a sharp *clang* of metal to reveal a staircase descending into the gloom, illuminated by the faint glow of torches.

Well I'll be fucking damned...

She looked up to the Forgotten One. "Do you think this is the Cellar that was mentioned in the letter we found?"

The pale figure relinquished the general's grip on the handle and placed the hatch door against the back wall. "Well, this is either the

Cellar itself… or the passage to it," they replied, hovering their hand over the first step and sensing the air. "And as there appears to be no soul-trap placed over it… I don't think the Butcher believed we would ever find this. That, and we have the footprints to prove it…"

Cavara looked down the staircase again, feeling the numb pull of the Rapture across her skin, and saw the blue prints of the spirit-trail continue on down into the dark.

So this is where they've been hiding all this time, she concluded, lifting to a stand. *And we were never meant to find it, because that would've been too obvious.* She smiled.

What a shame.

"Are you ready, general?" the Forgotten One asked, placing a hand on her shoulder.

Cavara took a deep breath. "For Evelyn… always."

And into the dark, she went.

†

Chapter 42

Bleed Them Dry

They will pay. They will all pay for what they've done to us. I will make them suffer in ways they didn't think were possible... bleed them in ways that make the agony last hours. Every last one of them... men, women, children. Every single survivor that we drag from the corpses of their kinsman, blood-soaked and screaming... all shall suffer our wrath, and face the consequences of the sins they've committed. They shall bleed, and they shall burn, and they shall die, by my hand and the hands of the faithful... and oh, I shall revel in it when we do. Mark my words...

The medical officer looked up from their station, a hammer primed in their hand. "Ready, sir?" he asked.

General Ferreus grit his teeth. "Do it."

The officer drew the hammer back like a drawstring, and swung it against the bolt sat adjacent to the general's damaged knee.

A grating sound of metal echoed out between them. The iron leg-brace attached to the bolt constricted sharply like a pair of jaws, as it fastened across the general's shin and thigh and locked in place. Ferreus growled, biting his tongue as his ruptured kneecap slotted back into place, and the ligaments along the back of his knee throbbed with an uneasy numbness.

Gods, that fucking hurt.

Leaning heavily against the table to his left, the general eased to a stand and wavered for a moment as his right leg adjusted to the brace.

Strikes of pain rippled up and down his knee, bulging awkwardly against his ankle. The pressure threatened to tear his leg in two; the general swore a delicate prayer under his breath. But as that same pain slowly subsided, and he flexed the brace a second time without any problem, Ferreus nodded his head and smiled.

Well how about that...

"The procedure... appears to have been a success, sir," the medical officer chirped, returning the hammer to their toolbox and closing the lid. "The leg should now provoke only minimal discomfort."

"It certainly feels minimal," Ferreus acknowledged, taking another step to test the weight.

"I will warn, it will take some getting used to, as the iron brace will naturally set you off-balance on that side, sir."

"I see what you mean... although, I'm still able to manoeuvre it quite well, and seem to have my full range of movement, so that's a blessing at least." Ferreus reached out and placed a hand on the officer's shoulder. "And so for that, you have my thanks. You have served me well, and I shall make sure you're paid handsomely when this is over." He leaned in close. "*Well, at least a hell of a lot more than the rest of these lot...*"

The medical officer said nothing, chuckling softly and lowering their gaze.

"Anyway, you're dismissed," Ferreus pronounced. "Thank you for your service, officer. I'm sure we'll be seeing each other again very soon."

"Indeed. A pleasure, sir."

They turned and ducked out of his command tent, pitched in a small square in the eastern reaches of the town at the general's behest. As the tent flap opened for a moment, Ferreus heard the distinct rattle of fastening armour just outside, and the charming sound of a whetstone sliding the length of someone's blade. The early morning glow of autumn sun glanced across the stone slabs underfoot, illuminating the tent around him in beige and porcelain hues. The Imperial Land Army amassed all around him with the dogged determination of ants, making their preparations for the next – *and hopefully last* – day of battle against the battered rebel fighters, still clinging to the hope of victory somewhere amongst the streets to the west.

Pitiful fools, Ferreus grumbled, adjusting his own chest-plate with a pull of leather straps. *Vagrants and whores, the lot of them. We'll grind them under our boots and send them to the mud for their idiocy.* He smiled. *I'll take great pleasure in watching Eli squirm as I drive my blade between his fingers.*

Great pleasure indeed...

"You seem spirited, sir."

General Ferreus pulled back from his thoughts and rolled his eyes. He looked toward the back of the tent, balling his hands into fists as he did so, to look upon the lead palace guard stood there with his arms crossed against his chest, holding a firm expression like that of chiselled stone.

I had hoped you'd gone and died somewhere...

"I am indeed spirited soldier... and with good reason too," Ferreus replied, trumpeting confidence. "I am spirited, because today is the day that we'll drive those bastards into the ground for good, and end this *shambolic* interlude in our plans. We'll drive the knife in deep, and show them exactly what the new regime is all about..."

The guard nodded slowly, producing a coy smile. "Very well, sir... but, forgive me if I'm wrong, but I thought that plan was yesterday's plan?"

Ferreus ground his jaw together. "It *was* yesterday's plan, yes soldier, and you fucking well know it was."

"And as far as I'm aware, the plan in question was also... *unsuccessful*."

"It was *not* unsuccessful, I will have you know. Certainly not from a military perspective. The battle yesterday was simply... *inconclusive.* Things got out of hand, the enemy changed position and tactics... and things just got messy. That's just one of the realities of engagement."

"Agreed... however, we weren't expecting you to charge in there and engage with their leader directly, without first securing the upper balconies and dealing with their firepower. I would've thought that was common sense."

The brace across his knee nagged stupidly. *Gods, you boil my fucking blood.* "I had every right to engage with Eli at the earliest convenience, because if I was able to kill him then the rebel cause would disintegrate before our very eyes. He is their centrepiece, and without him there is no rebellion. So, *soldier,* I believe that I did what was right to secure the situation best..."

"Perhaps." A deafening pause carried out between them. "However, some would see your actions during the fighting yesterday as a fatal tactical error... one that in turn forced our retreat and meant that we lost the fight—"

"*We did not lose the fight*!" Ferreus bellowed, storming over to the guard and pressing a finger down against their chest-plate. "We have lost *nothing,* officer, do you understand that? The battle was hard fought; the rebels lost the town square and much of the northern quarter; their leader was badly wounded, and their forces were decimated. We won the day, and we fought heroically... so don't you fucking *dare* say that we lost anything."

The palace guard held still, looking down on Ferreus with dour, disappointed eyes. "That may be so to you," the guard said quietly, "but the Governor does not see it that way one bit."

The general's eyes bulged like rotting fruit. "*What?*"

"The Governor has expressed his concern over your leadership and the utilisation of resources in the battle yesterday... he said that you were *sloppy* in command, and reckless in your engagement."

"And who the *fuck* gave you permission to have private correspondence with the Governor?"

"The Governor did, sir. We were asked to make our reports and dispatch them straight to him." He produced a dissuading smile. "I apologise if this upsets you, sir... I'm just following *orders*."

The general took a step back, gritting his teeth, with the biting, gnawing anger pumping through his veins like magma.

How dare they, he muttered soundlessly. *How dare they overrule my command. How dare they disrespect me like that. I am their leader, out here. I am the one who decides our engagement.*

Not them.

"Very well, *soldier.*" Ferreus tightened his knuckles until his palms bled. "If you are having correspondence with the Governor directly without my knowledge, then please feel free to tell him *this:* we shall exterminate the rebels in their entirety by dusk today. We shall hunt down and execute every last one of them. We shall hang their flayed corpses from the spires of the baron's hall where they shelter like rats. I shall gouge the nails from the fingers of their leaders, and feed them to them like pellets. I shall carve out Eli's intestines and shove them down his throat as he slowly asphyxiates, and then I shall begin carving his limbs off like the branches of a tree. I will make an example of them, and I will exact my will *absolutely* when I do so." He turned to the tent's opening, his forked tongue sensing the air. "You can tell him all of that... and you can tell him no-one shall stand in my way, or I shall start making people disappear ..."

He gave one last look to the palace guard, trying to hide a wicked grin.

Including you.

†

Chapter 43

The Masterplan

Eli rolled his shoulders and chewed on the inner shelf of his lip. Tensed his hands; uncurled them like the fronds of a fern. A biting, spiteful pain cracked down his spine, echoing a poor night's sleep tossing-and-turning in the dark. His eyes were bloodshot, straining to focus in the low ebb of candlelight. Toes crunched in his boots like a boxer's fists, sensing the danger that would come and wholly aware of the uncertainty of it.

I don't want them to do this. He paused reflectively. *No: I don't want to* ask *them to do this. They've hurt enough… lost enough, without me demanding more of them.* He placed his hands flat against the table, in an act of self-admittance. *But I also know that, if I don't ask it of them and we turn away from this… then they will be hunted down and murdered anyway. The regime will not cease until every one of us is dead.*

And this, right now, is the only way we can avert it.

They stood in the baron's chamber surrounding the old oak table, with the same maps as before sprawled out in front of them like a pale coat of winter snow. The officers present – *the four who remain after all this* – had already spent some time looking over the maps and notes to determine why they had been summoned at such short notice, producing numerous quizzical frowns as they did so, muttering amongst each other like priests. None of them could make sense of it, and the confusion proved all-encompassing. So, when Eli then entered the room donned in his finest armour with a sword at his hip, they had turned to him expectantly like students, quiet and resolute but wearing the same perturbed expression that begged the question.

Are we actually going to fight on?

"I know this seems… *odd*, that I have summoned you here, considering no more than twelve hours ago there was word about a managed retreat, and I imagine you have a lot of questions as to why this change has come about," Eli explained, raising his hands. "But, I assure you all, that there is good reason for it."

The officers squared their shoulders and stood to attention, looking between each other with undetermined stares.

Eli blinked slowly.

Here we go.

"The simple answer is, we believe we've found a way to win this war that the enemy don't know about… a way to get behind them and decimate their back lines while we press from the front. And we have concluded from this, that this battle may not yet be lost…"

"Who's *we?*" one of the officers asked.

"That would be me…"

Heads turned like swivels, searching through the hazy orange glow to watch Jinx emerge from the gloom, strapped in light steel armour. A crossbow sat neatly at her side; a short-handled sword sat in a woven scabbard against her back. From the shadows beside her, the well-cut figure of Castan also appeared, bowing his head to Eli and placing his hand against the table next to them.

"Well met, Alva," the Chief pronounced, receiving her smile with one of his own. "Perhaps I best leave it to you to explain our new plans, as you're the one who designed them."

"Gladly," she said, her voice echoing strongly against the chamber walls. She levelled her gaze at each officer in turn before speaking. "We have found a way to outmanoeuvre, outflank and outsmart our enemy, and cripple them to the point of defeat in doing so. Maps that we found in the baron's vaults indicate that, as part of a redevelopment programme for the towns across Provenci, a number of underground tunnel systems called 'The Warrens' were constructed to allow quick and secretive evacuation of the towns in the event of an invasion. In our case, these Warrens stretch right across Marcheg, and have several hidden entrance points in various locations. From what we gather from the maps, one such entrance lies at the back of a small square somewhere in the east of the town – which, if accessed, would put our forces directly behind the enemy lines." She paused, allowing a coy grin. "And the entrance to said tunnel, and our chance at victory against the imperial regime… lies right behind us."

The officers frowned as a collective; they turned suddenly to study the shadows at their backs, trying to make sense of what she meant. Finding nothing but hollowness in the gloom…

Drawing their attention back with a rap of knuckles against the table, Eli stood to one side and opened his hand toward the hearth. "See here," he boomed, using the end of his boot to flick the rug aside and reveal the small hatch beneath it.

A number of gasps diced between the officers; a few even managed smiles.

"Do the enemy know of this?" one of them inquired: a rotund man with a splattering of rings across his hands.

"Not that we're aware of, no," Eli replied, drawing the room back to him. "If they had known about this before now, they would not have expended so much energy trying to take the square." *And Ferreus wouldn't be stupid enough to put his life on the line to siege this hall.*

Well, actually…

"Is that a certainty or a possibility, Chief?" another asked: a black-haired woman with blistered palms and a deep-set collar. "Do we know how many of these plans were made, and where they were kept?"

"Several plans were made that we know of, and there are copies likely residing in the vaults of Casantri's palace as we speak," Jinx explained. "But the chance of Alvarez having seen those plans and then drawn up a battle strategy with them, are incredibly slim."

"Such is the arrogance of liars and traitors..."

Jinx allowed a grin. "Precisely so."

"So there's a chance?" the rotund officer spluttered, eyes glowing hopefully. "We could actually... y'know, *win* this?"

"Providing the plans are correct, and the enemy don't know of them... we will most likely win the day today and cripple the Imperial Land Army for good," Eli explained, letting his words echo out through the baron's chamber like the rumbles of a church organ.

"What's the plan then, sir?" a third officer asked, with striking blue eyes and a knot of blonde hair pinned up with iron needles. "How does this work in practice?"

The Chief of the Mountains smirked and exhaled shakily through his nose.

Ah yes... the easy words before the very hard actions.

"We will fight as a double-offensive," he began, "utilising what numbers we have left over the widest possible area. You four and I shall engage the enemy as we've done before: hold the square, apply pressure on the flanks, keep the palace guards busy for as long as possible. Our main duty is to hold the street outside this hall with our lives, if this plan is to work. Because, while we engage the enemy on the streets above, Alva and Castan will lead a small flanking unit through the Warrens beneath our feet and locate this secondary exit in the small square to the east. Once there, providing everything goes to plan, they will fan out and attack the enemy from the rear, and we shall throw everything we've got at them from the front in the hopes we cripple their morale and force their retreat." He pressed his thumbs against the tabletop and nodded slowly. "It's the best chance we've got at this... so let's make it count."

A silence descended, like the moments before a coffin was lowered into the earth and the dead were finally put to rest. A couple of smiles appeared, dotting faces like pearls, as the revelation of hope rose in their hearts.

Eli looked on, feeling the weight in his chest grow heavier. *Hope is a fearful deception… replacing sense with ignorance. Hope is a beautiful thing in so many ways.*

But it may also be our undoing.

"I do have one question, though, Chief," the black-haired officer said softly, the swell of her chest indicating a long breath. "What happens if this *doesn't* work? What will that mean for us?"

The Chief sensed the arrow wound in his arm tug, the twine that held it together itching and straining against his skin.

Reality is a cruel mistress, as ever.

"I would not ask any of you to do this, were it not our last resort, and if the odds were not in our favour," he thundered. "But I believe what Alva has discovered may prove to be the lifeline that we need to finish this battle and emerge victorious… and I have faith that this plan, and the task that lies ahead, is not as insurmountable as it seems. We have come so far already, as a cause, in challenging the regime openly and standing up for our way of life. We have done so with honour, and good intention. We have shown already that the Imperial Army is not some behemoth intent on crushing our spirits: it is just another force, made up of people just like you or I, fighting for their institution and on behalf of those in power. They're just human, in the end." He looked to the dark-haired officer opposite him. "So, in answer to your question, if the plan doesn't work and we are caught out in the upcoming fight… then many of us will likely die, and the cause will meet the heel of the regime in its final breaths. That is the reality, and that is our situation, and it is best we don't shy away from that." He braced a hand against his steel breast-plate. "But I believe, regardless of the odds, that it won't come to that. That if we fight, and if we fight with our hearts in it, then the day will be won, and the Imperial Army will be ruptured beyond salvation. We have the opportunity before us to change the course of history… and all we need do, is try."

The officers before him, trounced with doubt before, nodded among themselves with fire in their eyes and the light of the cause in their souls. The Chief looked to them, passing from face to face –

meeting the gaze of Jinx and Castan, who smiled at each other and bowed their heads to him, acknowledging the task at hand and welcoming it gladly.

An honour to serve with you all, as ever.

Now let's get this done.

"So I ask of you all: rally the rebels, and tell them of the fight to come," Eli exclaimed, crashing his fist against his chest. "Tell them we shall press on, and we shall do so with fire in our hearts, and we shall emerge victorious in the end." He paused. "Tell them the army should fear us..."

For we are coming for them.

The officers departed through the main doors into the baron's hall beyond some time later, leaving Eli in the dark of the antechamber with a barrage of fears to spare. Once he was alone, he had paced over to the thick burgundy rug and pulled it aside, revealing the stone hatch beneath with a rasp of dust and stagnant air. Curling his nose up, the Chief had bent low and peeled it open to reveal the dark recess beneath: a passage no wider than a sewer, opening out somewhere beneath the hearth just ahead. He had stood then wondering, in the anxious cracks of his mind, about what kind of dangers awaited down there; how safe it was, in a place unseen for sixty years; whether the enemy knew of it, and were laying their traps down ready for them...

No, he spat, rolling his shoulders. *This is not the time for fear. Lives are on the line.*

This is it now.

Sensing a presence, Eli turned to watch the doors open and a line of some thirty rebels pace into the chamber toward him, bowing their heads one after the other with Castan arriving at the helm.

"Well met, Chief," his second-in-command said, bracing Eli's forearm with a firm grip. "How are you?"

"Hoping this is not a mistake," Eli replied, rolling his tongue. "And that we actually have a chance of winning this."

"Well, we have the advantage now… I mean, the enemy don't even know these tunnels exist. So providing we can get to the other end unscathed, I say we have a very good chance of winning this."

Eli nodded. "You're a good man for doing this, Castan."

"It's an honour, Chief."

"And… thank you for looking after Alva. I mean it."

Castan placed a hand on his shoulder. "For you, my friend, I'd go to the ends of the known world to keep her safe. You have my word on that."

"Thank you, always. I'll never forget it."

He stepped past the Chief and winked. "You better bloody not…"

Eli stifled a laugh, as Castan descended into the passage at his back and guided the other rebels down after him. They filtered in one by one, offering their well-wishes to the Chief as they passed – although Eli found himself distracted, fighting with the unease building in his throat, as a swell of ginger hair pulled the doors closed at the back of the room and approached him with elegant strides.

Here it is.

"Hi, Alva," he said softly, holding his breath.

"Hi Eli," she replied, tucking her arms under his and pulling in close for a hug.

The Chief returned the embrace, his massive hands pressing against the frame of her back, with his cheek perched against her head. He sensed the knots in his stomach and the heat in his skull; tears pulled at his eyes, threatening a torrent that he kept steady with a long breath. Holding her still – so small in his arms – he imagined Arrenso's smile seeing them both together.

Remembering the man he loved.

"Please be safe, Alva," he whispered, rubbing her back. "Please be safe…"

Jinx stepped away from him and held him by the shoulders, smiling through her own tears with a flash of hazel eyes.

"I will be, don't worry," she said. "Remember, I'm Arrenso's sister, aren't I? And you know what that means."

"Tough as fucking nails."

"Tough as *fucking* nails, exactly." She nodded once, once only, and looked to the hatch next to him. "Now, go lead your people Chief. May fate be on your side, and may it kick the bastards in the teeth for the both us."

Eli steeled himself and breathed. "Good luck Alva."

"Good luck."

She released her grip and moved off toward the hatch, stepping down with a graceful motion onto the packed earth beneath. Torches had been lit, illuminating the passageway in amber hues like the rise of dawn. Jinx's hair seemed to ignite like firewood under their glow.

Eli turned to the hatch and gave a final smile to her, taking a deep breath as he pulled the lid down and sealed the passage shut once more, burying his fears beneath the mellow tones of duty and the resolve to see the job done.

Because that's what this is, he acknowledged, pulling the rug back across and turning to the far doors. *A job to be done, and an enemy to defeat. We have the advantage, and we have the strategy to win… all we have left is to do it.*

Looking to the left slightly, he spied the silver round of his bludgeon propped against the doorframe and smiled.

The place is here, and the time is now.

So let's get this done.

†

Chapter 44

Tyrant's Game

Endless corridors passed her by, glossed by the hands of shadows. Rising steps and ancient covings, woven into the rock by long-forgotten hands. The echoes of the many who had come before, chiming out to those who followed.

Gone again without a whisper, like the grace of autumn wind.

Savanta paced the corridors like a hound baying for blood, starved of sustenance and longing for the hunt to begin. She wasn't sure how long she had been searching, or how deep beneath the earth she had ventured. Every space that she entered was a near-mirror image of its predecessor: on and on, down into the impossible depths, alone and hungry with the burning flash of hate in her eyes.

No guards had come looking for her since she had escaped from her chambers. There had been no alarms or marching feet or pursuit through the winding corridors. As a matter of fact, she had not even encountered another soul thus-far, whether by accident or not. Each turn revealed a space as dormant as the last; every door lay locked and silent, no matter how many times she cracked a fist against it and bellowed for answers that never came. The keep remained uncaring, despite her best efforts to challenge it, as she pressed on into the dark wondering where it would end.

And whether the shadows would finally stop following her, just out of sight.

As the thought came, Savanta turned sharply to spy one drift elegantly from view, just behind her. A haunting presence; a narrow frame of curves and coiling skin. A whisper seemed to catch at the air nearby.

And yet when she spun to meet it with her knife primed, hoping to gut the shadow like a fish, there was nothing but empty stone there to welcome her, as it had done for what felt like days on end. No movement. No sound.

Just effortless silence again.

Savanta scowled, descending the next staircase with a flash of her teeth. *She's toying with me,* she thought, finding comfort in the knife tensed firmly in her grasp. *Like a cat chewing on a mouse: wanting to keep it alive while it's slowly maimed to death, just to savour the fun of the hunt.* She allowed a quiet smile. *Well, let's see how long this little game lasts then, shall we, your Highness?*

Let's see who bleeds in the end.

She disappeared into the shadows, seeking the steps in the dark as she descended, turning the corner at the bottom to see the corridor beyond—

Where a figure slipped through a doorway, trailing a sword as they went, with laughter ricocheting off the high walls and through Savanta's ears like a jester.

Drawing still, the Champion blinked slowly and scowled, moving off toward the door with long, fiery strides. The clatter of her boots echoed like drums against the walls; the tiny specks of mineral deposits glistened across the ceiling. An ire burned within her, pulsing to life like a furnace as she approached the door and tried the handle.

Only to find it locked, sealing its secrets within.

Savanta turned back to the corridor she had just walked down, and pulled her knife close to her.

"You think this is a game, don't you?" she cried out, not caring for who heard. "You think it will bring you some kind of satisfaction, don't you?"

Turning on her heel, she looked back the other way into the gloom and found nothing there.

"Well, it doesn't. It never has. It's weak and cruel... you are pathetic for cowering in these shadows."

The Champion lifted her fist and smacked it against the iron door, sending blasts of sound down the corridor like the clash of blades.

"Show yourself, you cowardly *bitch*! If you are the great Queen you claim to be – the mighty Gaza of Tarrazi legend – then do me a fucking favour, and *prove it!"*

Silence answered; her fist clattered harder against the door.

"Show yourself! Fucking *show yourself!"*

Silence was all that—

"Prove it, you fucking bitch! Prove it!"

Silence—

"*SHOW YOURSELF!"*

Sil—

Footfalls, approaching from her right. Turning suddenly, to spy a black cuirass and shimmering leg-guards pace across the stone. The pale round of a tyrant's skull, glowing like the moon. Piercing eyes and a forked tongue between flesh-pink lips and a steel jaw. The menace of the madness, cast in shadow, with the thin strike of a rapier twisting at her side.

Gaza Minesk, the Iron Queen of Tarraz, drew to a halt and smiled.

"Hello again, Champion," she cooed.

Savanta glared her way, the fear and ire convulsing in her throat like a blocked steam vent. The glint of the knife in her hand was almost hypnotic.

"No games," the Champion growled. "No games anymore."

"Who said anything about games?" The Queen stood perfectly still, the thin blade twitching delicately in her hand. "I had reports of someone breaking out of their chambers and killing one of my guards – I am not here on account of any *games,* my dear, I assure you. I am here chasing a wild animal that has not been brought to *heel*."

"I am not yours to control."

"You are, and always will be, whatever the *fuck* I tell you to be."

A hint of venom laced from her tongue. "Now why don't you be a good girl and come with me back to your chambers… make this nice and easy for everyone."

Savanta shook her head. "No more games."

She started approaching, gaining speed as she went.

The Iron Queen's fangs appeared between the folds of her lips.

"Well, if you *insist*…"

Savanta screeched, near-enough tearing the stone from the walls as she hurtled toward the Queen and struck out with her small blade.

With a deft turn of the heel, Gaza flicked the knife away with her rapier and stepped aside, allowing the Champion space to fly past her and skid across the stonework like a bull.

Digging her heels in to skim over the slabs underfoot, Savanta twisted quicker than Gaza had anticipated and lunged out again toward the Queen's exposed flank. A darkness crossed the moon's of her eyes, and the Queen adjusted by the tiniest fraction to avoid the knife impaling her chest.

Then the rapier swept up, rallying to counterattack; Savanta lurched sideways and manipulated the knife through her fingers, using the opening to strike down toward Gaza's orb-like skull.

The Queen made no attempt to block it – she hardly moved at all, it seemed – until the knife was inches from stabbing into her brow and—

Gaza's free hand pulled up to grapple Savanta's wrist, twisting it until her elbow-joint creaked and a whimper escaped her lips. The knife dropped out of her hand. The breath seemed to leave her body. The Champion, boggle-eyed, looked up at the tyrant's shadow—

As a balled fist clutching the rapier snapped across her jaw, the knuckles biting into the metal plate laced through her cheek.

Savanta screamed. Her eye sagged grotesquely. Something in her mouth ballooned and popped. Blood threaded over her gums. A vessel popped in her nose from the force tugging against her skin. Dark patches flooded her vision, threatening to drag her down into a murky slumber.

The Iron Queen relinquished her grip on the Champion's wrist, letting her sway awkwardly on haggard legs as she dipped in and out of consciousness.

"Anger is to the soul, what the sun is to the eyes," Gaza mused, kicking the knife away with her boot. "Raw and fiery, capable of a great many sins… but so blinding to us, when we gaze into its maw for too long." She took a single step back. "It's a pity, really, to watch someone so *capable* brought so low by her fury and hate…"

With tears leaking from her eyes, Savanta ran forward as if to tackle the Queen to the ground—

Facing the crack of knuckles, as Gaza landed a punch against the back of her head, sending the Champion sprawling out across the stone slabs below, wheezing painfully.

"It is a *pity* to watch you behave like such an animal when you refuse to bow the knee. All I ask is for a little respect… and for your *total* subordination… but still you refuse, blinded by your own self-interests. How *sad*…"

Savanta brought her knees up and propelled backwards, hoping to crash against the Queen's legs and fell her like a tree—

A sharp kick snapped against her shoulder, with enough force to buckle her arms. Crashing down across the stone again; bones bending beneath her skin. Head bouncing like dropped pellets. The high ceiling spinning in beautiful circles far above…

The Iron Queen stepped over her, grabbing a knot of her hair and pulling her up. Savanta sensed the fight rise within her, but her limbs would not rally to meet it: like a lifeless husk, she looked deep into the pale circles of the tyrant's eyes and sensed the shame therein.

"You're supposed to be my Champion… bringing honour to a rank not held in nearly a century," the Iron Queen spat. "Do you understand the weight resting on your shoulders? Do you understand the power you wield, by my side? You have capabilities beyond even your wildest dreams… you have access to a life that no other mortal could dare comprehend. You have everything, you can be anything you wish… and yet this is where you are. This is where I find you.

Skulking through the shadows, murdering my guards, treating this keep like your own personal hunting range. Like some cruel little psychopath. Do you ever wonder why I put you in that fucking chamber in the first place, and locked the door? Because you're a mess… you're a grief-ridden, vengeful, blood-lusting coward. You are a monster, calling the darkness your home, and you are a disgrace. You disgust me with your actions, and how blinded you are by your pain…"

A metallic echo clipped in her ears for a moment; Savanta followed the Queen's gaze off to her right where a doorway had opened and orange light flooded the corridor from within. A shadow appeared and disappeared through it – faster than the blink of an eye – but from the shape of their body and the folds of their robes, Savanta knew who it was without any other suspicion, pulling at her heartstrings like chains.

"He's ashamed of you, you know… ashamed of what you've become," the Iron Queen said softly, stroking her head. "He wishes he could tell you… if only you'd ever listen. But you just scream, and cry… and rot. So, we made something of a deal, that allows you to prove to us just who you can be… someone he can actually feel a sense of pride for. Not the hate-filled bitch you've become… but something more." The stroking stopped. "And it all starts with a serpent's fangs…"

Savanta felt herself slip from the world.

"And the snap, of one's fingers…"

A click in her ear, and she was gone.

†

Chapter 45

Truth Lies In Shadows

He had not washed in days, and his skin had taken on the unusual texture of bone marrow. Hair matted with grease, plastered to his skull like wet leather. Black dust in the pits of his ears, thick as mucus.

And an ugly ire burning in his chest, as he traipsed the outskirts of the camp like a feral stray baying for mischief and blood.

Commander Revek of the Imperial Army of Provenci gave an admiring nod of approval as he surveyed the construction of the barricades along the northern edge of their camp. Wood carted up from the lowlands in the south had been butchered down into poles and interlocked to form the main walls. Platforms had then been constructed sporadically along them, facing out toward the dense trees where crossbowmen traced their shots. There were even a few pitfalls dug out along the treeline, hidden beneath dirt and sticks.

And what seemed most impressive of all, was that even in the midday heat of the Ozban Forest – with swarms of biting flies darting over their heads – the soldiers continued to work tirelessly on with resolute smiles on their faces. It was surprising, almost.

To everyone except the commander, that was.

"How are we, my friends?" Revek inquired to one group of them, stooping down to their level as they set more poles into the earth.

"Working on and working hard sir!" one replied enthusiastically.

"First time I've felt genuinely pleased with my work in a while, if I'm honest, sir," another said.

"Certainly hoping it keeps the bastards out," muttered a third.

"You're acting most fortuitously in your work, I must say," Revek mused. "Is this entire section yours?"

The men nodded in unison.

"Three layers of barricading? That's an impressive feat." He slapped one of them across the back, receiving a chortling laugh in response. "Almost making the rest of 'em look bad, ay!"

"We'd never dream of it sir," one of them said with a grin.

"Well met, soldier, very good." Revek squeezed the man's shoulder and released. "Well, do come and find me when you're done out here, won't you? I'll be sure to reward you for your efforts, as you've made a stoic effort on these defences so far. Keep it up."

A splutter of 'thank you sirs' were clucked his way as the commander stood and brushed his breeches, smiling off at the sun.

"Oh, and on that note," Revek added, "let's... keep the rewards thing between us, ay? Don't think the other officers need to know, or would appreciate it if they did."

The workmen beneath him looked among each other and smiled.

"We only take orders from you anyway, sir," one of them said proudly. "Only man with any sense of order round here after all."

The commander produced a grin, proud and vengeful.

Good.

He bowed his head to them and turned away, following the curve of the barricades as they banked slowly to the right, with a thousand tiny droplets of thought tapping through his mind as he went.

Loyalty is a beautiful thing, he considered, clasping his hands behind his back. *Loyalty breeds subservience... subservience breeds control. With every ounce of faith they place in me, they lose more of their own morality. What is theirs, becomes mine. Until they are nothing more than dogs on leashes...*

Their life and their steel in my hands.

He rolled his tongue across his teeth, swatting a swarm of flies away. *That's the bit the others don't understand... the bit Lazaerys can't seem to get into her thick, stubborn skull. Just because you hold the rank and fly the flag, it doesn't mean shit out here where the world is very real and very terrifying. The soldiers don't seek out whoever's in charge; there is no uniform command structure. They seek a familiar face, and someone they can trust.*

Someone like me, you feckless bitch.

His eyes wandered briefly, lost in a daze of self-aggrandisement, when he spied the silver plates of an officer shifting between the carts just ahead, taking note of their supplies.

The commander grinned seditiously, his strides lengthening as he approached. *Well, well, well...*

Just the woman I wanted to see.

"Zespa!" he exclaimed, raising his hands to her disdainful glare. "How are the defences coming along, my fellow officer? It seems to be going rather well I would have said. They're a determined bunch at any rate..."

"They're going well," she replied bluntly, pulling aside another ream of cloth to note the contents of the cart next to her. "Do you need anything, commander?"

"No, not at all... I simply wished to speak with you is all. I like to have good rapport with my fellow officers, you see. Good for the soul, and all that."

She raised an eyebrow. "Is that so?"

"Yes, of course... you seem unsure?"

Zespa smiled. "Forgive me, sir, but I've uh... been warned that anyone who forms any kind of working relationship with you usually ends up being killed... or at least, ends up disappearing."

"Is *that* so?" he said venomously. "Well, how strange. Do you care to tell me who told you *that?*" *So I can string them up and feed them to the fucking rats...*

"Just some joking around among colleagues, sir... nothing of any great importance, I assure you." The smile fell away conceitedly.

"I see." He placed a hand against the cart beside him, making it very apparent that he had no intention of leaving. Studying her for some moments, he watched her go about her business without question or thought: just fulfilling orders, rank and file, almost without conscience.

What's the use of someone like you, hm? Revek queried. *What purpose do you actually serve? An officer of the army just... following commands. An ant in the colony, ready to return to the mother once the task is done, only to be sent off again as soon as you can. No personal thought or resourcefulness... no intuition. Just blind, brain-dead servitude.* He sighed, before an idea sprung to mind. *Unless that's just a front.*

Let's see what you're really thinking...

"Can I ask you a more personal question, Zespa?"

The general produced a concerned scowl. "If you must."

Revek leaned in closer, lowering his voice. "How do you feel, with Marshal Lazaerys around, breathing down our necks at every turn? Does it make you uneasy?"

She lowered the cloth back onto the cart, rolling her shoulders slowly. "I wouldn't have said so, not in particular. Her presence has little meaning to me... I take orders from Xol and yourself. She's just another officer in the end."

"But doesn't that get under your skin?" the commander pried. "To have two commanding officers giving you orders – a mess in itself, if you ask me – and now a third officer has shown up, who not only gives you even more shit to do, but also chastises Xol and I for doing our jobs. It's all a bit strange, wouldn't you say? A bit of a mess. Almost like the top is a bit... *crowded,* you know?"

"Such is the nature of command," she said simply. "Everyone has to answer to someone in the end."

"Perhaps, yes... but *who* one chooses to listen to in command, is the important part."

"I suppose it is."

"So... who do *you* listen to, Zespa?"

Her eyes levelled with his, challenging the question; her hand tensed against the lip of the cart. "I listen to whoever the Supreme

Governor of Provenci says I should listen to. I follow orders. I'm an officer. The truth doesn't lie in shadows: it lies in order and discipline." She paused. "Perhaps you should learn that someday..."

Revek ground his teeth, a sudden heat pulling up his neck. "What's *that* supposed to mean?"

"You don't need to hide it, sir... we can all see it," she muttered, rolling her thumb and finger together. "You've been slighted ever since the Marshal appeared and splintered your command. Ever since she sent you out here, on a death-whim with three officers chosen to keep an eye on you, you've had a look in your eye that spells *traitor.* Because you long for power, and you long for *complete* power, and you will do whatever it takes to get it." She shrugged. "Perhaps Oslo died in the snapping jaws of that beast by the Acolyte's Tower... or perhaps he didn't. Perhaps I don't care; perhaps he was foolish enough to go there in the first place and tempt fate." A silent smile. "But what I do know, commander... is that no matter how the last officer died, and by what circumstance, if any other generals of this army go missing over the coming days... it will, without a doubt, be by your hand and your blade."

She stepped away from the carts, dropping her gaze to the floor, her hand never steering far from the sword at her hip. "Anyway, I'm finished up here, so I'll report to Xol and the Marshal about our progress and fill you in on any orders given," she explained, turning from him and offering one final look. "All the best, sir... I'm sure you won't need it."

Zespa paced off into the wider camp without a word more, slipping between the ruins and disappearing moments later.

Revek stood for some time after she had left, staring absently at the spot where she'd stood. Frozen in time; frozen in thought. A cold wind whipped up through the trees suddenly and dousing him with thin autumnal air. It took some force – and a shiver biting down his spine vigorous enough to crack his vertebrae – for the commander to finally return to reality again.

And when he did so, he found himself smiling, looking up to the sun in the sky.

So she sees it, he admitted. *She sees the desire in me for what's rightfully mine. For the power I once had… and the power that was so cruelly taken from me. My determination to get it back, and to reign supreme.* He sighed. *It's a shame, really, that she didn't long for that same power too. A shame she didn't display that same lust as I have. I mean, I would have quite liked to fuck her and make her my second-in-command, it's true…* A playful turn of his cheek. *But alas, such things are trivial in the grand scheme. People, like expectations, are often expendable. And I have no time for such things.* The commander looked out to the wider camp again and felt the blade burn against his hip. *Because she's right: the next person to disappear will be by my hand.*

And she won't live to know it.

†

Chapter 46

Under Pressure

Cavara drew to a halt with a long sigh and put her hands on her hips, surveying the tunnel ahead with pinpoint eyes.

Where the fuck are we?

The tunnels they had uncovered were a series of short, interconnected passages, narrow at the sides but unnaturally high above, built like a crosshatch just beneath the city streets. Sconces lined the walls, haphazardly lit so that some passages lay bathed in a warm orange glow while others surrendered to the dark. It was an eerie place: somewhere foreboding, where not even the rats dared venture. It felt like the underbelly of a derelict keep.

And that wasn't even the strangest part.

What's going on with the walls? Cavara thought, placing her hand against the stone and letting several streams of water trickle over her knuckles. Every surface was coated with a sheen of water, either stagnant or mobile, sliding over the walls and pooling at their feet. The dripping droplets echoed out down the passages like rainwater; the splashing tides of a breach somewhere ahead sounded like a river breaking its banks. All around them, thick furrows of moss coated the walls and amalgamated in cold corners, swelling and contracting like lungs; green algae spewed from the grout holding the tunnels in place like seaweed. It was a marvel to witness, Cavara found. The passages seemed to possess an environment that was entirely unique to the world beyond: a flooded biome, only a few hundred feet across, unlike anything she had ever seen before.

It's so strange, she pondered, pulling her hand away. *I wonder what's causing it?*

"The walls seem to be weeping," the Forgotten One said behind her, studying the high ceiling like a saint regarding the stars. "How unusual..."

"I've never seen anything like it," Cavara replied, sidestepping a large puddle coated in thick green slime. "We aren't near any water sources, are we?"

"I don't imagine so. With our altitude and the angle of the City, I doubt any water is able to accumulate properly before its swept down beyond the walls in the east. Everything is in a constant run-off."

"But there are still water systems in the City... I mean, people have working pumps in their houses, and lots of the interlocking sewers underground." Cavara shuddered suddenly, grimacing at the pools of liquid around her feet.

Although I really hope this isn't piss.

"That is true... but even a reservoir basin would not cause this much leakage, and the waters would not be rich enough to allow vegetation to grow. You wouldn't have this much... *moss*, I believe you call it... down here if there was."

The general nodded. "Maybe there's a natural spring somewhere in the City that we don't know about, causing the plants to form?"

"It is certainly a possibility."

"Or maybe..." Cavara held her lips shut for a moment, pondering the options – realising, suddenly, what was really going on. "I know where we are!"

The Forgotten One frowned. "What do you mean, Successor?"

"It's not so much where we are... but rather what we're *under*." She tapped one of the walls, pointing to the ceiling. "We're beneath the bathhouse... the one that Evelyn went running off to a few weeks ago, just before I was captured. That's why there's so much natural growth down here: the waters have been infused with stuff, and the thermal baths mean that they can germinate when they settle."

A smile graced the pale figure's face. "Very intuitive. I think you might be right."

"But that still doesn't explain why these tunnels are here. I mean, why build them if they're just going to leak and damage the building above? It doesn't make any sense..."

"I'm not sure of the answer, I'm afraid, Successor." The Forgotten One looked down the next interlocking passage, spying the faint glow of a sconce at the end. "But I do believe that, whatever we are searching for, will be found somewhere here."

"And all we have to do, is keep walking..."

And pray we aren't too late.

Cavara turned on her heel and paced off in the direction of the orange glow, dicing over puddles of tepid water illuminated like fish scales on the stone. The echoing expanse shifted ahead; the tip-tapping of water carried on incessantly somewhere in the dark. Like wraiths, the shadows played tricks on her eyes, forming into bodies and creatures that dissipated seconds later, setting her heart racing. Unease crawled up her spine, with every tiny footstep she made.

"I don't like it down here," she admitted, rolling her shoulders. "Not one bit."

"It has a number of rather unpleasant qualities, I do concur," the Forgotten One said at her back.

"That's one way of putting it."

"A rather odd design to this place, however... would you not say?"

Cavara nodded. "Definitely so. My father used to tell me that some human endeavours tread a thin line between idiocy and torture... and I think I'm starting to realise what he meant." A particularly-heavy droplet of water splashed against her scalp suddenly, as if to illustrate the point. "I used to think he was just pessimistic... now though, I'm not so sure."

"He sounds like a wise man. What was he referring to at the time?"

Cavara bristled, sensing emotions she had long forgotten raise their heads from slumber, as she exhaled weightily and pressed on. *Now is not the time.* "He was in construction, specialising in land management. Very good at his job, I might add. And just after I was born, he surveyed an area close to the mountains that they had plans to build an aqueduct on, drawing rainwater down from the peaks to improve irrigation. It was a good idea, and one that would greatly benefit the local area… in theory, that was. My father laughed at them when they suggested it, saying the whole operation was ridiculous: the land was rocky with soft-clay soil, and wouldn't be able to hold a structure of such size. It just wouldn't work." Cavara sighed. "But, as expected, they went ahead with it anyway. Ignoring my father; ignoring sense and safety precautions along the way. I would go and visit the construction site regularly with him, and he'd remind me just how foolish the whole thing was. I mean, I was only young, so I didn't really know what he meant at the time…"

"And what became of the aqueduct, in the end?"

"It was built" – she leapt over a larger puddle covering the passage floor – "and the local barons were all mighty impressed with themselves for it. Called my dad a quack and said he should be stripped of his titles, too… there was even talk of a court trial at one point. My mother was livid with him, and… well she…" – *threatened to beat him to a pulp* – "she couldn't believe it. But regardless, my dad remained certain he was right – and when the hot season came along, and the aqueduct was finally put to use, that became very apparent very quickly…" She allowed a quiet smile. "As the water rushed down the channel from the mountains, the legs suspending the thing over the rocks sunk into the soft soil, and cracked the joins that held it in place. And when it broke, there was chaos: enough water to turn Casantri into a soup-dish, crashing down on the land below, destroying farmlands and villages for miles across. It was a disaster, and cost dozens of lives." She shook her head. "And the irony was, we were waiting at the end with everyone else to watch the first lot of water come through… and we didn't get so much as a drop of it that day, all because my father had been right…"

The Forgotten One considered. "Your father should never have been second-guessed."

Cavara managed a laugh. "Yea, that's for sure."

"He sounds like a decent man."

"Yea..." Her lips drew still, breath quivering in her lungs.

He was.

The general blinked rapidly, stifling the emotions that came, facing down the shadows that engulfed her on all sides. *Now isn't the time... this isn't the time,* she cursed. *I don't need this. We're in the passages, hunting an assassin, hoping to find a child still alive at the end of it. The grief can wait for now. It can wait.*

As it has, and always will.

She ground her jaw, shaking loose any thoughts that remained. Dismissing her past; stamping it beneath her heel like a bug. Pressing on into the dark – approaching the orange glow just ahead – pulling air through her nostrils in great heaves...

Realising, then, just how heavy it had become in her lungs, and how it seemed to stick to her skin like tar.

Wait... what's going on?

Vapour started rising from the walls all around her, like the tiny vents of a hot spring; a faint hissing sound issued from somewhere on the ceiling high above, as pressure released through the cracks. Her cloth undergarments lay plastered across her skin suddenly, itching and pulling against her like lice.

What the fuck is this?

She stumbled forward, stalling for a moment, trying to find her footing. Water splashed up around her boots; cracks continued to hiss overhead. The sudden humidity of the tunnels forced her to stop and brace against the wall, wedging her hands between florets of moss. Wondering what was going on, as she sucked air through her teeth and fought with her conscience to stay awake. Wondering if it was just a trick of the eye, or if the walls were closing in all around her...

This is horrible, she acknowledged, struggling to string together a competent thought. *I must be right beneath the burners that they use to heat the baths. There is no way in hell it could be anything else. I'm near enough dying in here. I just pray it doesn't get any worse just ahead.*

I wonder how the Forgotten One's getting on—

She turned and stopped, her heart stalling in her chest.

Realising the Forgotten One had gone.

"Hello?" she cried out, sensing the horrific darkness pull in like a net, gazing down empty passages bathed in absolute shadows. "What is this? Where are you?"

The silence made no attempt to reply, echoing back to her through the waterlogged tunnels.

"Hello! Please, are you there?"

Her words were laced with panic; the fatigue caused by the humidity was quickly overwhelmed by the sudden surge of adrenaline. Cavara reached for the sword at her hip.

"*Hello!*"

Lurching about with the orange light overhead, she stared off into the dark, fear-stricken and lost. Imagining things that weren't there. Interpreting sounds that never happened. Praying for the pale figure to return – praying for their safety, too. Sensing the dark pulse and ripple around her, threatening to swallow her whole.

Where are—

She turned for a moment, searching the gloom down the passage beside her, and paused.

Was that there before?

There was a light, yellowy in tone, at the far end of the passage, that seemed to pass through the barred window of an old iron door. It was incredibly bright even from a distance, meaning that whatever lay on the other side was very well-lit.

And also probably occupied. Cavara looked back along the tunnel she had just passed through and ground her teeth, the orange light above her head spitting like a roasted pig.

I could go searching for them, she considered. *That would be the sensible option in this. Because I don't know what lies ahead… I don't know how much danger I'll be in. The Forgotten One can help...*

But I could be down here for hours. This could be another soul-trap, and I'm all alone anyway. Pacing about in the dark is a sure bloody way of getting myself killed as it is. The transmitter could be anywhere down here, just waiting for me. I don't know what really lurks in the dark here...

She turned to the passage with the door at the far end.

So it's best that I see what I'm dealing with, and pray it's enough...

The general drew her blade from its sheath and wiped the sweat from her brow, pacing toward the door at the end of the tunnel with a prayer marked on her lips.

Knowing survival was never guaranteed.

†

Chapter 47

A Coward to the End

The reflection of a blade; the reflection of oneself. Quiet realities painted pure in a man's eye. An insight into another world. Words spoken and expressions made; the mirage of the truth merged between. The face they consoled with; the face they looked up to.

The face that led, whether he liked it or not.

I am not up to this, Eli considered, studying himself in the fractured mirror of his steel bludgeon. Despite its unforgiving angles, the Chief saw the cracked trenches across his skin; the harshness of his wrinkles, marked under his eyes in charcoal lines; the wiry, untamed texture of his beard; the rash-splattered sunburn scalding his scalp like spilt wine. The haggard expression of a man under siege, betraying his better nature for the will of a cause he had brought forth into the world and now commanded on its last legs. A painter, looking upon his masterpiece as it went up in flames. Aware, suddenly, of the nagging wound just below his shoulder – the crunching twist of his knees – the scabbed callouses across his palms. Realising just how damaged he was by the fighting that had occurred; wondering how much more damage was yet to be done.

Perhaps I am a true reflection of this fight, he scoffed, *ruining myself for the sake of a belief.* Studying his reflection again, he saw that cost worn heavy against his skin: he saw what it meant to be Chief of the

Mountains, with the weight of the fell squarely on one's shoulders.

What it meant to lead, no matter the cost.

"Enemy soldiers have been spotted mobilising down the road opposite, sir," the rotund officer said from beside him, donning his helm. "Are we ready?"

Eli adjusted the bludgeon in his hands and sighed, a grave expression trouncing his face. "No-one is ready for a fight like this, my friend," the Chief said sombrely. "Yesterday was a mercy… today, may not be so."

"Do you think we'll prevail?"

He shrugged. "We can only hope we last long enough for the others to outflank them and reinforce us in the square… and that is by no means a guarantee." A sudden stutter in his heart caught him like a gut-punch, as he thought of Alva down in the Warrens below, and the potential hell that could await her if the enemy knew of their plans. *They could be cornered, or ambushed.* A knot formed in his throat.

She could already be dead.

He ground his teeth, furrowing his brow, gripping the bludgeon tighter in his hands. *She is stronger than that, I know. She has persevered through far worse and come out the other side fighting. She will be fine.* A quiet, peaceful smile pierced through the veil of his face.

And she's Arrenso's sister, after all.

Tough as fucking nails.

"We're ready and waiting for you, sir," the officer exclaimed, bowing his head. "Just give the word."

The Chief rolled his shoulders and exhaled through his nose, tightening his chest against the glow of the morning sun.

Here we go…

"*FORWARD TO THE SQUARE!*"

Like a titan on the fields of oblivion, Eli strode forward in defiance, with the clatter and jeer of three hundred other voices tracing his steps just behind. Mismatched steel boots and fragmented armour plates covering their bodies; cloth undercoats and baker's aprons refashioned into garments of war; brass rings interlocking across their knuckles wielding short, half-rusted blades. Scars lacing their arms; bruises across their chests and faces. The rebels of the west – those passionate, violent few who remained – rallied behind their leader with an imperious order that would make even the most prestigious field commander blush.

And for a brief moment, Eli looked back to them: their glowing, wanderlust faces with gritted teeth and steely eyes, an aura of vigour radiating from them like the glow of dragon embers. An army of farmers and cooks; of blacksmiths and merchants and cobblers and craftsmen. The common people, alighted by a common cause – standing against the tyranny of the Imperial Land Army who formed across the square from them in tight rows, clashing fists against their chests with hateful glares.

The Chief stopped at the end of the street to face them, as the rebels fanned out behind him in haphazard rows, and the distinctive *clicks* of loading crossbows echoed down from the baron's hall above. He looked out across the enemy with the wind billowing through his beard, to find tired eyes and trembling hands against polished blades – fidgety motions to adjust uncomfortable armour, with perspiration already forming across their foreheads and cheeks – a concern mounting among them, as more of the rebels appeared.

They almost look scared, the Chief thought with a smile. But he found the moment of pride drift away almost as fast as it appeared, as he laid eyes on the enemy vanguard emerging in their shimmering red-rimmed steel.

The palace guards, he grimaced, clenching his bludgeon tighter. Ten of them emerged from the throng of bodies to form an arrow at the head of the enemy, their pronged helmets remaining mute and malicious staring off at the rebels nearby. *Ten… that's more than I had hoped. They must be here to hold the line when we engage.*

No doubt protecting that creature they call a general.

As the thought came, his gaze drifted just beyond their shoulders, and he tracked the path of a silver-haired man stalking just behind like a wolf, gesticulating awkwardly with sweeping arms and a clear limp affecting his stride.

The smile returned. *A small victory.*

Now I just gotta get the other knee…

"We're ready on your command, sir," the officer at his side said, steadying his blade in his hands. "It's now or never."

Eli smirked.

No hiding from this now.

"*READY!*"

There was a cacophony of motion at his back as the rebel force locked into shape, forcing a rumble of shock from the soldiers stood opposite. A silence spread among them, fickle and all-encompassing. The Chief watched the crowds opposite; watched as General Ferreus appeared at the centre of the vanguard, peering through a narrow gap like a goblin, and grinned wickedly toward Eli with a blood-stained venom.

The Chief cracked his neck.

Time to get my revenge, asshole.

Lifting his bludgeon skyward, he watched as Ferreus slapped the two palace guards across the back and slipped back behind them out of sight.

A coward to the end. Eli grit his teeth.

Well let's see if you can match this.

A step; a breath; thumping against his chest. Bellowing at the top of his lungs—

"*CHARGE!*"

The chaos began again.

†

Chapter 48

Rats in the Sewer

Tunnels, dark as clotted blood. Walls alive with tiny motions: crawling insects with many hundreds of legs skittering through the shadows. Cobwebs bigger than sails, skimming the upper reaches of the passage like tapestries. Snapped tiles underfoot, covered in oily smears and stone shrapnel as the walls slowly rotted around them. A heavy, corrupting smell of damp tainted the air; flourishes of fungus crawled through the cracks in an explosion of pink-red-white. Like a fresh wound bitten by infection. Like a birthed child clutching for pitiless life. It was a grim, despairing alcove of a dark, forgotten world. A hell of intertwining tunnels and sealed chasms.

And the resonant glow of torchlight swelling suddenly at the far end.

Jinx drew the wicker flame up to eye-level, and stopped for a moment to sense the air. The shadows danced with the torchlight in her hand like an inquisitive animal. Water dripping from the ceiling hissed and crackled against the flame.

The thief smirked.

Interesting.

"What is it?" Castan inquired at her back, looking ahead into the dark with the contingent of rebels snaking behind. "Have you seen something?"

"No… but listen," she replied, lifting her free hand to the ceiling with an extended finger – acknowledging the minute sounds of scraping boots and the near imperceptible whisper of voices somewhere above. "We're beneath them… the enemy army. We've crossed underneath the town square."

"That's good… will they hear us?" he asked quietly, peering up across the spider webs.

"Not at this depth… and certainly not with the noise they're making. We've got about six feet of dirt over our heads and they have no idea that we're even here."

"You're certain?"

She smiled at him. "Why, are you afraid?"

"Not afraid for my life, no." Castan met her eyes. "To protect you, more than anything."

"You feel I need protection?"

"You know that I can't let anything happen to you, Alva… I could never forgive myself, and I couldn't bring such pain on Eli to put you in harm's way."

"As honourable as ever." She said with a grin, her eyes shimmered like stardust. "So you will protect me, Castan, through thick and thin? Is that what you're saying?"

The dark-haired rebel laced his arm around her own and clasped it tightly, leaning in closer.

"*With my life, Alva… I shall protect you always*," he whispered, bowing his head and letting go.

Jinx sensed a flutter in her stomach like feathers, feeling the warmth rise in her cheeks. She turned from him and tried to hide her joy, exhaling slowly.

"Thank you, Castan," she replied eventually. "You are a most noble companion."

"Anything for you, my dear."

Jinx pursed her lips.

I'm quite liking this.

She absently adjusted the torch in her hand, spilling light into the shadowy reaches where beady-eyed insects scuttled into the dark or dug their way back into the cracks in the wall. Trickling reams of residue spilled over the black-stone blocks, glistening like tiny stars. The flame spat and quivered, as its light peered deeper into the recesses ahead.

Where the shadows seemed to shift, rising and falling like the tide.

As if something had just slipped out of sight.

Jinx held her breath, drawn away from her thoughts, and stared into the gloom intently. "Castan?"

The chiselled face looked up and placed his head alongside hers. "What is it? Is something wrong?"

"Did Eli say anything to you about things living down here... y'know, *non-human* things?"

"I don't believe so... why?"

Jinx held her lips still, sensing the air.

"Alva, *why*—"

A scraping sound echoed out somewhere ahead; the clicking of mandibles ricocheted down the tunnel toward them, before fading out into nothingness.

Jinx gasped.

What the fuck was that.

"Draw your weapons," Jinx exclaimed. "*Now.*"

Castan unsheathed his blade next to her; behind them, the snaps of drawn steel pierced the silent veil as the other rebels did likewise. Whispers passed between them, disconcerted and fearful. Their eyes speared the shadows, in search of movement.

The movement of a great something, somewhere in the dark ahead.

Castan placed his hand on the small of Jinx's back. "What do you suggest?" he whispered, a tremble in his breath.

"We carry on as we are, and stick to the plan... but we must keep our guard up," she replied, looking down the tunnel where her torchlight couldn't reach. "Because even though the enemy aren't down here with us... it doesn't mean we're alone..."

*

They continued to descend through the tunnels with their swords raised, banking left and right at random intervals as the Warrens snaked off through the earth. There was no uniformity to how the passages had been built: like the burrowing holes of a mole, they construed at awkward angles to slip deeper into the earth and then bolted suddenly upright to the surface, meandering in some places as if they had once been riverbeds. Disappearing off into the dark, with the hope of light at the end.

This is an exercise in patience, Jinx thought, rolling her eyes. A pain pulled up her leg suddenly, as she almost rolled her ankle against an incline – scolding her lack of focus, she pressed on nonetheless. *Either the maps were wrong and we're lost, the town is a lot bigger than we expected, or these passages are taking their jolly-fucking-time getting to the point. Because we should have come across something by now. Surely. Unless we've gone the complete wrong way.*

And condemned the others to death…

She bristled, a shiver running up her spine at the thought of it. *I pray this is the right way, for Eli's sake. For the sake of everything he's sacrificed in this. For Camilla, and for Davo, I pray.*

For my brother, too.

They twisted through another passage – like the long, shimmering coils of an undulating snake – as Jinx held herself steady, holding the torch aloft to view what emerged just ahead. Picking apart the shadows; picking through the haze in her eyes. Studying as the stones seemed to curve gently outwards in the near distance.

And an opening appeared ahead of them, cast in a blue-grey gloom.

Jinx dug her heels in and ground to a halt, holding up a fist to alert those behind her to stop too, frowning at the wide cavern just ahead.

"What is it?" Castan inquired.

"There's something ahead… the tunnel opens out into some other place," she replied. "Was there anything on the maps in the baron's hall about a cavern or chamber?"

The dark-haired rebel shook his head. "None that I can recall, no. What does it mean?"

"Well, there's no way that we could've gone the wrong way, because there have been no other passages that we've had to choose between. It's been one route, straight under the roads of the town. So we're still on the right path... but whatever this is ahead of us, was either not marked on the initial plans..."

"Or something has carved it out in the time since."

Jinx ground her teeth – *I was afraid you'd say that.*

"What do you advise?" he asked.

She looked back to him. "We don't really have a choice: it's press on, or let the others die." Peering behind him to the idle faces of their fellow rebels, she opened her fist and waved. "Let's continue, everyone! Hold formation, and keep your wits about you..."

Because we don't know what's about to happen.

They moved along the passage with cautious strides, grimacing at the slimy surface of the stone floor beneath their feet. The blue-grey haze of light grew steadily as they approached, like the parting of a storm. The echoey drips of water channelled down the tunnel toward them, indicating that the room ahead was nothing short of colossal.

Out of the frying pan, Jinx mused.

And into the fire...

She walked out into the light, and stood for a moment in awe as she laid her eyes on a massive ravine – larger than anything she had ever known – descending into the impossible depths below.

"What the fuck is this...?"

The walls rose around them like sheer cliffs, curving at the top to give way to the winding streets of Marcheg. The remains of pillars lay across the stone around them like fossils, from an ancient time in the forgotten annals of history where humanity still occupied the recesses of the world. And, gazing down into the abyss beneath them, Jinx couldn't dream of why they'd ever want to...

"This definitely wasn't on the maps," Castan whispered alongside her, gesturing ahead of them. "And neither was that..."

A walkway, clearing the ravine in a single stretch, linked the two openings of the tunnel system like a spider's-web. The stone looked incredibly old and cracked, and the supports against the wall holding it in place were laced with scars of neglect. But it was the only way forward, in the end, for the rebels: a bridge across certain death, into a tunnel that seemed to glow with the faintest light somewhere in the distance within.

"Is it just me, or is there daylight at the end of the tunnel opposite us?" Jinx said, her heart jumping suddenly with anticipation.

Castan squinted, and nodded his head slowly. "I reckon you might be right in that," he replied. "And with how close we are to surface, it would make sense."

"Which means we're nearly there." She looked down into the depths below.

And the last bit is always the worst.

"How should we go about this?"

Jinx looked back to the other rebels. "You go first: get them across safely and work out what that light is in the next tunnel. I'll follow up the rear once everyone's through."

"That sounds good to me." He squeezed her hand, turning to nearest dozen rebels and smiling. "Well, you heard the lady! Let's get moving! No time to waste."

With the composure of a righteous king, Castan stepped past her with a wink and strode out onto the bridge beyond. As his full weight fell upon the stone, a heavy layer of dust shifted from the underside and drifted down into the abyss below, but the bridge itself held steadfast and allowed him to cross without issue.

Looking across to him as he slipped under the alcove of the other tunnel, Jinx realised she'd been holding her breath the entire time, and coughed as she turned to the next man and ushered him across the gap.

He can be quite charming, that's for sure, she thought, watching him assist the rebels across with open arms and reassuring words. *But I shouldn't get ahead of myself. He cares for my safety, and has a duty to protect me on behalf of Eli... that may be all it is.* She crossed her fingers.

Although I'm rather hoping it's not.

One by one, the leather bracers and cautious faces crossed the bridge without complaint, darting across it like mice for fear it might collapse beneath them. And although the bridge gave no grievances, Castan proved as thorough as ever in the safety of his people, leaving a short window between each crossing to ensure the stone would hold.

So, as the first dozen crossed, Jinx produced a sigh of relief that things appeared to be running smoothly, and allowed her gaze to drift somewhat down into the chasm below.

Where the shadows shifted suddenly, like running fingers through soot, and tentacle-like shapes pulled down into the dark without a whisper of sound.

Jinx thrust an arm out and stopped the next rebel from crossing, scanning beneath the bridge for signs of movement.

"What is it?" Castan called across to her, looking down as she was.

The thief remained silent for some moments – discerning what was truth and what was a trick of the eye – before relaxing her shoulders again.

"It's all good!" she said, letting the next person cross. "Just... keep an eye out, is all."

And pray it's just the shadows...

Another rebel crossed without issue shortly after, finding their way into Castan's arms and skittering off into the tunnel beyond. Another one followed, and another, and the fourth was much the same.

Jinx continued staring into the dark.

The tenth person whispered a quiet prayer before they started walking, setting off across the bridge at a good pace to the supportive jeers of their comrades, marking the halfway point—

Jinx's head snapped around as a yelp of fear escaped their lips, and their foot slipped across a polished stone jutting out above the rest.

Sending them tumbling toward the darkness beyond…

Before she had a chance to react, Castan had propelled himself from the tunnel opposite and caught the rebel's hand as they fell. Bracing his fingers; gritting his teeth. Tightening his grip around his hand, then his forearm. On uneasy legs, he managed to swing the man back onto the bridge and settled him down with an exhausted thud…

As the shimmering star of his unholstered knife tumbled down into the chasm below, disappearing into the gloom in seconds.

Almost caught in a trance, with the others unaware of what had just happened, Jinx hardly realised as Castan guided the rebel across the bridge and summoned the next group to follow. Her eyes remained transfixed on the void beneath them – waiting with terror, in the hopes that the knife would hit the bottom and skitter across the stone as expected. Waiting for normality to return; waiting for her fears to be proven wrong. Waiting for anything, in the end, as the knife made no noise. No clatter, no whisper.

Echoes.

Silence.

Patience.

Grace.

And then the tentacles started crawling up the walls.

Jinx lifted her head and bellowed, shoving rebels across the gap as dozens of barbed appendages pulled up from the chasm beneath them, each one littered with spines the length of her forearm.

Fuck this.

Castan roared his own command in return, near-throwing each person into the tunnel as they appeared, staring wide-eyed as the limbs spread across the ravine around them like rot.

Fuck this.

Something shifted in the depths below as they made the pass to the alcove opposite, a tortuous mass of flesh and ruin twisting at their feet, rising with predatory intent like shivering trees—

One of the tentacles shot across the bridge suddenly, moving out from the shadows with heart-stopping speed, and impaled one of the rebels through the chest like a skewer.

Behind, someone screamed, dropping onto their back; the person in front, caught by the impact, slipped against the old stone and tumbled over the edge of the bridge.

Jinx could do nothing, coercing the last of the rebels onto the bridge, as they fell into the depths flailing wildly and clattered against whatever mass writhed within, lost to the shadows.

Heartbeats passed; another two rebels reached the far side.

She allowed herself a breath—

A hollow screech echoed out from beneath, as the sound of chiselling bone caught in their ears.

And a droning bellow like a slumbering titan shook the walls around them, devouring all conscious thought beyond one single syllable, ruminating through their collective ears like a fear-stricken child.

"*RUN!*"

Jinx gasped for air, pushing the last rebel onto the bridge as another tentacle shot across just ahead and tore another soul from the world. Lurching in horror, she planted her feet on the quivering stone and hurried forward, sweat beading on her cheeks—

More tentacles appeared around them, hooked on the ends, rising from the dark and lunging out toward the rebels—

Lunging out toward her; Jinx ducked as a talon the size of her head swept through the air where her neck had just been, where it then swung back across and tore another body off the bridge just ahead.

She was upright again in moments, dragging at air, stumbling over broken rock as the tunnel loomed just ahead. Bellows echoed from beneath her. Shadows burst with flurries of motion. The undulating horror just beyond the edge of the bridge spasmed sharply.

Jinx sensed everything. Felt everything. Bodies and blood and barbs; the barbaric dereliction of the natural order of things, present in the hell-pit beneath them. Aching darkness; another rebel safe in the tunnel. Counting her breaths in turn.

Fifteen strides away.

Twelve.

Nine—

The tendrilled arms of a terrifying behemoth, of blue flesh and oily skin, rising around her like a deadly embrace.

Crashing down across the bridge at her back, ripping the stone out from beneath her.

Six strides away; Jinx lost her footing. Screamed. Wide-eyed, gazing up at Castan. His outstretched arm. The bodies swarming up the tunnel behind.

A light at the far end.

Heartbeats ticking by. Barbed tentacles creeping up the walls around her like vines. Stone crashing down against stone.

The bridge slipping out like a carpet beneath her.

She heard his voice then, for a moment. All of them at once, in fact: Castan, calling for her to jump; Eli, telling her to be safe and strong.

Arrenso, embracing her tightly, and telling her how he missed her.

"How far you have come, little sister."

Bending at the knees, Alva propelled from the last stones and leapt out over the chasm, away from the tentacles swarming toward her, reaching for the rebel's outstretched arm and the path toward safety.

Light swelling suddenly in her gaze—

†

Chapter 49

Skulls in the Walls

She awoke to a yellow haze and a burning tightness pulling against her cheek like needles. Her limbs were numb, almost arthritic, fused into place like a mannequin. Balled up in a foetal position, every half-draw of air felt clogged and heavy, with no wind nor cold brushing against her skin. She tried to recall what had happened to leave her in such a sorry place with her eyes fused shut, but for a long time her mind lay blank.

Until the ripples of a laugh plucked at her ears from somewhere high above, and her eyes snapped open to a wash of golden light.

With skulls coating the walls in their thousands.

Savanta lay on a floor of sand and gravel with a column of metal plates rising in front of her, its interconnected segments like the scales of a coiling serpent. Torches adorned the upper reaches, where a viewing platform peered down on the circular room below – no doubt used for the vile entertainments of the tyrant and her fools.

Gazing up there as she dragged herself to a stand, Savanta struggled to focus. Blinking furiously, she found her vision fade in and out as a seizure of pain hit her skull, likely where the…

She stopped.

Where the Queen knocked me out.

A memory resurfaced, slowly but surely, of where she had been before.

Stalking the corridors, I had escaped, she recalled. *Followed by shadows, and a haunting laugh…*

She steadied herself, wiping the grit from her face and matted hair – pulling the hand away to reveal a shade of deep red, as blood lay plastered across her scalp.

She came for me… I attacked, hoping I could best her. I was wrong, and I failed. She had me in her grasp and… and…

That door opened.

Savanta turned on her heel, reciting the memory in her head, and found a heavy wooden door in the wall just behind her, lined with iron beams and several impressive locks.

So this is the door I saw before, the one that I saw the shadow move through before the Queen knocked me out. Meaning this is where the light was coming from.

Meaning my father was here too.

She turned back to the fore, acknowledging the room around her, and silenced a shiver creeping up her spine.

In this pit of sand and gravel, with galleries for the despot to see.

Where skulls line the walls in their thousands…

With a spot destined for me.

And there were thousands of them. Empty sockets and yellowed teeth. Cracked cavities and bolted jaws. Dents and scrapes and scars, deep as ravines. Pasted to the walls like grim ornaments, stacked atop each other in great wavering lines. A room of death: more so than she could even begin to fathom – and the exact purposes of which she could never know.

This place makes Val Darbesh look like a fucking mansion, she thought facetiously, rolling her shoulders. *And even though that fighting pit had a hell of a lot more monsters, I doubt it has any creature quite as venomous as—*

"Champion…"

A wave of anger shuddered through her system, at the sound of the woman's voice. Echoing out from somewhere in the galleries above. Looking to her; looking *down* on her. All pride and supremacy and arrogance. Savanta grit her teeth and threw her hands out, almost to challenge the very room itself.

"I thought we were done with games, you *bitch!*" she cried, snarling at the shadows. "Why don't you show yourself? We can get this over with nice and quick…"

"But it'll be you who's buried come the end of it, if I do…"

The voice came from behind her; Savanta spun suddenly in the blind glee of the hunt, hoping to make her kill and savage the tyrant's flesh.

Yet all she found when she did turn, was an empty patch of sand, and a door stood watching her dumbly as if nothing really mattered.

"Where are you, then, you fucking coward!" she challenged. "Why won't you show yourself—"

"I am everywhere, my dear, in ways you could never understand…"

A voice to her left; Savanta turned to find nothing there.

"I am the shadow in the alcoves…"

The tyrant's words, drifting along the gallery above.

"I am the sword at your side…"

Savanta frowned, before she reached down to her waist and realised to her shock that she was armed – with her own blade, at that, from when she had first been taken at the lake-house.

How the fuck…

"I am the whisper in your ear…"

She winced, as if tiny mites were burrowing into her scalp.

"I am the noose about your neck…"

The air thinned in her lungs, until she was almost gasping.

"I am the venom that slithers through your veins…"

Something moved beyond the column in front of her, twisting out of sight. She couldn't discern what it was, as her vision fuzzed and blurred. Fighting for air, Savanta closed her eyes and took a moment to—

"I am the demon Markus warned you of…"

Her eyes flicked open, as something bitter and cold pulled at the rage in her heart. She stared out across the tiny space where the Iron Queen now stood, as if it were the opposite end of the sea. Breaching waves opened her chest like a surgical knife, threatening to wash everything away. She blinked and swallowed and could hardly move her limbs.

Markus...

She reached down for her blade, pulling the leather strap away from the sheath and twisting her hand across the hilt, sliding it into the light in all its blunted, shimmering glory—

To find it was snapped and awkwardly weighted, and not much longer than her hand in total. Studying it in the golden light; realising it was not her blade after all.

The weight of horror wrenching at her soul, as she realised—

This isn't my blade...

It's his.

"You really need to understand who you are, Savanta of Provenci," the Iron Queen said simply, with no harshness or mockery in her voice. "And you need to understand not only who you've become... but how you fashioned it from the beginning."

Savanta's eyes bulged, as she met the tyrant's gaze.

"You think we're so different, you and I. But in reality, we are almost exactly the same. Cut from the same cloth... burnt by the same hand... broken by the same malice. I just rose to the top... and you haven't quite got there yet."

She couldn't breathe; she could hardly think.

"Because what this is – what you *are* – didn't start when you entered this keep and were bent to my whim, did it? Nor did it start when you fought in those pits, and drove a blade through that poor fucker's chest. I don't remember his name really..."

Savanta blinked.

Did I imagine she said his name?

"But the point I'm making is, whether it was your false pretence of revenge or the revocation of your feminine beauty when you had that metal plate lodged in your jaw, you can never put a marker on when things really started to go… *wrong,* can you? Almost like it doesn't add up." A smile graced the Queen's lips. "Almost like you're *forgetting* something…"

Savanta longed to scream but her throat lay closed and broken. Her eyes stung; pains jabbed at her skull and through the nerves of her fingers. Memories ballooned to the surface that she forced back into her skull, but the tide was relentless and its waves were all-encompassing and something had to give—

"You used to butcher things as a child, didn't you, Sav?" Gaza said softly, almost like a prayer. "You liked to pick apart dead rodents you found in the barn where you lived. You liked to pry them apart and see what was inside. It gave you a sense of joy, maybe, toying with the cat's food before they ate it." She paused for consideration. "And then, over time, you would start doing it to the cat too… and the ducks in the pond outside. And the neighbour's dog, that you strangled with it's own leash and strung up outside your room, where by the morning after the corpse was so infested with maggots that you had to move and burn the place down, didn't you?"

Savanta held her ears, but the noise still got in.

"They wondered where they went wrong, your parents… your father in particular," the Queen continued. "What could cause a sweet little girl to do something so barbaric? What could they do to solve it? They had no answers, in the end, but once you moved house you seemed much more settled… I mean, the odd knife still disappeared from the kitchen drawers, but that was normal for seven year old children, now wasn't it?"

Gaza shook her head; Savanta could hardly breathe.

"Yes, perfectly normal… until that boy came in over winter one year. So cold and starved and alone… and your good-willing family offered him a place to stay to see out the worst of it, hoping to find his real parents when the snow cleared. How charming he was… and how *silent* you became. Seething, in your own little horror, planning your masterpiece at last. The fruition of your years of butchery… a single subject to make yours. Your father walking into the barn, wondering where the little boy had gone..."

Stop... no...

"To find him murdered and flayed like a roast pig on a workbench, with you carving his heart out with a *knife*."

Savanta swayed. The room spun. The floor seemed to open up and swallow her.

A carving knife. A child's dead eyes. Blood in her mouth and on her hands.

The despair in her father's eyes. The betrayal of everything he had known. Fear and terror and disgust.

You are no daughter of mine.

"He knew after that moment that he could never see you again... and you knew it too, didn't you?"

You are no daughter of mine.

"So you wrote him a letter, hoping he'd understand your pain inside, and why you did it, and what was wrong... but he never read it. He never so much as *looked* at it..."

You are no daughter of mine.

The Iron Queen held her gaze for several moments, as coiling shapes moved across the sand behind her.

The next words came almost like the wind.

"*So is that why you cut off his ear?*"

The weight fell upon her, and the world lay swamped in shadows. Savanta looked down to her hand, her entire body dead still and remorseless, recalling the memory as if it were poetry at a funeral. the bloodied ear with three gold rings pierced on the lobe; the letter in her—

The knife in her other hand, serrated along its edge, with the terror-stricken face of her father just beyond kicking out toward the open door...

It was all a lie.

"You are a monster, Savanta... through and through. It's what you were born to be, and what you will always become..."

Gaza sidestepped slowly, as the sound of shifting sand caught in Savanta's ear and something emerged from behind the column.

"You have been called many things, amounting to the same thing. A butcher. A traitor. A murderer... *'serpent-soul'*." The Queen allowed a smile. "Your father unknowingly called you that when you were born, without realising what you'd become. So perhaps we should see if you really are a serpent-soul..."

Savanta blinked, and she was gone.

"*Let us see what happens when you face some real poison...*"

Rising up in front of her, at least twenty feet in length, a serpentine shape of jade-green scales flashed its pearlescent fangs and looked down upon her with beady orange eyes. Towering above her, coiling to strike...

The basilisk flicked its forked tongue and hissed with a hateful glee.

The Champion stumbled around, unaware of which reality she walked through, and gazed at the torchlight twinkling above. The lies she had lived; the falsehood that she had premised her entire life upon.

I am a monster, she thought, giggling quietly with tears in her eyes. *I am a monster... and a monster is me.*

And now everything must die.

With the basilisk making ready to lunge above her, Savanta studied it in awe. Wielding the blade of the friend she had murdered – that she would use to kill her traumatised father who could not live with the knowledge of her horror – with a fellow monster looking down from the galleries in a lustful, tempestuous glee.

The Champion screamed, tears and hate and love and fury streaming from her eyes.

I am a monster.

The basilisk attacked.

And a monster, is me.

†

Chapter 50

The Traitor

Another shall die today…

And they shall die by my hand.

Silence. Dead shadows. Clouds scuttling overhead in thin trails, slipping past the high sun off toward the sea. The rustle of branches. The Ozban echoing like a stream through a cavern. The buzz of human enterprise carrying off from the main camp, as dozens of blushed faces sat down for food and liquor. A cool serenity held the world in that moment: so unusual to find in a place so cruel. The cry of an eagle sounded somewhere in the skies high above.

As the crunch of footsteps passed in fitful strides, crackling like embers in a hearth.

Revek craned his neck like a vulture, clasping his hands at his back with mutinous intent. His eyes crossed the bare earth over to the camp in the distance, scanning for movement as he went. The sun beat down overhead; somewhere off over the hills to the west, a storm threatened to break. Thunder rallied over the peaks. The commander grinned, and stepped lightly to leave no marks in the earth. He passed supply carts and wood piles and barricades criss-crossing trenches like stitches over wounds. Turning a corner behind an old stone wall – flinching as a raven spiralled into the air and swept off over the trees.

His destination appearing suddenly, only a few steps away.

A single tent, erected along the outskirts of a ruined stone house, with the red-green standard of Provenci billowing in the wind at its peak. No guards stood watch; there was not another soul present, in fact. Just the crunching of his steel boots and the rustle of branches to his left. The cool serenity of the world slowly imploding.

And it's all just too easy for me.

Revek entered the tent without a sound, pulling the length of fabric to a gentle close as if it had never been touched. With lips pursed into a smile, he turned to survey the barren interior beyond: the personal items clumped together in an opened sack in one corner; a few oil candles sat unlit along the left side; an armour chest-plate and boots straddling the opposite wall.

And the bed-throw splayed out at his feet, padded with handfuls of straw, where the calm, unconscious body of Officer Zespa lay sleeping, mumbling softly to the gods.

The commander's smile widened.

Oh how peaceful you look, sleeping there, he mused, rolling his fingers against the hilt of his knife. *How innocent and unrepentant... like a child cradled in their mother's arms. As if there is nothing wrong in the world, and there never has been.*

His grin turned to a growl.

Lies...

He stooped low, studying her face intently: the delicate curves of her cheeks; the roundness in her eyes; the blossomed hearts of her lips. Lying there as if placed on an altar, hands clasped to her chest gazing to the heavens. The ripples of her breath tickled in his ear.

Revek blinked slowly.

So beautiful, in your own forsaken little way, he acknowledged, tilting his head. *So much potential... so much power that you could've had at my side. If only you'd chosen ambition over duty.*

It will almost be a shame to kill you.

Like a seductress, the commander folded his hand around the knife in his belt and slid it gently from its sheath. Glistening like the surface of a lake under stars, he brought the blade across his body and held it aloft over Zespa's chest. He couldn't help but notice how there was not a single quiver in his hand, nor any objection in his act.

You brought it on yourself, you know. You are the arbiter of your own demise. He exhaled through his nostrils, savouring the moment. *It wouldn't have taken much to spare you, really: a bit more faith in your feelings... a bit of moral flexibility, perhaps. To not make yourself a puppet of the cause. Such little ambition... and so much unnecessary blood because of it.* A shrug, suppressing a wild laugh.

But, such is the way of the world. There are those that follow, and those that butcher. You fall on the wrong side of that line.

And that is a sin I must amend.

Lifting the blade over her head, Revek drew a deep breath and levelled his gaze.

Another shall die today.

The knife dropped.

And they shall die by my hand—

Zespa's eyes snapped open like split fruit, grappling the knife from beneath the folds of her bed-throw and twisting Revek's arm violently.

The commander squealed – some guttural sound like a neutered pig – and felt his wrist bone bulge. Fire ignited in his eyes; he nearly threw up.

With a heave of muscle, Zespa threw the thin quilt aside and lurched upwards. Grappling Revek's collar in the meat of her hand, she pinned him against her forearm and spun him so he landed on his back beneath her, the air exploding from his lungs like a burst valve. He thrashed about in a contorted mess suddenly, hissing spittle through his teeth, wild-eyed and adrenaline-strained and very, very afraid. As if the doors were closing on his life ahead.

This wasn't supposed to be!

Zespa pressed the knife blade flat against his chest, veins pulsing to life across her forehead as she braced the traitor against the floor with a snarl. Looking up from him for a moment, she tensed her neck and howled off toward the entranceway for help—

The sound of moving metal echoed out from somewhere beyond shortly after, accompanied by the bellows of command. Revek had a moment to breathe and gasp.

And then all was chaos and motion.

Bodies piled into the tent: armoured helmets leering down toward the commander and grappling at his arms. Swords stood shimmering behind them, readying for a fight. The entranceway exploded with sunlight as more people appeared to see what the commotion was all about.

Revek started bellowing, terror shivering through his body, demanding they stop and unhand him, proclaiming his innocence – but they were faceless and emotionless in response, uncaring of his demands, carrying out their work with dead eyes and sad souls. He whimpered for a moment at their silence – whimpered at how little power he had left over them – and the horror of his reality dawned like a blood-red sky.

You brought it on yourself, you know...

Zespa rose to her feet and shook her head, as the soldiers dragged the commander toward the entrance kicking and roaring like a hound.

Such is the way of the world...

Bright, lustrous light screeched overhead, forcing Revek to squint at the shadows that loomed all around him. He heaved air down his throat, dragging his heart along the ground at his feet.

Another shall die today.

Suddenly falling, he was thrown to the floor in a crumbled heap of dust and twisted metal. Kicking out like a mule, he rolled onto his knees, blinking heavily into the light to decipher the figures stood there.

Holding his breath, as his eyes nearly popped from their sockets.

And it shall be because of my hand...

"Hello, commander," Marshal Lazaerys exclaimed with a smug grin, tilting her head as if reprimanding a child. "Fancy seeing you here..."

"I… I…" He swallowed, coughing suddenly, dripping sweat and bile. Nausea bit in his chest. "I…"

"Lost for words, commander?" General Xol said from beside her, uncrossing their arms and shaking their head. "Must say we were quite the same, when we got word that you were here…"

"I… don't understand…"

"Then allow us to *explain*," Zespa grumbled from behind him, kicking him in the side as she passed to join the others. "We had reason to believe you were a danger to our operation out here, after General Oslo's untimely and highly unusual death, alongside other reports from soldiers about your… *erratic* behaviour. We were thus concerned about whether you would seek to harm any other officers of the army now that we're all together in one camp… so we decided to set a trap." She rolled her shoulders, presenting an expression of indifference. "You would join me in managing the fortification of the northern border, and I would then threaten you with the accusation that you killed General Oslo… an accusation that you couldn't *possibly* let slide, as that would give me leverage over you and whatever *power* you still possessed. And so, with that in motion, General Xol here informed a small group of loyalists of our plans… and had them stationed in the trenches next to us, right outside my tent." She produced rye smile. "All we had to do then was wait for our killer… and lo-and-behold, there you appeared… you filthy fucking *traitor*."

She loomed overhead and spat at him, a huge gobbet of phlegm stringing its way across his nose.

Revek lifted his hand and smeared it away, his face an ugly shade of taupe as if he'd be sick.

Wearing the look of a desperate man who realised he had been bested.

"You've lost, commander," Lazaerys muttered. "You've been revealed to be the very thing we always knew you were… a power-lusting coward and a backstabbing villain. I knew it since the first day I was assigned here… the first day I looked into those manipulative, conceiting eyes of yours. I knew from that moment, that you would ruin yourself. That you were nothing more than a rot, and a threat to all of us." She clicked her knuckles. "And now you've been caught, weapon in-hand, attempting to murder one of our own…"

A curling fist cracked across Revek's cheek; his head snapped back like a crossbow string. He spat, and drew his tongue over his teeth. Felt a tooth wiggle under the pressure.

You'll pay for that.

"You're pathetic, commander… reckless and pathetic. You have brought nothing but a corrupting hate to your office, and now… now you will pay the price for it."

Revek looked up at her, sneering, the venom of a thousand blood-stained blades biting in his eyes.

"What will you *do to me?*" he rasped, his eye twitching.

"You will receive the martial punishment befitting the *disgrace* you've inflicted on your rank," General Xol proclaimed, their pale face blank and resentful. "You will be brought before the combined forces of this detachment, and in the sight of your people and the gods above you shall confess to your crimes against this army… and you shall be executed by decapitation for your sins."

The bubble in Revek's throat popped. "*Decapitation…?*"

"You have lost, commander." They stepped closer. "And may the souls of those you have betrayed to get here, watch with glee at your *demise…*"

Lazaerys raised her hand to the east. "Bring him to the block!"

The commander writhed. "*Wait*! Wait, *no*! No… this can't… *PLEASE*!"

Hands grappled around his arms, pinning them to his back, dragging him up to his feet—

He bucked, pulling away, whimpering and begging, the grotesque swell of salty water biting in his eyes.

"*NO!* This can't be, I can't… I can't *die*! I can't…"

Xol, with a face of sheer disappointment; Zespa, with one of glee.

They're gonna kill me.

Turning to face him, Marshal Lazaerys grinned, using her thumb to imitate a throat being slit.

"NO!" he wailed.

Please, no…

Thunder rattled somewhere in the sky high above.

Even the gods were laughing.

†

Chapter 51

Traitors Come in Pairs

Mustard-yellow light from sconces as large as fruit-bowls. Silver chains like a dowager's jewellery suspended from the ceiling in braids. Ugly wooden shelves eaten by mould wedged awkwardly at the edges. The invariable hiss of steam pushing through cracks somewhere in the stonework above.

And a single chair in the middle of the room, sat adjacent to a locked steel door.

Cavara stepped into the room with hesitant steps, checking her corners with her blade held close to her chest. Along her spine, she could sense the pull of the Rapture against her skin as it deciphered the shadows around her, seeking assassins in the dark. It gave some courage knowing that her powers were still with her, as she shifted left and skirted along the walls of the room. But even that courage proved momentary, as the general took a long draw of breath and studied the floor beneath her, letting her heart grow quiet and still.

Beneath her, the remnants of spirit-trails criss-crossed the room like deer tracks in the snow. There were over a dozen of them, circumnavigating the space between the chair and the steel door, and then disappearing off into the tunnel that she had emerged from. All indicating the presence of another – the *recent* presence of another, at that.

The transmitter has definitely been here, Cavara inferred, approaching the door, *and they've used this space frequently. But for what reason, and how they found it in the first place, I have no idea.* She stopped next to the metal door embedded in the wall and studied the chair opposite, noting how the arm-rests had cuffs bolted to them. *What was this place even used for? An empty cell at the end of winding tunnels, accessed by a trap-door at the back of a storehouse…*

What were they hiding here?

She turned and placed a hand against the cold steel door at her back, pressing her ear against one of the metal locks to hear what was inside. It took some time for her heart to stop drumming in her head, and for her anxious breaths to reach a quiet tedium, but eventually a silence claimed her mind and she could concentrate on the space beyond. However, for several long moments a murky nothingness was all that prevailed, no different than the room around her. Frowning, the general was about to dismiss the idea that the cell was occupied at all…

When the tiny, fractious whisper of a breath slipped through and prickled in her ear.

And she blinked, almost in disbelief, before ushering a single word in reply.

"… Evelyn?"

And something stirred in the beyond, just on the opposite side of the door from her.

"*Miss Cavara?*"

Her heart jolted.

Oh gods…

"Evelyn is that you? Are you there?"

A pause. "*It's me, Miss Cavara, I… it's very dark in here.*"

"It's okay, it's okay… I understand." The general couldn't believe that it was real – *I found him.* "It's okay, are… are you hurt? Are you safe?"

"*I have bruises… my leg is very swollen. Painful…*"

"Okay… okay, it's gonna be alright, just keep it still for me, won't you? We're gonna get you out."

"Be quick, the... the bad man might be back soon."

"I will I promise, I will, he won't get to you. Don't worry..."

"I want my mumma..."

Cavara closed her eyes and stilled the fear roaring in her chest. "It's okay, you'll be back with her soon, okay? Everything is gonna be okay—"

"Well, well, well... would you look who it *is*..."

The general stopped as her heart dropped through the floor. The pain and loss she had felt hearing the fear in Evelyn's voice, gave way to a tumultuous rage burning bright in her chest.

With a slow turn – blade coiling tight against her side – Cavara looked back to the doorway she had entered through, and saw there perched against the door-frame the unmistakable form of the Butcher studying her intently.

"I see you've found my little lair..."

The cleaving knives down his throat curled as he grinned, disappearing beneath his bloodied apron. The same pair of grisly blades sat in sheaths across his waist, as well as a number of dissection tools strapped down his leg.

"You never fail to surprise me with your tenacity, *usurper,*" the transmitter muttered, stepping into the room. "But I suppose that'll make carving you all the sweeter..."

"You'll do no such thing," Cavara said defiantly. "We are matched evenly here, and the Forgotten One is not far behind me... and I know you wouldn't *dare* drag me into the Rapture, knowing the powers I have. So if you think I'll just roll over and let you gut me like a fish, then you are in for one serious disappointment..."

The Butcher smirked. "Those are brave words, for someone so maladjusted to her powers."

"Well how about you come over here and I'll show your organs what *maladjusted* looks like, you bastard."

"And as *tempting* as that may be... I think I'll let you make the first move."

"And why's that?"

Raising his hand into the light, he jangled a set of small iron keys on a ring toward her. "Because I already have what you want... and *you* have to come get it."

Cavara ground her teeth, glancing for a moment at the meticulous-looking locks along the edge of the steel cell.

"Just let the boy go," she muttered, easing her grip on her blade. "He doesn't have to be involved in this anymore. Just let him go back to his mother and we can settle this here on our own."

The Butcher raised his eyebrows, almost considering the option, before laughing and shaking his head. "I'm afraid not, usurper... I'm afraid not. Because, you must understand, I need *guarantees* in my line of business. The Coven never gave me that, long ago, and in this new lease of life I hope to rectify that. So the child will remain exactly as they are, and your hand will be forced into confrontation for the sake of saving them." He paused. "It's almost poetic, is it not? Risking the world for the sake of one pathetic little boy... you are truly not worthy of the powers you hold."

Cavara steeled herself. "The boy deserves to live."

The Butcher grinned. "Then you will die."

She lifted her arms, challenging him. "Well, it's just me and you, you foul little creature... so *do it.* What are you so afraid of?"

"It is not fear that guides me..." Without breaking his gaze, the transmitter reached across and tapped the door next to him. "It's the joy of the hunt, that satisfies me most..."

The general drew in a long breath, flinching suddenly as footsteps approached from the tunnel beyond. The sword felt abruptly hot and heavy in her hand, almost vibrating through her knuckles. She stooped into a fighter's stance, levelling her blade at the tunnel entrance opposite.

"Did you ever wonder how we found Brutus, and how we knew he was communicating with you through the Rapture?" the Butcher explained, stepping to one side. "Did it ever cross your mind, general?"

Cavara remained silent with sweat beading across her skin.

"Because, as far as we know, you've only seen him once since coming to the City, haven't you? Out on the plains, practicing your shadow step… he came and spoke to you. He was probably warning you that he had seen me traversing the Rapture… probably wanted to keep you nice and safe. Such a kind and doting friend… such a shame his life ended so abruptly…"

Cavara heard whispers behind the door next to her and felt her throat burn—

"But how could we have known that, general? How could I know these things about you, when I hadn't even found you yet?" The Butcher paused and smiled. "It was almost like someone was watching you…"

A boot emerged at the tunnel entrance.

"Like a spyglass on a city wall…"

Cavara shuddered. A gasp escaped her lips. The sconces around the room flickered in disbelief.

One person entered the room, followed by another, to take up positions alongside the Butcher.

The room pulled in around her.

Ptolemy smiled.

"Hello again, general."

Cavara stared wide-eyed at him, her jaw hanging open in shock. "*You?*" she exclaimed.

"It is rather interesting, when the tides turn so suddenly… is it not?"

"And when the price is right," Amara said alongside him, studying the curve of her blade with a smile.

"You would do this… you would *abandon* your principles and your honour… all for the sake of a higher bidder?" Cavara spat. "He is a Tarrazi, you know? An ancient enemy."

"To you, perhaps." Ptolemy wagged a finger at her. "But for us, the Butcher here is just another piece in a puzzle between those vying for power in this world. There is no good or bad… only quantities that need to be measured. And I would sooner take my weight of gold than I would the polish on my soul..."

"You fucking *bastard.*"

"We don't *care,* general," Amara said. "That's the beauty of it. You can call us what you want, think of us however you wish... we don't care in the end. Money does the talking in this world, not any false notion you have about morality and righteousness..."

Cavara shook her head in disgust. "I should've known..."

"Known what? That you can't trust us?" Ptolemy scoffed. "You never did trust us, general, that's the thing... and yet we *still* walked all over you."

"And now they have the great pleasure of exacting my whim," the Butcher thundered from just behind, almost morphing through the shadows like a demon. "Two of my most loyal informants... here for their final task."

Ptolemy drew his sword suddenly; Cavara levelled her own blade out towards them with her heart in her throat.

"It doesn't have to be this way," the general said as both a plea and a warning. "You don't have to do this."

"Oh, but we *want* to," Amara hissed, a tormented glee in her eyes. "After the little incident in the brewing house... you deserve to be bled for disrespecting us."

"You had your chance at reconciliation, Cavara... and you broke my nose for it," Ptolemy growled, edging closer in tiny increments. "So the death you shall receive from our hands, is as exacting as it will be *warranted...*"

Cavara sighed, thinking of the little boy trapped in the cell behind her, terrified and longing for his mother. She tightened her jaw, channelling the energy within her.

"If you choose this path, then so be it," she proclaimed. "But when this is over, I will be walking out of here with a child in my arms" – she lifted her blade to the Butcher – "and your *head* to prove it..."

The Butcher smiled, welcoming the challenge.

A whisper escaped his lips.

"*Kill her...*"

†

Chapter 52

Death and Death and Death

Savanta felt the pressure against her shoulder-blades as she hit the wall of skulls, cracking like a chisel to limestone, shoved there absently by a twisting body as it snaked past the column and beyond. She managed a breath and a vulgar curse before the basilisk's head loomed into view once more, its tongue sensing the air with tiny flickers. It was patient and horrifying in equal measure, moving toward her with a calm, undulating certainty. Sensing her flesh and savouring the taste. Its fangs emerging between pink gums, beneath the raw intensity of two amber eyes. Studying her as prey.

Readying to strike once more.

The Champion roared, vaulting away from the wall of skulls as the basilisk lunged toward her. A rush of air twitched at her fingertips. She swept across the floor with an elegant precision, as the serpent rounded at her back and slid across the gritty earth toward her.

Prickles twinged up her back: Savanta inhaled sharply and side-stepped as a massive serpentine head pummelled the ground where she had just been, its tiny angular teeth glinting like knives. Wasting no time, she cut across and slid her sword between the rivets of its scales, fighting to keep a hold as the blade scored a line through its flank, oozing blueish blood.

Flicking the sword away almost immediately, Savanta caught sight of a shadow lurking in the galleries high above, studying the Champion as she turned and darted off toward the basilisk's tail in the hopes of scoring another easy wound.

She's enjoying this, Savanta scoffed, gritting her teeth as her heart pumped through her chest. *Of course she is, the sly bitch.*

Well, let's give her a show then.

Tracking the passage of the creature's massive head as it slid past the column at her back, Savanta allowed a tiny grin as she speared her blade out toward the basilisk's tail.

It punctured like a ripe fruit; somewhere behind her, an anguished hiss escaped the serpent's jaw. The Champion drove the blade deeper still, digging between flesh and cartilage before she sensed the basilisk twitch next to her, and flicked the sword free with a slick of blood that painted the walls an ugly shade of amethyst.

Bunching her legs up, Savanta leapt forward and tucked into a tight roll, skidding against the gravel and regaining her balance a mere heartbeat later—

Turning to find the basilisk surging toward her with swollen eyes and gleaming fangs, moving at impossible speeds—

The serpent's head hit her across the side, knocking the wind from her chest and bruising her flesh. Scales grated against her side. She angled away and smacked the ground in a limp tangle of limbs. The skulls on the walls goggled at her whimsically, as if they contained the world's secrets.

Savanta curled her nose up and spat at them.

Fucking waste of my fucking time...

She was on her feet again in seconds, turning to find the basilisk coiling up on itself and sliding over its body toward her, hissing and rasping as it went. Savanta snarled in reply, sweat glistening over the metal plate in her cheek as she swept to the side and lunged at its head with her sword.

The strike met its mark seconds later: embedding in the serpent's nostril, it tore down into its jaw and whipped away just as fast, dispersing a number of teeth as it did so. Savanta smiled as the fangs scattered at her feet; the basilisk appeared to groan at her back as it coiled awkwardly about. The creature sounded like it was badly wounded.

Or so the Champion thought.

A grating sound echoed to her right: Savanta turned to watch the snaking body loop over itself, snapping against the metal ridges of the column as it did so.

Another sound, quivering over to her left: the basilisk slid out of view behind its own mass and hissed furiously as it went—

Sliding scales moved at her back.

To the left and right too.

The walls closing in.

Savanta swore and tightened her grip.

Shit!

She was running suddenly, without thought or direction, out toward the serpent's body with the sword glinting in her hand. Jumping mid-stride; her blade clasped above her head like a trident.

Impaling the basilisk. Pressing her feet against its sliding, scaly skin—

Baulking as the creature roared and its body started revolving beneath her, twisting her dishevelled corpse up toward the galleries where the tyrant lurked. Up toward the torches and the warm sunset hues, with skulls lining the walls in their hundreds.

And the central column looming suddenly before her, where she spied a tiny gap in the metal plates that looked oddly like a grappling point...

Savanta blinked, assessing her situation in immediate, all-encompassing detail. A moment passed. A moment more—

She let go of the sword and jumped.

Scrabbling against the wall, she clawed for purchase like a squirrel at the mercy of a fox. Digging her hands in against the metal; a sharp edge bit against her fingers and drew blood. She hissed; the basilisk hissed beneath her. She swore she heard someone laughing in the shadowy gloom just above her.

She's enjoying this.

Savanta smiled.

And maybe I am too...

She looked down to the grey, gravelly earth beneath her and traced the movements of the basilisk as it stared up at her with quiet, almost curious eyes. Despite the wounds it had sustained thus-far – and the sword that was still embedded in its side – the creature seemed entirely unphased by Savanta's efforts, and moved across the pit floor as enchantingly as it had done at the start.

The Champion sighed, adjusting her footing against the metal plates. *The sad thing is, as much as I enjoy this little dance we're having, this isn't what I want,* she thought. *I have greater desires in this world. I have more blood to shed. I want to kill my father and I want to maim that bitch tyrant and I want to massacre every little fucking blackcoat in this place with my bare fucking hands. I want them to hurt and I want them to see my hurt and I want them to understand. I want them to see the hollowness inside me, and watch it consume them.*

I want death and death and death and death.

She found herself revelling in the moment – near salivating at the blood she would carve from every victim she hunted down – and sensed a certain glee as the basilisk coiled up beneath her in preparation for another attack.

This is just the beginning... this is just the beginning! You, beast, are but the first of many. A test subject to the lust of death. You are the subject of my parting words. You are the altar, from which I begin my sacrifice.

And I long to watch you bleed for it.

Savanta closed her eyes and let the warmth pull up through her veins, giving in to the dark as the basilisk opened its jaws and lurched up toward her.

The serpent's fangs gleamed.

The coiling body rose from the ground in a lunging strike.

The Champion's eyes snapped open, fixed upon the sword buried in its back. She vaulted from the central column and slid over the brow of the beast's massive head, darting over the twisting scales and plummeting down toward the dry earth beneath—

Sticking an arm out, and locking her bloody fingers around the hilt of her buried weapon—

Feeling the blade give, as it carved between the scales and tore the serpent's stomach open like a burst sack of offal.

The massive creature screeched somewhere overhead, crashing against the metal column and spinning off to the left. Savanta landed with bent knees and whipped the sword free, barrelling on her side and making to stand as the beast's tail slid out of sight ahead of her.

Offering no time to recover, the Champion charged headlong at the basilisk with a sadistic grin plastered to her face. Rounding the column, she found it nursing its wounds with a forked tongue, completely oblivious to the impending danger of the monster and her blade—

Savanta screeched and drove her sword into its side again, cutting across in maniacal arcs as she ripped the creature to pieces. Scales and sinew splattered across the earth; blue blood spewed across the Champion's skin like war paint. An echo of a voice carried off from the galleries high above.

She marvelled at the beauty and the madness.

An agonised hiss echoed from the basilisk's throat, as it twisted away from the maw and snarled toward Savanta, studying its body with solemn acceptance. Looking between the wounds and the blood and the broken scales. There was a courage in its eye, then: an indefatigable vigour that still longed for the hunt, as it turned back to her and bared its fangs. The Champion almost found herself admiring it for a moment, for how much it still had to give.

And I pity it, too... for how futile the next bit will be.

Savanta dropped into a fighter's stance, poising her blade in her left hand with her right pulled in close to her chest.

Sensing the challenge, the basilisk pulled their coils tight beneath their head, sliding them through and over each other in one massive revolving torrent. Its eyes were furnaces; its skin was cooling metal. A hiss trickled through the gaps in its fangs.

Savanta inhaled deeply, letting her pulse slow as the darkness coursed through her system. Facing down a creature of legend, with a tyrant watching on from the alcoves. Blood, slick between her fingers and dripping down the steel blade in her grasp, dotting the floor at her feet.

The fractious, ticking moments that passed, as the inevitable became true.

The basilisk lunged toward her with its mouth agape, hoping to break her spine and engulf her body in one—

Savanta bellowed like thunder and drove her blade up into the roof of its mouth, cutting her arm against the creature's fangs as she rammed the sword deeper and deeper—

The ground swept out from underneath her, pressed against the serpent's mouth, bellowing louder into its amber eyes as she was hauled backwards—

The basilisk howled as the sword pierced its brain cavity, and its jaw unhinged like a snapped door—

Savanta slammed into the metal column and blacked out on impact, as the opposing jolt and the pain tearing through her forearm swung her mind back to reality—

She screeched, pushing against the sword and the fangs embedding in her wrist as the serpent howled and spasmed across the dirt, fighting against impending death—

Its eyes bulged; Savanta roared.

"*FUCK YOU, YOU BASTARD!*"

And the sword slid through into its brain.

Silence consumed the pit suddenly, like the morning after a storm. The pressure eased from Savanta's chest, as she stood panting and reeling against the metal column. Beyond, the coils of the massive serpent lay suddenly very still, and a certain warmth in the creature's eye dissipated like stardust.

On quivering legs, the Champion relinquished the grip on her blade, and watched as the basilisk dropped to the earth into a pool of amethyst blood.

It is... done, Savanta thought, looking across the beast's huge body and up to the skulls on the walls. *The first blood has been spilt... the first sacrifice has been made.*

Lifting her forearm, she stood for a moment entirely mesmerised by the blood leaking down from her wrist. With her other hand, she traced lines through it, and rolled the crimson liquid across her fingers like it was a paste. Savouring its beauty, with a tiny voice in the back of her head telling her to drink it...

Blood and death and blood... as all things will become.

Savanta dismissed the thought, shaking her head clear and looking up to the back wall instead, where she spied an ancient metal door that she hadn't recognised from before. It stood amongst the skulls like a portal, with rusted hinges and an ugly-looking lock down its middle. Studying it more closely, she also realised that the door stood ajar, revealing a cold room of deep blues beyond.

Almost like someone had left the room and slipped through the door when she wasn't looking...

Savanta smiled: *so this is the game you want to play.* She looked down to the serpent's corpse for a moment, and sighed lamely. *Well, if it is, it's a shame that you wish to rush me, tyrant. I was rather looking forward to carving this thing up and feeding its organs to the walls...*

But anyway, perhaps another time.

She ran her tongue across her teeth and spat into the dust at her feet, rolling her shoulders as she did so.

Now, we must face the music, and acknowledge the truth for what it is, she pronounced. *We must seek out the evil that rots this world, and tear it out from its roots...*

She stepped past the basilisk's head and paced off toward the open door.

Death and death and death.

†

Chapter 53

Retribution

This is hell.

Beads of sweat lined his scalp like rainwater, spilling over the rivets of his forehead as another cloud of dust kicked up across the square. The sweat twinged over his eyebrows, pooling in the black bags under his eyes which he wiped away with absent hands, hardly aware of his own existence. For a moment, he squinted up into the massive sun as it crossed from afternoon to evening, belching its yellow rays across the town of Marcheg as a cacophony of violence filled the skies. He swat at his face, as swarms of bugs skimmed across the battlefield around him, feeding on the dead and circling higher only to be picked off by birds perched along the gutters. By ravens, no doubt.

The harbingers of death.

Eli held an arm up and coughed. *This is hell,* he thought, rolling his shoulder. *From the heat to the flies to the sheer bloody ruin of it all. It's just hell.*

And here we are, neck-deep in the middle of it.

He studied the scene convulsing before him, looking up to the rooftops of the houses opposite. Against the haze of light, he spied the small, hunched shapes of imperial archers peeking over the lip of the roof, with the thin lines of their bowstrings like needles in the clouds. They shifted delicately, surveying the battle below with studious eyes, and knocked their arrows once a target had been found. It only took a matter of moments, and Eli watched as they lifted from their stoop and loosed into the crowds beneath, where the sudden and quickly-silenced cries of his people indicated they had met their mark.

The Chief grunted under his breath.

Need to do something about them.

But, almost as soon as the thought came, a whistling sound passed across the sky above him, and one of the archers toppled backwards in a jetting arc of their own blood. Sliding down the tiles, the body disappeared from sight – and somewhere above him, Eli swore he heard a cheer go up.

He allowed himself a slight smile.

It's good to see they're still hopeful...

Looking back down to the battle unfolding before him, he clocked a figure approaching and sighed.

Because I sure-as-shit ain't...

Like a titan wading through a massacre, the palace-guard stopped a few paces before him and lowered into a fighter's stance. A short-sword glinted in their left hand, already slick with someone's blood, and a number of scrapes lined their chest-plate to match it.

Eli sized them up – noting how, even without a suit of armour, he stood slightly taller than his opponent – and felt a warmth pull across his fingers as he gripped his bludgeon tighter. Closing his eyes for a moment, he managed a short prayer and hefted the weapon into his other hand, sliding his feet across the stone slabs.

Let's have it.

He roared, charging forward with his bludgeon swinging, strafing across his body toward the guard's silver chest-piece.

They reacted with agility, sliding just out of reach and lunging out with their blade, forcing Eli to grind his heels in and deflect the blow. The sound of metal chimed in his ears, as he grappled his hefty weapon and brought it across for a short sweep.

It connected with the guard's arm with a hefty *crack*, dislodging several pieces of armour that fell across the stone at their feet like shells. The palace guard hissed, bringing their blade up in a sudden, erratic strike that narrowly missed carving Eli's wrist open.

The Chief sucked a breath through his teeth.

Best watch out for that.

He stepped back for a second and assessed his options, deciding another sweeping attack was his best bet, arcing down toward the opponent's knees.

The guard lurched away as the bludgeon impacted, narrowly avoiding the spiked ball that would've mangled their toes to oblivion. They grunted with frustration, digging their heels in and sliding their blade up suddenly toward Eli's exposed neck—

As the Chief quickly sidestepped, bunching his shoulders together and ramming into the guard's chest, forcing them to teeter backwards and lose control—

He pressed the advantage, gritting his teeth and hefting his weapon skyward, pulling back suddenly as the guard readjusted and jabbed their sword toward his head—

Ignorant of the metal ball spinning toward their arm at frightening speed—

Snapping across their knuckle with a horrific crunch of bone, as Eli watched the wrist bulge out of its socket and disintegrate under the strain.

The guard howled, wailing beneath their helmet. They released the short-sword still lodged in their broken hand and seized it with the other like a circus act, slicing up suddenly toward the Chief in a tear-bitten rage.

Eli brought the bludgeon up to deflect the attack with a grin. Using the weapon's handle, he jabbed out at the guard twice, pressing down against their chest to force another backstep, much to the opponent's disgust.

The Chief squinted against the sun.

Let's work some magic…

Using the momentum of the jabs, he stepped forward into the

guard's circle and spun his weapon like a flail, as the spiked metal ball scraped up across their chest-plate and connected sharply with their helmet—

Ripping the entire thing off from the base; flinging it skyward to reveal a woman's shocked expression, with gritted teeth and a sweat-sheened brow.

Eli stared, wide-eyed.

Well how about that...

The palace guard roared and diced her blade across in several long strokes, forcing the Chief to backstep and use his weapon as a baton. He deflected several attacks – wincing as one skimmed the bracer on his forearm – before bringing his own weapon about to counter. It was a quick striking motion, pressing between the woman's chest and shoulder. The spikes ripped between the metal plates, tearing at flesh and cloth and sinew. The guard hissed, swaying to one side—

Wasting no time, Eli brought the handle of the bludgeon across and caught her across the jaw with the brace of a punch.

The woman collapsed onto all fours suddenly, blinking stupidly as her tongue ran over the broken teeth and blood now meshing in her jaw.

The Chief allowed a grin; he kicked the palace guard's flank with the end of his boot, spilling her onto her side.

Staring up into the blue sky above with little sense left in her mind, the guard blinked slowly and seemed to accept her fate.

"Have... mercy..." she spluttered.

"Eat shit," Eli spat.

Hefting the bludgeon, eclipsing the sun at his back, he cast it low across the stone slabs at his feet.

And caved her face in like an eggshell.

He stood then for a moment, wavering in the heat, gazing down at the corpse and the sticky brain matter now smeared across his weapon like hideous artwork. A bite of nausea pulled in his stomach that he quickly swallowed down. Every fibre of his being ached in some melancholic way: not enough to render him useless, but enough to exact a toll on each movement thereon.

Getting too old for this.

Hefting the huge weapon onto his shoulder and stepping over the palace-guard's stricken corpse, Eli took in the musty air and the din of battle, and drew one definitive conclusion from it.

We're losing.

Everywhere he looked, steel stood glinting: soldiers and swords cutting down his people, who fought for their lives with broken stares and butchered limbs. Gasping as they fell, collapsing to a ground already littered with corpses from the day before and the one before that. Swarms of flies circled the air around them in thick clouds, descending amongst the dead every so often to ply their bodies with maggots, accompanied by crows and rats who glutted themselves on the feast of human idiocy.

Stood at the centre of it all, watching almost as a bystander, Eli shook his head and felt a tug at his heart. *So much death... so much waste... and for what?* he thought, wincing at the wounds on his shoulder and stomach. *We lose, and continue to lose until the inevitable end comes, where our only hope lies in a fate we cannot ascertain.* He closed his eyes solemnly and looked up to the skies.

Where are you Alva?

The thought came and went like a shooting star, forming shadows in his mind, as the orbit of the battle spun his way once again. Opening his eyes slowly, he looked out across the square opposite and found two squat brutes in steel plates approaching him, grinning moronically with their swords raised.

The Chief cursed under his breath and blasphemed the gods.

Getting too fucking old for this...

He swung the bludgeon to the left and caught the first one across the wrist, watching as their sword snapped from their grip and spun off into the crowds beyond.

Releasing the hold on his weapon, Eli formed a fist and clocked the second soldier in the nose, where his metal guard cracked the cartilage in an explosion of blood and residue.

A squeal; the soldier stumbled backwards clasping for their nose, whimpering quietly in their arrogance—

Grappling the bludgeon, the Chief swung upwards with a toothy snarl and tore through the enemy like carving bread. The soldier's elbows cracked under the pressure; their jaw snapped off its hinges, ramming teeth and gums up into their skull like pellets; squashing the eyes in their sockets, dismantling the brain until everything was gore and hell and the light of hate left their eyes. A single breath passed their ruined lips.

And they crumpled to the floor in seconds.

The Chief grimaced and spat at the body, glaring at the other soldier with a venomous eye. They stumbled backwards, fearful and desperate, holding their wrist with wide-eyed horror. Like a fox caught in the gutter, they turned and ambled off into the throng of bodies behind, hoping to escape the murderous melee and the destructive terror of the bludgeon.

Eli watched them scamper away, and shrugged tiredly.

Some cowards are more obvious than others, it seems.

He stepped back, leaning against his massive weapon, and drew in a long breath. Assessing his situation; sensing the air. Acknowledging the clash of steel blades and the *caw* of ravens and the thrum of crossbow strings from the balcony above him. The blood that pooled at his feet in tiny rivers; the beautiful blue sky smudged with smoke above. The quiet passage of the sun, drifting between the clouds, watching on from another world.

Gazing up at its eternal beneficence, Eli almost believed it too—

"Well, well, well... the Chief of the Mountains! We were wondering where you'd got to..."

Eli silenced the thought and lowered his gaze, scanning the square ahead to find another palace guard approaching him, brandishing a broadsword as wide as his leg.

Oh joy...

And then, from behind, another guard appeared.

And another behind them.

Oh…

Fuck.

"We have orders for your execution, Chief!" the middle one thundered, levelling their blade at his head, "as a traitor to the nation and its people."

"I'm no traitor, officer!" the Chief roared back, hefting his weapon to his shoulder. "I'm a man of the nation."

"You're a man of *nothing*."

All three of them started approaching.

Eli ground his heel. "I'm a man who's gonna break your face in if you get any closer, *officer*. I'm warning you…"

Striding toward him, unphased by his threats, the palace guards closed him down, corralling him like wolves with cackles and smiles.

For a moment, as the Chief faced down the spectre of death that now approached him, time seemed to slow down. The end emerged, like a subtle knife slowly breaching his ribs. The possibility of survival fell away, and a lonesome foreboding claimed Eli's heart. As the battlefield chimed behind them and the calamity of war raged on, the weight of the world came down across his shoulders: it ground at his knees and ankles; wept from the wounds on his arm and chest; pounded through his skull in the high-sun heat; and chiselled across his teeth until his tongue bled.

We were so close, he mused as they closed him down. *We were so close to beating them. Victory was there: for a brief, beautiful moment, it was in our grasp. We could all see it and taste it.*

We were so close…

I don't know where Alva is. I don't know where Castan and the others are. I don't know if they've survived, or what happened down there in the Warrens. I don't know a thing.

And it seems I will never know. I'll be dead in a matter of minutes. I'll never know the fate of the only person left alive who reminds me of him. Tears streaked his face, cold against his cheeks.

I'm so sorry, Arrenso… I failed you.

I'm so sorry…

He closed his eyes, then, and thought of all things: of his life, and the cause, and those who fought and died around him for it.

Of his people, down in the depths beneath their feet, knowing they could never be saved.

His only living relative, down there with them, screaming for help with no answer to come.

His dead husband, murdered by a tyrant and his pet general, who now skulked the square before him plucking at dead men's eyes and laughing.

Thinking of Camille and Daro, waiting in a quiet camp some twenty miles west...

And how their father will never return.

With numb motion, he drew into a fighter's stance, his eyes red with tears like autumn leaves – facing the death that came in steel plates with polished swords and hate in their minds.

I'm sorry, my beautiful children. I'm sorry Arrenso. I couldn't do it. I'm so sorry...

The guards lifted their blades.

I'm sorry.

His heart stopped—

And his prayers were suddenly answered.

A crackle like cinder snapped in his ear, and the entire stretch of buildings lining the square's eastern edge exploded in a maw of fire. Tiles shot from the rooftops like bullets. The crack of wooden beams tore across the skyline as dust and debris filled the air. The entire second-storey started sliding off its hinges, with the archers in the windows screaming in terror as the building swung sidelong and ruptured across the street below. Shrapnel and the vicious smell of ignition powder clouded the air. The entire battle seemed to gravitate suddenly to the east.

Where a swarm of rebels appeared in reinforcement, tearing through the enemy lines with steel blades shining.

Eli stood in disbelief, his cheeks aching from his smile.

They actually did it.

They're alive.

The rebels collided with what remained of the Imperial Army like a battering ram, breaking faces and armour with a brute simplicity that the enemy could not match, emerging from the smog-filled air of the ruined buildings roaring with pride. Eli watched the palace-guards turn from him to face the incoming tide, roaring orders as arrows channelled their way and embedded between plates of steel. Fire and light seemed to explode before him. armour clattered to the ground across the square: steel helmets slapping against dead bodies to paint the floor with blots of red-gold-green. The surge of the rebels channelling all around them.

Perhaps all is not lost after all.

With a long draw of breath, opening out his chest like a giant, the Chief of the Mountains lifted his bludgeon and prepared to join the fray—

When a body stepped out from the crush a dozen steps ahead of him, and turned to face him with a look of hate-filled horror. Combing a hand through their silver, rolling hair, they snarled and lifted a short-sword toward Eli's head.

General Ferreus growled.

"You'll die for this, you *bastard!*"

The Chief clasped his bludgeon and smiled.

Let's see about that.

†

Chapter 54

When the Lights Go Out

He fights aggressively, proactively, preferring long, arcing swings to small jabs and counter-manoeuvres. He holds his blade close to his body, using his arm-span to attack but never physically entering my circle – meaning he's afraid of close-quarters combat, and that this is not his preferred setting for engagement. We could also infer that he has limited confidence in his ability at hand-to-hand fighting, which is balanced by the sheer strength he exudes behind each attack. If I were to parry him, however, and enter his circle... he'd be on the floor in seconds.

Ptolemy grit his teeth and swung down toward Cavara, who stepped aside and lunged forward in retaliation, forcing him to disengage and backstep awkwardly, exactly as she'd expected.

Predictable... good to know.

As she thought it, she sensed motion to her right and brought her blade across, connecting with Amara's dual-rapiers and smacking them aside.

With visible frustration, the honour-guard slunk back into the shadows and circled behind Ptolemy like a wolf.

She is the moon to Ptolemy's sun, Cavara inferred. *Uneasy in her attacks, preferring someone else to do the dirty work as she nips in for the kill. That's likely the reason why she hunts with dogs outside the city limits: the dogs maim the victim so she can savour the end. She's more of an assassin, keeping to the shadows and waiting for an opening.*

Cavara snarled and deflected another of Ptolemy's attacks.

Not that I'll give her the chance.

In fact, I'll go for you first.

"You can give in now, you know, and make our lives easier," the Butcher said from the chamber door, watching on with obvious amusement. "This can all be over soon..."

"I won't give you the *satisfaction,*" Cavara muttered, deflecting another attack from the front and countering Amara to her left.

The Butcher smiled. "So *be it.*"

And the honour-guard advanced again.

Ptolemy attacked first, sensing her wavering resolve. He cut across in one motion, forcing Cavara to backstep; he sliced up in the next, the general's sword juddering in her hand as the blades snapped together and slid apart. Cavara readjusted her footing, circling to the left with gliding steps, taking a sharp intake of breath as Ptolemy carved across for a third time, opening up space in the middle—

She lunged out, spearing up toward his neck, forcing the honour-guard to lose balance and step away with a frustrated grunt on his lips.

A heartbeat passed, allowing the general a moment to breathe, before Amara emerged to her right and howled with her blades spinning.

Cavara registered the angle and ducked, as one of the rapiers skimmed just above her head and frayed the hairs on her scalp. Bringing her own sword up across her chest, she pushed out as if wielding a staff and blocked the second blade, lifting again to counter—

Ptolemy stepped in to attack behind her, lunging down toward her back—

The general tensed up and kicked out like a horse, snapping her heel against the man's shin as he groaned and recoiled his attack.

Looking up suddenly, Cavara propelled up into Amara's circle before she could intercept with her blades and headbutted her in the nose, the crunch of cartilage ricocheting through her ears.

Amara hissed and stepped away, bringing a hand up to a nose that was still intact but now leaked blood like a tap across her lips.

"You'll pay for *that*," she screeched, shifting back into the shadow.

Cavara shrugged.

We'll see.

She took several steps back, now facing the entranceway where the Butcher loomed and the honour-guards approached from both sides. To her right, the cell door stood watching in anticipation, with the occupant inside fearing for the general's life probably as much as they feared for their own. Trapped in the darkness, as their fate played out in the room beyond.

It'll be okay, little one, Cavara thought in a moment of quiet, with a dutiful warmth in her soul. *You'll be safe again soon.*

I have a plan, after all.

She held her weapon down against her hip, edging slowly backwards as Ptolemy approached from the front with a smug grin on his face.

A heartbeat later, and the honour-guard pounced, striking across with several venomous attacks that forced Cavara to lurch backwards and deflect them with her blade. Pain crawled up her arm in shockwaves: lightning strikes screaming across her shoulder and reverberating through her collarbone. She lunged out again toward his chest, hoping to force a retreat, but Ptolemy saw past it and skimmed his blade along her own toward her exposed hands. Cavara flinched and stalled; Ptolemy hefted his weapon over his shoulder and carved down toward her face. She stepped backwards in fear and knocked against something, looking down to find the chair there, not paying attention—

Not watching her opponent, who speared out toward her stomach and slit a line across her side, withdrawing the blade with blood along its edge.

Cavara hissed, wincing at the pain now twinging above her hip and the warm blood now spreading across her skin.

"Very poor, general, very poor," Ptolemy mocked, shaking his head with a smile. "I thought you knew better than that."

Cavara grit her teeth. "Lucky hit..." she managed with a smile.
Ptolemy stepped forward. "Any last words, general?"
The general smirked. "Yes, in fact..."
She grabbed the chair at her back and winked.
"*Catch.*"
Hefting it across her body with a roar of strength, Cavara swung the chair and smashed it across Ptolemy's head, wooden shrapnel flying across the chamber toward Amara and the Butcher. The metal buckles on the arms and legs smacked into the honour-guard's skull, tearing chunks of his skin off. Thrown across the room by the impact – his sword spinning off across the floor – Ptolemy connected with the far stone wall in a disgusting contortion of limbs.
And with a single *crack* of bone, his head split open like an egg.
Amara screamed.
The Butcher frowned.
Cavara suppressed her nausea and whispered a prayer.
One down...
The general rolled her shoulders and tensed the sword in her hand – wincing at the angry muscles pulsing in her elbow – and turned to the remaining honour-guard who emerged suddenly from the gloom.
"I'm gonna fucking *kill you!*" Amara screeched, sliding her blades together and storming forward.
Cavara lowered her body and stared her down.
Come on then, you bitch...
Amara spun on her heel with her blades dicing through, stepping into the general's circle like a hurricane of knives. Cavara baulked for a moment and sliced down through the blades, knocking one aside and catching the other close to her wrist, withdrawing to avoid any injuries.
Steadying herself, Amara paced forward relentlessly, channelling the anger burning through her eyes into malicious and vengeful strikes. Cavara screwed her nose up and speared through the middle toward the honour-guard's throat – missing by a hair's-breadth, with

the only result being to piss her off even more.

Amara recoiled and carved up again, the swords coming at the general in torrents. She batted them aside in a flurry of panic, unable to keep track of the thin blades as they dissected the air around her. Knocking one aside; ducking the next; spinning the third, only to backstep and parry the fourth. Their feet sliding across the stone below: a dance of death, almost. The torches around them flushing and biting against the shadows, as light and dark clashed once more.

Playing out an ancient battle, eons old, in the chamber between them.

Cavara broke another of her attacks and sought an opening to utilise, only to hiss in frustration as Amara brought another blade across and forced her back on the defensive. Both rapiers skimmed inches from her chest; the general pushed them back and swung heavily with her left, receiving an angry spasm from her elbow in reply. Amara snarled with spittle on her lips, and rammed forward with her shoulder, connecting with Cavara's chest and knocking the wind from her system.

Stumbling backwards, the general spat across the stone and sighed through her teeth.

The anger has changed her, she acknowledged, beating back another wave of attacks. *She's become... more erratic... fights more in my circle... I can't find space... I can't...*

Cavara growled and beat down with her sword once – twice – three times, forcing the honour-guard to step away only by the sheer force of her movements. The general hoped, in a facetious part of her mind, that it might make her more cautious when she next attacked.

But when that attack came seconds later, and Amara intertwined her strikes like dicing meat, Cavara realised just how foolish that notion was.

There's no holding her back... she just keeps... fighting—

A lunge toward her stomach; Cavara leaned back and slammed a fist into Amara's shoulder, suddenly on the offensive.

I just have to beat her back. I just… need… I…

Fuck sake!

She sensed her anger rise, and the volatility burned in her veins as she tried to press an advantage.

Come on, come on!

Grinding her jaw until her gums hurt, she lashed out in her rage against the flailing honour-guard, forcing her back inch-by-inch, hoping to find some breakthrough.

Come on—!

She lunged and overextended suddenly, exposing her entire left side to the mercy of Amara.

Giggling with mania, the honour-guard pressed her rapier into the small of the general's back and shoved her away, allowing the fall to carve a deep line along Cavara's waist and send her crashing out across the stone.

Cavara screamed, cursing herself, and rose quickly to her feet. Resistance across her back from where she had fallen sent shivers of pain over her ribs; sickness bubbled in her stomach. An excruciating tension pulled across her shoulders. For a reflective moment, she thought back to her time with the Forgotten One sparring on the hillside to the north, and re-called one of their teachings.

"Control that rage, Successor… if the rage wishes to fight, let it be in the mastery of one's blade…"

…and not in the screech of their mind.

She drew in a long breath, pushing down into her diaphragm, and the world seemed to slow around her. The chamber opened out, with the lights flickering in the alcoves high above. The pain coursing through her body numbed to a quiet tedium, as the enemy charged toward her with their blades primed.

The mastery of one's blade…

She studied Amara as she approached, as a master watches an apprentice: the adjustment of her feet; the angle of her arms; the positioning of her swords. Every droplet of hate flying from her mouth. Cavara saw it unravel, slowly but surely, and could almost imagine what came next. Pre-emptive measures and second-guesses and the randomness of chance.

A realisation, toying in her mind suddenly, as the way of the Rapture took hold.

Levelling her blade, and closing her eyes…

Amara screeched and crossed her blades, aiming up to slice the stunned general through the neck—

Cavara's eyes snapped open suddenly; sliding the blade between the two rapiers, she dragged them apart—

Lunging across with a fist suddenly, the general swung into Amara's side and impacted like a bullet—

Craning her neck a heartbeat later; breaking the woman's nose completely. Watching her stumble back—

Exhaling, as the general tore her blade down and sliced straight through Amara's wrist, watching her hand still clutching the rapier slap against the cold stone below.

Let the rage be transgressed…

Amara screamed as blood jetted from the stump of her forearm, dropping her other sword to clutch it and stare in disbelief. Her skin became sickly white; the fury that had boiled in her eyes simmered away to nothingness. The severed hand twitched grotesquely at their feet.

…let the sins be undone.

The honour-guard glared at the general on trembling legs, hissing and gnashing her teeth together.

"*I'LL FUCKING KILL YOU!*" she roared, opening her arms out to charge forward—

When a huge blade impaled her back and speared out her chest like a parasite, as her limbs went limp at her sides and she choked on her own spit.

Staring at them in shock, Cavara watched as the weapon lowered and Amara's corpse slid from the blade.

From behind, a figure emerged covered in robes, with something resembling a smile on their face.

The Forgotten One smiled. "Did you miss me?"

Cavara found it in her to laugh, as a deep relief claimed her heart once more. "More than you can know, my frie—"

She stopped suddenly, shuddering, looking past them to the empty doorway beyond.

"Where is *he*…?" she muttered, her throat closing.

The pale figure blinked.

"Who?"

She didn't find time to respond, let alone think. Her skin crawled, as the Rapture sensed a presence in the room around them and beckoned her into its embrace.

Tensing for a moment, and offering one final glance to the Forgotten One before her, Cavara closed her eyes and stepped forward into an all-consuming darkness—

~

Lifting her hand suddenly to conjure the flaming sword, as the Butcher emerged from the void with a cleaver aimed at her head…

†

Chapter 55

You Know What You Must Do

Savanta entered the throne-room with quiet, limping steps, looking up into the cavernous ceiling and wishing it would swallow her whole. Ornaments lined the walls alongside her: tapestries and metal sheets depicting beasts and tribal demons that looked upon her as one of their own, as if she were no different than them. The blue-grey light of the chamber swirled and vibrated around her, devoid of light or solace –yet she felt so much darker than the gloom she traversed, like an eclipsing moon swallow-ing the sun. And she realised, then, that the shimmering eyes of the tapestry demons did not look upon her as their equals, but rather cowered from her as something greater. As if she were a shadow, or a wraith. A creature that rivalled even their mythical barbarity.

A monster, of man's own making.

Here to exact a toll…

Before her, stood in a haggard robe with his beard rolling down his chest, the hunched form of her disconsolate father stood awaiting her arrival. He seemed unphased by her presence – unphased by the sheer bloody ruin painted across her expression – and stared lowly at his feet. Savanta sensed a burning pain rise in her stomach as she gazed upon him: a feeling only made worse, when the Iron Queen materialised to her right and stood adjacent to them, rolling her tongue across her teeth like a viper.

The Champion stood opposite the ghostly visage of her father, levelling her eyes with the shadows hidden beneath his cowl. Wondering what machinations consumed his mind then.

Hiding from the truth of your own daughter.

"Well, well… you're alive," the Iron Queen mused next her, with a hint of surprise in her voice. "I was beginning to wonder what had happened to you…"

"I did what I needed to survive," Savanta said plainly, holding her gaze on the robes opposite. "That's all."

"Perhaps, yes." Gaza paused. "Then again, perhaps you should tell that to the basilisk that's been filleted like a fish, spewing blue blood all over my beautiful arena…"

Savanta pursed her lips and offered nothing in reply, suppressing the rage that burned in her soul.

The Queen studied her for a moment and smiled. "What's wrong, Champion? For someone so full of hate and menace and the desire to burn the world to ashes… you seem so quiet all of a sudden. You're not the grovelling, spitting, flea-ridden dog I remember anymore. I'm almost hurt."

She scoffed. "Apologies for *disappointing* you, your Highness."

"I shouldn't worry… this isn't the first time you've disappointed me, and I somewhat doubt it'll be the last."

Savanta recoiled at her words, shocked that she felt so influenced by them. Almost like she cared about what the Queen thought of her.

As if I find value in her command.

"It's no matter, in reality," Gaza continued, lifting a hand and flicking dirt from under her nail. "The world does not care for you, and neither should I. It will continue its relentless cycle all the same, tearing itself apart until we are nothing but bones and dust. Your place in it really means nothing."

"I'm just your fighting whore then, am I?" Savanta spat, unable to control it. "I'm just your creature, that you push around and get bloody and use at your whim, until I'm burnt out and no longer fit for purpose. Is that what it is?"

"What you are, is a fighter, chosen by my loyal envoys in Val Darbesh..."

"I am a *Champion* fighter, who has bested every single task you've thrown against me and still lives to tell the fucking story. Do not wash your hands with my potential because it isn't convenient with your notions of *grandeur*."

Something twitched beneath the cowl before her; the Queen lost the humour and wickedness in her eye for a moment.

"I knew there was still some venom in you, Champion... but like an abandoned child, it had just lost its way," Gaza said softly. "And in so many ways, you are still just like the child you were the day your father left." Her eyes darted over to the robed man and back. "Addled by pain, and by grief... by *lies,* and a false understanding of self-importance. Mired by the fickle nothings of a monster... and still now grappling for that same supremacy you sought when you butchered that child before—"

"*Enough,*" Savanta muttered, as nerves twitched and spasmed across her skull, rekindling a foul memory she had hoped to bury. "Enough..."

"This is what you are though, isn't it? The part you keep forgetting – you are a Champion fighter, besting all of my challenges, of course, but you're also so much more. You're a butcher, and a traitor, and a disgusting monster to your own parents. You're a liar, and have buried your head in those lies for your entire life. You are nothing but madness, and *hate*—"

"*Enough!*" Savanta quivered, pulling air through her teeth, like her soul was erupting from her chest. The shadows of the room spun high above, tightening at the edge like a choke-hold. Suffocating her. Pulling her deeper and deeper into the dark...

This can't be, she pleaded. *Please no... please, gods, no. What is this? What is any of this? Wha... what can I do? What does it all mean? A monster of flesh, rotted by the shadows, ruined by grief. Never to recover.*

Death and death and death...

"You want it to stop, Savanta... don't you?" the Iron Queen cooed with a malicious glint in her eye. "You want it all to end..."

The Champion looked off into the shadows beyond, lost in a void of her own making.

"Then you have to end things, as you always started them..." Reaching behind her back, Gaza drew something into the light and held it out for her to see.

Savanta saw it and gasped.

The Queen grinned.

"You must end it, with *blood*."

A knife, twinkling like the gemstones on a dead king's crown, lay against the palm of her hand. A subtle weapon, with a finely-sharpened blade and a handle made of leather and blackened steel. It seemed so small in her hand, almost forgoing the pain it could inflict. Savanta looked upon its glinting blade, and took it from the Queen's pale hands.

To find herself reunited suddenly, with the blade she had intended for Gaza's throat.

All those hours sharpening and practicing, praying for a moment just like this, she considered. *And then I'm handed the weapon by the very same woman I sought to use it against...*

The Champion smiled quietly.

How cruel fate has become.

"The blade you carried all this way has now returned to you, Champion... and before you, lies a choice," the Queen pronounced beside her. "Wield the knife, and kill the man who caused you so much pain, so you may be free of its curse forever... or let him live, and carve your own throat out in his place." She paused. "A sacrifice must be made, Champion... and the choice, is *yours*."

Savanta stared at the knife, puzzling at her own hands and the fate they sealed. Lost in a maze of her own mind; corrupted vessels and broken faith. A sensation pulling over her body, almost like her skin was flaking away.

How cruel...

"This is no idle task, Champion… I understand as much." The Queen nodded slowly. "This is a momentous thing… something to savour and consider. The ties you have to your past are strong, and I imagine there is great rift in your heart staring at the knife in your hand. But, just think of the—"

Savanta lunged forward and speared her father in the chest, driving the knife deep until blood exploded across her hand and arm and fountained across the stone beneath—

Withdrawing and driving up again, stabbing into his stomach, piercing intestines as his gasping head lurched across her shoulder—

She kicked out at his knees with a snap of bones: her father buckled to a kneel before her, where she clasped his hair through his cowl and dragged him up—

Spearing the knife into his face, over and over and over with gritted teeth and quiet eyes and a terror coursing through her body, impaling sockets and ripping teeth from gums, puncturing his skull cavity—

Lifting his haggard body up against her own, her arms bulging ferociously—

Carving his throat to a bloody pulp, bathed in her father's blood.

Like a discarded toy, Savanta dropped the body at her feet and cast the knife spinning across the stone toward Gaza.

Watching it stop at the end of her foot, the Queen looked up at her Champion with shock and horror, her eyes never lingering far from the robed body crumpled against the stone beneath.

Savanta lifted a hand to her face and studied the blood webbing through her fingers, watching it fray and congeal over her skin. Something verging on pride glowed in her eye, as the drums in her head finally drew still.

Breathing slowly, she lifted her gaze and regarded the tyrant stood nearby.

"In blood, your will is done…"

Savanta smiled; the tyrant smiled back.

My Queen.

†

Chapter 56

Heir of the Ozban

Only death remains now.

In the murky desecration of the Ozban, the rain tore from the skies like arrowheads, and swept across the lowlands in a vortex of surging waves. Slate-black skies roared overhead, casting long shadows over the freshly mudded earth. The bare trees of the massive forest braced silently against the elements, as the murky depths between their boughs rippled and squirmed. The ruined stone walls of the rotten buildings swayed drunkenly in the swell. It was almost as if the world were retching, and the sin of man convulsed into itself once more. Even hell appeared more peaceful than the depths of the Forest then.

And the gods seemed to be laughing, as Revek was dragged to his death.

Silver helmets like studs glistened with sheens of rainwater, spread over the bare earth before the platform like a field of thorns. Jostling against one another with grey faces and tired eyes: phantoms in the dark illuminated only by the dead moon breaching the storm high above. Solemn and despairing, they traced the procession as it passed: spying among their ranks – dragged by his arms through the mud and rain and piss and ruin – a commander they had fought and bled for. A good man; a terrible man; a true leader; a vicious tyrant.

A mirage now, in the depths of the quaking thunder. A traitor, or something.

The gods roared high above.

The platform ahead shimmered like the surface of a lake, illuminated by weak torchlight on either side. Rising suddenly before him; the commander ascended the steps on withered legs, his boots struggling for purchase. He slipped for a second, stumbling and righting himself with an exhale of breath. From behind, Zespa's laugh echoed in his ears. The commander didn't register it, as he studied the maelstrom of light and steel spinning furiously overhead. Realising he was a witness to hell, as it descended upon the mortal realm.

On their thrones, the gods raised their glasses.

On the platform before him, a wooden stock had been erected facing the soldiers, and the glint of an executioner's axe lay embedded in the platform just beyond. Shadows danced around it, as if the harbinger of death had conjured from the storm to make merry in his demise. Watching as he was led to the stock; watching him kneel before it as if in prayer. The rain blanketing his face: a moment's respite, as thunder ripped the skyline above and the officers fanned out behind him with vengeful grins.

To his right, Lazaerys approached the front of the platform.

The gods stilled themselves to listen.

"Soldiers… officers of this army!" the Marshal bellowed over the din, throwing her hands out wide for all to bear witness. "We have brought you here today, before this executioner's block… because one of our highest-ranking officials has committed an act of treason, and attempted to take the life of another officer for their own personal, vindictive gain. Commander Revek *here*…" – she turned to him with a venomous smile pulling across her cheeks – "…was found in General Zespa's tent before the storm hit, with a knife in his clutches, aiming it down toward her sleeping head. And it was only the general's bravery and quick thinking that kept her alive, as we stormed the tent and apprehended the commander before he could commit his *atrocity*."

Lightning rallied overhead. Xol stepped forward with hands clasped tightly at their back, offering no emotion in their disconsolate gaze.

"What the commander has done here," Lazaerys continued, "is tantamount to *treason*. He is a traitor to our army… a traitor to his rank… and a traitor to you *all* for his actions!" Drenched in rain, the Marshal leered over the edge of the platform, spearing a finger toward Revek. "And, as is *befitting* his rank, he shall receive the due punishment for a *traitor* of Provenci… and you shall be here to bear witness as this great sin is finally condemned."

Quiet eyes looked up through the storm; somewhere high above, one could almost hear laughter.

"Commander Revek!" Xol proclaimed, turning side on to the soldiers and their fallen tyrant. "You have been found guilty of high treason under the Provenci Imperial Code, for the attempted murder of General Zespa, the probable murder of General Oslo, and the wanton abandonment of your post during the tragic retreat from the Grey Plains, costing near seven-hundred Provenci lives. For your crimes against the army and nation… you are to be executed by decapitation, and buried in an unmarked grave where you lie." Xol lowered their head. "This is our decree… and by our decree you shall be put to death."

Xol nodded over to the Marshal. In turn the Marshal bowed her head to Zespa, who took a single step forward and hefted the massive axe out of the platform floor, studying the silver curved blade with a sadistic pleasure. The two other officers dropped from the platform and splashed down into the mud, wading their way forward to stand before the amassed forces as the traitor awaited his end.

Revek lay his neck in the small inlay, feeling cold, sodden wood against the ball of his throat, which tensed rhythmically every time he tried to swallow. The air seemed cooler there, crisp and unburdened, as the rain ricocheted across his back and peeled across his scalp in tiny rivers. It was almost peaceful, he felt, knelt there waiting to die.

Almost.

It all could've been so different, the commander thought, as he closed his eyes and exhaled slowly. *This didn't have to be this way. I could've murdered that bitch in her sleep and slipped away without a sound. I could've got Oslo lost in the camp during the attack – fed him to the creature on a fucking plate. I could've killed Lazaerys, somewhere, somehow.*

Zespa stood beside him, with the axe locked tightly in her fists.

They all had to die... they all still have to die. That's how it should be: none left but me, the god of the army, the triumphant commander brought back from his lowly exile. I should be leading them. I should have this power. I can't do that... when they're alive. They should all just die...

Whispered insults from Zespa were half lost in the howl of the storm – she raised the axe blade over her shoulder.

They will all die. They must die. Blood and hell and fire and fucking blind murder. Death must come. Death like the savages in their camps. Death like Darius. Death like Oslo. I am the arbiter here; there is no god but me. Death shall come for all.

Like the Ozban that surrounds us...

†

"What are we gonna do?"

"They're dead... the army's destroyed... we, we might be the only ones left, the only ones alive...."

"Where are they now? The... the enemy. All around us."

"They could be in the trees, stalking us like wolves... behind us! Anywhere! What are we..."

"What are we gonna do, commander?"

Revek sat against the tree opposite them, sharpening his sword with a whetstone, the malevolent dark of night cast heavy across his face.

He ground his teeth together and screwed his nose up, as the image of their retreat into the Forest corrupted in his mind: stumbling through the undergrowth, flailing and sweat-soaked, directionless and terrified. Pressing on into the dark, evermore. He had no idea how long he had ran for; no idea where in the vastness of the Ozban he had ended up. Only that, in a small grove of trees laced with congealed-purple vines, he had stumbled upon a cluster of his soldiers who lit up at the sight of him. They had been in there for a number of days, likely just trying to survive. Upon his arrival, they leapt up from their hovel with hopeful smiles, opening their arms in prayer, looking over to him, through him with…

With bleeding pupils. Tiny trickles, black as night, leaking across their irises. Each and every one of them, possessing the same affliction.

Rotting away inside…

No-one really knew what drove people mad within the shadows of the Ozban. No-one had lived long enough there to find out. Surveyors, sent across from the capital when Tarraz was little more than a colony, had made their guesses as to what lurked within the shadows of the skeletal trees: wraiths that crawled out of the roots and dragged people in; pools of acidic liquid that bubbled to the surface and dissolved all life above; noxious gas releasing from spores in the leaves. They had theorised, and they had suggested, but it had all been inconclusive in the end, pointing more to the ignorance of the surveyors than to any tangible answer.

So when the commander watched the soldier's pupils slowly leak into their skulls, and watched as their faces started to sag and rot inside like decaying corpses, he had initially thought he was going mad. How could it be happening? What did it mean?

And, even more so: how could they not notice?

As the hours ticked by, very little changed in their demeanour: they made no acknowledgement of their condition, as their minds slowly gave over to the Forest and its curse. Part of Revek thought he was imagining it all – part of him thought he was the one going insane.

That was, until they started flinching and sweating one day, as if seizing from electric shocks. Weeping in their sleep that night, and several nights after until they didn't sleep at all. Screaming mid-conversation with no clear reason, scratching at their faces like rash-bitten dogs. A cycle of madness, circling over and over in the gloom.

Never to end.

"I don't know what we should do," Revek had replied to them, never quite meeting their eye for fear of the insanity screeching through their bones. "All I know, is that we need to keep moving... and that the longer we stand idle, the more the trees consume us..."

After that day, he had spent long nights and broken days staring into the shimmering reflections of chest-plates and swords and shields, fearful and despairing. Waiting for his own pupils to start to weep, and the rot to take hold through his system. Waiting patiently, almost inquisitively. Watching those around him – those few soldiers who followed him like rodents – as their eyes became nothing but falling stars and their nails were lined with their own skin. The commander sat sharpening his blades, watching on.

Questioning why his own did not do the same.

"They say insanity takes all," one of them prophesised one night, sat cross-legged stabbing his palm with a knife, producing little welts of blood. "They say it claims us, bores within us like maggots. Claiming so many. Claiming... but not all of them! Never all of them. No: some may survive it, perhaps. Those lucky ones who tread the line of madness already. They live to tell the tale... but at what cost? No-one knows. No... no-one can ever know..."

And Revek had listened for a moment to the mad ramblings of the doomed man, wondering what chaotic oblivion their brain was devising, when they said something in passing – so callous and lost – that twisted in his heart and clung to his mind like a fungus. A single, coherent thought, passing their lips.

And suddenly everything made sense.

"Perhaps those that survive," the soldier muttered, laying the knife down and licking his palm, "are already insane..."

Revek had stopped looking at his pupils after that. In fact, he had stopped assessing the descent into madness altogether. And he had stopped assessing it, because he already felt it: coursing through his veins, blackening his heart, catalysing in his soul like a demon. He realised that the Forest was no longer something to be feared – because he was *the fear that the Ozban consumed. It was within him. It had already consumed him. He was free of it, like the Tarrazi were. The Tarrazi who could traverse the Ozban without question, untethered to the maddening rot, hunting them through the trees with their pale, pupil-less eyes.*

Revek could only grin at the beauty of it.

"We shall all die eventually," another soldier had muttered, staring at a tree that they must have thought was a person. "Whether by a blackcoat's blade or a beast of the dark or the rot of the Forest that surrounds us. All will be sent to the mud in the end, one way or the other…"

Revek had considered his options – considered the power within his grasp – and, under the moon-streaked canopy of the trees where they had decided to rest for the night, he had made a deal with the Ozban. An exchange, sacrificial almost: a life, chosen for extracting death. That for his continued survival – for the tired, broken remains of his sanity – the commander would cast off his soldiers and feed them to the Ozban, so he may walk free from its borders and survive. He would please the Forest, and the Forest would forgive him in turn. It would be a great rebalancing. A mercy, almost. Looking to the soldiers in the dark: knowing they would die soon anyway regardless of his intentions, screaming in their own shit and piss as they scraped at the earth and snapped their ribs open like sticks. It would be a mercy that he would be enacting, in the end. A gesture to the gods.

Or at least, that was what he told the reflection of his sword, as he sat rocking beneath a dead tree whistling to the stars.

Awaiting the mercy that would come.

So Revek had smiled, without a trickle of guilt in his blood, as he lit a torch in the tiny grove and slipped away, drawing the Tarrazi hunters to the rotten soldiers sat quivering in the gloom. And he had laughed, hearing their whimpering deaths as the enemy ran them through, knowing they were clueless and rotten and that nothing would remain come morning.

Where Revek would start all over again.

And so for countless nights and unending days – like a malicious demon crawling through the dark of the trees – the commander had yielded to the cruelty of the Ozban and hunted his comrades like rats. Dicing amongst the shadows like a hound in a frenzy, sensing the air with a nervous glee. Slicing tendons and slitting throats and watching the fear take hold of them as he arrived. A spectre of death, hands coated in blood.

On and on and on…

And then he had heard the hooves of a horse one day, echoing through the night air behind him, and the Ozban seemed to whisper in his ear that the time had nearly come to be free. That his work had finally paid off.

And only one last death awaited.

"Sir!" they had cried as they approached, so innocent and calm, with the terrible leeching blackness staining their irises like tar. "Sir, I... you're here, alive... I... there are bodies everywhere. So many have died. We... we're all going to die*..."*

"It's okay, soldier, be calm," he muttered with a smile. "It will be okay. Just... just come to me now, come to me... it will all be okay."

So innocent and calm, they had approached him, hope glowing in their face. That the commander was here, and he was saved, and everything would be okay. Ignoring the horse, as it stamped and snorted next to him, sensing the corruption spewing from the commander like a burst artery, just beneath the surface.

So innocent and calm...

"Will it really be okay sir?" they had whispered softly to him. "Will we live to see the end?"

"It will all be okay." Revek placed a hand against his forearm. "You will live to see the end..."

"Thank you sir, I—"

"As the Ozban demands another."

Revek's sword had speared up through the man's neck, piercing the top of his skull as if impaling the moon high above.

"Behold it's beauty..."

Dragging the body from the startled horse, he had slid his sword free of their skull and started prizing their intestines open, stringing them out like lines of rope. Impaling both eyes; snapping his nose.

Roaring to the Ozban for its beauty.

Sometime later, Revek had clambered atop the horse and spurred it on, his haunted eyes locked to the path unravelling before him as the Forest forgave him and showed the way. The blood slick across his hand and blade, coating them like clay, flaring like rashes over his hands. Tears streamed over his cheeks.

He whistled into the dark.

They all died. They had to die. Blood and hell and fire and fucking blind murder. Death had come. Death like the savages in their camps. Death like Darius. Death like Oslo. An arbiter. A god. Rotten to the core and bleeding from his eyes.

Broken like the Ozban, spiralling all around…

†

And knelt there on the platform in the heart of the storm, with rain hailing down across his back like tiny needles, the commander looked down at his reflection in the rainwater that pooled across the wood beneath his head—

And saw there a blackness leaking from his pupil, flooding his irises slowly.

Revek felt his heart tense.

The Ozban has claimed me after all…

At his side, Zespa swung the axe over her shoulder and drew it down toward his neck.

The commander let out a cackle, and grinned.

But death has other plans—

Above the howl of the rising wind, the thrum of six arrows caught in his ear, followed by a startled gasp and a wet explosion of blood.

Looking up, he watched Zespa topple sideways, seized by black-shafted arrows, crumpling like a landed fish across the platform beneath where the axe clattered into the mud.

Gasps echoed before him: the soldiers and officers recoiled in fear—

A howl issued from the trees at his back.

The Ozban seemed to hold its breath around them.

Revek closed his eyes.

They all must die.

Mounting the platform at his back, a Kazbak Hound broke from the tree-line and charged into the crowds of soldiers wedged in the mud before him. Screams flashed across the sky; the soldiers broke ranks and fled. More Hounds piled into the fray, skirting the edge of the platform with gnashing teeth and wicked eyes. The storm rallied and raged overhead.

The Tarrazi emerged from the shadows of the Ozban, ready for blood and broken skulls

In a quivering mass of sodden limbs, Commander Revek rolled from the block onto the hard platform and drew in sharp draws of air. Like a traumatised puppy, he lay staring at the maelstrom above, his hands held tight against his chest shaking in weak spasms. He watched as dark shadows passed overhead – passing him entirely, with no acknowledgement that he was even alive, as they dropped from the platform and speared their swords into the terrified crowd. He rolled onto his front, pulling himself up to a swaying stand, beaten and battered by the storm that swept through in vicious tides. He watched the scene unfold before him: General Xol attempted to rally their soldiers as the blackcoats descended on them, cutting through dumbstruck men and women like lambs in an abattoir. Orders were bellowed and lost in the howling wind; screams meshed with cracks of thunder that split the skyline high above. Blood and rain became one and the same, as swords butchered flesh. The dead piled higher and higher, paving the floor for other's to stand.

Here lies our greatest sin.

Revek took it all in for a moment, as the soldiers he once called comrades were slaughtered before his very eyes. Sensing the wind whip up across his face, burning his cheeks; the rain digging into his eyelids like nails; the Ozban Forest flexing and contorting all around him like a pulsing heart, as it exacted its bloody vengeance.

The Ozban demands a sacrifice…

The commander watched Xol fight on, pushed back by the enemy: watched as he stumbled over a low wall and fell into a ruined building, with three blackcoats surging over after him and disappearing out of sight. He looked elsewhere, as a man had a serrated blade run through his intestines, pulling out with a string of his guts trailing off like bunting. Watched as a woman had a sword plunged through her mouth, her eyes rolling back as it disconnected her spine from her head—

As footsteps approached from behind him suddenly, and a pale hand landed on his shoulder.

"Quite a sight, is it not?"

The commander turned at the voice, sensing a weight in his chest, and saw there a familiar face that made his skull explode.

A pale, earless head with eyes like moons, and concentric circles laced around the right eye down to their chin. Black robes concealed the body; a deadly black-steel blade hung limp at their side. Their grey lips were perched in a smile, studying the violence unfold with a resolute glee.

"So much death… so much *savagery,*" the pale figure cooed softly, turning to Revek. "You survived the Ozban, didn't you?"

With fearful eyes and no words to give, the commander nodded absently.

The smile widened. "I have not yet seen a survivor of your kind… the rot must run deep within you to walk out of that place alive."

Still he said nothing.

"Insanity is the perfect motivator, you know? It's what we've always known. It takes from us our worst instincts, and breeds them into the world, until our own corruption is all that we can see… and we don't even know it anymore."

Revek blinked.

"So, *commander,* tell me: what do you want more than anything in this world? What do you wish to *take* from it, and exact in your name?"

The commander gulped. "I… I want power. *Power…*"

"Power?" Their teeth bared, white as frost. "A truly *exquisite* motivator, is power. Power alone can drive any man insane, if they do not act upon the instincts that drive them." They nodded. "Tell me: in that dark and violent part of your rotten, ruined head, commander… where does this *power* lie?"

"With the death of my enemies... taking my *rightful* place once more," he spat, grinning without thought.

Death shall come.

"Your rightful place? What happened to it?"

"They stole it from me." He said it almost as an admittance. "They took from a god, his place in the sun..."

"And I think they intend to again." A deep terror sounded in its voice, rattling Revek to his core.

They gestured out to the bloodbath beyond.

"Just look for yourself..."

He followed the pale figure's hand, adjusting to the ethereal light that carved through the storm-clouds above, and registered where they were pointing: out beyond the fighting, to the far reaches of the camp where a few tired souls fled, hoping to spare the inevitable. Watching as they piled into the trees or into the ruins or back down the road they had come from. To be anywhere but there. Out at the edge of the fighting...

Where a steel-plated woman with a look of horror on her face dived right toward the makeshift stable-block, to drag a horse from under the canopy and adjust their saddle with stricken hands.

Revek ground his jaw.

Lazaerys.

"All that hard work... all the loyalty and trust you have in this army," the figure muttered. "It could all be destroyed by a single order that leaves that woman's mouth. They don't know what has happened here, back at the command post... they'll believe anything they hear. Especially from a superior officer." They paused. "You're a commander, aren't you? And so is she..."

They drew close to his ear with the smell of decay on their breath.

"*So tell me, Revek: who will live to tell the tale? Who will take what is rightfully theirs?*"

The commander stood in silence, looking out on the bloodshed beneath him, and felt the blood roar through his veins. A quiet, trickling venom leaked from his pores, dissolving against the rain.

Some vile, decrepit part of his mind snapped, as he looked off into the distance and spied the Marshal mounting an old horse, kicking off down the narrow southern path with terror in her eyes.

Who will live to tell it?

He sensed the pale figure pull away at his side, and bristled as the wind sliced across him. But, in that same moment a shaft of light speared through the clouds above, and graced his body in glorious light and heavenly warmth.

Returning a god to his place in the sun.

Revek inhaled slowly, rolling his shoulders. Soft drops of rain danced over his skin. The dead screeched below him, dying in their droves.

He looked to the southern road, and grinned.

Death shall come to all.

†

Chapter 57

The General

Eli roared – louder than even the dragons residing in the distant peaks could fathom – and curled his bludgeon up across his body like a club, the veins in his forearms tensing like a swollen delta.

Ahead, General Ferreus smirked and glided elegantly backwards, his knee brace clunking into place as he planted a foot down and lunged forward with a short-sword.

The Chief twisted, watching the blade skim past his stomach, and swung the bludgeon across again, stepping out of the general's circle as he did so.

Ferreus ducked the attack – gazing up fearfully as a huge metal sphere skimmed just above his head – and lashed out with a kick to Eli's shin, forcing a grunt from the rebel leader as he stepped backwards and adjusted his grip.

"Come on, *old man,*" Ferreus cooed, licking his teeth. "Thought you were better than that."

Eli growled. "Your move, asshole."

The general took the offer almost immediately, rushing the Chief and carving his blade across like an axe.

Batting it away with the bludgeon's handle, Eli managed a short swing toward his head that missed by a matter of inches, skimming the general's shoulder guard instead and nudging him off balance for a moment. Hoping to capitalise on it, the Chief lunged in for a shoulder charge in the next breath, but was forced to bat a stray blade away as Ferreus launched his next assault.

The short-sword cut across in several powerful motions; Eli used his bludgeon as a paddle to dish them aside as they fell, straining under the awkward weight. Ferreus grinned and lunged out suddenly – slipping past the Chief's defences toward his stomach – and it was only the chainmail buried beneath the rebel's armour that saved him from being impaled—

As he angled the hilt of his bludgeon down toward the general's head, connecting with his temple like a punch.

Ferreus stumbled backwards, hissing with a hand against the side of his head, and snarled at the Chief.

"You'll fucking pay for that," he snapped.

Eli rolled his shoulders. "Try me."

The general charged forward; watching his approach, the Chief hefted the weapon and swung upwards toward the glaring sun, hoping to crack his jaw.

Ferreus dodged, striking out toward Eli's throat with a glinting blade; using the handle once again, the Chief squirmed at the grating metal just in front of his face and slapped the weapon away—

Startled by the general's recovery, as he slung the blade round and speared in at Eli's ribcage, misjudging the angle slightly and grazing the inside of his arm.

The blade retracted, and the Chief hissed at the tingling nerves shooting across his underarm, indicating a deeper wound that now wept a steady stream of blood.

Little bastard.

Stepping back for a moment – watching the general's foul smirk stain his face like sick – Eli tightened the grip on the bludgeon and imitated another overhead swing. And, as expected, Ferreus reacted by stepping forward and slicing his blade through—

Only to find the Chief lower his weapon suddenly, drawing it into the space between them as it locked against the general's arm and wedged his sword flat against his chest.

Ferreus seized up, fearful and suddenly very pale, as the rebel leader grinned.

"Weren't expecting that, were you, you little *shit*."

The Chief lifted his leg and kneed the general in the stomach, relinquishing his grip on his arm and shoving him backwards across the square. Ferreus keeled over in pain and retched at the nausea now bulging in his intestines, drawing in great lengths of air to try and steady the flow.

That's what you get, Eli thought, taking a moment to savour the general's pain – knowing that he would have to move fast if he was going to last much longer. *Need this over soon.* Sensing the warmth of blood under one arm, and the nagging sensation of a reopened wound on the opposite, he sighed and accepted the truth.

These wounds will be the death of me if this goes on much longer: I will fight on no matter what, but with these cuts sapping my energy I can't see my strength holding out.

He studied the metal sphere above his head again, and smiled.

I just hope I live to see Alva again—

A scream clipped the air to his right.

Lost in the moment, Eli registered slowly, and by the time he reacted it was already too late.

A soldier – some lone hero without a weapon, sensing his leader in danger – charged at the Chief with his arms outstretched, hoping to tackle him to the ground. Eli baulked at the sight of them, tensing his back, hoping to heft his weapon up in time and send the attacker spinning off across the stone—

But as he turned, the soldier was already upon him, their arms flailing wildly against his arms and chest. Trying to readjust, they stumbled suddenly against the slabs underfoot and skimmed past him, bundling the bludgeon in their grasp like an awkward hug—

Snatching it from the Chief's grip, as the soldier spilled across the dusted ground alongside him and knocked themselves unconscious on the spiked metal ball.

Eli looked at the crumpled body in disbelief.

Oh fuck.

Hissing as his wounds twinged, he cursed at his awful luck and looked up to the general opposite, who grinned maliciously toward him and paced forward with his weapon primed.

"Weren't expecting that, now *were you?*" Ferreus taunted.

Eli sucked in a breath and raised his fists.

Fuck!

Two strikes fell; the rebel leader dodged both, turning sideways as the short-sword glanced against his chainmail. Another one looped overhead, intending to mash his skull; the Chief lurched down, crunching his knees, and stepped into the general's circle.

Ferreus backstepped, dodging a punch intended for his kidney, and swung upwards with a howl of glee.

Eli stumbled, sliding across the stone as the sword skimmed through his beard. A flush of tiny, wiry hairs were cast to the wind between them. Grinding his jaw together, the Chief growled, readying for the next attack.

Just one wrong move…

Ferreus covered the distance between them in seconds, raining down two more attacks that narrowly missed his neck.

Come on, you bastard…

Gliding gracefully through the space in front of him, the general stepped into the Chief's circle, the sword-point channelling toward his exposed gut—

Now!

Eli snaked an arm around the general's wrist and jarred his elbow, manoeuvring with enough power to break his arm.

Ferreus screeched, his eyes on stilts, as the Chief loomed before him and stepped closer—

Craning his neck; headbutting the general in the nose.

Blood shrapnel crunched against his brow. A squeal escaped the man's parched lips. The old wolf tilted backwards; under the pressure of Eli's grasp, his sword spilled from his hand and skittered off over the slabs to his left.

They separated, Ferreus holding his nose and swaying dumbly, looking off toward the baron's hall and the imposing shape of the rebel leader with his fists raised towards him.

"You fight dirty," the general spat. "Where is your *honour*—"

"To hell with honour!" Eli bellowed. "You had my husband murdered in cold blood – had him beaten in a prison cell, half-starved to death – all because you failed to have one of your own killed with no witnesses. All because of lies, and the corruption of a regime that was never fit for purpose to begin with. You're a coward, and a butcher, and an abhorrence to the rank you hold… and now, for those sins, you'll die for it, you little *prick*…"

The general looked to his hand for a moment, bloodied and bruised, and smiled. With a wipe of his sleeve against the mashed cartilage of his nose, he then started laughing. A high-pitched, maniacal laugh, like the final words before an execution.

He turned to Eli, and shrugged.

"I don't care," he said plainly, scoffing. "Don't you get it? I don't give a shit about what you think is *right* and *wrong* or whatever else. There is no moral high-ground; there is no better cause. We do our duties, and we kill those who don't approve of it. You don't approve of mine… and I don't care about yours. I see your death as a means to an end, exactly the same as that bitch husband of yours when I watched the Governor drive a blade through his chest. Another death, another body… another sin amended. And here you are grovelling over it, sending people to die for him…"

"These men and women joined of their own accord, and they fight of their own accord," Eli challenged. "You can't say the same about yours: beaten into submission and choked by propaganda, so terrified of your 'means to an end' that they have no conscious thought of their own!"

"*Order is the righteous path!*" the general bellowed, turning the heads of those fighting around him. "For *years,* I have earned my honour, and for *years* I have followed the orders of my superiors. And I have emerged victorious from that, *every single time.*"

"And for what? Glory? A lust for power? Your own chronic insecurities?"

Ferreus bared his teeth. "Because good fucking *soldiers* follow their fucking *orders.*"

Eli shook his head, squinting at the sun as it faded to dusk. Red rays glistened across his skin.

The colour of blood.

"You are truly lost, general," the Chief said sombrely. "The entire regime is. This has all gone too far. We're on the verge of civil war, for gods' sake. This has to end now."

"And it *will,*" he growled in reply, lowering his hands. "It will end with the righteous path… it will end as the orders dictate. It will *end* as it should have done all along…" The general inhaled slowly, shivering and spasming with hate. "With the iron fist of the imperial regime ending this rebellion…"

Ferreus smiled.

"And a knife stabbing through the heart of their *RULER!*"

Eli flinched; he noticed the small blade only as it left the general's hand, darting toward him like a shimmering bullet.

Death waited.

Death watched

Dea—

A body moved in front of him, levelling a shield to smack the knife aside, standing out against the sun—

Jinx snarled.

"Back away from him you *bastard!*"

Ferreus gasped, wide-eyed, staring her down in disbelief.

"You little bitch…"

Turning suddenly, aware of the damage to his body, the general bellowed in frustration and ambled off into the crowds of people, making for the northern road and the last exit out of the square.

Letting him go with a snarl, Jinx turned to the Chief, and gazed up at him for a moment.

"Hi Eli," she said softly.

The rebel leader smiled, tears forming in the pits of his eyes, and placed a hand on her shoulder. "Hi Alva."

"I told you I'd make it."

"Yes you did… tough as fucking nails."

Jinx placed her head on his chest for a moment, a warmth spreading through her heart. Eli returned the gesture and pulled her in closer, awash with rays of glorious orange sunlight. A quiet moment – a quiet prayer echoing out – a recognition that they were both still alive.

And hope still remained.

As they parted again, Jinx looked off to the north and allowed herself to smirk, gesturing there with a nod of her head.

"Well… now that all the fun is over and we've won the battle at hand," she mused, "what say we finish this, and finally give that bastard what he deserves?"

Eli stooped low and collected the bludgeon from the unconscious soldier, watching the wave of silver hair slip through the last of the crowds and out onto Marcheg's north road.

"I couldn't have said it better myself," the Chief of the Mountains said with a smile, pulling his weapon over his shoulder.

Let's finish this.

†

Chapter 58

The Butcher's Block

Cavara's arms strained, tightening and tensing as she stared into the eyes of the transmitter, their face billowing with light as the flaming blade pulsed and ignited between them, holding the butcher's knife at bay mere inches from her chest. She stood level, gritting her teeth, fighting against an assassin who had been shipped halfway around the known world and smuggled into a city, all at the whim of a murderous tyrant in a land bathed in war and ruin. A distant land that ravaged her own, killing her people in their hundreds. Her nation was one under siege by its own corruption, mired with greed and imperial ignorance, slowly tearing itself apart in a bitter conflict with an ancient enemy that knew no bounds. An ancient enemy led by a foul woman intent on enslaving the world, whose hate and malevolence lay embodied in a singular aim and the shimmering cleavers of the trans-mitter stood before her. One aim; one target.

Her head, and the Ascendent Soul.

With a bellow, Cavara shoved the transmitter away and spun the sword in her hand, watching the Butcher prime his knives and study the swirling burns on his arm.

"That blade is rather a nuisance, wouldn't you say?" they mused, wincing as they pressed a finger into the burn marks and felt the tender flesh there. "It seems to be doing a good job at keeping your head on your shoulders."

"I'd say it was rather fit for purpose, then, wouldn't you?" Cavara retorted, sensing the Rapture's power ebbing through the weapon in her hands.

"Yes… although that doesn't make my task any easier. The Queen demands results, after all, and with the price she's paying for your head… well, I can't go back empty handed."

"Then I'll make sure to send her my regards, when I deliver your head back to her on a spike."

The Butcher smiled, striking his knives together.

"You'll rue the day I found you, usurper…"

They came together with a burst of flame and the rhythmic chime of steel, the transmitter wielding their cleavers deftly to stave off the general's far stronger weapon. As they connected, the void seemed to ripple and tense around them like a sheet of cloth, reacting to the vibrations their weapons produced. Striking out in wide arcs, Cavara attempted to break the Butcher's defences and catch them in the side, but with every manipulation of her blade her opponent was there to meet it, using their physical strength to knock her aside and press on with a counter of their own.

Focusing on her attacks and the motions of her blade, the general surprised herself with how adept she was at using it compared to the times before. Every strike against the Butcher's knives was her own, and every block she made against him was done without the assistance of the void. The ethereal, flame-kindled weapon dancing in her grasp was as much her own as it was belonging to the Rapture. And, thinking back to her first encounter with the Iron Queen, and the strain she had undergone just wielding the blade, the progress she witnessed against the transmitter gave her some semblance of hope.

A hope that she approached cautiously, knowing how easily it could be snatched away.

Cavara diced across with several quick attacks and forced the Butcher to sway backwards, gritting his teeth in frustration and wiping his brow with his hand.

"Just give in, general… it will make things so much easier for every-one…"

"And let my people become enslaved back home, at the hands of that murderous witch you call a leader? Over my dead body."

The transmitter shrugged, striding forward once more.

"We can arrange that…"

Using both of the knives in parallel with each other, the Butcher growled and slashed across in long, sweeping motions toward the general's neck.

Cavara parried them comfortably and lunged out into his stomach, narrowly missing as the transmitter glided backwards and advanced once again.

Several more attacks followed, the flame-sword spitting and roaring in her hand as Cavara wore her opponent down and paced slowly backwards, giving herself plenty of space and keeping her circle well-guarded. She knew fighters like the transmitter, and knew their attack patterns almost as well as her own: keeping close-quarters where the length of her sword was a liability, panicking her with the intensity until a knife slipped past and buried in her stomach. She had every faith that the flaming-sword would keep her safe in that scenario and deflect any attacks no matter how close they were, but she wasn't about to put that faith to the test anytime soon.

And certainly not with her life on the line.

Cavara clasped the hilt of the blade in both hands and speared it forward suddenly, catching the Butcher off-guard and forcing them to sidestep, the flaming edge singeing the fabric of their apron and scolding a layer of skin beneath.

The transmitter groaned and turned for the next attack – angered further by the wicked smile perched neatly across Cavara's face.

The general levelled her weapon, trying to ignore the nagging pains biting through her shoulders. She backstepped again, readying for the next onslaught – when she spied the huge, grey impression of the Forgotten One pacing the room ahead in the real world, moving over to the impression of the steel door where Evelyn was being held and bracing against it with their shoulder. Offering words of calm and support no doubt, and assessing the locks to see if the boy could be freed. A warmth graced her heart then for a moment, looking upon the rigid shadow of the pale figure trying to save the child, thinking back to a time when they could hardly understand human emotion and seeing how far they had come.

And, as the Butcher carved the knives down for another attack, she saw how much was then at stake if she failed.

She backstepped once, then again, knocking their cleavers aside with sweeping counters and balancing her weight on her toes.

"Into the tunnels we go, then, general..." the transmitter cooed, driving forward suddenly with a destitution in their eye. "Let's see what secrets await in the dark..."

Cavara flinched suddenly, tensing her back, unsure of what the Butcher meant – but as she stepped back once more, she realised that the void had darkened all around her, and the vibrant white chamber they had occupied previously was now little more than a glowing chasm just ahead.

As she stepped back again, a weird, percussive sound issued from the ground at her feet, and looking down she saw how the void vibrated beneath her toes where she assumed there were pools of water. In fact, as she moved through them, she noted how many of the features of the tunnel did not translate properly into the Rapture: there was sweat dappled across her arms, but none of the humidity to cause it; water trickled down the walls and puddled at her feet, but without the properties of liquid to match it; the occasional rasp of pressurised steam in pipes above them, were little more than a rumble of thunder in the back of her head. She found it so strange, to occupy the same space and yet experience it so differently. To feel so many abstract sensations, and yet to also feel nothing at all. Part of her wondered what it would be like to experience the Rapture in places she had come to know very well.

And a quiet, solemn part of her soul wondered how different home would feel too.

Blinking frantically, shaking the thoughts from her head, she raised the flaming sword up to her face and carved down toward the Butcher, aware of the narrowness in the tunnel around them and how careful she now needed to be.

"You look afraid, usurper," the transmitter taunted, slapping her blade against the wall and striking out with his knives. "Are you afraid?"

"I'm not afraid, no..." She lowered her weapon suddenly and struck out with a fist, connecting with the Butcher's side like a hammer. "But you should be..."

The transmitter bellowed and carved down with their blades in alternating directions, forcing Cavara to engage the sword's powers and deflect each strike. Almost immediately, she felt her wrist tense under the pressure, guided by the blade to near-impossible angles as it sought to protect her. A low hissing sound caught in her ear, as the blade cut through the humid air like butter; vaporous smudges rose from its edge as steam swelled in the air between them. Her fingers twisted and bulged as the blade opened up space between them, finally giving her some room to manoeuvre.

"You don't have to do this, you know," she said softly, taking control over the blade once more. "This isn't the only choice. You have a unique gift of the Rapture, far surpassing that of any other person I've ever known. The options at your disposal are limitless. If you were to slip away from here and live out a life someplace else, there's no way for the Iron Queen to ever know——"

"Don't try and manipulate me," the Butcher growled, rolling their shoulders. "I don't do this because I'm forced to. I do this because of the powers I possess, and the money that can earn me. I have my weight in gold waiting for me back in Val Azbann… and with your corpse, I can claim that for myself and grow fat and old in the hills as the world destroys itself. That sounds idyllic to me."

"And you'd be willing to watch the world burn, just to line your pockets?"

The Butcher shrugged. "Welcome to the real world, darling… where've you been?"

The butcher knives carved up suddenly, catching the general off guard. The flaming sword in her hand adjusted sporadically and nearly tore her arm off, twisting again in a half-hearted attempt to perform a counter and stave off the next round of—

The Butcher surged forward with the blades levelled, ready to cut down and slice her arms open like slabs of steak, forcing Cavara to slide backwards suddenly and slip against the wet stone floor, lurching out toward the tunnel walls to try and regain her balance—

Her sword embedding between several rocks, producing a dramatic hiss as steam enveloped her hand and choked the air between them.

Cavara baulked fearfully – the void ahead of her lost within reams of grey-black vapour – and tried prizing her sword back out of the wall where it had fused into place like a metal strut. Planting both of her hands against the handle with rapid breaths and sweat pouring across her scalp, she planted a boot against the impression of stone and pulled back with every fibre in her limbs, the void tensing and contracting all around her—

The blade suddenly slipping free, throwing her against the opposing wall with the force of it—

Carrying with it several large stones that had held the tunnel in place, and a sudden explosion of warm water cascaded out of the wall.

Cavara blinked once, and felt the numbness slip at through fingers.

"Oh, fuck..."

~

Torn from the Rapture, nausea ballooned in her stomach. Lights flooded her vision; textures pricked against her fingers. The heavy, drowning, swamping heat smacked into her like a gut-punch. Her skull pulsed, adjusting to the thin stretch of tunnel that she pressed up against, as steam clogged the air and pressurised gas hissed in the rocks above her.

And the entire wall opposite seemed to bulge suddenly, exploding with torrents of water.

Sensing the stone roof tremble overhead – fearing being buried alive – Cavara turned back to the glowing chamber where she had just been, abandoning any concerns she had about the Butcher as she swung away from the wall and dragged her way out the tunnel—

Swept out by water surging against her knees, dragging up to her waist as she lost her footing and spun out against the tunnel walls, crashing against them in a tangle of limbs—

Warm liquid submerging her for a moment; striking her head out to gasp a breath of air and spin backwards—

Barrelling out into the torch-lit chamber, as a terrifying crash erupted down the tunnel and the entire structure caved in behind her, dragging whatever was above it down into the depths below—

Spluttering and gasping for air, choking on the humidity that engulfed the room around her, Cavara kicked out against the stone at her feet and rolled against a far wall, pain shooting through her back—

Hit with another wave of water, as it collided with the rear wall of the chamber and rebounded back toward them—

Smacking her head against the stone; lights blinkering in her vision. On all fours, staring at the dirty liquid as it swelled and eddied beneath her, she tried to stay conscious and regain some semblance of time. Acknowledging the bruises that now rose all across her body, and the throbbing headache now chiselling at her skull.

Alive, at least, she managed, coughing and clearing her lungs. *Alive...*

Where's—

A boot rammed into her side, throwing her back against the wall and into the sloshing waters below.

Spluttering, she screeched as the attacker grabbed a knot of her hair and dragged her over to the middle of the room, where she was thrown down and kicked again for good measure.

For some time she remained sprawled there, dipping in and out of consciousness, with the hissing light of the torches flick-ering across the ceiling high above. Lost in a daze – almost as if the break in the Rapture had stolen part of her soul – she slowly turned over to observe the room beyond: the lights and the dark tunnel she had just escaped from, where thin shreds of light pulled down from an opening somewhere above. The undulating waters and spasmodic ripples in the dark, pushing against her skin.

And the Butcher, looming over her with a foul, twisted grin, a cleaving knife taut in their hand.

Alive... for now.

"At every turn, in every unfathomable way... fate still shines on you, *skal-thüm!"* the transmitter bellowed, gritting their teeth. "Why does it take so much, to kill one measly little fucking woman!"

Cavara groaned, holding a hand against her stomach as it throbbed painfully.

"You should've listened, you know, you should've—"

The Butcher stalled, looking up across the chamber with wild eyes, and speared the knife out as something shifted at the general's back.

"Ah, ah! You stay right where you are you traitorous *scum*! If you take one step closer, I will not hesitate in gutting this bitch, do you understand me?"

Somewhere behind her, she sensed the Forgotten One tense up and stand down, groaning at whatever wounds they had sustained during the flooding.

I hope they're okay—

"Now, where was I… oh *yes*," the transmitter continued, glaring at her with venom and hate. "You should've listened, general, at the very beginning. You should have gone through with my offer. You should have handed yourself over and spared that child the misery of this place, and spared us all the patient *agony* of you finally keeling over to die. This all could've been over *so* much sooner…" He clicked his tongue. "But – as is the beauty of inevitability – no matter how hard you tried to subvert me, and how close you came to actually outsmarting me… you are still in the same place I always expected you to end up. Broken and bruised, failing all those who put so much faith in you… preparing to *die*."

Cavara reached out toward him, as a dying saint reaches out to the gods for mercy, and the Butcher kicked her hand away and flipped her over like a fish.

"So I will kill you now, general, as I should have done some time ago, and fulfil my contract with the Tarrazi Queen," the transmitter pronounced, lifting their knife. "And when I'm done with you, I will go into that cell, and murder that child you hold so dearly, knowing he will never see his mother again. I will take *everything* from you… and you won't even *know* it."

The general tried to scream, to fight back, but her throat had sealed and her limbs lay straddled in the water, numb and lost. The lights spun above her sickeningly. The shadows pulled in at the edges.

I've failed you, she thought, as tears formed in her eyes. *I've failed you, Evelyn. I'm so sorry.*

I'm so sorry…

Above her, the Butcher grinned, the knife glinting over her head like an executioner's axe.

"You were no match in the end, usurper," he cooed. "I was always one step ahead…"

He stepped forward, lunging down—

Water sloshed at his back—

A hand grappled his chest, as a blade coiled around his neck.

A face pressed against his cheek—

Azura snarled.

"*But you never thought to look behind.*"

The Butcher opened his mouth to scream; the blade slit his throat.

Like a felled giant, the transmitter buckled at the knees and collapsed into the murky waters below, his blood ebbing out in purple waves as the light left his eyes.

Azura wiped her blade and spat on his body.

"That's for my *fucking son.*"

The general watched her step over his body with disgust and approach her with a stern face, offering a hand out that she gladly accepted and lifted up from the blood-tainted waters. For a moment, Cavara balanced on shaking legs, assessing the bruises that littered her body like a skin disease, and inhaled gently. At her back, two heavy boots splashed over and a hand hooked under her arm, the Forgotten One holding her steady as she looked up to her saviour and smiled.

"How did you know… that we'd be here?" Cavara muttered quietly, stretching her back out.

"Well, it wasn't easy, I'll admit," Azura said, sheathing her blade. "But luckily I had a bit of help from a certain towering figure…"

Cavara looked up to her guardian, who gazed down on her with moons for eyes and nodded. "I left a note on her table," the Forgotten One explained, "just in case anything was to go wrong. It said that if we had not returned by the setting of the sun, then she must go to the storehouse and find us..."

"Thinking so many awful things like, *'I wonder if they're still alive?'* and *'I wonder whose blood I'll find staining every wall of some poor man's house?'*" Azura shook her head and smiled. "And I almost didn't find the storehouse, too: I can't say your friend's instructions here were exactly *succinct*. But I went in search of it nonetheless... and as the sun set lower I thought I was too late, and everything would be over. I just didn't know..." She stood to one side and gestured to the collapsed tunnel at her back. "Until I heard screams echo out the bath-house, and something about a sinkhole... and I knew, there and then, that it just *had* to be you two."

Cavara coughed, laughing for a moment. "Well, I mean... we do have a habit of causing a mess wherever we go."

"Don't you just!" Azura said, laughing herself. "First you get yourself arrested, then you go down into the ruins searching for secret doors. And that's not even including the storehouse and the assassins—"

Her voice cut out, extinguishing suddenly as a metallic knocking caught in their ears from the cell alongside them. Tiny, repetitive sounds.

Tears formed in the knots of Azura's eyes almost by instinct. She looked up to the general.

"Is... is he...?"

Cavara said nothing, smiling with her own tears, and bent low to the water at her feet. Reaching down into the murky, berry-red liquid, she felt across the stone until she reached the unmistakable softness of flesh, and wormed her way down to the Butcher's waist – where she unhooked a key from his belt and drew it out into the light.

"You can do the honours," the general said, placing the huge iron key in the woman's palm. "May you be reunited again..."

Azura studied the item and wrapped her fingers round it, looking up to Cavara with glistening eyes and a warmth in her cheeks like roses.

She stepped forward then and wrapped her arms around the general, pulling her in tight. Cavara returned the gesture and placed her head against the woman's shoulder, pulling air through her teeth in slow bursts as Azura sagged with relief in her arms.

"Thank you for returning him to me," she whispered, step-ping back and bowing her head.

Cavara couldn't find the words to respond, choosing instead to smile and wave a hand toward the cell door, which the elder woman turned towards and paced over to with tired, unsteady strides, raising the key to lock as she did so.

Allowing them their moment in peace, Cavara found the weight grow heavier in her chest, refusing to let go.

This was my fault, she acknowledged, looking up to the Forgotten One. *Evelyn may be saved, but I was the one who put him in danger in the first place. I haven't added anything to the world with my actions: I've just averted a catastrophe caused by my own hand. This was all my fault.*

As the door slid open behind her, and Azura rushed into the room to bundle her child into her arms, Cavara clamped her jaw together and sighed.

I can't do this anymore.

"What will you do now?" the Forgotten One asked her, almost looking through her with the intensity of their gaze.

What will I do? "I have to warn the Alderbane of the honour-guard's treachery, and inform them of what's happened with the Butcher," she replied dutifully. "We don't know how deep this goes, or if the Alderbane's life is in danger. If the honour-guard were working with the Tarrazi, then who knows how many of the City guards are too..."

"A good plan, Successor, indeed. I promise to stay and make sure Azura and the child return safely to their home. Do what you need to... and be safe."

"Thank you. I'll return soon."

The Forgotten One bowed their head and gestured to the collapsed tunnel; steeling herself, Cavara turned toward it and trudged through the murky waters, intent on getting back to the palace as soon as possible and averting another potential crisis.

Not that I feel particularly inclined to, she admitted. *With how they've treated me, I should let them get their comeuppance… but for the sake of stability within the City, the last thing we need is—*

"Miss Cavara?"

The general blinked, realising she had stopped just before the entrance to the tunnel, and recognised the voice at her back almost immediately.

Turning slowly – lowering to a crouch instinctively – she brightened her face and looked into the quiet little eyes of Evelyn: thinner than he had been before, with a few small bruises on his arms and a nasty scratch across his knee.

"Hi, Evelyn," Cavara replied with a tremble in her voice. "Did you need something?"

The little boy tilted his head like an inquisitive pup, studying her intently. And then, in an honest, near-silent voice, he said something to her that plucked at the strings in her soul.

"It's not your fault, you know."

The general blinked, rolling her tongue around her mouth. "I don't know what you mean, Evelyn… I don't—"

"It's not your fault, Miss Cavara." For a moment, he smiled. "It never was. You did your best… and that's all that matters."

And, without another word, the little boy stepped forward and wrapped his arms around her, his beautiful head tucking under her chin.

His hands grabbed at her shirt.

"*You're a hero.*"

Cavara wrapped her arms around him and pulled him in close, squeezing him with tears streaming down her cheeks and a knot of emotion in her throat. The world stopped for a moment, as her heart found a tiny bit of peace.

It's not my fault… she closed her eyes.

That's all that matters…

She let him go and stepped back; the little boy gave one last smile before wading off toward his mother, who bowed her head to the general and nestled Evelyn against her leg.

Cavara wiped her eyes. "I'll be back soon."

"We know you will," Azura replied, ruffling Evelyn's hair. "Now go be a hero, won't you? The world needs one right about now…"

The general looked between the three of them with a smile pulling at her cheeks, and turned to the tunnel beyond.

She took a deep breath, and let the relief wash through her.

One last step.

PART IV

Dawn of the Coming Storm

†

Chapter 59

The Chief of the Mountains

The end was inevitable, as Ferreus always imagined it would be.

Dark thunderclouds rumbled over the distant lowland hills of Tarraz, drifting imperviously toward them. The sun was little more than a glowing mirage passing beyond the distant peaks to the west, engulfing the world below in amber rivers of light. Shadows flecked the air high above as crows circled him, *caw*ing to each other insipidly.

The folly before the fall.

The general reached the edge of town and watched the streets of Marcheg unfurl before him into dirt tracks and misshapen roads, each lined with low stone walls and the wide rolling plains of greater Provenci. The grass blustered wickedly in the wind, sensing a coming storm. The rattle of violence still erupting behind him twinged through the branches of the sparse beech trees dotting the landscape ahead.

To the far east – tracing the ugly black line of the Tarrazi border to the north – his gaze fixed hopefully on the pearlescent walls and towering spires of Casantri, bathed in dusk light. The land before it fell away like an unravelled scroll before him: undulating over hillocks and through tough knots of trees, until finally reaching a ridge about a league ahead of him where the fluttering flags of the command post poked up like waving hands. With a calculated determination and adrenaline pumping through his veins, Ferreus saw the path ahead that would mean the difference between life and death.

The probability of which remained far from certain.

Just need to get to the command post, the general snarled, applying pressure to his nose as it continued to weep profusely. *Just need to get there and alert the Governor of what's happened, then he can send in the reserves and wipe the floor with the survivors. Execute them all and annihilate this outrage to our regime. All I need do is get to the command post.*

That's it.

Attempting to run, General Ferreus turned west and started limping toward the nearest outcrop of rocks jutting from the earth just ahead. His body ached all over as he moved, more than he had acknowledged at any other point in his life.

Fucking rebels, using tunnels to outflank us. He spat bloody phlegm into the grass. *Why was I never told there were evacuation routes under the town? Why did the field strategists not know? They had maps, copies of plans in the capital vaults… why were we not warned?* He stumbled on a small ditch and jarred his ankle, a fresh spurt of blood erupting from his nose as a result.

Fucking traitorous shits, the lot of them. If I get out of this I'll personally execute every single one them…

And I will enjoy every single second of it.

He turned for a second, looking back on the desolation of the town in the setting dusk—

To see a bludgeon round the street corner there, as a figure appeared just behind him.

"Where do you think you're going, general!" the voice bellowed from behind him, as the scraping sounds of running legs echoed in the old wolf's ears. "Surely you're not abandoning your people to die?"

Ferreus felt his heart squirm in his throat.

Fuck!

He tried kicking out faster, straining his body in a desperate attempt to survive. The nag in his ankle continued to burn; the blood spouting from his nose lined his gums like tar.

This can't be.

The running intensified behind him.

Why can't they just die!

The rocks bundled across the earth just ahead of him, so close yet so far. It could act as cover, maybe, or a place to hide. Something to survive, to live just a few moments longer.

The running stopped at his back for a second.

Anything, anything—

A pain shot across his injured knee, as something sheared through the metal bracer holding it in place and burrowed deep into the bone beneath.

The sensation of something snapping ignited in his tendons; an explosion of agony pulled up his thigh as the knee-joint collapsed in on itself.

Squeaking, horrified, the general swung sidelong into the dirt, lying there with his face planted in the grass and the tension of death creeping ever-closer at his back...

†

Eli watched on with a smug satisfaction as the bolt left Jinx's crossbow and whistled through the air, tearing through the general's knee as he toppled like a dead tree into the dirt.

"Nice shot, that," the Chief acknowledged, nodding his head.

"Should've gone for his head really," Jinx replied, rising to a stand at his side.

"Now where's the fun in that?"

She smirked. "Lead on, Chief."

They paced down the dirt track toward the felled general, who had managed to pull up onto his elbows and edged slowly toward the outcrop of rocks just ahead of him. Eli studied the broken metal plates and the pale, thread-bare skin of the wolf as he dragged his body away, and relished the sight of a creature brought so low.

Years of taking orders and killing innocents… years of cruelty and abuse of power… years of covetous schemes and manipulating lies.

That all ends today.

Walking up alongside Ferreus, Jinx flashed her teeth and kicked him across the shoulder, turning him over like a landed fish and stepping back to observe the result.

"This ends now, general," Eli growled, looming over him. "All of it."

The general scoffed, a bruise across his cheek twitching angrily. "You don't get it, do you?" Ferreus spat, wincing at his knee. "This doesn't *end.* None of this ends. You've won one battle, in one town, in one square. You've achieved next to *nothing* in the grand scheme of things, and for what? Near eight-hundred rebels dead, and a legion of soldiers staining the street tiles purple with their blood. All of that ruin you've inflicted – all the dead bodies piled up in your name – and this isn't even the *beginning…*"

"This isn't the beginning of anything, general… this is the end, both of you and your tyranny."

He shook his head with bloodshot eyes. "Ah, you see, even that isn't true. I am but one cog in this great war machine of ours. I am but a conduit of the power and control exerted by those residing in the capital. My end is nothing, in all this. Because they will still come for you, you *bastard…* they will come for you mounted on horseback with scythes and lances; on the back of artillery tracks tearing down your homes; rows upon rows behind interlocking shields tearing your pathetic *rebellion* to shreds. Your people, and your *cause…* it'll all be sent to the mud and left unburied where it belongs. You cannot survive this; you cannot survive what will come for *you…*"

Eli looked down on him – the spiteful, bitter man led incapacitated in the dust – and shrugged.

"You're right," the Chief admitted. "This isn't the end of the war: this is simply a battle, and it is the first of many, I don't doubt. We are a decimated force… we have been hit hard by the days of fighting through Marcheg's streets. The dead number in their hundreds. We are, to the absent observer's eye, too weak to go on." He paused. "Except, general, there is also the bit you don't see… that this is not just a fighting force, loyal to one person, given orders and sent to march. This isn't an army as you know it. This is a *cause*. An idea. A rebellion against those who have failed us, time and time again. It is a choice: a creed that people ascribe to; follow; fight for. And it is with *hope* that these people are guided." He locked eyes with the general. "So, every single person who has given their life to this cause, will have done so knowing they are doing what they believe in, protecting what they *love*. They are noble, honourable people: people I am proud to stand by and die beside. They are free thinkers of a better world… and I don't think you or your *legion* can say the same—"

Ferreus launched up on his hands suddenly, snarling and spitting like an animal, aiming to bind his hands around the Chief's bearded throat. He made it a few inches, edging closer, before Jinx lay her blade across his neck and coerced him back to the ground with a scoff.

"And *you,*" Ferreus sneered, "a daft little girl way in over her head, so desperate and addled with grief. Arrenso would be *ashamed*—"

Jinx brought her leg up and kicked him across the chin, jamming his teeth into his sagging tongue. He recoiled sharply, smiling, licking blood from his gums.

"That's for underestimating me, you son of a *bitch*," Jinx growled.

"Hm… you'll pay for that, you know…"

"She'll pay for *nothing*," Eli commanded.

"Ah yes, my apologies, *hero,*" Ferreus said bitterly, turning back to him. "I forgot you were judge, jury and executioner around here." He paused, then grinned. "But what kind of hero are you, really, hm? A hero of corpses? A hero of grieving families? Reigning supreme from your kingdom of ash… the rebel leader sending so many families to their deaths. And you thought the Governor was a tyrant..."

"I don't murder my own officers," the Chief challenged. "I don't make people disappear, just because they have a few concerns. I don't conscript innocent people and send them marching north into a hellscape they neither understand nor have any right to be in, and watch them be butchered in their *thousands* by blackcoat steel." Eli gripped the shaft of the bludgeon until his knuckles drew white. "And that's leaving out the worst one..."

"Oh, is it?" Ferreus asked sarcastically. "And what would that be, *hm?*"

The rebel leader studied him intently, hiding a smile.

"I don't leave people abandoned in the mountains starving to death, while the soldiers of a *rearmament* programme march west on a madman's whim..." He rolled his tongue; the smile appeared. "But I tell you what, I think I know someone who did..."

The general shrunk down suddenly, wide-eyed and deathly white as the Chief ushered his last remark. A frozen fear crept over him, beyond the realms of fathomable possibility. It was the look of a man who had been outsmarted.

And knew exactly what the rebel leader meant.

Without a word more, Eli reached down to his side and prized a telescopic lens from his belt, handing it over to the general with quiet eyes.

"Take a look at the mountains for me, general," the Chief boomed. "Tell me what you see."

Ferreus lifted the lens to his eye slowly, glaring at Eli as he did so – not that he needed to, because since it had been brought to his attention the general could see what the Chief meant even from afar.

And the telescopic lens that he now gazed through just made to illustrate his worst fears.

Billowing columns of smoke trailed down the mountainside. Fires formed in marching lines, wedged at the end of long poles. The tiny, shimmering marks of steel helmets, dotted between the wrenching wheels and wooden struts of massive artillery machines. There were hundreds of them, thousands even, snaking down the mountainside and out onto the scorched plains of Provenci. Emerging from the ruins of the secret camp that had been built there ten years before.

Orchestrated and materialised by the general's own hand.

"You and that fool Revek were so pleased, when the taxes swept into the palace coffers from Tarraz and the king gave you the all-clear to start rearming," Eli charged. "It was remarkable, to think of how many thousands of people you tore from their homes and marched up there, with some as young as six years old, just to feed into your criminal masterplan. There were blacksmiths, artificers, hunters. Butchers and bread-makers. Even criminals: shipped off in the back of armoured carts, destined for the 'exclusion zones' you built in the mountains, far from the prying eyes of the innocent masses like us. Training them to fight, and lead, and kill. Brainwashing them in their droves...." He shook his head. "Ten *years,* they spent on that mountainside... ten years under your cruel, neglectful reign, destroying all hope they had of a life outside the perimeter walls. Ten years... and what did you do with all of those workers and trainees when the king died and war was proclaimed?" Eli gritted his teeth and speared a finger down. "You sent the soldiers off to war, didn't you? And you left the rest of them *to die...*"

Ferreus blinked. "I... *no...*"

"Several days later – having watched the hordes of soldiers descend from the mountainside, fearing for our lives – I gathered a group of volunteers, and lead the recovery mission up into the camps to get the abandoned workers out." He steadied his emotions, closing his eyes for a moment. "And you know what? I cannot even *begin* to explain the horrors I witnessed walking up that mountain pass: to see *hundreds* of people, half-starved and freezing to death, sleeping on goat-skin mats by the roadside. Half of them were delirious, ravaged by illness and disease... some of them I knew would never make it off that mountainside alive. We got there... *horrified* by what we were witnessing... and we set up staging posts and hospitals for them; shipped food up the mountain to them on the backs of mules;

dragged medics all the way from the borders of Rodenia to try and save them from dying in their sleep. We lit fires and shared drinks with them, and brought them in as our own. We saved hundreds of lives from imminent death… and we saved them, when the people in power did not. When people like *you,* left innocents to *die…*"

Ferreus trembled, looking between them, the lens slipping from his hand into the dirt below.

"And when I spoke to these people, general… when I saw them there, half-dead and freezing… they did not ask for food or water or shelter when we arrived. Not one of them, in that moment, cared for the bare necessities of existence. Because, *general,* do you know what they instead asked me for?"

He leaned in close, right up to the wolf's ear.

"They asked me, for *revenge…"*

"No…" Ferreus muttered, looking into the Chief's cold, venomous eyes. "No, this isn't… they… *no…*"

"So when I got the letter through from Arrenso, saying the capital was under martial law and that people were being dragged from their homes by our own army, we returned to those mountains with the people you had abandoned… and we rebuilt your training camps," Eli said. "We organised the workers: we offered them a choice, and they committed to our cause of freedom. They honed their skills. They united as one common people. And they built for us weapons and artillery machines the likes of which this world has never *known…*" Eli pointed out to the mountainside. "Those people you abandoned up there, became our fighters, and our builders, and our engineers by *choice*. By choice, your people became *our* people. They worked hard, and they worked with honour, and they worked knowing that, come the end of it, they would have the revenge they so fervently desired. And I made a promise to them, before I departed to come here… a single statement to guide their hopes in the perilous times ahead." He slammed a hand against his chest-plate. "That if we survive, and defeat the armies of the field… then they will come down from the mountains with their swords gleaming, ready to march on the capital…"

"No… *no!*" Ferreus spat, bellowing, erupting with fury and disbelief. "This can't be! *No!*"

"And so it shall be that, by the hands of the masses, we shall tear down the walls of Casantri and right the wrongs brought against us. We shall end the reign of the ruinous tyrants who beat us down and leave us to our demise. For this is the cause we fight for… and you, general, have *lost*."

Ferreus looked up to him – through him – with fearful tears in his eyes, reaching up with blood-stained hands.

"Please," he grovelled, breathing shallowly. "*Please—*"

"So in the name of revenge, and with the gods as my witness," Eli thundered, tensing the bludgeon in his hand, "I condemn you, General Ferreus, to death…"

"*No…*"

"For crimes against this nation, and in memory of those we have lost…"

The bludgeon sailed skyward, hurtling back down toward the stricken body—

"*For my love, Arrenso.*"

"*NO!*"

The weapon landed like a meteorite, pulverising the general's face into a mesh of bone and blood and teeth. His squirming limbs were suddenly still, slapping against the stone beneath him. His screech, effortlessly silenced, still rang in the Chief's ears as he dragged the bludgeon aside and exhaled shakily, relief washing through him like a deluge.

He offered a prayer to the gods, and let the wind wash over his skin.

"It's done," he said quietly, proclaiming the truth to the world. "The pain is over."

At his side, Jinx hooked an arm around his back and pulled in close, trails of tears trickling down her cheeks beneath the orange frizz of her hair. Eli wrapped his huge arms around her and stood in silence for a moment, studying the autumnal shades rippling across the sky.

No more grief... no more sorrow. He closed his eyes. *Vengeance has been served, and my heart need not bleed. The perpetrator has been killed, and the land army has been destroyed.*

A sister may finally have her peace.

Feeling her warmth in his arms, a prideful determination built in his chest.

But this is not the end of our plight, and we must not let up on our true purpose. The regime still prevails, and we have an even bigger fight on our hands. The true enemy now lies on the eastern horizon, within the walls of a city we hope to topple.

And I suppose it rather begs the question...

"So, what happens now?"

Jinx slipped her arms apart and looked up to him inquisitively, wiping the tears away that dangled from her lip.

Thinking on her question, the Chief drew himself up to full height and sighed, sensing the warmth of the dying sun blanche across his face.

"What happens now, is we fight on," came his defiant response. "We regroup and rearm, and we march. We will face down the regime as one united front, as we take this war to them at last." He opened his eyes, looking off to the dense silhouette of the city by the sea, draped in the shadows of night and the treachery of a mad tyrant. "Our target, will be Casantri's walls..."

The Chief of the Mountains smiled, tightening his grip on the bludgeon.

"But our aim, will be the Governor's *head*..."

†

Chapter 60

A Throne of Lies

She had been a prisoner once, stood in that long hallway of headpieces and vaulted ceiling windows: dragged from a dungeon in chains, passing through dark stone corridors to make audience with the mysterious creature residing behind the far doors. All around her then, the pale carvings along the walls were like gnarled roots. The shimmer of armoured headpieces were like shoals of scattering fish, glinting across the tiled floors. General Cavara entered the long hallway with bated breath, bathed in colours of rust-red, scanning the inlets and covings for signs of the enemy.

For even the slimmest shadows could hide killing knives.

There are no guards, she acknowledged with a frown, pacing forward slowly. *There are never no guards... what's happened here?* She listened out for a moment, but heard no noise emanating from the Alderbane's chamber. *No sign or sound of a struggle...*

I hope I'm not too late.

Cavara approached the doors at the far end and pressed her hands against them, whispering a silent prayer as she pushed out and prized them apart. A crank of hinges, and a breath of stale air swelled out from the room beyond.

The general stepped inside.

There was the empty throne of dragon bones, black as the deepest trenches. The single, remarkable stretch of coarse-cut stone set on wooden struts, spanning the length of the room before her. Polished glass like ripples along the back wall, diced with orange light.

And the jarring shadow of the Alderbane stood at the right-hand window, looking off over the City through the visor of its skull.

Cavara studied them for a moment, dissecting the rivets in their black robe and the haunting grey aura that seemed to suck the colour out of everything surrounding them. There was a sense of fear within her, looking upon their form, that penetrated even the deepest resolve of her mind. Looking upon a being of great power and mystery, rivalled only by the Mothers of the Rapture, who stood looking out upon the bustling streets and pale houses of the city they had lorded over for decades. A master – an heir apparent – lost in a world of their own.

A world that was also slowly coming undone.

"I have been expecting you," it thundered suddenly, the shadows of its body billowing like flames.

"I came as soon as I could," Cavara replied. "I came to warn you… there's been a betrayal, among your ranks. Lots of people have died."

"Tell me everything."

"There was a plan in place, between the Forgotten One and I, to apprehend and kill the assassin who came ashore aboard the Tarrazi ship. We found signs of him in the storehouse where I was attacked last time" – she recalled their previous conversation and sighed, burying her grievances – "and we investigated from there. We found an underground tunnel system at the back of the room, that we assumed had been built to perform maintenance on the city bath-houses, but it had also been frequented by the assassin in question and was likely used as their hideout. We went down there in search of them and I… I lost sight of the Forgotten One… but then I found this room with lots of lights and a cell door…"

"What did you find there?"

Cavara exhaled. "I found the child. The boy who'd been taken, he… he was being kept down there by the assassin, waiting to be used as leverage to get to me. And I was hoping to free him, and return him to his mother… but then the assassin appeared, and…"

She stopped herself, squaring her jaw.

Here we go…

"Ptolemy and Amara are traitors, and they've been working with the Tarrazi the entire time," she admitted. "They were there when the assassin appeared in the chamber, and they were set upon me like dogs. All for a bit of *money*…"

"And what has become of the honour-guards? And of this *assassin* you speak of…" The Alderbane still refused to turn to her, staring out onto the city beyond almost in some kind of trance.

"They're all dead… they died in the chamber, by my hand. The assassin is gone, and the child has been returned to their mother. It's… well, it's over."

A pause echoed out between them for some time, deafening and vibrant, until the Alderbane produced a single word in reply.

"*Interesting.*"

Cavara flinched. *Interesting? What does that mean?*

She ignored it, considering the danger at hand. "But the reason why I came here now, is to warn you about the betrayal of your guardsmen and the potential threat to your life," she said. "If the honour-guard were working for the assassin, then others may be too. I'm concerned about people's lives… I'm concerned for the safety and security of your palace, too. I don't know how many of your guards have had any contact with them, or could be working with them already…"

"At least a dozen, I believe."

"Exactly, so we—"

She froze; her heart stopped.

Wait.

"*What did you say?*"

Facing away from her, gazing out the window onto the bloody-red streets beyond, the Alderbane started to laugh. A painful, cruel, terrifying thing that rattled her bones and pried a spear through her soul. A baritone horror that reverberated through the chamber and back again, growing deeper and more covetous the second time round. It was a mocking, venomous thing, burrowing deep into her chest.

Threatening to tear her apart.

"When the ship came ashore, in the dead of night," the Alderbane muttered, "I told you that we sent it away before it had a chance to offload. I told you that anyone, or any*thing,* that left its deck in the short time it was docked, would have done so without our knowledge." They paused. "I now acknowledge that that statement, which I relayed to you, was not entirely true." The figure suddenly turned, a spiral of shadow orbiting to face her, with the mangled half-skull glowing gold and grey. "Because we did in fact receive a letter from the captain of that ship, which was sent directly to my chamber by one of my guards and was only opened by my hand. And I want you to know, that the contents of that letter said nothing of the assassin aboard the ship, nor the plot to end your life, nor the war that rages on in your homeland. What lay within its folded pages said nothing concerning any of the plights you have faced, in fact... but what it did tell me, general, is the truth about what you really *are,* and about the unimaginable power you possess. A power that I found most intriguing, and desired to covet *myself...*"

Cavara swallowed loudly.

"So, when I told the captain of my decision, I allied with the transmitter, and I hired the honour-guard from a group of mercenaries to draw you into a trap. I told the assassin to use the child you hold so dear as bait, and I gave him access to the underground tunnels as a hideout. I orchestrated the entire chain of events that led you to that storehouse in the first place, where you faced down those hooded figures intent on your demise." They stopped for a moment, almost in disgust. "Yet, it seems the single most important facet of that plan, did not manifest in the end..." Whatever eyes it possessed burrowed deep into her own like knives. "...because *you* did not *die.*"

The general stepped back.

"You see, I heard a story some time ago, about the nature of the

Rapture and the power it holds… perhaps you have heard of it too," the Alderbane rumbled. "It is said that when the Mother dies, a successor is chosen from the ruler of the nation in which they reside. And as far as I understand it, *general,* that means that if I were to kill you now, as successor to the All-Mother… that mantle you currently possess would not go back to your homeland. It would transfer unto *me…*"

"That isn't true!" Cavara yelled, reaching for her weapon. "That… I *trusted* you!"

"It means nothing anymore. None of this does."

"This is all *wrong…*"

"You are a foreigner in my City – a refugee of your homeland – possessing an unimaginable power that you can hardly control. The dead fear you, and yet the living do not even know you exist."

"The Ascendency cannot be yours…"

"It is a power I covet, and a power I must have. Such envious *control* over the world… an immortality unlike any other. You are not deserving of its *majesty*."

"Don't do this…"

"The soul of the All-Mother is the greatest force known to the world around us…"

The Alderbane unhooked the robe along its chest.

"And with your death, that power shall be *mine.*"

The robes slipped from its shoulders, spilling across the floor at its feet, and Cavara beheld the true nature of the Alderbane in all its debauchery and horror.

A broken skull of interlocking horns plated with gold, its mangled fangs twitching above a chasm of shadow. A neck brace of silver and gold plates, welded to a damaged knot of fabric spilling down its front. A skeletal ribcage protecting blackened, half-rotten organs consumed with spores of fungus. Six massive skeletal arms unfolding from one another, drawing curved blades of dark, menacing steel. Studded feet like a dragon's, with claws as long as sabres that clicked across the stone floors.

Cavara reeled backwards, eyes bulging from their sockets, beholden to the false god in all its terror. She pulled at her belt, reaching for her sword locked away in its sheath.

And as her blade finally emerged and she levelled it to her chest, the creature before her stooped into a fighting stance.

"*Behold your death.*"

With revolving metal blades interlocking and dicing through like a torture machine, the Alderbane surged toward her menacingly with its head stooped, the dragon claws scraping against the polished porcelain underfoot.

Cavara forgot to breathe.

What the fuck...

She blinked once and leapt sideways, launching over the table acrobatically as the blades tore toward her with relentless motion. With little direction or control, she bundled toward the shadowy throne opposite and collapsed into its seat, tucking her legs in behind her to avoid the revolving weapons that scraped across the table inches from her feet.

Inches from death.

Cavara rolled out the seat and stood gasping, turning to the Alderbane—

As the creature mounted the table with a single leap, exuding a snarl and driving its curved blades down toward her.

The general ducked with a shriek; the swords darted past her and carved trenches through the throne at her back. She propelled herself to the side, rolling across the porcelain and back to a stand – turning again, to watch the Alderbane pace slowly down the table toward her, manipulating the blades together with explosions of sparks.

It was all a lie, she spluttered, adrenaline coursing through her body as the creature approached. *They all wanted me dead... this was all just a ruse to claim my power. The Alderbane never cared about any of it. They never trusted me or accepted me in his City... they used me, and held me here like a prisoner just long enough to have me killed.*

It was all a lie...

Cavara shook her head, steadying the frantic pulse of her heart, and found swords raining down toward her once again, the dead black eyes of the creature looming down upon her like hell.

Lies...

She struck up in a wide arc to deflect one side of the attacks, and then managed to curl the sword back through to deflect another two—

Where she gasped and stumbled backwards, avoiding the sixth blade as it speared through the middle toward her heart.

And the first three blades were already coming round for another attack.

Her sword crossed weakly, snapping across the creature's weapons as she crept slowly backward, rounding the end of the table with the Alderbane looming large above—

With outstretched arms like a bat's wings, the creature launched from the table towards her, a murderous bellow escaping the vortex of its mouth as the blades spiralled down across her body.

Cavara fell onto her side, kicking away toward the back wall suddenly in a fearful sprawl of limbs. The swords rained down in terrifying arcs before her, drawing closer with each snap of the creature's claws: blades scraping against her shin plates, slicing against her boots—

She hissed and cried, as the needle-thin edge of one blade slid across her ankle and cut through the flesh there into her bone.

Pain shot through her foot and calf; tears strained at the edges of her vision, as a welt of blood stained her sage leggings.

This is impossible...

Registering the danger still present, the general pushed herself back to a stand and stumbled backwards, tensing the ankle painfully to maintain her balance with her sword wavering in her hand.

Cavara looked up into its dead eyes. "What the fuck *are* you!" she screeched.

The Alderbane turned towards her, glaring and snarling with a premeditative glee.

The blades diced across in dismembering strikes.

"*I am death and hell...*"

Cavara deflected the attacks as they came with terrified swipes of her sword, as the Alderbane's blades revolved relentlessly before her in a dissecting wall of motion. She remained on the defensive, backstepping with each attack; the room diminished around her as she skimmed along the back wall. Her strikes slowed as she lost ground and poise and form. Her skin crawled with sweat and her muscles were tearing at the seams. The components of her fighting form – the one thing she knew she could rely on more than anything else – broke down before her very eyes in the wake of the creature's ungodly onslaught.

I don't know how much more I can take—

Shapes suddenly loomed up beside her; startled, she turned for a moment to see the huge double-doors skim against her shoulder. The gold, shimmering carvings and the dark stone frames, gazing down upon her inquisitively. Slow, delicate moments ticked by, with the creature tearing through the air ahead of her. The room narrowing before her – her life, narrowing all around. Slow, delicate moments ticked by...

Between life and death and a doorway.

The general grit her teeth and snapped her blade across suddenly, pressing deep into the Alderbane's circle. The creature backstepped for a moment, relinquishing their attacks with a snarl of frustration. Cavara stepped backwards, staring wide-eyed at the demon before her, pressing her shoulder down against the metal door.

To pass into the hallway beyond, and run.

Almost immediately, the snap of hinges echoed at her back; she grated to a halt and turned to watch the door behind blast open, the top hinges flying in a glaze of shrapnel and snapped wooden beams.

From beyond, the Alderbane stepped through and growled, swords drawn close across its back to imitate spines.

"Where do you think *you're* going..." it snapped, its horns glistening against the dusk. "You can't run from *me*..."

Cavara stood her ground, screwing her nose up, whispering a prayer to whichever poor, feckless god was listening. Her gaze locked to the hollow dark of the Alderbane's sockets, emotionless and deathly, as the arbiter of hell paced toward her with sliding claws and shimmering blades in the orange-red haze of end-times. A place where shadows ruled supreme.

And her existence would be snuffed out in seconds.

The general exhaled slowly, grasping the sword tight in her hands, and wondered whether it was worth it to run. To turn tail and bolt out the doors and try her luck fleeing the city. To survive another day, or even another hour, hoping the city gates wouldn't seal shut and roving assassins wouldn't hunt her down in the streets.

Or that she wouldn't die at the hands of a monster, the likes of which she had never known.

But I can't. Within her chest, a defiance rose to the surface, unbroken and steadfast. *I can't back down now. I have to finish this. Too much is at stake. If I go now, there's no guarantee Azura and Evelyn will be safe. I have to finish this here and now.*

For their lives, as much as my own.

She gritted her teeth and rolled her shoulders, sensing the numbness rise in the room around her—

Stopping suddenly; frowning.

A numbness?

A chill swept down her spine; something echoed in her mind.

'Incoming.'

The grating of doors echoed at her back as the words entered her mind: turning, she stepped to one side—

Watching, as the Forgotten One appeared, draped in dusk's warm gloom, smiling with their sword levelled at the creature snarling down the corridor opposite.

"What do we have here?" the pale figure goaded, twisting the blade in their hand.

"Stay out of this, *beast,*" the Alderbane warned. "This does not concern you."

"I hate to disappoint you, your greatness, but I don't believe that's entirely true. Because you stand here, with your swords raised, intent on the Successor's demise..." They stooped low, gliding into a fighter's stance. "And *that* is something I sadly cannot allow."

"If you wish to stand in the way of this, and deny my right to the true power of the world that resides in her wayward soul, then *so be it*." The Alderbane stooped down into a counter stance, their swords primed like scorpion pincers. "I shall simply have to end your life first..."

The Forgotten One shrugged.

"I'd like to see you try..."

The two demigods collided into one another in a ferocious storm of weapons, six intersecting blades striking a single massive sabre conducted with impossible speed in the counter. The Forgotten One drove deep into the Alderbane's circle, pressing fearlessly, forcing the six rotating arms in close to their body to protect the rotten organs therein.

Several exchanges passed, threading through the air before the general as she looked on and studied their movements. Under the might of the Forgotten One's sabre, the Alderbane was forced to retreat slowly, their claws scraping against the stone floors underfoot in tiny, fractious steps. Hissing, growling sounds escaped from the shadowy envelopment of their neck; their attacks spiralled and darted through, in feigned attempts to slip past the pale figure's defences. Nothing appeared to work, as the violence escalated and the Forgotten One pressed the advantage.

Until the creature changed stance and lifted on the balls of its feet, levelling its horned skull like a bull and charging.

The Forgotten One lurched backwards, steering off-balance as the creature jarred toward them, driving the blades down in lunging motions toward their robed chest. The pale figure diced each strike to the side with gritted teeth, as sparks flecked off their weapons like the embers of a great fire—

In the chaos that followed, one of the creature's blades fell aside and struck a plinth displaying a steel helmet: it teetered for a moment, balancing on a precipice, before rolling sidelong over the edge of the column—

In a frantic turn, the Forgotten One swept the headpiece up onto their hand and locked into a fist.

A heartbeat later, and they swung the helmet through to strike the Alderbane across the jaw.

A stream of black smoke seemed to rise from the impact point; the creature swayed back on their claws for a moment to steady themself—

Driving the sabre down to their side, the pale figure connected with one of the Alderbane's clawed hands.

Severing the bones away entirely.

A column of smoke billowed out across the Forgotten One's blade. Shards of bone sprayed across the walls like tiny bullets. The *clang* of steel hitting stone chimed in their ears.

A venomous hiss; the creature growled and studied the remains of their hand.

"*Time to die…*"

Bellowing like a dragon, the Alderbane made their counter.

Blades rained down like hails of arrow-fire, skating against stone pillars as the Forgotten One was forced into a retreat, lost in the interchanging motions of the spinning, spiralling swords.

Suddenly on the back foot, ribbons started to flay from their robes: lacerations tearing the sleeves apart, with one significant strike going deeper and catching at the skin beneath. The Forgotten One winced uneasily, striking out with greater intensity but finding no way to make a mark. Suddenly on the back foot.

Cavara gasped.

I have to do something.

With guttural sounds escaping the maw of their mouth, the Alderbane relished the fear worn heavy across the Forgotten One's face, as they continued to strike out at the pale figure's robes seeking the touch of flesh.

Stalling for a moment, the creature slowed its attacks, listening out to the corridor—

To hear the thud of footsteps approaching quickly from behind.

Turning suddenly with two blades adjusting into a block, Cavara's sweeping sword clattered into them with the force of a tidal wave. A second – third – fourth strike then followed, meandering around the creature as it was forced to relinquish its defence, opening out to reveal the concave of black organs pulsing within. Sensing opportunity, the general lunged out to try and pluck at them like gulls picking through the surf for shells – but met instead the ferocious counter-attacks of three intertwining blades.

'This is hell,' Cavara exclaimed through the Rapture, lunging out and darting away before the swords could carve her into strips.

'This creature is a very strong fighter,' the Forgotten One admitted, their feet gliding across the stone. *'Neither of us are skilled enough to kill it as we are. Too many blades…'*

'Their swords are like torrents, I… I can't get past.'

'It holds a defensive guard around its organs; that's where its weakest.'

'Then that's our place to strike.'

'The question is: how?'

Striking out again, a single, fleeting light opened in Cavara's mind, radiant in the red-orange glow of dusk.

'I know how to kill it.'

'Okay – what do you need?'

'Keep it distracted and be aware of my positioning. On my signal, disengage.'

'Understood.'

The Forgotten One charged forward into the maw of steel, dicing the blade through with a renewed vigour. The sabre snapped with sparks of silver against the spine-like ends of the Alderbane's weapons, with the creature's skeleton now impossibly dark in the vast hallway of shadow. With every attack, the pale figure struck down closer to the creature's hands, hoping to enact the same luck as before and disarm another blade.

But it came to little avail, as the Alderbane snarled and snapped with rage, their joints clunking like an unloaded crossbow as they made to counter.

Cavara stood back and observed the demigods and their violence, calculating with every step where the opening would come. She tightened her shoulder-blades, sensing the tension in the air with outstretched palms. Her heart thundered in her chest, syphoning down through her body in ripples.

Summoning the Rapture within her.

Cavara opened her hands wider, the numbness channelling up from her fingertips, quivering through her larynx with every breath. The hallway before her seemed to pulse; her skin crawled with energy. Studying the demigods locked in their struggle just ahead of her, she saw the Forgotten One step back—

'Now!'

The pale-figure sidestepped suddenly, as the full terror of the Alderbane loomed ahead of the general.

Cavara held her blade across her side, kicking out into a sprint, charging at the creature in what seemed to be an act of suicide, skittering across the stone with a ferocious bellow spilling from her lips.

The Alderbane lowered their blades, grumbling quietly, making to strike out through the middle—

Cavara waved her hand.

A whisper escaped her lips.

And the darkness rose to claim her, once again.

~

A single step later, from shadow to the void, and the Rapture was all she could see.

Adjusting to the new axis, she planted her feet on half-realised stone floors and ground her heels. Blinking, breathing, rasping. Her sensations rallied, pulsing and fighting through her system. The gloomy dissemblance of a massive figure, that she stepped into and passed through like a stream of fog, loomed behind her. A mirror of a reality, shifted silently through her vision.

Counting seconds with heartbeats.

She slot her blade against her forearm. Planting her feet, spinning on her toes. Extending the weapon with her twisting body, controlling the numbness as it swarmed back through her like a breached dam. Tensing across her fingers; nothing and everything all at once. Striking out toward the shadow.

The darkness caving in again.

~

Crimson lights and spiralling pillars and the manifestations of hell all around.

Cavara drove her blade up between the Alderbane's ribs, eviscerating organs and rotten tendons in a spew of porous black fumes.

The creature roared like a bear; shadowy, viscous blood exploded through its chest cavity, dripping down her blade like slicks of oil. The shadows of its neck erupted with sinews of light, extending up and through its skull like arteries.

With arms extended outwards like wings staring up at the gods, the Alderbane screeched at an impossibly high pitch, glowing with such an intense profusion of light until the shadows seemed to combust entirely, snapping from the world into nothingness. The entire body seized and radiated like the sun; Cavara withdrew her blade and covered her eyes as white light consumed her vision. Everything seemed set to explode—

A crackle like cinder caught in her ears.

Silence was all that followed.

The general pulled her arm away and watched as the creature's gnarled, skeletal corpse collapsed across the stone tiles below, levelling like a stack of cards. She studied the mound of bones with an expression of shock, spying the gold-plated skull as it rolled off to one side and stopped suddenly, staring through her with dead, hollow eyes.

Cavara closed her eyes, and let the last of the dusk warmth wash over her skin from the windows above.

"It's done," Cavara gasped, steadying herself, lost in the hollow sockets of the dead god's skull.

It's finally done.

†

Chapter 61

Commander of No Legion

Death came as dusk descended, and the storm tore the low-lands apart before the Marshal's very eyes. Lashing rain like tiny pincers butchered the earth at her feet, unleashing a quagmire of mud and broken stones in every direction. The deluge ripped through branches and felled trees, forming huge pools where artillery fire had ripped the landscape apart many nights before. A howling wind carried down from the thunderclouds above and decimated any life that remained below. And then there was the lightning, the most impervious will of nature, scattering across the skyline in a delta of blue light and flame, bellowing furiously against the gods' wrath. For death came as dusk descended.

And the world just seemed to die.

Marshal Lazaerys peeled the hair away that had welded to her face and squinted into the storm. Strikes of cold bit up her spine and across her shoulders in tight spasms as she moved. She struggled to see, or even to think in that moment, as the path ahead was torn away at the seams and the earth seemed to regurgitate itself.

It's all going wrong…

She lurched suddenly, as the lame horse beneath her whinnied and slid across the mud, struggling to steady itself. Lazaerys swore, dig-ging her heels into the horse's flank, only to receive a snort of disgust in response. The beast stood exhausted, its front legs splayed in the mud with streams of air billowing from its nostrils like dragon's breath. The Marshal made a few more attempts to stir the horse on, swearing and pleading under her breath that it would shift from the mud.

But each one came to no avail.

Fuck.

Lazaerys pulled herself down from the saddle, dropping into knee-deep swamps of mud, and waded from the scene, leaving the horse to die in the storm.

That scheming piece of shit. Shadows lay heavy across her back, like the many prying hands of the dead ripping up from the earth to claim her. *That scheming, traitorous, power-lusting piece of shit.* She clawed at a branch, using it to drag her sodden carcass out of a pit and up onto a grassy bank. *He sought to betray us all along. To kill us, one by one... and to kill me, in the end, claiming the commandership back for himself. All of it, just for power... just for his own greed.*

What a monster.

Lazaerys crested a small ridge where a tree trunk had been blown to shreds, standing atop the shrapnel and looking south through the grey maw. There, she spied the beige canopies and tired barricades of the command post still standing beyond the storm, several rises and bows ahead of her atop a wide plateau. With the imposing smear of the border wall rising beyond it, the camp looked almost like a watercolour painting: a haze of inter-changing, often-merging colours and shapes that seemed to bleed into each other in great blotches. An abstract disconcertion, splattered on a blank canvas. And Lazaerys found, much like life, that nothing seemed to take much shape anymore.

As we stand inches from death, it's no surprise.

She stepped forward off of the broken log and planted a foot cautiously against the soil beneath. A pool of water formed around the heel of her boot, but it seemed to hold for now. She smirked.

Perhaps we'll get back after all.

Especially because that rotten shit of a general is dead now, back in that hellscape they call the Ozban. She spat into the mud and screwed her nose up. *There's no way he could've survived that attack. No matter how stupid, lucky or blind he is, I don't see him selling himself out to the Tarrazi anytime soon. He's far too proud for that.* She scoffed.

Then again, I thought he was far too proud to let a change in the order of leadership get to him, and I was wrong about that. She shook her head, pulling her hair from her face again. *So who really knows what's happened—*

Pain erupted in her leg suddenly like a small detonation, and the sky exploded with lightning above her.

She screeched suddenly, lurching forward as a crossbow bolt embedded itself in her hip and lodged against the bone. She tried to take another step with sick frothing in her mouth, only to tense the entry wound and nearly collapse with shock. The haze of the storm ahead seemed to darken and slide. A furore of agony carved across her pelvis and down through her feet. Marshal Lazaerys turned slowly to face the Ozban, trying to seek out where the bolt had come from...

And heard the cackling of maniacal laughter, long before she saw him appear.

Her eyes opened like swollen fruits.

That's impossible...

Only a few dozen steps away, stumbling toward the horse still stood lamely in the mud, Commander Revek passed along its flank tugging at its saddle with mud-coated hands. Reaching its head, he drew a knife from a small sheath at his waist, whispering a quiet prayer – and in a single dicing stab, he impaled the horse through the eyes, giggling to himself as it squealed and tottered sidelong into the mud, never to rise again.

Lazaerys felt her throat tighten.

You should be dead.

She turned from him and started hobbling through the storm toward camp, sweating and heaving, the adrenaline coursing through her veins providing just enough strength to overcome the bile punching through her throat. It seemed impossible; it should have *been* impossible. Reality felt fickle and twisted in her head.

This can't be... how have you survived? Ambling, legs pumping beneath her, the Marshal hissed and groaned at the incising pain biting into her leg with each stride. The warmth of her own blood balanced with the cold rain, reminding her of life and mortality and how precious little she had left. *He was on the platform when they first attacked... the hounds swarmed around him. He should have been killed.* She stumbled over a stone, barking with agony. *How has he got away? How is any of this possible?*

How can—

Lazaerys stalled, pushing her weight down across her heels as she swayed over a ridge and nearly fell headlong into a pit of snapped branches and muddy water. She inhaled sharply, her eyes boggling out of her skull. The wind seemed to change around her, elucidating the storm in bitter tones. Drawing up to the skies like a hurricane; drawing still around her.

As a whistling sound snapped in her eardrum, and all was lost.

The second bolt punctured her side, snagging between leather straps and burrowing deep into the flesh beneath. With a frightful gasp of air, Lazaerys twinged as the tiny shred of metal pierced one of her organs, lodging deep within her chest, and all light seemed to shimmer overhead in delicate, fastidious rays.

And then she found herself falling, toppling into the ditch of broken branches and mud-slick ooze. Adrenaline coursed into her brain; she slapped against the filthy water and buckled her shoulders against stumps of wood. Embedded in the mud; sinking suddenly; fighting to stay conscious; putrid waste leaking into her wounds like a cancer. Her eyes blinkered, lost to the world. Coated in mud and sweat and bile. Ripples of lightning and thunder blasted across the grey clouds high above.

And a shadow manifested at the edge of the pit above her, with an unloaded crossbow swinging limply in their hand.

"You thought... you thought you could stop me!" Revek howled, cackling madly into the hail. "You thought you could stop me from getting what I *deserve?* You thought you could just take it from me, and leave me for dead? You stupid, naïve little *bitch.*" He flashed his teeth, a haunted tension in his gaze. "You denied me what is rightfully mine… and look where it *got you.*"

"You're a monster…" she spluttered, nearly vomiting, the ugly taste of iron lathered on her tongue.

"*Wrong!* Wrong! Don't you get it? Don't you understand? I am no *monster!* I have never been a monster: I am a man of the army, a man of order and control and *justice* against the wrath of contempt. You despise me for my power; you hate me for it. So you and your petty *officers* dragged me through the mud so you could have what's yours, all because of a lust to see me fail." He speared a finger down to her. "And you call *me* a traitor…"

"I did… as I was ordered to…"

"Then you have *failed.*" With spluttering, scoffing laughter, Revek skid down the pit's edge to face her, submerging his shins in the foul water just to get close. "I cannot tell you how long I have *waited* for this moment. The miserable days spent plotting, targeting people, toeing the line and following commands… all in the hopes I would find myself in the position to end your life and take back what's *mine* at the end of it." He lifted his arms. "And here we are, on the cusp of hell…"

He grinned like daggers.

"How long I have waited to do this…"

He pounced on her with hands outstretched, ringing a knot of her hair in his hand and plunging her head down into the mud-water below. Straining suddenly, shocked at the speed of it all, a boot pressed down against her back and held her in the cesspit like a felled boar. The Marshal was writhing, kicking out with immense splashes and scrabbling with her hands for any purchase, as the blood left her body and the wounds ballooned with infection and her face pressed deeper into the mud below. Eyes opened, stinging violently as splinters and tiny stones embedded in her pupils – gasping suddenly with no air to come, taking on volumes of shit-brown liquid that choked and dissolved her airways like acid. The taste of iron replaced by the taste of sodden earth. Splashing limbs becoming numb, little more than a patter against the water's surface, slowly submerging. Squinting eyes like the sun through clouds. The rapidity of the unconscious void slowly claiming her, swallowing her, another soul lost to the hell of Tarraz.

Murdered by one of her own...

Commander Revek watched the Marshal's twitching body grow still, until the bubbles ceased to rise from her head and the final spasms of death drew to a close. He gazed upon her drowned corpse malevolently and in silence, with the mad humour that had claimed him long departed.

What came instead, was a moment of utter peace, and the bloated relief of restoring order. That now he alone was the single commander of the Imperial Army of Provenci. That he alone, now held a position he had earned righteously through honour and merit.

And one that he had then retained, through butchery and blood.

Looking up to the skies, he closed his eyes and let the heavy droplets dash across his face like a new-born child's first bath. The cold tingle of ice hitting their skin; the bubbly, chirpy, satisfied noises they made. A relinquishment washed over him, coating his damaged heart with rivers of gold.

He knew what had to come next.

Drawing a quick breath, lowering his gaze back to the cesspit below, Commander Revek dragged the Marshal's corpse to the edge of the pit, and began the long walk back to camp.

†

They stood in the main command tent sipping brandy, discussing how bad the weather was. Five groups of them, soldiers and officers of the army reserve clinking glasses and bumbling to themselves with red cheeks and bulbous grins. Commenting on the wider camp: how soldiers had been forced to double up their tents to shield them from the elements, weighing down larger canopies with boxes just to stop them taking flight. Expressing their sympathies for families back home, wondering how their fathers and sisters fared out in the wilds of Tarraz. The occasional whisper of how things were at the front, quickly batted away as 'business talk' and not something for such a gathering. Wandering eyes passing between them, ignorant and blissful, as the storm howled on outside. A few of the more observant ones looking on, noting a shadow approaching the entranceway, and the sound of marching boots dragging something heavy toward them…

Commander Revek ducked under the opening with a gust of frozen wind and a look that could melt steel. Without ushering a word of greeting to any of them, he slung the Marshal's mud-coated corpse around and threw it on the dirt floor at his feet.

A unified gasp passed the soldiers' lips. Chairs scraped against the dry earth below. A number of faces turned from cherry red to milk white in seconds, looking about ready to spew their drinks across the tent like fountains. A few even dared to lower their drinks and reach for their swords instead.

"Evening, officers," Revek muttered facetiously, rubbing his muddy face with a bloody hand. "How fares the back-line?"

"What's happened, sir?" one of them blustered, reaching for their sword hilt. "Has there been an attack?"

He looked down at the body of his former co-commander and snorted. "Yes… I suppose there has been."

He paused, meeting the eye of every single person in the command tent around him, seeing if any would dare offer a challenge to the lie that would fall from his lips.

"There has been a betrayal among the ranks of the army, and it has been committed by the hand of the person who now lies dead before you," he began. "Because out in the Ozban, in the depths of crisis, I was framed by the Marshal here for the death of one General Oslo, who died after a terrible accident when securing a waypoint further north from camp. I was told I was guilty, by officers who were not there to witness his horrific fate, and sentenced to a public execution without any legal investigation made. But before they could swing the axe down and take my head from my neck… the Tarrazi swarmed our camp in their droves, and decimated those soldiers who remained. Both General Zespa and General Xol died in the subsequent retreat, while Marshal Lazaerys here made off on the last horse and left us all to be slaughtered." He sucked air through his teeth, hiding his smile. "She intended to return to this camp, and lie to you about the events that occurred, placing the blame wholly at my feet for the Tarrazi attack and for the dozens of lives lost on this day. But I found her, having escaped from the ambush myself, stumbling through the storm with a demon in her eye. And as soon as she lay eyes on me… she attacked me, hoping to finish the job off and bury the truth with my blood. But, to my luck, I was not as poor a fighter as she had hoped, and I bested her in combat out on the lowland plains." He paused. "There was nothing I could do, you see. Such are the perils of treachery. She was, in the end, a traitor… and there was no other *way*…"

As the commander finished his monologue, and the hail of the storm snapped venomously outside, the officers and soldiers amassed under the canopy looked to each other with cautious glances. Assessing, in their own silent, contemptuous ways, whether the mud-slick man who had charged into their tent was telling the truth – or whether what he said was simply a fabrication, offering a mirage of blood and lies for them to indulge upon. There were no witnesses; there was no claim against him. With wounds in his eyes and a dead innocence in his smile, the commander seemed sincere. And the soldiers saw it, beneath the earth and blood that stained his skin. They saw a man who had overcome adversity, stood over the muddy corpse of one of their own who now gathered swarms of flies like medals. She was a traitor, supposedly. A coward, so he said. There had been no other choice.

And who were they to say any different?

"Can't have traitors in our ranks sir… no matter who it is," one of them suddenly exclaimed, stepping forward with a bow of the head. "You were right to do her in."

"Can hardly blame you for a Tarrazi attack, now can we?" another said. "We've been with you the whole time so far, after all. I mean, watching your valour on the Grey Plains... you ain't the type to sell us out to them really."

"If she betrayed you, she got what she deserved, ay?" a third proposed, to the jeers and nods of many others.

Revek masked his grin and inhaled slowly. "Your understanding is most appreciated, officers, thank you," the Commander replied. "Your resilience and *loyalty* will be rewarded in due time, I assure you."

"Although, if this has all gone on, sir," the first asked him, "then... what happens now? The Marshal is dead, and the army is basically all gone. So... what do we do now?"

Now the smile appeared, tight across his cheeks like knives. "Well... the answer to your question, my friend, is in fact quite *simple*." Revek opened his hands out to them. "With the Marshal dead, *I* am now the lead commander of this army, and thereby hold power within this camp and across the entire front-line of this war. I am the arbiter here, and I have the final say. And what I tell you – each and every one of you – is this: we shall return to Casantri in the next week, gathering our camps and leaving this godforsaken place to the hands of the savages who reside here. We will cross the border, and regroup within our city's walls, and make our triumphant return out here in the coming months with my command fully reinstated. We shall strike at them again with the might of our imperial force, and we shall emerge *victorious*." He clapped his hands together. "Now, do I make myself clear?"

A few shocked expressions emerged, as mutters passed between them—

"*Do I make myself clear!*"

Fear gripped them – affirmatives and salutes spluttered from their mouths like bile – their faces flushed with colour under the commander's punishing gaze. Revek reeled violently in the entranceway to the tent, challenging them with wild eyes and hatred burning across his lips.

"Good. I'm glad we're at an *understanding* about that. Now, if you would please, don't waste any time: go out and tell the soldiers of the change in command, and tell them to be ready to depart. We leave in the coming days. I expect this to be done swiftly and effectively, or there will be *consequences* for tardiness. Do *not* disappoint me. Understood?"

The same muttered affirmatives emerged in reply, accompanied by the same doleful stares.

Revek pursed his lips.

Good.

He turned from the officers, looking down to the dead Marshal's corpse at his feet, and on to the maelstrom surging across the lowlands just outside the door.

"It is time we return to our homeland, my friends," he proclaimed to the storm. "It is time we get our dues, and have our power acknowledged once more..."

As he spoke, lightning cracked the sky above.

Revek smiled.

And no-one will stand in my way...

†

Chapter 62

The Unravelling

The wind picked up as dusk descended, and the world grew cold and still. Clouds as dark as caverns scuttled across the sky overhead, edged by the golden blossom of a deep setting sun. The mountains in the distance rose like black spears along the horizon, bathing the scorched plains to the west in swamping reams of shadow. Turrets of smoke wisped faintly upwards from there, marking the burnt inlets of trees and the ruined stretches of farmer's fields. In the dark, the grass beneath them seemed to lie tossing in its sleep as a chill rasp of wind swept up the ridge to signify a coming storm.

And at the centre, nestled in the bowl of the valley, lay the shattered homes and bloodied streets of Marcheg: a desolation, scarred by the advent of war, where survivors now fled with hanging heads back to the refuge they called home.

Supreme Governor Alvarez stood with his generals to the east of their camp, and watched with a deepening sorrow as the stragglers of his Imperial Land Army limped their way up the slope toward him. There were near a hundred of them approaching: solitary, swaying corpses staring at their feet, bruised and beaten and dripping blood from wounds big enough to mark graves. Their rustling steps reached the crest of the ridge one after the other like ants – and one after the other, they made no acknowledgement of their Governor and his subordinates, stood with torches raised to guide them back to sanctuary. There was, in the end, not a flick of the eye nor a turn of the head between them. They simply paced on, moving down into what remained of the command post behind, with most of it packed up and loaded onto carts, anticipating a return to the capital soon.

Alvarez pulled at the knots in his thin hair, easing a hand across his scalp to stem the headache knocking within.

Need more drink, he grumbled, pinching his nose. *Anything to forget this mess.*

As the thought came, one of the soldiers ascending the hill turned to approach them, dragging a limp left leg through the grass like a plough, the shin visibly bulging beneath their armour. He stalled just before the Governor, sucking air through his teeth and lifting his head.

"What has happened, officer?" one of the generals at Alvarez's side muttered.

"We were routed, sir," came the hollow, dejected reply. "They used the emergency tunnels underground an' crept up behind us. We had no rear-guard left to stop 'em… they just swept through and cut us to pieces. We got out when we had the chance… and only the lucky ones survived."

"What's the situation in Marcheg now?"

"It's in rebel hands." The soldier readjusted his broken leg. "There ain't a soul left down there still wavin' a sword with the imperial standard on their chest, that's for sure. It's done."

A pause passed amongst the officers, long and foreboding.

"Where's General Ferreus?" Alvarez said slowly as little more than a whisper, refusing to meet the man's gaze.

The soldier clicked his tongue. "Dead, sir. By the hand of their leader." He shook his head, hands twitching. "It's over…"

Stepping between them, the soldier passed Alvarez without a word more, hobbling down the ridge behind them with agonised steps. The Governor watched him for a long while before turning back to his generals.

"What do we do now, sir?" the same officer as before asked with fear lining his face.

The Governor let the darkness wash over him, pulling his tongue across his teeth to taste bile and ethanol there.

"We return to the capital, general," Alvarez said morbidly, lost in a realm of his own. "This fight is lost…"

He looked up to the clouds above, and felt the tiny specks of rain tap across his cheeks. A rising storm, no doubt.

Civil war, has come.

†

Chapter 63

Champion's Ruin

It is done, at last…

A Champion is born.

Gaza watched her approach through the shadows of her throne room with blood still dripping from her hands. An elegant darkness, creeping through the gloom like a ghost. She noted how her fingers twitched occasionally, flexing and bunching together again as if she still clutched the killing blade. How the metal plate embedded in her cheek shimmered like the moon, underlining the grooves of her soulless, hateful eyes. Her expression was one of subservience; the Queen wondered if her single act of sheer brutality had finally gifted her some peace. And as she strode forward with slow, measured steps to the base of the throne and dropped to one knee without question, Gaza could see there just how far the Champion had come in her journey since the fighting pits.

And how much I've taken from you in doing so…

"Rise, Champion," Gaza exclaimed. "There's no need to kneel. Let us see you for what you are… for the monster you *really* are."

Savanta stood before her with her gaze lowered, inhaling slowly like the rhythmic beats of a child's heart. Despite the warmth of her face, her skin almost looked frostbitten in the low light.

"There we are… how magnificent. You look exactly like the Champion I envisaged at the beginning of all this. You have proven yourself worth of such a title now… and I am most pleased."

"Thank you, my Queen," she replied despondently, refusing to look at her.

Gaza clenched her jaw, rolling her shoulders and sighing.

Still some work to do then.

She crossed to her desk and studied the maps sprawled across its surface, stroking her fingers over them meticulously. "Have you heard anything of the war, Champion?" the Queen asked. "Of what goes on in our lands and beyond?"

"I have not, my Queen, no," she replied, nodding slowly. "I chose to stay away from all that after the incident. I was a scout, and the war was not mine, so to speak."

"Well, although that may have been true… it is not true with your new place at my side. As Champion, you have a part to play in all strategic and military matters of this nation, including the current conflict raging at our southern border." She paused. "This is not something any of us can escape, after all…"

"I understand, your highness. Please, enlighten me."

Gaza blinked slowly. "We're fighting a war on multiple fronts, with different levels of engagement in each location. We have the war in the south at our border, as I'm sure you're aware, against the Provencian Imperial Army. As far as my reports indicate, their forces are currently corralled along the border wall and we hope to secure that area in the coming weeks, while executing any survivors we find roaming the Kazbaks to the west.

"Alongside that, we have spies and assassins in the City of the Sun in Sevica – about a dozen hired hands in total, I believe. They're there to tie up some loose ends and alleviate a particularly irritable problem that I am unable to solve by my own hand. But, once that's put to rest, the entire eastern side of the known world should be neutralised against us."

"It's a wide network, it seems," Savanta assessed.

"Yes… and one that needs to broaden in scope still. We need spies in the forests of Rodenia to keep a watch on their activity… someone within the imperial regime currently in power in Casantri, to mislead and inform… more civilian vessels along our shores to monitor any ships leaving Provencian waters…" She shrugged with a wicked grin. "So much *potential* out there… so much work and influence to exact… and we seem the only ones with the guts to do it. I will do whatever it takes to tear the Provencians to the ground for what they've done to us… and no-one else has the guts to fight back. No-one will *stop* me…"

"It is fear that makes them weak, your highness… I know it, because I once felt it too." She finally lifted her gaze, staring deep into the Queen's pale eyes. "They fear you, and the power you have conjured. They fear becoming another of your victims."

"Then perhaps they still have some sense left in them. No-one challenges the true heir of the All-Mother's throne – the Iron Queen of all Tarraz – with the armies I have at my disposal and the dark secrets I keep locked away…"

Gaza watched the Champion flinch at her words, and smiled.

Oh, you haven't seen the half of it.

"What will you have me do, my Queen?" Savanta muttered, placing her hands flat against her thighs uneasily. "What is my first task?"

The Queen nodded, somewhat impressed. *So loyal already…*

This shall be good.

"Well, Champion, with the war churning on in the south and our forces closing in around the Ozban Forest, the plan is that you'll—"

The sound of metal latches drew her attention away suddenly, echoing out from the back of the room. Gaza screwed her nose up as the door slipped ajar at the far end, and one of her generals scuttled in with a frightful sweat across his brow.

"Well, general… this better be good!" the Queen scolded, tapping her finger against the desk. "I am not one for interruptions, as you well know…"

The general gulped loudly. "My apologies, my liege, but this… this is rather urgent," he muttered as he crossed the chamber, standing alongside Savanta and looking disgusted at her bloody hand.

Gaza frowned deeply. "What is it?"

"An urgent report from the City of the Sun, my Queen, concerning the… the um…" The general looked frightfully between Gaza and her Champion.

"Yes, she knows about the assassin in Sevica, general, so please dispense with the hesitation… and tell me what's *happened*."

"We've… we've heard back from one of the locals we hired to assist the Butcher, my liege. The report came in via the hold of a stray merchant ship this morning." He paused weightily. "I regret to inform you that the operation has failed, my Queen… the assassin was killed by the general's hand. All of our personnel have been evacuated… I am sorry to bring you such news."

Gaza stood for a moment, her eyes sealed shut, and swayed soundlessly in the gloom. Ironclad clouds drifted across the skyline just beyond her window; the drums of thunder hailed off over the distant mountain peaks. The smog of her vast war machine clogged the air outside with entrails of smoke.

And none of it could quite portray the dark and malicious fire that now burned through her veins, and crawled its way across her cold, beating heart.

Gaza grappled the edge of her desk and flung it from the platform, snapping the legs and casting the ledgers across the chamber in a great fury-driven cloud. Wood shards spilt over the stone like broken rivers. Inkpots smashed. The room pulsed as the Iron Queen turned back to them, a grey effluvial shimmer coalescing in her eye.

Wishing the world dead and rotten with every breath.

"What will it take to bring that traitorous pretender to her knees, and slit her fucking *throat!*" she bellowed, gritting her teeth. "I hunt her down myself, only for one of those rogue god-champions to come and rip her away. I send my best transmitter to hunt her down – a trained assassin of Tarrazi blood – and that half-apt *maggot* bests him with a fucking *sword*. She doesn't even understand her powers; she doesn't even understand what's at stake here. She has no fucking idea what she's doing. And yet she still has the audacity to *resist* me..." She sighed at length, funnelling the anger coursing through her system. "*FUCK!*"

"What will you do, my liege?" the general whimpered, cowering from the Queen and the Mother's spirit roaring within her.

Ah yes, Gaza thought, almost laughing.

What will I do...

"General?" she spat.

"Yes... my Queen?"

"At dawn-break tomorrow, ready the armada. Load them with every cannon and mortar we have. Dismantle those on the outer walls of the capital if you have to, and load them onto the cargo ships that will accompany them. I want them out at sea in ten days... and we'll have my new Champion here at the helm to lead them."

The general appeared dumbstruck, mouthing a response that never came, shuffling on his feet like an impatient toddler.

And next to him, Savanta steadied her gaze, unsure of the mission that lay ahead. "I shall do as you wish, my Queen," she said. "Where will we be departing to?"

Gaza Minesk grinned: the kind of grin that snapped bones and conjured fire.

"You shall go to the City of the Sun," she pronounced. "You shall sail my armada – seventy vessels and twenty supply ships – to the Sevica coastline, and you shall rain down every shell and shot we have in our arsenal against their pretty pale walls... until the entire fucking thing *crashes* into the *sea!*" Veins bulged in her throat, bursting across her temples. "I want that usurper general dead, and I want my rightful place as heir to the known world pronounced... and I will rip every stone out from under her feet, and murder every soul she holds dear to get it."

Savanta gulped. "Understood, your Highness."

"We shall destroy *everything* they have, and I will stop at nothing until she is dead and buried under the rubble..."

She looked off to the thundering skies outside, and to the burning red embers glowing between the distant peaks.

Gaza smiled to herself.

Mark my words…

†

Chapter 64

Dawn of the Coming Storm

"What happens now?"

The palace of the City of the Sun lay silent and still, glossed by moonlight that shimmered across its domes like sand-coated hills. The tall palace spires speared up into the stars with a calm iridescence, dispelling the shadows all around. There was a certain poetry to it, almost like the gods had ordained it. A certain beauty in its madness.

And had it not been for the demon's remains scattered about its corridors, they could almost believe it too.

The inner chambers had been vacated by all residents and workers after the fighting had stopped, as they were told to return to their homes and remain there until summoned come morning. Initially, when the Alderbane had been killed, soldiers had charged in with their weapons drawn hoping to arrest any perpetrator they could find, sensing treachery was afoot and that the refugee was at the heart of it. Although, after entering the main corridor and facing down the Forgotten One, who stood like a domineering shadow at the end of the room, they accepted the reality for what it was, and agreed to guard the outer courtyards while the situation was assessed. Indeed, the only person to have entered the palace since then – much to the disgust of the guards – had been Azura: summoned by the general via messenger, the old mother had drifted through the quiet streets while the rest of the citizenry lay sleeping, ascending the steps and slipping into the palace chamber like a ghost. Walking the halls with a timid unease; directed down the long corridor to the gold-carved doors at the end.

And when she had entered the throne room, and seen the general's expression long before any words had been spoken, Cavara had watched a quiet acceptance wash over the old woman's face as if she had known it all along: that the Alderbane had been a traitor like the rest; that the Alderbane had fought the general in the hope of claiming her powers; that the Alderbane now lay dead and maimed in a burial crypt several hundred feet below them. That the City of the Sun, and Sevica as a whole, was now leaderless.

And would collapse into carnage, if it was not restored.

"Where do we go from here?" Cavara asked, planting her hands flat against the tabletop. "The nation is without a ruler… the City is completely unaware of what's happened… and you have no means of succession in sight. So, as far as I see it, come sunrise this entire place will tear itself apart."

"An apocalyptic outcome, with the threat of the Iron Queen still at large," the Forgotten One added from the back of the room. "Should the realm of Sevica collapse, it will be easy for the Tarrazi to seize it and add a new tract of land to its empire…"

"Exactly so." Cavara looked up to Azura, a plea in her eyes. "So, Azura, you know this place better than anyone… what do we do?"

The old woman considered for a moment, the tired whites of her eyes drawing still and solemn like an owl's.

But then a smile appeared, and almost a laugh to follow.

"Under usual circumstance, as a born-and-bred Sevican, the answer of what to do next would be simple," she replied. "Let the country tear itself apart: let it be subjugated and then oppressed and then let us overthrow the oppressors and establish a new governing body for the people and watch it all crumble again. Let nature – *human* nature that is – take its course." She shrugged; her smile faded. "But I also understand that this is no ordinary circumstance… and the nature of what has happened is as impossible as it is unbelievable. But such is life, I suppose… and there is, therefore, only one option left to us."

"What's that?"

Azura met the general's gaze. "Do you remember, when you awoke on my ship in the middle of the sea… you asked me if the stories about this place were true. If the Alderbane was really as brutal as they were; if we were as oppressed as your lords deemed us to be. And I told you about it all, and about the lies they propagated… and I told you about our way of life being in a constant state of flux…"

"… and how the next leader may come by the will of the people, forming a council to govern together for the good of the nation." She paused. "Are you saying that's the way forward?"

Azura lay her hand against the table and sighed exhaustedly, with weight spread heavy across her shoulders. "I believe that is the only option available to us, yes. They only way out of this mess…"

"Then how do we go about it? How do we initiate something so monumental – something that hasn't been done before in the history of the known world?"

"It must be done tactfully, and it must be done with a show of honesty and force." Azura's smile returned. "And that is why *you* must be the one to do it."

Cavara pressed a hand to her chest, frowning furiously. "*Me?* Why me? What part do I have to play in this! I'm a former-general, here as a refugee… I mean, I'm not even *from* Sevica. What good will *I* do?"

"You can act as legate – a neutral ambassador here to oversee the handover of power. Every nation of the Icebreaker Sea has had one at some point in their history, and now you have the chance to… and more than that, you have the chance to do it *properly* so everything doesn't go to shit. You can address the City tomorrow and tell them what's really happened here: tell them about the betrayal; about the fate of the known world; about your powers, even. Tell them *all* of it. Make them understand… and if they don't, threaten them until they do. Call for public order: for people to step forward and offer themselves up to serve the City and their homeland. Provide the framework for a council, and put them to a vote. Make this *work*."

"But why *me?*"

"Because if one of us were to do it, it would be seen as nothing more than a palace coup, and the city would burn in weeks… but if *you* were to do it, with the Forgotten One by your side, people would listen. They would *have* to listen." She sighed, pursing her lips. "You are the key to saving Sevica, Cavara. You are the key to our future… and perhaps the future of our world too."

Cavara clasped her hands shakily and looked out to the City beyond. Bathed in the moon's glow, it looked like a chalk painting drawn across the walls of a cave. A mosaic of sliding pieces, shifting with the light.

Much like my life has become, in so many ways, she thought anxiously. *So many pieces sliding together, with me in the middle of it.*

Wondering when it's all gonna go wrong…

"It's a lot to take in," Cavara admitted. "I mean… who would even offer themselves up to such a task? Their ruler has just been killed, and a massive corruption scheme has been unveiled… who would want to step up and right those wrongs?"

"I would," Azura said assuredly in reply. "I would do it if I had to. And if all else fails, I would do it single-handedly. The City needs leadership… it needs to prepare, and manage its defences, and protect its people. It needs to protect *you,* above all else, and the fate you hold in your hands." She nodded as if condemned. "So yes, I would do it… for the good of the nation, if I have to."

"Reluctance is often the sign of a born leader," the Forgotten One said stoically. "Those who serve the nation for the people, often serve its interests best."

Cavara acknowledged the remark, smiling. "You prove to be more remarkable every time we speak, Azura."

"Old age does wonders to the soul," the old woman said, flicking her hair with a smirk.

The general bowed her head in recognition.

Truer words were never said...

"So will you do it, general? Will you become our legate, and bind the wounds the Alderbane left with their treachery?"

Cavara drew still and closed her eyes for a moment, sensing the pain shift through her body from various wounds and numb bruises congealing just below the surface. Sensing the tiredness in her mind; the cautious relief still flooding her heart. The knife wound, still knotted across her stomach. Knowing that the life she had known long ago, would never return. Accepting, from that condemning place, that things would only get more out of her depth from there. Realising there was nothing else left for her, in the end.

Other than to be alone, cast out to sea, with the world in the palm of her hands...

"I'll do it," she said plainly, snuffing the thoughts out with a single strike. "I'll see that it's done... and bring order before chaos. And I'll do it, on the understanding that *you* will be the one to lead them, so that we may prepare for whatever comes next."

"I'll do it then, general," Azura replied softly, bowing her head in relief. "You have my word."

"As do you have mine," the Forgotten One said beside them, the etchings of a smile on its face.

"Then it's settled: tomorrow at midday I'll address the City as the neutral ambassador, and let them know that I'm here to oversee the transition of power to an elected council by a vote of the people," Cavara exclaimed. "And from there, providing the correct preparations are in place, it'll only be a matter... a matter of..."

She stopped, as her words seemed to fail her suddenly. As the room seemed to darken, and the walls closed in. She breathed slowly.

Exhaled.

Gasped.

What is—

A numb wave fell over her, engulfing her: swamping her body as if she were falling unconscious. Passing up from her chest to her body; exploding in ribbons across her soul.

Silencing, as quickly as it had appeared. Disappearing in moments.

Cavara stopped.

Breathed slowly.

"What the fuck was *that?*"

The pale figure, looking almost nauseous, placed a hand on the table next to her, swallowing heavily. "I see you felt it too, Successor."

"Yea, I did…"

"What's happened?" Azura asked, her eyes darting between them.

"I don't really know… it's never happened before. Everything went numb and swollen, passing like a wave and gone again. As if we were talking through the Rapture, but no words were spoken…"

"That's because something was," the Forgotten One said forebodingly.

"*What?*"

"Someone has established a connection to the Rapture… someone very powerful, back in your homeland. They possess a strength that goes beyond that of a simple transmitter, which has allowed them to contact us even from this distance. It is very strange… almost like…"

The pale figure stopped speaking, as a look of shock crossed their face.

"What? What is it?"

"It's… *happened.*"

"What! What's happened?"

The Forgotten One turned to her.

"Mother Katastro's soul has found a successor…"

†

Epilogue

The Horns of Grief

He pulled the cloth gaiter up over his mouth as another gust of sand swept through, clawing at his eyes and biting through his lungs like tiny pincers of steel. Adjusting the pronged shovel in his hands, he winced at the grinding of raw skin across his palms from endless weeks of work, and grimaced as they oozed an odd, discoloured liquid across his fingers like sap. He would have to get it checked out soon, knowing what kind of infections one could get out there in the desert. He knew that was the safest bet. Knowing it… and yet also knowing he probably wouldn't get it checked at all. Not that anyone would particularly care either way. He was just another cleaner, after all.

Another body like the rest.

Lifting an arm skyward, he shied away from the raging sun that boiled overhead, morphing across the sands in an ungodly haze of yellow and bleaching grey. Sweat gleaned across his forehead and streamed down his back under its onslaught; the scabs of a hundred rashes grew steadily worse across his shoulders and spine. It was a foul day at the best of times, when caught in the high heat of the desert.

But it was even more so, when surrounded by a pit of bodies decaying in their thousands.

"Keep sifting through the top layer!" he cried out to his associate several feet to his left, wading over the corpses with awkward strides. "We need to expose the underside so they can decompose faster!"

He drove his shovel down between two bodies, flipping one over to expose the layer of the dead beneath. He saw eyes goggling therein: gaunt faces and hollowed cheeks and the tiny forms of maggots wriggling across exposed stomachs. There were the shapes of animals, too: some no bigger than rabbits, curled up in foetal positions with snapped legs, while others were as large as Kazbak Hounds with serrated jaws and stab wounds to spare. He lifted a hand to his mouth at the sight of it, relenting against reality, reeling as the stench of rotten flesh lurched skyward and assaulted his nostrils. It was impressive how, even with ten years in the business and a gaiter to cover his mouth, his stomach still twisted violently every time the smell appeared.

It never gets easier, he thought quietly, prying the other body aside to reveal more wretched filth beneath, curling his nose up in disgust.

"How much longer are we out here!" his friend cried out, kicking at a Hound's head with its tongue lolling vacantly to the side. "This heat is unbearable..."

"Another four hours!" he cried back, spearing the shovel down to split some bulbous sack open at his feet – and proceeding to swear as the contents exploded all over his boots. "They'll pay us handsomely for this, don't worry!"

"Not handsomely enough for what it's worth! It stinks of shit around here."

"I thought you'd be used to it... have you smelt your wife?"

His friend raised a fist. "Go fuck yourself!"

He grinned like a child in reply.

It's good to acknowledge life's little joys.

Stepping over the next ridge of bodies on cautious feet, he was startled suddenly by a murder of crows alighting across the sky, their black wings beating heavy against the sun.

Strange... they don't usually fear us, he thought, turning to survey the horizon just ahead...

To spy a massive, bloated carcass there, the size of a three-storey house.

"Bloody hell!" he cried with an expression of genuine shock.

"What is it?" the friend replied, lowering her shovel.

"Look at that huge thing over there!" He speared a finger out to the horizon. "Must've been brought in fresh with the last lot!"

Struggling to see, she waded over to him on shaky legs, using her shovel as a prop to navigate over the rift.

"By the gods, it's huge..." she said, standing alongside him with wide, shimmering eyes. "And, by the looks of it... it's covered in those massive metal bracers too. There may be a gemstone or two locked away under all that bloated skin..."

"That's a good point, yea." A shiver ran up his back, and he winced into the light. "Although, I can't say I'd ever want to face something like that in a fight, even if my life depended on it."

"Agreed... because it looks like whoever *did* face that thing, had a hell of a time bringing it down..."

They crossed the rotting pit towards the beast as a ship navigates a storm, traversing the troughs and peaks with their shovels outstretched to hold steady. It was slow, tedious work, picking between bodies and trying to find their footing: but they knew also, that any misstep could mean they disappeared beneath the corpses and would likely never emerge again. Consumed by the dead, just to become one of them.

Such a profound way to die.

As they moved toward the outskirts of the corpse pit, picking their way through the limbs, the gaunt and threadbare faces of the long-deceased were replaced by the ugly, blue-bloated ones of the recently living. Their skin peeled away like layers of a vegetable, where the burrowing trails of beetles could be seen; hair lay matted and greasy across faces and torsos, growing patchy on the hides of various animals; the wounds that had finished them off had turned a crimson red colour in the heat, seeping yellow puss with ugly blemishes of curdled green. The crunching of bones underfoot were replaced by the squelch of muscle and skin, and it made his skin crawl beneath his cloth slacks with ever passing moment that came.

Such is the nature of our people, he thought whimsically, looking out to the desert beyond.

They always demand a quota in blood...

The beast they had spied from afar was significantly bigger up close: even with its body half-buried among the dead, he still had to crane his neck up to meet one of its many eyes. It towered over everything else in the pit like a titan, sat hunched as if it were lost in a deep slumber. Studying it from beneath its great shadow, he also saw what had been done to kill the creature in the first place: the gouge of a cutting blade ran from its forehead down across its skull, splitting its slathering mouth open and ruining whatever brain-mass lay inside. He grimaced at the wounds, repulsed by the sheer size of the thing: from the towering tumour of its massive head, to the arms sprawled over the corpses to either side like logs.

I've never seen something so grotesque in my life.

"Wonder where they found this thing?" his friend asked, using the end of her shovel to cut a small hole in its skin and watching a trickle of pale liquid seep out of it. "It's gross..."

"Probably in a sewer, or in some cave under the sand," he replied, pursing his lips. "Because that's the thing about this desert: no matter where you look, it manages to churn up all manner of wonderful things..."

"Hm. Yea... I mean, I dread to think what's crawling beneath our feet even now, feasting on the bodies of the dead."

He looked down through the gaps at his feet and shivered.

Don't say that.

"Look! What's that over there?"

He followed her finger, tracing the outstretched arm of the beast to their left, unable to determine what she meant.

"What am I looking for?" he asked.

"Look there! Right there! On the end of its index finger... you see that thing glowing?" she exclaimed, hopping down the ridge of corpses to get a better look. "You see it?"

"I…" He squinted, banishing the intensity of the sun, and gasped. "Oh wait, I can see it! Yes I… I…"

What the hell is it?

Whatever it was, it was something very vibrant, pulsing and shimmering in the sun like the undulating waves of the sea. From afar, he couldn't determine exactly what it was, or to what it had once belonged – all he knew was that, if it was shiny, the chances were that it would also be valuable.

"Let's hope it's worth something!" his friend cried out from the bottom of the ridge, shifting along the edge of the beast's arm as if traversing a mountain pass.

"Go steady there!" he warned, moving over to the colossal corpse.

We could be walking into a trap…

Using the outstretched arm as a guide, they clung to its strange, liquidised skin and shuffled inelegantly toward the fingers at the end, blessed to be under its looming shadow and out from the strain of the sun. Their eyes fuzzed in their sockets; shivers crept up their spines as the sweat cooled across their skin. The unrelenting stench of decay still consumed their senses, digging through the cloth gaiters to reach their noses and pull at the back of their throats. But, with the glint of something shiny in their eyes and the acknowledgement of their empty pockets, neither of them seemed to care much for the stench at that moment.

There is no smell sweeter than money, after all, he thought with a grin. *That much I do know.*

They emerged back out into the sun at the creature's fingertip as the heat beat down across their backs once more, burning their eyes with its ferocity. They lifted hands across their brows, turning to the pulsing light now only a dozen feet away and bounding excitedly toward it, hoping their prayers would be answered.

But as they approached, and the jubilation of their find ebbed away, a deep unease set in and their prayers were left unsaid.

What the hell is that?

It was an arm, or what looked like an arm, reaching up as if ready to pluck the sun from the sky. Fused in place, it was covered in sun-blisters and scars with ugly cracks across the fingernails. It was an grim ornament, he admitted, but was not in of itself that impressive or unique.

Or that would have been the case, had it not been for the striking blue rivers of effluvial liquid branching up the veins, lacing under the skin like crystals in a mineshaft. They were dazzling, twinkling like stars: looking closer, he saw something almost like lightning spur through them.

"It's beautiful," his friend exclaimed with glowing eyes, "and yet so horrifying at the same time."

"It looks bloody valuable, is what I think you mean," he snorted. "You think how much they'd pay back in Val Azbann for something like this? It's like nothing I've ever seen before."

"It is remarkable."

"We'd never have to work a day in our lives again."

"Is it dangerous?"

He scoffed. "C'mon! It's a corpse… there's nothing dangerous about it." He drew a knife from his belt and clicked his tongue. "Dead is dead, anyway…"

And that's sometimes worth some coin.

He stooped down low, grappling the arm by the wrist, twinging at the sharp pains tapping through his fingers.

Thinking nothing of it, with the blade twisting in his free hand, he drew it low to the elbow and—

Felt the hand twitch in his grasp.

Wait—

The fingers locked around his wrist.

"What the *fuck—*"

Staring wide-eyed in horror off to one side, the woman watched as the blue liquid pulsed up the veins of the buried arm and seized across the man's hand like tendrils. The lights flickered rapidly, accelerating like the drumming hooves of a horse; an ugly shade of blue clawed up the man's arm, bulging under the skin.

The knife slipped from his fingers.

He threw his head back, screaming at the top of his lungs.

Blue light surged up his throat and exploded from his mouth, tearing across his eyes, the pulse accelerating on and on with no end in sight—

Until his head imploded like a vortex, fizzing with electrical blue light.

And a body began to emerge from the pit below, clawing slowly up toward the surface.

Studying the decapitated corpse of her friend, she screeched like a banshee and ambled off over the cesspit of bodies, with her eyes swelling and her lungs heaving and the terrible weight of the sun bearing down across her skull. Wanting to be free. To disappear.

To be anywhere but there.

Behind, the body wrenched itself free of the corpses, swaying on shaky legs as it made to stand. It inhaled slowly, agonisingly – surprised, almost, by the revelation that it was alive. Adjusting to the world once more, like reacquainting an old friend: stepping over the body of the now-dead scavenger, and looking out to the edge of the pit where the other one now made her escape. The figure produced a grunt, visibly unimpressed, and then smiled.

Something crackled in the sky above.

Muscles rippled across its shoulder, spilling down its arm to the glowing fingertips flexing slowly in the light. Tendons bunched in its throat, grinding its jaw together as a pain swept through its system. It raised its hand like an orator, with tiny twists of metallic light glinting between its fingers. The pulse of the liquid accelerated again, tightening across its chest. Beating through its heart.

A moment of complete silence came, save for the gusts of wind pulling across the vast desert sea.

And then, with a thunderous roar like a dragon, lightning lanced from the sky toward the distant horizon, and turned the fleeing scavenger into dust.

And all was still again.

He lowered his hand, studying his arm and the blue-white liquid knotting through it. He tracked its movements, as it circulated in through his chest and up into the wells of his skull. Like a whisper, it tapped across his mind, heightening his senses, almost as if he were ascending. He had seen the world all over: its vastness and its depravity. And in the beating heat of the corpse-pits on the outskirts of Val Darbesh, he stood alone on shaking legs as a conqueror of worlds.

And now, perhaps, I can have my peace.

Markus flexed his fingers and smiled.

And now, at last…

I can have my revenge.

ACKNOWLEDGEMENTS

This book was one of the hardest things I've ever written, and has taught me a lot about writing and how to approach my future projects. Despite setbacks, delays, and a rewrite of two entire storylines, I am incredibly pleased with the final product, and hope you have enjoyed this next instalment in the Blood and Steel Saga as much as I have.

I want to give thanks to two main people here, who have done me a great service during the writing of this book:
Firstly, I want to thank my illustrator Diego Spezzoni, for his tireless work and for the incredible cover design he produced – it was beyond anything I could have imagined, and I can't wait to see what comes next.
Secondly, I want to thank my beautiful partner, Charlotte, for her patience and dedication to my dream, and for keeping me motivated to carry on even when I felt like giving in. I am grateful for you every single day.

And, finally, I want to give thanks to my ARC readers: Jennifer, Rebecca, Karl, Chris, Vedang, Harry and Mel, for being amazing supporters of my work, and for making the Indie Writing Community an even better place.

So, thank you all, and until next time…

Happy adventures!

AUTHOR'S NOTE

Read below for a brief overview of the events in Chapter 49, as indicated by the 'content warning' at the beginning of the book:

Savanta awakens in a sandy pit where skulls line the walls, and a viewing gallery overlooks the small arena from above. She senses another presence in the room around her, and after some searching the Iron Queen reveals herself from behind a central pillar.
The Queen charges Savanta with being a monster, and losing her grip on reality. But she then reveals that the problems Savanta faces, and the madness she feels, goes back further than any of the events that have occurred since the injury that damaged her face: she has displayed a form of madness her entire life, ever since she was a child.
The Queen explains a number of terrible things Savanta did, and how her father was forced to abandon them out of disgust for his daughter's actions.
And then Savanta realises the truth of it all: that the story of the letter with her father's ear in it [from the first book] was a fabrication. It was Savanta who wrote the letter, and it was she who removed his ear as a threat against him leaving. She had fabricated the story as a child, to cover up for the terrible things she did.
The Queen explains that she's been a monster all along, and the injury at the border simply reactivated the true self she had buried as a child: the grief-stricken, evil person she really was.
As Savanta faces this revelation, the Iron Queen slips from view, and from behind the pillar emerges a huge basilisk, ready to tear the Champion to pieces…

THE HONOURS LIST

Giving a massive thanks to:

Jennifer Sutton
Ross MacBaisey
Henry Sinclair
Glenn Dove
Ganesh Subramanian Alwarappa
Jake Wilson
Joseph McLachlan
Sean Doty
Claudia May
Rebecca King
&
Charlotte Macbean

For their support and contributions to the production and publication of this book and my future projects. You are remarkable people, and have made a young man's dream come true.

I hope to do you proud.

Printed in the USA
CPSIA information can be obtained
at www.ICGtesting.com
LVHW011029070224
771186LV00083B/3196

9 781399 947954